EYE OF THE
WOLF

EYE OF THE
WOLF

MARGARET COEL

BERKLEY PRIME CRIME, NEW YORK

THE BERKLEY PUBLISHING GROUP
Published by the Penguin Group
Penguin Group (USA) Inc.
375 Hudson Street, New York, New York 10014, USA
Penguin Group (Canada), 90 Eglinton Avenue East, Suite 700, Toronto, Ontario M4P 2Y3, Canada
(a division of Pearson Penguin Canada Inc.)
Penguin Books Ltd., 80 Strand, London WC2R 0RL, England
Penguin Group Ireland, 25 St. Stephen's Green, Dublin 2, Ireland (a division of Penguin Books Ltd.)
Penguin Group (Australia), 250 Camberwell Road, Camberwell, Victoria 3124, Australia
(a division of Pearson Australia Group Pty, Ltd.)
Penguin Books India Pvt. Ltd., 11 Community Centre, Panchsheel Park, New Delhi—110 017, India
Penguin Group (NZ), Cnr. Airborne and Rosedale Roads, Albany, Auckland 1310, New Zealand
(a division of Pearson New Zealand Ltd.)
Penguin Books (South Africa) (Pty.) Ltd., 24 Sturdee Avenue, Rosebank, Johannesburg 2196,
South Africa

Penguin Books Ltd., Registered Offices: 80 Strand, London WC2R 0RL, England

This book is an original publication of The Berkley Publishing Group.

This is a work of fiction. Names, characters, places, and incidents either are the product of the author's imagination or are used fictitiously, and any resemblance to actual persons, living or dead, business establishments, events, or locales is entirely coincidental. The publisher does not have any control over and does not assume any responsibility for author or third-party websites or their content.

BERKLEY® PRIME CRIME
The name BERKLEY PRIME CRIME and the BERKLEY PRIME CRIME design are trademarks belonging to Penguin Group (USA) Inc.

PRINTING HISTORY
Berkley Prime Crime hardcover edition / September 2005

Library of Congress Cataloging-in-Publication Data

Coel, Margaret, 1937-
    Eye of the wolf / Margaret Coel.
       p. cm.
    ISBN 0-425-20546-0
    1. O'Malley, John (Fictitious character)—Fiction.   2. Holden, Vicky (Fictitious character)—
Fiction.   3. Wind River Indian Reservation (Wyo.)—Fiction.   4. Shoshoni Indians—Crimes
against—Fiction.   5. Arapaho Indians—Fiction.   6. Women lawyers—Fiction.   7. Indian
women—Fiction.   8. Massacres—Fiction.   9. Wyoming—Fiction.   10. Clergy—Fiction.
I. Title.

PS3553.0347E97 2005
813'.54—dc22

                                                                                2005044064

PRINTED IN THE UNITED STATES OF AMERICA

10   9   8   7   6   5   4   3   2   1

ACKNOWLEDGMENTS

My deepest thanks to the people on the Wind River Reservation who took the time to talk with me about many aspects of this novel: Merle Haas, Director, Sky People Higher Education; Douglas Noseep, Chief, Wind River Law Enforcement; Richard Ortiz; and Harold Smith. A special thank you to Brian Smith for guiding me to the remote and beautiful area of the Bates Battlefield.

My thanks also to Detective Sergeant Roger Rizor, Fremont County Sheriff's Department, Wyoming; to Robert Pickering, Ph.D., forensic anthropologist, Deputy Director, Buffalo Bill Historical Center, Cody, Wyoming; and to Gail Rogers, LPN, Boulder, Colorado.

And thanks to Carl Schneider, Boulder, for his always astute advice; to Fred Walker, for educating me about guns, also of Boulder; to Stephan and Julie Edwards in Riverton for showing me around the beautiful campus of Central Wyoming College; and to Anthony Short, S.J., former pastor at St. Stephen's Mission on the Wind River Reservation, for suggestions that keep me on track.

And to my friends who read parts or all of the manuscript and made many suggestions which, in almost every case, I took: Virginia Sutter of the Arapaho tribe; Karen Gilleland, Beverly Carrigan, and Sheila Carrigan, Boulder. And to Philip F. Myers, Silver Lake, Ohio, for his perceptive comments.

And to my husband, George, the clearest-eyed critic of all.

This is for Violet Katherine Henderson.
Welcome to our world; we have been waiting for you.

AUTHOR'S NOTE

The Bates Battlefield is located in Hot Springs County, Wyoming, three miles from the border of Fremont County. For the purposes of this story, I have placed the site of the battlefield in Fremont County.

The Indian thought of the wolf as "an animal who moved like liquid across the plains, silent, without effort, but with purpose. He was alert to the smallest changes in his world. He could see very far—'two looks away.'"

— *OF WOLVES AND MEN* BY BARRY LOPEZ

"We reached the old wolf in time to watch a fierce green fire dying in her eyes. I realized then, and have known ever since, that there was something new to me in those eyes—something known only to her and to the mountain."

—*A SAND COUNTY ALMANAC* BY ALDO LEOPOLD

The place where crying begins,
The thi'aya,
The thi'aya.
When I see the thi'aya,
I begin to lament.
—ARAPAHO SONG

1

THE CALL HAD come at precisely two minutes after nine this morning, everything about it marked with urgency, even the way the black plastic phone seemed to shudder with each ring. Father John Aloysius O'Malley, the Jesuit pastor of St. Francis Mission on the Wind River Reservation, could still feel the knot of dread that had tightened in his chest as his hand shot across the desk for the receiver. There were so many emergency calls—*Father, there's been an accident! Father, could you get over to the hospital? Father, we need help*—that he'd developed a sixth sense, like an invisible antenna capable of detecting the type of call even before he'd picked up the phone.

"Father John," he'd said, the usual greeting, but he'd hurried it, he remembered, anxious to hear what had happened.

And on the other end, the calm, deliberate voice of Nathan Owens, the Episcopal priest at St. Aiden's Mission in Ethete. "I think I've got something for you, John," he'd said. "Could you come over as soon as possible?"

Now Father John squinted into the sun exploding off the snow and aimed the front wheels of the ancient Toyota pickup into the tracks that marked the Blue Sky Highway. It had snowed during the night, a late gasp of winter that intruded into spring after a week of clear skies and sunshine and wild grasses sprouting green in the fields. Now the gray sagebrush poked out of the snow that blanketed the ground as far as he could see. The feeling of snow still hung in the air. Intermittent bursts of warmth from the vents punctuated the music of *Il Trovatore* blasting from the tape player on the seat beside him and barely cut through the cold that crept past the windows and into the cab. It was the first Monday in April, the Moon of Ice Breaking in the River in the way that the Arapahos marked the passing time.

Small houses began flashing past—gray one-story here, tan bi-level over there. He was on the outskirts of Ethete, the humped foothills of the Wind River Mountains, lined with snow, in the distance to the west. He knew the roads that crisscrossed the reservation by heart. He'd spent the last nine years at St. Francis Mission, almost the entire decade of his forties and three years longer than the Jesuits usually left a man on assignment. Not a day went by that he didn't listen for the phone call that would send him on to some other place. The call would have its own peculiar sound, he thought. He would sense it.

He didn't want the call to come. He was at home here, a fact that still took him by surprise when he thought about it. He, the tall, redheaded priest from Boston, descended from a long line of redheaded Irishmen, at home in the vast openness of the Wyoming plains with brown-skinned Arapahos, the blood of warriors coursing through their veins. He'd never imagined himself a mission priest. He'd been on an academic track, teaching American history at a Jesuit prep school with a doctorate and a university position ahead. Instead there had been the year spent at Grace House becoming a recovering alcoholic, followed by the search for a job with a Jesuit superior willing to take a gamble, or maybe just desperate for help. Finally, the call had come: a position available on an Indian reservation. Did he want the job? He'd flown into the Riverton airport, still wobbly on his feet with his newfound sobriety.

The center of Ethete was ahead—a stoplight swinging over the junction of two roads with a gas station and convenience store on the southwest corner. Father John began easing on the brake, then took a right into the grounds of St. Aiden's, and wound around the narrow, circular road past a series of small buildings, past the hundred-year-old log-cabin church rooted in the earth and the snow. He parked in front of the cream-colored residence and turned off the tape player, the melody still running through his head as he hurried up the sidewalk.

They were similar, the two missions, he thought, knocking on the front door and glancing around. One Episcopalian, the other Catholic, separated by thirty miles, both with a circle of dormitories, schools, and cookhouses that had metamorphosed into offices, museums, and meeting halls. St. Aiden's had come first, but Father John Roberts, the Episcopal priest who founded the mission, had welcomed the Jesuits in 1884 when they built St. Francis close to Arapaho settlements in the eastern part of the reservation. "Now the Indians are surrounded by Christianity," he'd said.

The door squealed open, and a small woman peered upward, sending him a look of expectation. She was that indeterminate age—somewhere between fifty and seventy—and everything about her looked soft, from the gray color of her hair to the milky blue eyes and the tiny lines cushioned in the folds of her face.

"Come in, Father," she said, backing into a small entry and pulling the door with her. "Nathan's waiting in the study." She tossed her head toward the closed door on the left, then started down a narrow hallway toward the kitchen in back.

"How do you like your coffee?" she called over one shoulder. He could see the edge of the dark cabinets beyond her, the small table still littered with what looked like the plates and mugs from breakfast. The sharp aromas of bacon and fresh coffee mingled in the air. Somewhere in the house, a washing machine was rumbling.

"A little milk. Thanks." He rolled his jacket into a bulky ball and set it on the chair in the corner, then balanced his cowboy hat on top. Before he could rap on the door, it swung inward. Filling up the opening was the large figure of Nathan Owens, dressed in blue jeans and a denim shirt that strained across his barrel chest. The man's round, puffy face was marked by a prominent nose and flushed cheeks beneath the thin strands of fading brown hair combed back from his forehead. He was in his seventies, he'd once confided to Father John, beyond the age of retirement, a fact that he hoped would continue to escape the Episcopal powers-that-be. He liked working on the reservation, even though he hadn't wanted the assignment here twenty years ago—another fact that he'd confided. A Philadelphia WASP on an Indian reservation? The Lord works in strange ways.

"He brought me from Boston," Father John had said, and they'd both laughed.

Now Father Nathan motioned him into a cramped study, not unlike his own. Papers spilled over the surface of the desk and onto the chair pulled close to one side. "Have a seat," the other priest said, scooping another pile of papers from the upholstered chair against a bookcase crammed with books stacked on one another.

Father John dropped onto the chair as the Episcopal priest swung his girth around the desk and settled into a swivel chair. "I appreciate your coming, John," he said, shoveling his fingers through his thin hair before patting it back into place.

"What's going on?"

Father Nathan raised a fleshy hand, fingers outstretched. His wife was coming through the door, holding out two coffee mugs like offerings.

"Don't worry about me," she said, handing one mug to Father John. She smiled at him. "The priest's wife sees nothing and tells nothing." She pushed aside a stack of papers and set the other mug on the desk.

"Thank you, dear." Nathan waited until the woman had retraced her steps and closed the door behind her. "I don't want Hilda worrying about this," he said. "It'll only upset her. She knows there's something I wanted to talk over with you. That's all."

Father John sipped at his coffee. It was fresh and hot. He could feel the burning strand of liquid dropping into his chest.

"I'm going to cut to the chase, John," Father Nathan was saying. "A very disturbing call came in late Saturday night. The minute I answered the phone, a voice on the other end—if you can call it a voice—said, 'Listen carefully and pay attention.' I tell you, a chill ran through me. I hit the record button on instinct." The man paused, his gaze fastened on the phone next to his untouched mug of coffee.

"You'd better hear this," he said, jamming a fleshy finger on one of the buttons.

There was a half-second of whirring, followed by a clicking noise, then . . .

"This is for the Indian priest."

The voice of a machine, Father John thought, a monotone, high-pitched and rapid. And inhuman. The voice of a robot or an alien in a B movie. Father John shifted forward, set his mug on the desk, and dipped his head toward the phone, not taking his eyes from the tiny microphone spilling out the words:

Once they fell in heat.
Revenge is sweet
And cold.
Bodies in the snow.
Frozen enemy of old
Dead in the gorge
Attacks no more.

The whirring continued for a moment followed by silence. The walls seemed to close in; the cold of the dead gripped the room.

"Well, what do you make of it?" Nathan sat back in his chair, one hand resting against the base of the phone.

Father John looked away. The tinny, mechanical voice, the clipped words were still in his head. *Bodies in the snow. Dead in the gorge.* A distorted, soulless voice. The voice of evil.

"It's very disturbing." He brought his gaze back to the man watching him from the other side of the desk.

"I would say frightening. The caller went to a lot of trouble to disguise the voice. Could be either a man or a woman." Then Father Nathan heaved himself to his feet, walked across the study, and stared out the window that framed a slice of the mission grounds. "I can tell you, I haven't gotten much sleep since that call came. Keep thinking that out there in the snow, some poor soul . . ." He turned back to Father John. "No," he corrected himself. "The caller said 'bodies.' "

Father Nathan lumbered back and sank into the chair, like a bear moving into his cave. He set his elbows on the desk and made a fist that he knocked against the palm of his other hand. "I must've played that tape a couple dozen times yesterday. I'm out of my depth, John. If the message is supposed to be a code that the caller thought I'd understand, well . . ." He threw up both hands in a gesture of surrender. "I don't get it. Enemy of old? Dead bodies in a gorge? Sometime around 2:00 a.m. this morning, I reached two conclusions. Either the call is a sick joke that somebody wanted to play on the mission priest, or I wasn't the priest who was supposed to get the message. The caller could have dialed the wrong mission. Makes sense, doesn't it? You're the one people hereabouts call the Indian priest. You're the one who used to be a history professor."

"I taught American history in a prep school," Father John said, shaking his head. He was always mistaken for the history professor he might have been.

"A historian nonetheless." The other priest waved away the clarification and shot a glance toward the window. "The caller wants the bodies found and figured you'd make sense of the message. I believe it was intended for you."

Now Father John got to his feet and walked to the window. It looked peaceful outside, the snow covering the ground and tracing the roofs of the old buildings, white flakes drifting like ash off the branches of the cottonwoods. Nathan's first conclusion could be right, he was thinking. The message was nothing more than a sick joke. He might even believe it, if it weren't for the voice, the soulless voice. *This is for the Indian priest.*

He turned back.

The other priest was slumped in his chair, staring at some point across the room, and for an instant, Father John had the sense that he was in the presence of an old man, weighted down by the long years and, now, consumed with an indefinable dread.

"Someone could have been killed," Father John said. His voice was soft, the voice of the confessional, of a counselor. "Perhaps, as you say, more than one person."

Father Nathan was quiet a moment. Then he said, "I was about to call the Wind River Police, but what will I tell them? A crank call about bodies in the snow? They'd fill out a report and file it with a hundred other vague reports. Nothing about the message makes sense. Bodies? Where are they? Enemies and attacks? What are we talking about?"

Father John let a beat pass while he chased the shadow of an idea forming at the edge of his mind. "Possibly about an Indian battle," he said. "The bodies could be on one of the old battlefields."

"How many battlefields are there?" The other priest seemed to be warming to the idea.

Father John walked over and dropped back into his chair. "Hundreds," he said. "The war on the plains lasted almost forty years." He ran his tongue over his lips. His mouth felt as dry as sand. *Hundreds of battle sites.* It would be like uncovering a pebble in the snow. But there were clues. The caller had imbedded clues in the message.

He let another moment pass before he said, "I'd like to take the message to the elders."

The other priest was nodding. "Yes, yes," he said, thumbing through a folder. He pulled out a sheet and handed it across the desk to Father

John. The telephone message was scrawled in black ink across the page. "I wrote down the words," Nathan said. "I also copied the tape." He rummaged through the center drawer. "You still keep that player in the pickup for your operas?"

Father John nodded.

"Good." Nathan handed him the tape. "It'll help if the elders hear the message. The voice will send chills down their spines."

Father John got to his feet and started for the door.

"John . . ."

He turned back.

Father Nathan gripped the armrests and began leveraging himself upright, his massive chest leaning over the desk. "I don't like the logic of where this might be going," he said. "If some crackpot gets his jollies from killing people and leaving the bodies on an old battlefield, there's no telling how many people might end up dead."

2

THE REDBRICK SENIOR citizens center stood in a snow-covered field off Seventeen-Mile Road, a deserted look about it except for the three pickups parked at various angles in front, as if they'd fallen out of the sky with the snow. Father John pulled in alongside one of the vehicles and hit the off button on the tape player. He'd been playing and replaying the message all the way from St. Aiden's, searching for the hidden meaning. Where was the meaning? Each time the tape started—*This is for the Indian priest*—he'd felt the same sense of foreboding. He couldn't get used to the voice. It always sounded different—the endless changeability of evil.

He took the tape player, slammed out into the crisp air, and made his way up the sidewalk, his boots kicking up fantails of white powder. A wedge of snow at the edge of the sloped roof threatened to drop onto the little mounds bunched against the building. He yanked open the front door and stepped into a large, open room, redolent of fresh coffee and hot fry bread. The round tables inside the door were vacant, metal chairs tilted on the front legs and pushed against the table edges, but two elders, Ethan Red Bull and Max Whiteman, sat hunched over Styrofoam cups at a table near the window in back. A gray-haired woman leaned into the door from the kitchen on the right and gave him a welcoming wave with a dishcloth as he started around the vacant tables.

"Help yourself to coffee, Father," Ethan called out. Both men had shifted in his direction, dark eyes watching him approach. They tossed their heads in unison toward the metal coffeepot and stack of Styrofoam cups on a cart pushed against the side wall, and Father John walked over, poured himself a cup of coffee, and—cup in one hand, tape player in the other—headed back to the elders.

Max Whiteman nudged a vacant chair away from the table with his boot. "Take a load off your feet," he said.

Father John set the coffee mug and player on the table, shrugged out of his jacket, and tossed it onto an adjacent table along with his cowboy hat. Then he took the chair between the two old men. It was hard to tell who was older, Max or Ethan. Both in their eighties, ranchers with cowboy hats perched on white heads and the outdoors etched in brown faces, brought up on stories told by their grandfathers of the days when Arapahos had lived free on the plains, warriors in feathered headdresses thundering across the empty spaces after the buffalo, protecting the villages from enemies.

"How are you, grandfathers?" Father John said, using the term of respect for men who had reached the fourth hill of life. From the top of the fourth hill, they could see great distances, which in the Arapaho Way, accounted for the wisdom of the elders.

"*Hi'zeti'*." Max shrugged. He was a stocky, compact man with eyes like narrow, black slits in a round, pudgy face, and a large head that sat directly between his shoulders. He had on a dark plaid shirt with the small bronze buffalo of his bolo tie riding halfway down the hump of his chest. "We're a couple of tough old buzzards," he went on, nodding at the man across the table. "Ain't that right?"

"Gotta be tough to outlast winter." Ethan Red Bull glanced at the window and the snow clinging to the edges of the pane, then lifted a fist and nudged at the brim of his cowboy hat, freeing tufts of white hair that spilled onto his forehead. He was a slight man, with dark, rheumy eyes, a prominent nose, and ropelike veins that pulsed in his thin neck. "How are things holding up at the mission?"

Things were holding up fine, Father John said. Then, sipping at his coffee, he launched into the pleasantries, the polite small talk that always preceded the real point of a visit. He talked on about the AA meetings, the religious education classes, the hospitality volunteers who checked on the shut-ins and made sure the elders had food stocked in their cabinets, and the after-school programs for kids, all the while his thoughts circling around the tape in the player that sat in the center of the table.

After a few minutes, Max rolled his massive head toward the player. "You ain't fixin' to play us some opera, are you?" he asked.

"No opera." Father John heard the serious note in his voice. He was aware of the elders working on their coffee, the dark eyes following him over the rims of Styrofoam cups. "I met with Father Nathan over at St. Aiden's this morning," he said. Then he told the elders about the phone call, the distorted voice, and the cryptic message, and as he talked, he pulled from his shirt pocket the folded piece of paper on which Nathan had written the message. He smoothed it in the middle of the table. Max pushed the paper toward Ethan, a gesture of respect, Father John realized, toward the elder man.

Ethan stared down at the sheet for several seconds, then slid it back. He waited until Max had read through the message and lifted his eyes before he said, "You got a tape of this?"

Father John nodded, then pushed the play button and listened to the sounds again: whirring, clicking, and finally the high-pitched, nonhuman voice speaking of bodies, enemy attacks, and death. When the voice stopped, he hit the off button. The tape cut off in the midst of the whir, leaving a sense of vacancy in the room, as if a large, empty space had settled around them. The rattle of metallic pans in the kitchen seemed to come from a long way off. Both of the old men wrapped their fingers around their cups, no longer drinking the coffee, just staring over the rims.

Father John waited. A long moment passed before Ethan set his cup down, cleared his throat, and said, "What does this tell you?"

"Somebody could have been killed and left on one of the old battle-fields," Father John said. "I don't know which battlefield."

"More bloodshed." Max glanced at the other elder. "This here voice"—he flicked his fingers at the tape player—"is an untrue voice, an evil spirit wanting to stir up trouble and bring us more death."

Several seconds went by—four, five, six—before Ethan refolded the sheet of paper along the creases and handed it back to Father John. "The bodies gotta get proper burials," he began, "so the spirits can go to the ancestors and the ancestors'll recognize them and lead 'em into the afterworld."

Father John didn't say anything. He understood that the elders always insisted that the dead receive proper burials, even bones from the Old Time, uncovered while a road was being built or the earth excavated for a new building, even the bones brought back to the reservation from the shelves of museums where they'd been stored. All were given proper burials, with the sacred red paint placed on the skulls and the smoke of burning cedar and the sound of pounding drums carrying the prayers to the Creator.

"You take this to the police," Max said, his gaze still on the tape player, "and they're gonna say, 'Bodies on a battlefield? They belong in the Old Time, so why should we worry?' "

"They're not from the Old Time." A fierceness had come into Ethan's tone. The elder pawed at his hat, this time pulling it forward. "This here evil is today. The untrue voice is saying people been killed now. The dead bodies are out there somewhere. You gotta find 'em, Father. You gotta find 'em so the spirits can get some peace."

Father John leaned into the back of his chair until the rim cut across his spine. He took a draw of coffee. "The battlefield could be in the area," he said, threading his way through the logic. "Father Nathan thinks the message was intended for me. I've been called the 'Indian priest.'"

The elders nodded at that.

"My parishioners are Arapahos. It could be an Arapaho battlefield."

"Could be one of the battles on the Powder River." Ethan sat back and crossed his arms over his thin chest. "My grandfather was in them battles. Warriors fought the soldiers all over the Powder River country. Soldiers killed a lot of the people. Burned our lodges and took our women and children. Grandfather said the medicine wolves was following the soldiers the whole time, dozens of wolves that made the nights hideous with their howling. Some of the soldiers got so scared, they took off, 'cause they knew them wolves was on the side of Arapahos, and if the warriors didn't get their revenge, the wolves was gonna get revenge for them."

Max drew in a long breath and sipped his coffee a moment. Finally he said, "There was some other battles. Arapahos joined up with the Sioux and Cheyenne and attacked wagon trains and stage stops up and down the Platte River. That's where the people found my grandfather, a little white boy wandering around lost after the warriors burned a wagon train. One of the warriors lifted him up onto his pony and took him to his lodge and made him his son. Called him Whiteman." He smiled, squinting into the distance, as if he might see the old man who had passed on the story of how he'd come to the tribe. "Could be one of them battles."

"Maybe," Father John said. He didn't think so. The Platte was a good hundred miles away.

Ethan pushed himself to his feet and stood over the table a moment, grasping the edges to steady himself, his breath coming in quick, sharp jabs. "Either you boys want some hot coffee?" he said.

"No, thanks," Father John said. Max was shaking his head, a wide hand still wrapped around the Styrofoam cup.

The other elder went over to the table, listing sideways a little as he planted one boot after the other. He refilled his cup and walked back. When he'd sat down, he said, "Soldiers weren't the people's only ene- mies in the Old Time. All them wagon trains heading across the hunting grounds, white men picking off the buffalo with their Winchesters and chasing the herds so far off the warriors had to ride for days to find 'em—some of them other tribes would've just as soon seen us dead, so they'd get whatever buffalo was left after the white people got done. There's battlefields around here where Indians was fighting Indians."

Max was nodding, his chin dipping into his chest. "Arapahos was always having to fight the Utes to keep 'em from making off with our ponies and our women. Then there was the battles we had with . . ." The old man stopped, his gaze fastened on the man across from him.

"Shoshones," Ethan said. Stillness settled over the room, like the stillness of night creeping over the plains, when not even the wind makes a sound. "Last fight our people had was out in the badlands by Bates Creek. You know where it is, northeast of the reservation?" He lifted a hand in the direction.

Father John nodded. Three or four years ago, one of the other elders had taken him out to the site of the Bates Battle—a deep canyon boxed in by steep, rock-strewn bluffs.

"Massacre is what it was." Max closed his eyes, as if he were watch- ing the images in his head. "The first light of day was just starting in the sky when the Shoshones come riding into the village. They wasn't alone. They brought troops with Captain Bates, and they was all firing rifles. They kept firing 'til lots of Arapahos was dead and lots more was wounded. Burned out the lodges, stole the food the people had stored up for winter, stampeded the ponies so the warriors couldn't hunt. Come close to destroying us. People said the sky turned the color of blood. Wolves was howling something terrible."

The old man paused. He opened his eyes and squinted at some point across the room. "We been here on the rez with the Shoshones for a long time now. We was a pitiful bunch when we come straggling in here.

Most of the people was more dead than alive, half starved, still mourning over all the relatives killed in the massacre. We been trying to get along with Shoshones ever since and forget about what happened. It's not good to talk about Bates. It might bring the evil back."

Father John picked up the folded sheet of paper and slipped it back inside his shirt pocket, part of the message burning in his mind. *The dead lie in the gorge.* He looked at Max, then at Ethan. "The Bates Battlefield," he said, his voice soft with certainty.

The elders were nodding in unison, as if they had already reached the same conclusion and had been waiting for him to catch up. Neither spoke, and for a long moment, the quiet running through the hall was as chilling as the howl of a wolf.

Finally Ethan said, "More bloodshed at that terrible place is just gonna bring back all the old evil we been trying to put behind us."

Father John got to his feet and leaned over the table, shaking the knobby hands, thanking the old men. Then he grabbed his coat and hat and headed for the door. The Bates Battlefield was in the middle of nowhere, over rough dirt roads that snaked across bluffs and down into valleys. Before he sent a platoon of law enforcement officers into the badlands on a wild-goose chase, he intended to check out the place himself.

3

THE MURMUR OF voices ran through the tribal courtroom, and every few minutes a new blast of cold air shot past the opened doors as someone filed inside. Vicky Holden squared the yellow notepad on the table and checked her watch. Almost one. At any moment, the door on the left would swing open and her client, Frankie Montana, would appear. Two tribal attorneys sat at the table across the aisle, pulling papers out of briefcases, heads tilted together in conversation. She glanced back at the knots of people—all related to Frankie, she suspected—settling onto benches arranged like pews in a church. Lucille, Frankie's mother, was two rows behind. Vicky managed what was meant as an encouraging smile.

The call had come this morning. Vicky had arrived at the office at seven-thirty, ahead of the secretary, Annie Bosey, who had followed her from the one-woman law practice she'd been struggling to keep afloat to the new firm that she and Adam Lone Eagle had started. Vicky was still shrugging out of her coat when the phone had started to ring. The answering machine would pick up, she remembered thinking. The ringing had stopped. A moment later, it started up again. What was it about an unanswered phone that had always bothered her? The unsettling sense of an emergency at the other end, a dread of the news? She'd reached across the desk and lifted the receiver.

"Vicky, it's Lucille. You gotta help us."

It had taken a moment to place the name and the voice. Lucille Montana. Lucille Yellow Plume when they'd gone to school together at St. Francis Mission. Vicky hadn't spoken to the woman since October, the last time Frankie was in trouble.

"What's going on?" she'd asked. Six months ago she'd gotten the circuit judge to dismiss a breaking and entering charge against Frankie. The sheriff's investigators had made the serious mistake of continuing to throw out questions after Frankie—who knew his rights cold—had asked for an attorney. A year ago, there had been a couple of DUIs and an assault complaint. It had taken all of her legal skills to keep the man out of prison. So far he'd spent only a few months in the Fremont County jail and another short time in the tribal jail.

"The rez police come and arrested Frankie last night" Lucille said. "I told 'em, he's a good boy, staying out of trouble, hardly drinking anymore." A rising screech of panic came into the woman's voice. "It's harassment, Vicky. That's all it is. You gotta get him out of jail."

"What are the charges?" Vicky kept her own voice calm.

"They say Frankie assaulted three Shoshones over at Fort Washakie Friday night. Assaulted!" The woman forced a laugh—she might have been clearing her throat. "It was those Shoshones assaulted Frankie. You gotta help him, Vicky. He's got a right to protect himself."

Vicky had told the woman that she'd look into the matter. Then she'd pulled her coat back on, stuffed a notepad inside her briefcase, and headed out of the office and down the flight of stairs to the entry of the office building on Main Street in Lander. She almost collided with Adam— coming through the door, the collar of his topcoat turned up, flecks of moisture shining in his black hair, the little scar on his face red with cold. A handsome, modern-day warrior, she'd thought, a man that women followed with their eyes when he walked down the street.

"Whoa!" Adam set both hands on her shoulders, as if she were a pony he wanted to corral. Specks of light flickered in his dark eyes. "You're going the wrong way."

"Frankie Montana's been arrested," she'd told him.

In an instant, the light disappeared and his eyes became opaque. A mixture of disgust and annoyance moved through his expression before his face settled into a blank and unreadable mask, the kind of mask that Indian people had presented to outsiders for centuries. She felt a spark of anger ignite inside her. Whenever she and Adam had a disagreement, he had a way of pulling on that mask reserved for outsiders.

"I'll explain later," she'd said, shouldering past. She hurried down the street and around the corner toward the parking lot where she'd left the Jeep, conscious of Adam's eyes boring a hole into her back before the door had thudded shut.

It had taken all morning to go through the legal maneuvers. She'd driven north on the reservation to Fort Washakie and obtained a copy of the charges from the Wind River Police: assault with a deadly weapon— a rifle—a detail that Lucille hadn't mentioned. Trent Hunter and two brothers, Rex and Joe Crispin, had filed the complaint. All were in their twenties—Frankie's age, the same age as her own kids, Susan and Lucas, which, she supposed, was one of the reasons why she'd always agreed to defend Frankie, hoping along with Lucille that he'd get his life straightened out. She'd driven to the tribal attorney's office in Ethete and demanded that Frankie be brought before the judge today—*He'd already been held for twenty-four hours.* Then she'd gone back to the low, reddish brick building with the sign in front that said, "Wind River Law Enforcement," where both the police headquarters and the jail were housed. She'd cooled her heels in the hot, cramped entry for what had seemed an hour and had probably been fifteen minutes, checking in at the office on her cell while she waited. "Boy, is Adam in a tear this morning," Annie had told her, the sound of a pencil tapping against the edge of a desk. "Dumped a pile of work on me and wanted it done yesterday. What's going on?"

What was going on? Adam Lone Eagle did not approve of clients like Frankie Montana, that's what was going on. He hadn't approved of Annie Bosey, either. "We need someone more professional," he'd argued. "More polished and less nosey." But Vicky had insisted upon bringing Annie to the new firm. Reliable, unafraid of hard work. Annie had a couple of kids. . . . And she'd seen herself in the woman. Vicky was barely twenty-eight when she'd divorced Ben Holden. Juggling classes at the University of Colorado in Denver, working nights as a waitress, trying to raise the kids. In the end, she'd given up and brought the kids to her mother on the reservation. By the time she'd finished her law degree, Susan and Lucas were old enough to be on their own, but the loss of their childhood—it was always there, like a dull ache.

Ignoring Annie's probing question, Vicky'd said that she wasn't sure when she'd get back to the office and pushed the end key. Finally, an officer in the dusty blue uniform of the Wind River Police had guided her through the steel doors and into the interview room in a corner of the jail.

Not exactly the picture of an innocent man, Frankie, tall and wiry, tattoos creeping below the sleeves of his tee shirt, black hair pulled back into a ponytail, striding around the interview room, threatening to break the hell out of there, shouting that he hadn't done anything wrong, just protecting himself was all. The Shoshones had gone to Fort Washakie looking for him, wanting to start trouble. They had a grudge against him. She'd been aware of the faint antiseptic odor that permeated the air, and the dull daylight filtering past the metal grille on the window. Outside was the empty exercise yard with the concrete floor and the razor wire on top of the high concrete walls.

When she'd asked Frankie about the rifle, he'd stared at her in slack-jawed disbelief. Rifle? There wasn't any rifle. How could he have a rifle when his deer rifle had been stolen out of the back of his pickup two weeks ago? Anybody said he'd pulled a rifle on those Shoshones was lying.

Vicky forced her attention back to the courtroom. The door on the left had swung open, and Frankie was heading her way, dressed in a tan jacket over a yellow shirt and dark trousers that Lucille had probably brought him this morning for the hearing, hair combed loose over his shoulders, head tilted to the side as he surveyed the courtroom. Close behind, in another dusty blue uniform, was a guard, the black belt weighted with a holstered gun on one hip. The guard nudged Frankie's arm, guiding him toward the vacant chair at the table.

Frankie slid in beside her, head still pivoting, narrowed black eyes roaming over the benches. Finally, a look of satisfaction imprinted itself on his features. He leaned sideways. "How long's this shit gonna take," he said.

Vicky could smell the sour odor of his breath. "As long as the judge wants."

"Yeah? Well, I want the hell outta that jail. The place stinks. You'd better get me out of there."

Vicky turned and faced the man. He and Lucas had ridden their ponies together in the summers when they were kids. God, what had happened? "Listen to me," she said. "I'll do what I can to get the charges against you dropped, but I don't work miracles. I'd suggest that you show respect for the court and act like you're sorry for the trouble you've caused."

"I was defending myself." Frankie squared himself to the front of the courtroom.

The court stenographer—a small woman with curly black hair and thick glasses—sat down at a table just as a short, stocky man stepped through the door behind the judge's bench. "Everybody rise," he called out, as if he were shouting through a megaphone. "The Shoshone-Arapaho tribal court is now in session."

Vicky got to her feet. From behind her came the scrape and shuffle of people rearranging coats and bags and standing up. She realized Frankie was still seated and tapped the man on the shoulder. Taking his time, he lumbered upward, still leaning forward when the tribal judge,

Harry Winslow, two hundred pounds of muscle encased in a black robe beneath a crown of white hair, emerged from the door, gripping a thick file folder in one hand. He glanced around the courtroom, then sat down in the high-backed leather chair behind the bench, and opened the folder.

"Take your seats," he barked, peering through glasses perched halfway down his nose. More scraping and shuffling as Frankie's relatives settled back onto the benches. Frankie dropped onto his chair and rolled his boots behind the front legs. Vicky shot him a warning glance as he started to lean back. The man lifted his eyes to the ceiling and clasped his hands across his chest.

"Looks like we've got three matters on the agenda this afternoon," the judge said, glancing over his glasses toward the back of the courtroom. "First matter before the tribal court is the assault charges against Frank Joseph Montana." A rattling noise drifted through the courtroom, like the sound of boots crunching dried leaves, as the judge thumbed through the papers in the folder.

"Mr. Montana?" He fixed Frankie with a hard stare over the top of his glasses.

Vicky stood up and, gesturing with her head, urged Frankie to his feet. The man pushed against the arms of his chair and lifted himself upward. "My client is present. I'm Vicky Holden, Mr. Montana's attorney." This was for the benefit of the court stenographer. She'd lost count of the times she'd appeared in Judge Winslow's court.

"Mr. Montana," the judge went on, "you've been charged with three counts of assault with a deadly weapon. Do you understand the charges?"

"This is crazy," Frankie said.

"I didn't ask for your opinion. I asked if you understand the charges."

"Yes, your honor," Vicky said. "My client understands the charges."

"Let your client speak."

"Yeah, I understand," Frankie said after a moment.

"Mr. Raven," the judge said, shifting his attention to one of the lawyers at the table across the aisle. "What are the specifics of the charges?"

Larry Raven. Vicky had met the man before, still in his twenties, with the ardent, eager-to-prove-himself manner of the law student he'd been only a few years ago.

"Your honor," the lawyer was saying, "the tribes have charged Frank Montana with three counts of assault on Shoshone tribal members, Trent Hunter, and Rex and Joe Crispin. The assault occurred last Friday evening on Stewart Road in Fort Washakie. While committing the assault, Mr. Montana brandished a rifle and threatened to kill the men."

"Bullshit!" Frankie shouted.

"Ms. Holden, if you can't restrain your client, I will see that he's returned to the jail until this hearing is concluded."

"I apologize, your honor," Vicky said. She shot a glance at Frankie and mouthed the words, *be quiet*.

"It had better not happen again." The judge was nodding his head, his glasses slipping farther down his nose. He lifted a puffy finger and pushed them upward. "What does your client say to these charges?"

"Your honor," Vicky began, "my client admits to an altercation. He was driving through Fort Washakie when three men in a pickup forced him to the side of the road, dragged him from his pickup, and began to strike him. He protected himself as best he could before he managed to get back in the pickup and drive his pickup across a yard behind his assailants' truck. He then drove out to the Wind River highway and escaped. My client denies brandishing a rifle, your honor. He admits that he owned a rifle, which he used for hunting, but his rifle was stolen from his pickup two weeks ago."

"Any witnesses to the altercation, Mr. Raven?" Judge Winslow peered through his glasses at the papers in front of him.

"The three complainants, your honor."

"Ah, the three complainants." Now the judge was staring out over the top rim. "Anybody call the police?"

"Not at the time. The three Shoshones came to the Wind River Police on Saturday morning and filed the complaint. They said they were afraid for their lives. It wasn't until Sunday that the police located Mr. Montana at his mother's home and arrested him."

Judge Winslow stayed quiet a moment, peering again at his papers. Finally he looked up. "Well, it looks like we have a case of Mr. Montana's word against the word of the complainants."

Larry Raven shifted from one foot to the other and glanced back at the rows of spectators. "Unfortunately, your honor, none of the complainants is here. I left messages at their homes this morning. I hoped they might show up so you could talk to them yourself."

"Your honor," Vicky cut in, "the tribal attorney knows that this is not an evidentiary hearing."

"I can only surmise your honor," the other lawyer continued, "that either the complainants didn't get the message as to the time of the hearing or that they are too intimidated by Mr. Montana to appear."

"Your honor . . ." Vicky said again.

"Out of line, Mr. Raven."

Vicky pushed on. "These are spurious charges made by three men who don't like my client. There is absolutely no evidence that my client attacked anyone. When the police arrested Mr. Montana, they searched his mother's house and his pickup. They did not find a rifle because there is no rifle. The only thing the tribal attorney has is the complainants' version of what happened, which contradicts my client's version. I intend to file a motion with the court to dismiss the charges for lack of probable cause. I ask the court to release Mr. Montana on a personal recognizance bond."

The judge was quiet a long moment. Finally he said, "I'm inclined to go along with you. The fact is, Mr. Raven"—he gave a half-nod the tribal attorney—"this is a case of one man's word against the word of three other men, who may or may not hold some kind of a grudge. I'm going to grant the bond."

The tribal attorney flinched backward, as if he'd been struck. "May I remind your honor," he managed, "that Frank Montana has a record . . ."

"I know all about Mr. Montana's record." The judge lifted one hand, then let it drop onto the bench top, making a loud, cracking noise. "You don't have a case here, Mr. Raven, and I'm stopping it from going forward until I consider the motion to dismiss."

Behind her, Vicky could hear the labored breathing and a muffled sob. Lucille, sobbing with relief. Vicky felt her own wave of relief washing over her.

Now the judge was staring at Frankie. "Let me remind you that this is not the first time I've seen you in this courtroom. The tribal attorney is correct in pointing out that you have a record of offenses against the people on this reservation going back at least two years. Not a pretty record. I have no doubt that you're capable of assaulting three men. Let me warn you that if you are convicted of the charges, I will see to it that you are banished from this reservation. Do you understand?"

Vicky turned to the man beside her. "Answer him," she whispered.

"Yeah, I understand."

"You're free to go," the judge said.

Vicky gathered her coat and briefcase and followed Frankie out into the side aisle. She waited until Lucille had stumbled after her son, coat thrown over her shoulders like a cape, glancing back with a look of gratitude on her face, dabbing a tissue at her eyes. Frankie's relatives crowded forward, patting him on the back as they moved through the double doors into the entry, where another small crowd was waiting for the next hearing.

"Thank you, Vicky," Lucille said. They were walking through the snow that skimmed the sidewalk in front of the tribal building. The woman reached out and grabbed Vicky's hand. Her fingers were like clumps of ice.

"Listen, Lucille," Vicky said, slowly removing her own hand from the woman's grip and keeping an eye on Frankie, striding around the group of relatives toward an old orange Ford sedan that Vicky guessed belonged to his mother. "I have to talk to Frankie a moment. Do you mind waiting?"

The woman blinked, then drew back, a look of fear shadowing her expression. "You go on," she said.

Vicky swung around and hurried through the family after the young man who had flung open the passenger door and was about to lower himself inside. "Frankie," she called.

Frankie Montana took a step back, then straightened his shoulders and rotated his head, flashing a victory grin back at the people clustered on the sidewalk. "Mom'll see you get paid, if that's what you're worried about," he said.

"Do you know what banishment means?" Vicky came around the front of the Ford and faced the man. The door hung between them, Frankie leaning over the top.

"What do I care? You heard the judge. I'm outta here."

"It means he has the power to keep you off this reservation."

"What?"

"You heard me, Frankie. Just like in the Old Time when the chiefs banished troublemakers from the villages. They couldn't see their families. They had to make their own way on the plains, hunt for their own food, find their own shelter. No one would talk to them. They were completely alone. Most of them died."

"He can't kick me off the rez."

"Yes, he can, Frankie. That's exactly what he can do."

The man shook his head and gave a snort of laughter. "I ain't worried," he said, ducking into the car and pulling the door after him.

"Take my advice, Frankie," Vicky shouted over the closing door. "Clean up your act."

4

FATHER JOHN GUIDED the pickup through the wash of snow that passed for a narrow road, bouncing over rocks and ridges, winding around frozen patches of sagebrush and wild grasses. The music of *Il Trovatore* washed through the cab. He'd been enjoying the opera lately, playing it over and over until the music had become as familiar as the music of *Aida, Rigoletto,* and *La Traviata.* He could see the wavy marks of fresh tracks ahead. One of the ranchers in the area, he thought. He'd driven through Lysite thirty minutes ago, the last place that resembled a town—general store, three or four houses, an abandoned gas station—and continued north into what the Arapahos called the badlands, a vast, empty expanse of bluffs that dropped into deep ravines a thousand feet below and ran uninterrupted into the sky all around. There were no trees as far as he could see. Gray clumps of sagebrush broke the monotony of the snow. From time to time, he spotted antelope tracks running alongside the road and, in the far distance, the dark cluster of ranch buildings. From time to time, the faint afternoon sun tried to break through a sky that had turned the color of lead.

This morning, pulling out of the senior center, he'd come close to calling the Fremont County sheriff. He'd punched in half the numbers on his cell before he'd hit the end button. What would he say? Father Nathan had gotten a strange telephone call that might refer to dead bodies? It was possible the bodies were at the Bates Battlefield? Or any one of hundreds of other battle sites? Might? Possible? And a whole platoon of sheriff's deputies and who knew how many other law enforcement officers could be off on a wild-goose chase.

He'd stopped at the mission before heading out to the battlefield. The moment Father John had let himself through the heavy wooden door of the administration building, Father Ian McCauley, his new assistant, had emerged from his own office at the far end of the corridor. A tall, narrow man with trimmed, blond hair and the usual serious expression stamped on his face, he was closing in on forty, younger than Father John by eight or nine years. When the Provincial had called and suggested the man for the assistant's job, Father John had been struck by the similarities. Nine years ago, he'd been like Ian McCauley, fresh out of rehab at Grace House, desperate for a job, desperate to prove himself. Oh, Father John remembered what that had been like. And he needed an assistant. The last priest had packed up and left almost three months ago—*You know I love it here, John, but a teaching position at Georgetown!*— leaving him to run the mission alone for most of the winter. A few weeks ago, Ian McCauley had arrived with a couple of bags, several cartons of books, and an eager gratitude stamped all over him, the kind that Father John recognized had been his own.

"There you are, John." Ian had come striding down the corridor with the bearing of a military general, waving a file folder. He'd followed Father John into his office on the right and launched into a speech about how they had to get their ducks in a row before tonight's parish council meeting so that they knew which programs the mission would have to cancel this summer. Naturally they'd have to back up their decisions with facts and figures.

"Naturally," Father John had agreed, flipping through the mail, checking the calls on the readout of the answering machine, half expecting to see an unidentified caller who would have a mechanical voice, making sure there wasn't anything that needed his attention before he drove out to Bates.

Father Ian had nudged a wooden chair across the study, sat down, and plopped the folder on the desk between them. "As I see it," he'd begun, riffling through the papers in the folder, "and believe me, John, I've spent a great deal of time going over the numbers, we're going to have to cut back on thirty percent of the summer's programs. Donations have dropped off." He whipped out a sheet from the center of the stack with the enthusiasm of the alcoholic intent on substituting one addiction for another. "Take a look." He'd pushed on. "AA, social committee, new parents group all meet at Eagle Hall, which means we need maintenance and electricity an additional eight hours a week. By cutting those hours, we can save . . ."

The other priest had stopped in midsentence, and Father John realized he'd been shaking his head the whole time. "What?" Ian had asked.

"We'll have to discuss this later," Father John had said, starting around the desk.

"Six new parents at last week's meeting." His assistant had followed him into the corridor. "No way do the numbers justify the expense."

Father John had yanked open the front door and glanced around at the man planted a few feet behind him. "I'll be back for the meeting," he'd said.

"For Godsakes, John. We have to talk about this before the meeting."

"Okay, then. I don't intend to cut any programs."

"Be reasonable, John. How can we pay for everything?" Ian had rolled his eyes skyward, and Father John had read the other priest's assessment of him: stubborn, refuses to see the facts smacking him in the face. He'd stepped outside, pulling the door shut behind him, and hurried to the pickup.

Now he realized that the narrow road had started winding downward. He was dropping off the top of a bluff, and the landscape was beginning to change. A thin line of trees—a black smudge in the whiteness—marked the banks of Bates Creek below. Tire tracks were still running ahead, which struck him as strange. Ranches out here were scattered over the bluffs. There was nothing in the valley, except the battlefield.

He was getting close, and yet, nothing was as close as it seemed in the empty spaces. He'd once decided to take a walk across the plains to the home of a parishioner—the direct route, the way the eagle flies. He figured it would take thirty minutes. It had taken more than two hours.

The road flattened out through the valley, the tracks heading west toward a canyon burrowing through slopes that rose like granite sky-scrapers. The snow was deeper, and the sky darker, so that he had a sense that he was plunging toward an abyss. It occurred to him that if another spring blizzard set in, he could be stuck out here for days. He'd meant to get new tires for the pickup during the winter; there'd never been enough money in the budget. He concentrated on working the accelerator—easing up when the road smoothed out, pressing down for the climb over the ridges, always aiming for the tracks that chased ahead.

He could feel the pickup balking in the snow, the back wheels slipping and churning. He jammed the accelerator into the floor and willed the old vehicle to keep going. A couple of hundred yards, it looked like—he couldn't be sure—to the mouth of the canyon. The pickup nosed into a ditch hidden under the snow and started crawling up the other side. Then it stopped, the wheels grinding in place. He shifted into reverse and tried to back up. The tires whined; the rear end shimmied sideways. It was no use. He was stuck.

He turned off the engine, hit the stop button on the tape player, and got out. He fished his gloves out of his jacket pocket and pulled them on. His hands felt stiff. The air was colder in the valley, the earth striped with blue shadows. Reaching back inside the pickup, he grabbed the cell phone and a pair of old binoculars that he kept in the glove compartment. He slammed the door shut—a loud crack through the sound of the wind rippling over the snow—and started out, stuffing the cell in his pocket, taking off his hat, looping the cord of the binoculars around his neck, and setting his hat back on. He walked in the packed snow of one of the tire tracks running ahead. Chances were that he could hitch a ride later with whoever was here, if he had to.

It looked as if the canyon had been swallowed by the black shadows falling down the rock-strewn slopes. He could see the scraggly line of trees veering right around the base of the mountain. And the tire tracks also veered right, he realized. They crossed the road and plunged toward the trees. Father John stopped. He stared after the tracks a moment, wondering where the driver was headed. Animal tracks danced around the tire tracks. Antelope. Deer. Maybe elk. And wolves, he knew, had also been seen in the badlands.

He dipped his chin into the folds of his jacket collar and set off at a half-run down the road, making his own tracks now, the snow swirling around his boots. He'd look for the other vehicle later.

It was like running into the night, he thought, as he headed into the narrow canyon, moving in and out of the shadows down a corridor of frozen air. The slopes closed in around him, clumps of rocks and boulders rising up to the flat faces of granite that towered overhead. Scattered among the rocks were a few junipers and limber pines that cast their own long shadows, like the shadows of dead men. Above, the sky was a milky strip of light. The snow-covered floor of the canyon was pockmarked with sagebrush and clumps of dead grass. There were a few trees along the edges of the canyon floor. Gusts of wind zigzagged over the snow, lifting white puffs into the air and dropping them back to the ground.

Father John stopped running. He was breathing hard, the air jabbing his lungs like icicles. This was a wild-goose chase, he told himself.

A crank call, just as Father Nathan had suspected. Nothing here but the emptiness and the pervasive quiet of remote places.

He lifted the binoculars and worked at adjusting the focus knob. His fingers felt as stiff as wood. Through the lens, the canyon dissolved into the sameness of snow wrapped in shadows, broken by a tree here and there and the gray hulks of sagebrush. The wind had picked up, howling across the slopes. No wonder that the elders said you could still hear the cries of the women and children at Bates and the howling of wolves.

He was about to turn around when the binoculars brought up something different—a long, horizontal shape, like a log partially covered with snow. Two round, dark smudges jutted from one end. He crept forward, keeping the shape in the lens. He'd gone about twenty feet when the smudges came into focus. He could see clearly—the black hair, the hump of a shoulder in a dark jacket, the long shape of a body.

He dropped the binoculars and started running, gulping in the icy air that ripped through his chest, the binoculars thudding against the front of his jacket. His heart pounded in his ears. A few feet from the body, he stopped. It was the body of a man, reclining on his side, right arm stretched over his head as if to ward off a blow. Little mounds of snow covered the gray jacket, the plaid shirt poking above the collar, the blue jeans, the tops of brown boots. There was no hat, no gloves, no footprints, which meant that the body had been here before last night's snowstorm, possibly since Saturday, when the temperature was in the sixties—hatless, gloveless weather.

Father John moved closer and went down on one knee in the snow. His breath stopped in his throat. The scavengers had already found the body—magpies, ravens maybe. They had picked at the eyes, so that the dead man seemed to be staring out through jagged, dark holes. Pieces of skin had been peeled away from the face and hands. Father John wondered how long it would be before the wolves came. They came with the ravens, he knew. They worked together.

He didn't take his eyes from the body. The man looked Indian, with prominent cheekbones, black hair falling over his forehead, wide nostrils.

A sheen of frost lay over what was left of the face, which looked leathery and gray, almost colorless. Even the right hand—half lost in the snow—had a gray pallor of frozen flesh. There was a hardened puddle of blood on the front of the jacket, another puddle on one shoulder. And there was something else—something familiar about the way the body lay, right arm pulled up above the head, left arm folded helplessly across the abdomen.

He'd seen dead bodies like this in old photographs of fallen warriors—soldiers moving across a battlefield in the stillness following an attack, snapping pictures of dead bodies lying on their side, right arms stretched overhead from the way they'd run forward, waving white pieces of cloth and American flags. But there was no surrender cloth here, no flag. Only the outstretched arm.

He understood then: The killer had *posed* the body.

"My God," he said out loud. The sound of his voice was almost lost in the quiet of the canyon.

He dropped his head and thumped a gloved fist against his forehead. In his mind, as clearly as if the tape had started to play, was the mechanical voice: *Frozen enemy of old. Dead in the gorge.* The voice of a madman who had re-created the battle scene from the past.

It was a moment before Father John could push past the horror. "May the good Lord have mercy on you," he said out loud. "May He forgive you your sins, whatever they may be, and may you live forever in His peace."

Finally he struggled to his feet and peered through the dim light along the canyon floor. *Bodies in the snow*, the voice had said, and he knew with a certainty that there were more bodies. He lifted the binoculars to his eyes and studied the floor again. Left. Right. The temperature must have dropped ten degrees, and the shadows were deepening, beginning the slow meld into dusk. It was going to be hard to spot any other bodies, he realized, sweeping the binoculars back to the left.

There it was—another horizontal shape interrupting the expanse of snow. The same dark, rounded smudges of a head and shoulders at one end.

Father John started walking, not taking the binoculars down, afraid of losing sight of the body. As he stumbled over something hard—a rock, a frozen stalk of sagebrush—the crack of his boots against the object lingered in the silence. He kept going until the body loomed up in front of him.

He went down on one knee again. Another man, judging by the wide shoulders beneath the dark jacket, the wide brown belt at the waist of the blue jeans, the heavy boot visible in the snow that had drifted over the legs. Hatless. Gloveless. There was the crusted blood, the torn black hole the size of a baseball in the back of the jacket. The body lay face down in the snow, both arms pulled high above the head so that the back of the jacket stretched into frozen wrinkles. Another pose, but this one was the pose of a chief running toward the enemy, both arms outstretched, palms up in the sign of peace—*We are friendly Indians*—before the bullet had slammed into his chest.

Father John said the same prayer out loud. His voice was tight with horror and dread. How many more bodies?

Another one, he realized, glancing over toward a clump of trees at the base of the slope on the left. How had he missed it? He pushed himself to his feet and walked over. Also a man, he could see, with the features of an Indian, dressed in blue jeans and a navy jacket opened over a light-colored shirt. In the center of the shirt, he saw the frozen puddle of blood. The scavengers had been here, too, pecking at the eyes and parts of the face. The body was propped upright against a tree stump, as if the man had sought a place to rest and had sat down, one hand relaxed in the snow. But the right hand was stuffed into the jacket pocket. A deliberate pose, Father John knew. He'd seen photographs of dead warriors, slumped against tree stumps and wagon wheels, one hand in a pocket.

Pulling aside one of the branches, he went down on both knees. "Lord, have mercy on us," he began.

Out of the corner of his eye, he saw something on the opposite slope—the faintest movement, like that of a wolf prowling an outcropping of rocks. He raised the binoculars and scoured the slope until he'd focused in on the spot. Hunched down among the rocks was the shape of someone in a dark jacket, a black hat pulled low over the forehead. It wasn't until the figure slid sideways behind a rock that he saw the rifle moving upward.

He threw himself down into the snow as the rifle shot cracked the air, the sound bouncing back and forth across the canyon. A nearby stump was hit, and little pieces of wood rained over his glove. He felt a sharp pain in his face, then something warm and moist trickling down his cheek. He ran his glove over the moisture; fingers and palm were smeared with dark red blood. The body had started to slump sideways, a slow falling into the snow. Father John inched himself around the body until he was behind a boulder where he pulled in his arms and legs and waited.

5

ANOTHER BURST OF gunshots reverberated across the canyon, explosions of noise. Father John could see the bullet lines catapulting through the snow. A nearby sagebrush shuddered, as a bullet thudded into the tree next to him. Pain stabbed at his face. He could feel the hot, wet blood trickling along his jaw. He held himself very still. Four seconds, five seconds passed—God, a lifetime—before the firing stopped and the silence closed in.

He stayed still. The slightest motion, he knew, and the shooter would pick him out in the shadows. Hunched over, curled around himself behind the boulder, the collar of his jacket damp with blood and his heart thumping in his ears, he waited for the next eruption of gunshots, counting off the seconds that turned into minutes, conscious of a scraggly line of trees running along the base of the mountain slope a few yards away. If he could crawl over to the trees, he might be able to work his way out of the canyon and make a dash for the pickup. Dear

God. The pickup was stuck. It would be impossible to dig it out with a madman shooting at him. He was ten, fifteen miles from the nearest ranch, the temperature dropping. Unless he could dig out the pickup, or get the cell phone to kick in, he was a dead man.

The sound of the wind skimming the snow melted into the quiet. Another thought now, the shooter could have surmised that he'd been hit and was coming for him, coming for him with a rifle, intending to fire another shot—to execute him—then pose his body like the others. Father John skimmed the landscape with his eyes and tried to tighten his fists, a reflex motion. His fingers had gone numb with cold; his gloves felt as stiff as cement. A sharp cramp had settled into one leg and the pain in his cheek had turned into a persistent throb. There was no sign of any movement anywhere, yet he could feel the shooter waiting and watching, like a wolf waiting and watching for its prey.

He considered darting across the open area for the trees, then dismissed the idea. A dark shape moving across the snow! He'd be the target in a shooting gallery. He remained still, trying to count off the minutes until probably three or four had passed. God, it seemed like three or four hours! The odor of his own blood was sharp in his nostrils. From somewhere far off came a high-pitched howling noise that drifted overhead, then dissolved into the quiet. The wind howling down the slopes, he told himself. And yet there were wolves in the area.

This is the way it had been at the massacre, he realized. Arapahos pinned inside the tipis and hunkering down in the grass and brush, with the troops and the Shoshones firing into the village, and wolves howling in the distance. Then, a few warriors had broken out and clambered up the slopes, dodging among the boulders. The advantage shifted. Arapahos had begun firing down on the enemy, eventually driving them from the village.

He tried to push away the images. Dear God! He had to keep his imagination in check and stay focused. He let a few more minutes pass, then began inching himself upward along the boulder, pulling his feet under him until they were firmly planted in the snow. Gripping his cowboy hat between two fingers, he moved his head away from the hat. To his right was a corridor of open space, no more than a few yards wide, he guessed, before the trees and the shadows began. With a flick of his wrist, he flung the brown cowboy hat like a Frisbee to the left. Gunshots cracked the air as he propelled himself across the open slot and into the trees. He crouched behind a small limber pine, more like a bush than a tree—a flimsy shelter—and held perfectly still, bullets streaking the air around him, smashing into the trees, furrowing the snow. There was some comfort in the realization that the shooter had to be shooting blind now, shooting into the shadows.

The afternoon light was fading fast, only a flush of light left in the sky and layers of black shadows dropping over the slopes and sweeping through the canyon. He waited another few minutes, conscious of the blood crusting on his face and neck, and then began moving along the trees, expecting the gunshots to explode again, but there was only silence and the muffled crunching of his boots in the snow. He kept going, sinking into a snowdrift at times and grabbing onto the branches to steady himself.

He was close to the mouth of the canyon when he heard the faint growl of an engine turning over. He stopped and bent his head in the direction of the noise. It seemed to come from far away, across a vast emptiness. And then it was a steady thrum that got louder for a moment before it began to fade, and he realized that the shooter was driving away.

Stiff fingered, he removed his right glove and fumbled in his pocket for the cell phone, nearly dropping it into the snow before he managed to grip the cold plastic. He jabbed at the on button and punched in 911, his eyes on the readout. Roaming. Roaming. Finally, the message, no service. He had to get out of the canyon.

He made a sharp left into a clearing and walked straight ahead toward the open expanse of snow and sagebrush, his muscles tense, waiting for the rifle shot—God, let the shooter be gone. There was no sound except for the *swoosh* of the wind. He tried the cell again and again. Still no service. He emerged from the canyon and started running. His legs felt like lead pipes pumping through the snow; his breath floated ahead in gray puffs. Down the road, the pickup looked as if it were part of the frozen landscape.

It took a good thirty minutes, he estimated. Extricating the collapsible shovel from the other tools in the lockbox in the pickup bed, shoveling snow out from the rear tires, spreading the bag of sand—half full, crammed in the corner of the box—behind the tires. Then jiggling the key in the ignition until the engine finally turned over and rocking the pickup backward and forward, the tires kicking out the sand and snow, until he was free. Craning his head around to stare out the rear window, driving in reverse along the tracks—his and the shooter's—until he came to a spot where he was able to manage a U-turn. And every few minutes, he pulled out the cell, jabbing in 911.

He was starting the climb out of the valley, the bluffs looming above, the phone pressed against his ear, when the cell came alive: "Fremont County Sheriff's Office." A woman's voice across a great distance.

"This is Father O'Malley," he said, and he told her that he'd found the bodies of three men at the site of the Bates Battle, near Bates Creek north of Lysite.

"Bates Battle," she repeated. "Deputies will be there as soon as possible, Father. It could take awhile."

He eased on the brake, looking for another place in which to make a U-turn, and told the operator that he would be waiting near the battlefield.

"THIS MIGHT HURT a little." The medic was bending so close that Father John could see the lint caught in the zipper of the man's gray jacket. He felt a crack of pain breaking across the side of his face.

"Okay, looks like that's the last splinter embedded in your cheek. Now for a little antiseptic," the man went on, swabbing Father John's cheek with a liquid that stung like acid. "You should get to emergency and have this stitched."

Father John stared into the dusk, his jaw clenched against the pain. Odors reminiscent of alcohol floated in front of him. "Just put on a Band-Aid," he managed.

The medic was probably in his twenties. He looked like a twelve-year-old, with slim, capable hands and traces of acne on his face. "If you don't get stitches, you'll carry a half-inch scar below your cheekbone," he said.

"Just the Band-Aid." Father John waited while the man pressed something adhesive over the top of his cheek, then he thanked him, swung off the gurney, and ducked out the opened rear doors of the ambulance into the cold air that crept through his jacket and into his bones. The pain had subsided into a mild stinging sensation. The Band-Aid felt like a poultice. Father John had the sense that he was peering across a white ridge. He patted at the gauzy patch and made his way toward the pickups parked in the mouth of the gorge.

"There you are, John." The man coming toward him, blue, red, and yellow lights swirling over his stocky frame and fleshy face, was Andy Burton, Fremont County detective. Head thrust forward, shoulders slightly hunched, a man not to be hurried. Father John had met him on numerous occasions, usually when Burton was investigating a crime that had occurred in the county but involved someone on the reservation. The battlefield was in Fremont County, outside the reservation boundaries. And Burton was in charge.

"I was about to head over to the ambulance to have a talk with you," he said. "What's the medic say? You gonna be okay?"

"He said I'm fit as a fiddle."

"Yeah, you look it." The detective moved in close and squinted at the Band-Aid. "You're lucky you aren't one of the bodies out there," he said, curving a gloved thumb back toward the canyon. "Could've been a bullet that hit your face instead of a piece of tree stump. You wanna explain why you didn't call us instead of heading out here alone?"

Father John jammed the sheet of paper with the message written on it into Burton's hand and told him that he'd wanted to check the battlefield and make certain the message wasn't some kind of a joke.

The detective held the paper up in the flashing lights. After a moment, he said, "Not unusual for a killer to return to the site of the crime, do a little gloating. Maybe he was hoping you'd show up after you got the message. Looks to me like the killer not only wanted the three Indians dead; he wanted the Indian priest dead, too, for some reason. I gotta tell you," he said, shaking his head, "you and Vicky Holden are a pair."

"Vicky!" Father John stared at the other man, surprised at the way the sound of her name had startled him, unlocking a flood of unwanted emotions. He and Vicky had worked together on dozens of cases over the past six years: DUIs, suicide attempts, domestic abuse, even homicides. They made a good team, priest and lawyer. So many cases and memories, and the feelings that he wished he could ignore. He'd made a point not to call her. It had been three months since he'd talked to her.

"What does Vicky have to do with this?" His voice sounded brittle in the cold.

"I'm just saying . . ." The flashing lights sparkled in the man's dark eyes. "You know that if Vicky had been the one to get that message, she would've been out looking around by herself, just like you. One of these days, you're liable to get yourselves in a situation you can't handle."

A procession had begun moving out of the shadows in the canyon: a line of men carrying three bags that bulged with the weight of bodies. The sound of boots on the snow and the low murmur of voices cut through the stillness. Groups of deputies stepped back, re-forming into new groups, as the procession came through the splash of lights, then moved off to the left toward the van that, Father John knew, belonged to the coroner.

"Since you figured out where the bodies were," Burton turned back, "what else have you figured out? What do you think happened out here?"

Father John was quiet a moment, marshalling his own thoughts into a logical order. Finally he said, "The killer intended to re-create the Bates Battle."

Burton was staring at him, perplexity and interest mingling in the man's expression, and Father John hurried on: "Eighteen-seventy-four. It was the last massacre of the Arapahos before they were sent to the reservation."

The doors of the coroner's van cracked shut, and Father John felt his muscles clench. For an instant, he'd thought it was a rifle shot. He said, "I think the killer posed the bodies to make them look like the bodies of warriors in the old photographs of battlefields. It's probably how the bodies looked after the Bates Battle."

"You're saying that somebody's reliving a battle from the nineteenth century?" Burton stared at the van that had come to life, yellow head-lights flaring ahead, red taillights blinking. He threw up both hands and looked back to Father John. "Well, that's just great. We got some nut running around trying to relive history. Any of the dead men look familiar to you?"

Father John shook his head. Across an expanse of grayness splotched with lights, the van was making a slow U-turn, the wheels digging a path through the snow, sagebrush raking the sides. Another moment, and the vehicle was heading out of the valley toward the dark shadows of the bluffs in the distance. He was thinking that he'd tried to identify the faces—the frozen faces—but he couldn't remember ever seeing them before. Maybe at a powwow or some other celebration, he couldn't be sure, but he didn't know them. And yet, over the years, he'd gotten to know most of the Arapahos . . .

"They could be Shoshone," he said.

"Same conclusion I been coming around to." The detective spoke hurriedly, pleased to confirm his own thoughts. "Hard to tell from the frozen faces what tribe they might belong to for sure, but Larry Miner over there"—he gestured with his head toward one of the deputies standing a few feet away—"says he thinks one of the dead men might've filed a complaint with the police on the rez against an Arapaho a couple of days ago. Can't be sure until the coroner gets the IDs. We found a pickup off in the trees. Might belong to one of the victims. Plates are gone. Glove compartment cleaned out. It'll take a while to ID the owner. What is it, John?" The detective leaned forward, his sour breath coming toward him.

"It makes sense," Father John said, thinking out loud now. Then he told the other man that it was Shoshones who had led Captain Bates and his troops to the Arapaho village. He stopped and drew in a couple of breaths. In his head was the tinny, mechanical voice. *Revenge is sweet . . .*

"So you're saying," the detective began, searching for the words, "that the murdered men represent Shoshones who attacked Arapahos a hundred and thirty years ago, and now we got a crazy Arapaho looking for revenge? Oh, my God." He started pounding one gloved fist against the other. "I don't want to go there, John. If the Shoshones think an Arapaho killed three of their men, there'll be full-out war on the reservation. One tribe fighting the other, just like in the past. God, John. Arapahos and Shoshones been getting along now for more than a hundred years. Maybe the tribes don't love each other, but they don't hate each other anymore. Kids go to school together. There's even some families that are intermarried. We can't have these homicides tearing people apart."

"It's a theory, that's all," Father John said, trying to ignore the sound of the mechanical voice in his head.

"Yeah, a theory." The detective jumped on that. "Let's not draw any conclusions until we get IDs and investigate why the men came out here. Could be a drug deal that went bad, or just plain bad blood between a few individuals. No sense in getting people riled up on the rez when we don't know what took place."

Father John let his gaze trail over the knots of deputies making their way toward the vehicles. Tomorrow they'd be back, he knew, searching the snow for bullets and cartridges and footprints, anything that might point to the killer, and they might come up with the same theory. Three dead Shoshones on the Bates Battlefield, revenge killings for a nineteenth-century massacre. And tomorrow the moccasin telegraph would flash the theory like lightning across the reservation.

God help us, he thought. The whole reservation could go to war.

6

VICKY CLIMBED THE flight of stairs and let herself through the wood door with the plaque at the side that read, "Holden and Lone Eagle, Attorneys-at-Law." Annie's chair was vacant, swiveled left toward Adam's office. The murmur of voices, low and serious, wafted past the closed door. Vicky headed toward her own office on the right, shut the door behind her, and dropped her briefcase on the desk. A curious lightness had come over her as she'd driven back across the reservation, eating up the miles between the tribal courthouse in Fort Washakie and her office in Lander, like an invisible weight gradually lifting from her shoulders as the snow-traced asphalt unrolled ahead.

Frankie Montana was lucky for now; the man didn't even know how lucky he was or how close he was to disaster. Banishment. It was hard to imagine anything worse. Even a prison sentence held the promise that, eventually, a man could return home. But banishment meant never again setting foot on the reservation, never attending the Sun Dance or the powwows, never going to family get-togethers, high school basketball games, church services. It meant being banished from the life of the *Hino'no ei.*

A door thumped shut in the outer office, followed by muffled footsteps crossing the carpet and the sharp rap of knuckles against her door. Vicky hung up her coat in the closet and turned back as the door swung inward. Adam Lone Eagle leaned into the opening a moment, then stepped inside and pushed the door closed behind him.

"Got a minute?" There was a hard, unsettling edge to his voice.

"What is it, Adam?" Vicky stepped over to the desk, not taking her eyes away. Adam's face might have been sculptured in stone, jaw thrust forward and light blazing in his black eyes, as if he had a fever. The little scar at the outer edge of his cheek was pulsing ragged and red. She knew him well enough to know when he was angry. It was like the force of storm clouds building over the mountains, about to explode over the plains. It had never exploded over her. Still Vicky could feel her muscles tense, the shadow of that other life with Ben Holden moving at the edge of her memory. She and Adam had been lovers now since the fall—lovers and law partners, a thin line to navigate, she'd argued, but Adam had tossed aside her objections. He wanted both, he'd said. He wanted all of her, and they would make it work out.

"We have to talk," he said.

"Have a seat." Vicky gestured with her head toward one of the side chairs, but it was clear that he had no intention of sitting down. She stopped herself from dropping onto her own chair and faced him across the desk.

"You'd better tell me what's bothering you," she said, trying for a placating tone. God, she hated that tone. *Ben, honey, what's bothering you?* The ultimate defensive position imprinted in her from that other life, ready to spring into action. Ironic. The tone had seldom worked.

"Bob Posey called again this morning." Adam waited a couple of beats, letting the information float between them. Director of natural resources on the Wind River Reservation, Posey was a Shoshone with the power to hire law firms for the important matters—water, oil and gas, gold mining, timber, exactly the type of law in which she and Adam intended to specialize. "We'll be the best damn Indian lawyers in the country," was the way he'd put it when they'd agreed to start a firm together. "Any tribe that has a problem protecting its natural resources will come to us."

"He wants an answer." Adam pushed on. "What's it going to be, Vicky? Are we handling the proposal to manage wolves on the reservation or is a law firm in Cheyenne going to get the retainer?"

"Of course we'll handle it." Vicky could hear the surprise in her voice. "We settled this last week, Adam."

"We don't have time to practice natural resource law and defend the two-bit criminals like Frankie Montana."

"The tribal judge released Frankie on a personal recognizance," she said, struggling to ignore Adam's tone. Then she told him the Shoshones who had filed the complaint were the only witnesses and that she would file a motion to dismiss.

"That's supposed to reassure me? How long before Montana's back here with some other charge? The man's a loser, Vicky. He's one step from being locked up, if not on this week's charges, then next week's. I don't get it. I thought we'd agreed to move away from defending two-bit criminals so we can concentrate on the kind of matters that make a difference to our people. Why are you bothering with Frankie Montana?"

"I told you, Adam." Vicky felt as if she were on the stand, an unwilling witness being badgered by the prosecutor. "I don't intend to see an innocent man go to prison. And Frankie's mother and I went to school together. She asked me to help her son. I'm not going to turn away from people I know."

"You know everybody on the reservation, Vicky." Adam swung around and walked over to the window. Through his blue shirt she could see the muscles of his back flex with each breath. The flecks of gray in his black hair shone in the light. For several seconds, he stared outside at the snow blowing across the flat roofs of the buildings across the street.

"I'm not saying that losers don't deserve an attorney," he said, turning back, "but we don't have the time to handle everything. How about the new lawyer down the street? Samantha Lowe? She just opened her office, and she's hungry for work. She called me last week, and we went to lunch . . ."

"Lunch?" Adam hadn't mentioned lunch with the new lawyer in town. The woman was beautiful, according to the gossip she'd heard from Annie. Great figure, flowing blond hair, in her twenties, not long out of law school. It didn't surprise her that a beautiful young attorney looking for work to be shuffled her way would invite the male partner in a firm out to lunch.

Adam came back across the office, something new in his expression, softer and placating and—was she imagining it?—guilty. "I'm not Ben Holden, chasing every skirt on the horizon."

Vicky exhaled a long breath that left her feeling as if there were still knots of hot air in her lungs. That was the problem, wasn't it? The shadows of her life with Ben blocking the light in this new relationship. God, would she ever be able to trust any man?

"I'm sorry, Adam," she managed.

He looked away at that, the muscles of his face shifting back into the hard, sculptured look he'd worn when he'd walked into the office. "Samantha needs work," he said.

Samantha. Something in the way that Adam pronounced the name made Vicky look away.

"All you have to do, Vicky, is refer people like Montana down the street to the new lawyer in town." Adam had turned away. "They'll have good representation, so your conscience will be clear, and we can practice the kind of law we agreed to practice."

"Samantha Lowe isn't native."

"That doesn't mean she isn't competent."

"It means Frankie wouldn't trust her."

"That would be his problem, Vicky." Adam locked eyes with her again. "What's it going to be?"

"We've met the deadlines." Now Vicky stepped around the desk, unable to hold herself still any longer, propelled across the office by the frustrations and suspicions churning inside her. She reached the window and let her eyes sweep across the traffic crawling through the slush on Main Street below, aware of the sound of the phone ringing in the outer office. Finally she looked back. Adam had perched on the edge of her desk, black eyes narrowed on her. "We filed the motion to appeal with the federal court in Cheyenne on the water management decision," she began, then she rattled off the other deadlines they'd met on the cases they were handling for the Wind River tribes.

Adam kept his face unreadable, not interrupting or giving any indication that she was going on about things he knew very well. When she'd finished, he said, "You work all the time, Vicky. You come in early. It's eight or nine in the evening when you leave. Last weekend, I suggested that we go to a lodge in Yellowstone where we could watch one of the wolf packs. You were too busy. You had work to finish up. No weekends off for you." He shook his head. "I miss you, Vicky. It's been almost two weeks since we've even had dinner together."

Vicky swung around and stared down at the traffic again. Adam was right. Frankie Montana had consumed the day, and for what? To keep him out of jail? To keep him from being banished? The man enjoyed teetering along the edge of a cliff from which, sooner or later, he was bound to plunge. There were other cases stretching back through the months since she and Adam had become partners. DUIs and adoptions and wills. Leases on small businesses that Arapahos were struggling to start in Lander or Riverton. The phone calls, the pleading, desperate voices—*Can you help me, Vicky?*—that had made up the bulk of her business when she'd practiced alone, the desperate voices that had followed her to the new firm.

She walked back to the desk. "Get me Samantha's number," she said.

Adam's face cracked into a smile. "How about a trip to see the wolves next weekend?"

"You're pushing, Adam." Vicky smiled back at him.

There was a double rap on the door and, not taking his gaze from her, Adam stepped backward and yanked the door open. Annie slid inside, moving into the line of sight between him and Vicky, head bobbing from one to the other.

"Oh, my God." The words came like an exhalation of air. She clasped her hands in front of her mouth and fixed her gaze on Adam. "My girlfriend just called me with the news. Her boyfriend works for the sheriff's department."

"Just tell us . . ." Vicky had to stop herself from saying the rest of it: *And skip the drama.* Every bit of gossip that floated off the moccasin telegraph and down the telephone line into the office was a monumental, earthshaking bit of news that Annie felt her duty to pass on immediately.

"They found three bodies," the woman blurted.

"What?" Adam tilted his head toward the young woman.

"Three men were found out in the middle of nowhere at the site of some old battle. Gates, Lakes, something like that."

"The Bates Battlefield?" Vicky caught the flash of recognition in Adam's eyes. He knew. The Bates Massacre had almost destroyed her people, sent the survivors scurrying around the plains to other tribes, willing to trade their customs and language, their very identity, for enough food to stay alive.

"Murdered, Vicky," Annie said. "Shot down just like warriors in the Old Time, like there was some kind of battle that went on again out there. Father John found them."

Vicky felt Adam's gaze shift toward her, and she made her own expression unreadable. *The face of a rock.* The sound of grandmother's voice in her head like the strain of a familiar melody. *Nobody can see inside a rock, Vicky. You remember that when you don't want anybody to know what you're thinking.*

John O'Malley, she was thinking, aware of the little stab of pain, like a needle pricking her heart. Someone must have called him and sent him out to the battlefield. Someone worried or in trouble. Someone who knew that he would go. John O'Malley would always go. She closed her eyes a moment. God, let me forget the man.

Then, another thought—the killer could have sent John O'Malley to find bodies that could have remained hidden in the snow for a week. The killer must have *wanted* the bodies found.

"What else did you hear?" Adam turned his full attention to Annie, and Vicky realized that he had deliberately turned away from her own rock-hard face. It struck her that grandmother could have been wrong, that someone might see inside a rock.

"They looked like warriors." Annie stumbled on. "I mean, the bodies were staged so they looked like they fell in battle. Somebody arranged their arms and legs. I mean, how weird is that? One of the bodies was propped up against a tree stump. And Father John . . ."

"What about him," Vicky cut in, ignoring the glance Adam threw her way.

"Somebody shot at him while he was out finding the bodies. He got hit."

Vicky gripped the edge of the desk. She felt as if the floor were moving beneath her, the walls of the office closing in, sucking out the air.

Adam's voice floated through the vacuum tightening around her. "Is he okay?"

Annie's voice "He's fine. Just a nick on his face. Didn't even go to the hospital. Too stubborn."

Oh, John O'Malley was a stubborn man, all right, Vicky was thinking, waves of relief washing over her. He knew *who* he was. A priest. He would never be other than who he was.

"Three men shot to death," Adam said, as if he were trying to wrap his mind around the immensity of the fact. "Who are they?"

Vicky stared at Adam, scarcely able to get her own thoughts around the notion that had flashed into her mind.

"If the sheriff's office knows," Annie went on, "they aren't saying. Waiting to notify relatives, I guess, but everybody thinks the dead guys must've been doing drugs. I mean, why else were they out in the bad-lands? My girlfriend said they looked like Shoshones."

Adam took hold of the edge of the door. "Thanks, Annie," he said, nodding toward the outer office. "Let us know if you hear anything else."

The secretary hesitated a moment, then, reluctance in the slope of her shoulders, she dodged past Adam and through the door.

"Vicky," he began, letting the door swing closed.

She held up one hand. "Don't say it. Frankie Montana might be a lot of things, but he's not capable of murdering three men to keep them from testifying against him."

"This isn't our battle, Vicky."

"It's quite a coincidence, wouldn't you say? What if the dead men turn out to be the Shoshones Frankie was accused of assaulting? Who do you think the sheriff's investigator is going to go after?"

"Frankie can always get another attorney, if he needs one."

"You expect me to leave him in the hands of a lawyer out of law school—how many years, Adam? Two, three?"

Adam didn't say anything, and for a long moment, silence hung between them like an invisible presence. Then he opened the door and went out, pulling the door shut behind him so slowly that Vicky could barely hear the lock click into place. She sank into her chair, her eyes glued to the door, a mute symbol of his contempt.

This could be nothing, she told herself. The murdered men could be anybody, any Shoshones on the reservation. And yet . . .

An indefinable dread, like an icy grip, had taken hold of her. If Lucille Montana called again and asked her to help Frankie, she knew that she would not turn the woman away.

FATHER JOHN POURED the last of the coffee into a mug and carried it down the hall and into his study. He dropped into the old leather chair behind his desk and took a draw of the coffee, barely warm and sharp with bitterness, left over from dinner a good four hours ago. He'd missed dinner—hamburger and mashed potatoes, which Elena, who had kept the residence running since long before he'd come to St. Francis, had piled on a plate and set in the refrigerator. He wasn't hungry. It was thirst that had taken hold of him somewhere in the darkness as he'd driven west on 26 and south on Highway 789, yellow headlights flickering over the snow, every cell in his body screaming for forgetfulness. A capful of whiskey was all he needed. There was courage in whiskey. He'd passed the bars in Riverton, the drive-in liquor stores, struggling not to notice them, and had kept going. Help me, help me, Lord.

He drained the last of the coffee and set the mug on a stack of papers. Shadows crawled down the walls over the bookcases and side chairs and crept across the carpet. Light from the streetlamps around Circle Drive splashed on the black panes of the windows. The small clock at the corner of his desk glowed red in the semidarkness: 10:53. His cheek burned with pain, and the Band-Aid was moist and cold with blood. He ached with exhaustion, but there would be no sleep tonight, nothing but the images glued to the backs of his eyelids of the blood-crusted bodies, the angles of arms and legs, the gray frozen hands and faces.

"God help us," he said out loud, surprised at the sound of his own voice in the quiet. His mouth was dry. He felt as if he were breathing dust.

He reached over and switched on the desk lamp. A puddle of yellow light spread across the piles of papers and envelopes—letters to answer, bills to pay, notes to himself about upcoming meetings, ideas for homilies. Swiveling sideways toward a bookcase, he glanced over the shelves until he spotted the title on the spine of the book he was looking for. He plucked the book out of its slot. The jacket was white, with a photograph of four warriors sitting on their ponies. It had been a black and white photo until someone had colored the ponies a golden bronze. The faces of the warriors, squinting into the sun, were also bronze, like their sinewy arms, the trousers and shirts were gray, the beaded vests, red and blue, and the eagle-feathered headdresses, white and brown against the blue sky. Emblazoned in red above the photograph was the title: *War on the Plains.* Below the photograph, also in red, was the name of the author: Charles Lambert, Ph.D.

Father John opened the book and flipped through the pages, stopping to study the photographs. Warriors with naked chests and arms sat astride their ponies, both warriors and ponies painted for war. Warriors galloping out of the villages. Women, children, and old people herding horses packed with household goods, trying to escape an attack. Soldiers standing outside their tents on the plains. An army officer bent over papers on a collapsible desk, the gas lantern glowing on the canvas walls. Wooden structures at army forts facing one another across the parade grounds, American flags lofted on poles in the center. And the battlefields, pages of photographs from battles, as if, after the killing, soldiers had dug cameras out of their knapsacks, wanting to fix in time everything that had taken place.

There was a sameness to the images, and for a moment Father John wondered if the soldiers had posed the bodies of fallen warriors before they'd snapped the pictures. He dismissed the idea. The bodies lay as they had fallen, arms and legs askew, heads wrenched sideways. He flipped to the back of the book and glanced down the index until he found Bates Battle. He turned to a page near the end of the book, just like the battle itself, which had come near the end of the plains war, and began reading through the double columns of text: One hundred and sixty Shoshone warriors and a company of cavalry under Captain Alfred E. Bates rode to the Arapaho village in the gorge near a creek. The attack began at dawn on July 4, 1874. Some Arapaho warriors managed to climb up the slopes, outflank the attackers, and drive them from the village. When the fighting ended, forty-seven Arapahos lay dead. Most of the tipis and household goods had been torched, and the horses had been stampeded. The Bates Battle became known as the day they killed the Arapahos.

Father John leaned back in his chair. He could hear the mechanical voice in his head. The attack had occurred in the middle of the summer, the hottest time of the year. *In the heat. Revenge is sweet.*

A large black and white photograph spread across the following two pages, a view of the canyon, the steep, rocky slopes rising on either side. It looked peaceful and quiet, wild grasses covering the canyon floor, the kind of place for a picnic, not a place of death. But on the following page, a photograph of death, the body of a man propped against the stump of a tree, arms flopped at his sides. He wore a canvas jacket, opened over a white shirt with the dark splotch of blood in the center. His right hand was stuffed into the jacket pocket.

Father John closed the book and stared past the circle of light into the shadows. The killer had seen the photograph. The killer had shot the man, propped him against the tree stump, and put his right hand into his jacket pocket. Detective Burton was right. There was a maniac out there.

7

FATHER JOHN SPOTTED the woman as he headed across the mission grounds for the administration building. A small figure outlined in the dull morning light, standing outside the door on the concrete stoop, hunched forward, as if she weren't sure whether to try the door or flee down the steps. Parked in front of the building was a blue Ford sedan with a dented passenger door and a side-view mirror suspended from a tangle of wires. The woman's head jerked around as he approached. She backpedaled toward the railing, black boots skidding over the snowy concrete.

"Can I help you?" Father John started up the steps. The first parishioner of the day, he was thinking, dropping by—*Father, do you have a minute? I have to talk to somebody.* Except that she wasn't a parishioner. She wasn't anyone he had ever met, and she was younger than he'd realized at first, probably no more than twenty. A girl more than a woman, her straw-colored hair brushing the collar of the gray coat that strained against the front buttons, as if it were a size too small for her slight frame. She squinted along the railing at him. A small circle of metal glinted in one nostril.

"You the Indian priest?" she said.

He felt a jolt of alarm. The mechanical voice clanged through the fog in his head. *This is for the Indian priest.*

"Some people call me that," he said, holding his place halfway up the steps. He was thinking that he spent more time with Indian people than with white people. His parishioners were Arapahos. Days passed when the only other white person he talked to was his assistant. But it was the whites in Lander, the town that abutted the reservation, and in Riverton—encircled by the reservation—who had given him the name. The girl probably came from one of the towns.

"I'm Father O'Malley." He nodded toward the door. "Would you like to come inside?"

"Yeah." The girl gulped at the word, watchful eyes still observing him—observing the Band-Aid on his cheek, he realized. She stood very still, arms dangling at her side. Her hands were bare and raw looking. The gray coat had a belt that looped in front, and for the first time, he noticed the little bulge below her waist.

Father John took the last two stairs, opened the door, and led the girl across the wide corridor crisscrossed with shadows and arrows of light from outdoors. He pushed open the door to his office and motioned her inside. She hesitated for a couple of seconds, then hurried past him and planted herself in the center of the room, her gaze taking in the desk piled with papers and folders, the old leather chair with the gray tape that he'd plastered over a small tear in the middle, the side chairs that he kept for visitors, the file cabinets topped with books and papers, the bookcases with shelves bowing under the double stacks of books.

"How about a cup of coffee?" The phone started ringing. He decided to let it go to the answering machine.

"Water would be okay." The girl shrugged.

"Make yourself at home." Father John hung his jacket over the coat tree, then took two Styrofoam cups from the little table that held a coffeepot and jars of coffee, sugar, and powdered cream and headed down the corridor for water. When he returned, the girl was sitting on a side chair, rubbing her hands together and staring into the center of the room. He handed her one of the cups, pulled the other side chair around, and sat down facing her.

"Suppose you start by telling me your name," he said.

"Edie." It was little more than a whisper. Then she added, "Bradbury." She was very pretty: startling blue eyes and wide cheekbones, lips a slash of red against her pale skin. He could see the faintest line of blue veins in her temples as she sipped at the water.

"Edie Bradbury," he said, not meaning to sound surprised. He took a drink of his own water, then set the cup on the edge of the desk. Short for Edith, he supposed. A girl with an old-fashioned name and a silver ring in her pierced nostril, as if she'd found herself stranded in the twenty-first century and decided to acclimate herself.

"Are you in some kind of trouble, Edie?" he asked, his thoughts already jumping ahead. A pregnant girl, alone, with no one to help her and no money. He could call the pastors at the churches in Riverton and Lander, get the names of families willing to take in a pregnant girl. He could put her in touch with an agency that would arrange for an adoption, if that was what she wanted.

He realized she was starting to weep. She set her cup on the floor and began patting at the moisture on her cheeks with the back of one hand, and he got to his feet and pulled a tissue out of a box almost hidden in the clutter on his desk.

"I can't find my boyfriend," she said finally.

"When did you last see him?" He handed her the tissue and sat back down.

"Last Friday when he left for work. He goes to work after we get out of class. We been going to Central Wyoming College." She blotted her cheeks with the tissue, then began lacing it through her fingers. "Trent's not like that. Just go off like that and not come home or call me or anything. Sometimes he has to work late, but he always calls me. That's how he is. We're really close. And he knows I get crazy with worry, with the baby coming. I get all scared if I don't hear from him. That's how I know something bad's happened to him. He's gotta be in some kind of trouble."

"Have you called his friends?" Father John began. Then he reeled off the rest of the logical sequence: Work? Family? There was a steadiness in logic, a way of plodding on that could keep fear at bay.

She was nodding. Quick, spasmodic movements loosening a piece of the straw hair that fell over one eye. She pushed the hair back. "He showed up for work Friday night, 'cause I talked to his boss. But he didn't go in on Saturday when he was supposed to get time and a half. Never showed up yesterday, either. All I know is, we went to class together Friday afternoon and everything was, you know, normal. Even if he was in trouble, no way was Trent gonna miss class. It's all about the Indian wars, and he really got into it, you know what I mean? The teacher is a big history guru I never heard of before Trent convinced me I oughtta sign up for the class. Professor Lambert's the name, and he's written lots of books. Trent says nobody knows more about the Indian wars."

Charles Lambert, Father John was thinking. Author of the book he'd pulled out last evening. He had no idea that the man was teaching at the local college.

The girl had realigned herself in the chair. She swallowed hard and went on, "I called a couple of guys from class that Trent likes to hang out with, but nobody was home. Trent wouldn't just take off, Father," she said, her eyes flitting about the room. "He really loves me. I mean . . ." Flitting. Flitting. "Me and the baby, we mean everything to him."

Father John was quiet. He wasn't the one that she was trying to convince, he realized.

"What did his family say?" he said.

The girl took a moment, squeezing her eyes against the tears beading at the corners. "I been calling and calling his folks, and the minute they hear my voice, they hang up. They don't even wait for me to tell 'em that something bad's happened to Trent. They told him, 'Don't ever bring that white trash on the rez, 'cause we don't wanna see her.' They don't even know about the baby. God, if they knew!" She lifted one hand and started pulling at her hair. "I get so scared thinking about it, sometimes I wake up in the middle of the night and I'm shaking and crying, like they're gonna find some way to get my baby, maybe kill me, or something . . ."

"Hold on, Edie." Father John held up one hand. "Trent's Arapaho?"

"Why do you think that?" She gave a little laugh that sounded like a strangled cry. "Trent's real proud he's Shoshone. He says his people and the Arapahos are traditional enemies, even though they live on the same reservation now and they gotta get along. Only reason his family hates me is 'cause I'm white. So they think Trent's gonna go off with me and they'll never see him again. Well, soon's he finishes school, we're gonna get outta here all right. We been talking about where we'll go." She started tearing up again, tearing up and blotting the moisture with the tissue. "Maybe go to Denver so Trent can get a job and we can live in one of them suburbs, you know, and have a backyard for the baby. I always thought that'd be great, you know, if you was a kid and had a backyard."

"What's Trent's last name?" Father John asked, trying to lead her back. He was aware of the front door thudding shut, the scrape of Father Ian's boots in the corridor.

"Hunter," the girl said. "Trent tol' me the name used to be Man Who Hunts Buffalo, but it got shortened."

He'd heard the name, Father John was thinking, but he didn't know the family. St. Francis Mission was on the southeastern edge of the reservation, close to the Arapaho communities. The Shoshones lived to the west and north. It was as if each tribe had staked out its own territory.

He reached over and dragged the phone across the desk. "Why don't I call Trent's family," he said.

"Oh, Father, would you?" The girl leaned so far forward that, for a moment, he feared she might topple headfirst out of the chair. Before he could dial for information, she was rattling off the number. He punched in the keys and listened to the rhythmic buzz of a ringing phone.

"I know the number by heart," the girl was saying. "I called it so many times."

The buzzing stopped. A loud clanking sound came down the line, as if somebody had dropped the phone at the other end. Then a cough, and finally a man's voice, deep and tinged with annoyance. "Hello."

Father John gave his name and asked to speak with Trent.

The line seemed to go dead. Finally, the voice came again. "You the priest over at the Arapaho mission?" Annoyance had given way to surprise. "My boy doesn't live here anymore, Father. He's going to school in Riverton, lives over in town. Got himself a job there. Keeps pretty busy. You want his number?"

"I was wondering if you saw him this weekend?"

"This weekend? Nah. Trent works on Saturdays, and spends all day Sunday studying, that is . . ." He hesitated, then plunged on. "Got himself a girlfriend that takes up his time, even though I been telling him, 'Son, you don't need to get yourself all tangled up with women now. Just gotta get yourself through school.' I want my boy to make something of himself, Father."

"When's the last time you saw him?"

"I don't know. Maybe couple weeks ago. What's going on, Father? Yesterday, the tribal attorney calls, says that Trent's supposed to show up at the court. I told that attorney he had the wrong Shoshone. Trent's over in Riverton, minding his own business, like I wish a lot of people around here would do."

"Listen, Mr. Hunter," Father John said. "Trent's girlfriend is here with me. She hasn't seen Trent since Friday, and she's worried about him. Do you have any idea where he might be?"

The line went quiet a moment before the man said, "Let me tell you something, Father. If I knew where Trent's holing up, I sure wouldn't tell that white girl. Sounds like Trent finally got away from her, all right. My guess is he doesn't want her knowing his whereabouts."

Father John thanked the man and set the receiver back in the cradle. The girl was still leaning forward, clasping her hands so tightly in her lap that her knuckles had turned bloodless.

"His father hasn't seen him," he told her.

"Oh, God." She sank back against her chair. "I did right, coming here. Trent always said to me, Edie, if there's any trouble, you go to the Indian priest at the Catholic mission. You ask anybody, they'll tell you how to find him. So I came here. I didn't know where else to go."

"What kind of trouble, Edie? Was Trent expecting trouble?"

She shrugged, lifted her chin, and locked eyes with him again. "There was some guy over at the Cowboy."

"The Cowboy?"

"Bar and grill over in Riverton. Sometimes we go there for a burger. So we're just sitting in the booth, me and Trent and these other guys from class, and this Indian at the bar starts mouthing off, saying how Shoshones oughtta get the hell outta there, that nobody wants 'em. And Trent told him to shut up, and the guy says, 'Yeah? You wanna go outside and party?' And Trent says for him to go . . ." She paused. "You know what I'm saying."

Father John nodded. "Any idea of who he was?"

"Arapaho, that's all I know. Trent says to me, 'Take a good look, 'cause that's an Arapaho and he's nothing but trouble. One of these days, we might have to teach him a lesson. All I know is, he was a skinny guy with tattoos on his arms and a long nose that made him look like a horse. He even had his hair pulled back in a ponytail."

Father John didn't say anything for a moment. He could think of two or three young men who might fit the description. Troublemakers, young men who got drunk and hung out at the park. Park rangers, they were called. Like the fort Indians in the Old Time, hanging out at the forts where the alcohol was always available. Usually harmless, except to themselves.

"That's it?" Father John said. But that wasn't all of it. He could tell from the way the girl's blue eyes shifted away. "Suppose you tell me the rest," he said.

"It's no big deal." The girl shrugged again. Moisture glistened on her cheeks. "I mean, we got things settled so there wasn't any more trouble from my boyfriend, I mean, before I met Trent. Jason Rizzo's his name. He's one of them white supremacist guys, always talking about the pure Aryan race and how it can't be contaminated, and all that crap. I don't know why I ever got involved with him, except I was real lonely, you know, and this girl I was working with over at the thrift shop says her boyfriend's in prison, and he's got this buddy, Jason, that's looking for somebody to write to. So I figure, what the heck. Poor guy's in prison, probably lonely like me, so we start sending letters back and forth, and he seems like a real nice guy. Then he gets out of prison and moves to Riverton, and he's expecting me to be his girlfriend, but I see he's real scary. I was his girl for a while, but I was looking to get away from him, and then I met Trent. He helped me get away. Said, 'Come on, Edie. You can go to school. You can make something of yourself.' Gave me the guts to walk out, 'cause I knew that he was gonna protect me if Jason came after me. So I moved in with Trent in a little house behind a big, old mansion over on Pershing." The girl caught her face in both hands. Her shoulders began shaking, the sobs coming in jerky spasms.

Father John waited until the sobs were quiet, and then he said, "What happened, Edie?"

She dropped her hands and started lacing and unlacing the tissue again, keeping her gaze on some point beyond his shoulder. A moment passed before she said, "It pissed Jason off real good, Trent being Indian and all. About a month ago, Jason and two guys he hung out with waited outside for Trent to get home from work. They beat him up real bad."

Father John sat back against the wood chair, turning over in his mind what the girl had said. Shoshone man, missing four days. And out at the Bates Battlefield, three dead Indian men who might be Shoshone. Dear God, was it possible? Somebody had followed Trent Hunter around, waiting for a chance to kill him? Finally corralling him and two other men and shooting all of them? Then mistaking Father Owens for the Indian priest and sending a message to make certain the bodies were found?

He tried to shake off the idea. He was catching the girl's fear. It was like a virus. The bodies hadn't been identified. There was no proof that they were Shoshone. No proof that Trent Hunter was dead.

The answer was probably simple, straightforward, logical. It was possible—he didn't like the idea—but it was possible that Trent had simply decided to disappear into the reservation. Maybe he'd had enough of the white world: classes, work, a pregnant, white girlfriend with a violent ex-boyfriend. Maybe he'd just walked away.

And yet the girl could be right. Maybe it wasn't like Trent Hunter to walk away.

He said, "I think you should go to the Riverton Police."

"Police?" Her voice rose in surprise. The blue eyes went large for an instant, then narrowed into slits of concentration. "Trent never wanted to call the police, even after Jason beat him up. He said the police don't like Indians. They never side with Indians."

"Listen, Edie." Father John tried to catch the girl's eyes, but they were darting about the office. "Trent could be hurt. He might have had an accident. His car could be off the road somewhere." He was thinking about the pickup Burton had found at the battlefield. He hurried on. "I know a detective who will take his disappearance very seriously. He'll check with the sheriff's office. He won't stop looking until he finds Trent."

He got to his feet, not waiting for a reply. Leaning across the desk, he picked up the receiver and tapped out the number to the Riverton Police Department. One ring, and an operator was on the other end. He gave his name and asked to speak to Detective Mike Perry.

The girl pushed her thin body out of the chair, stumbling forward a little, shaking her head. "I don't know," she said. "I don't know if I should go to the police."

"Hey, Father John. How's it going?" The detective's voice boomed down the line.

"Hang on a minute," Father John said. Then, cupping his hand over the mouthpiece he said, "I can go with you, Edie."

She stared at him a moment with bleary, hopeless eyes, then shrugged and turned away.

He removed his hand and said, "I have a young woman here, Mike." Then he told the detective that Edie Bradbury's boyfriend had been missing since last Friday. His name was Trent Hunter, Shoshone, a student at the college. He'd had a couple of run-ins recently with a white supremacist, and he might be in trouble.

The detective let out a little whistle. "Sounds like we better have a talk. How soon can she get over here."

"We're on the way." Father John replaced the receiver and turned to the girl who had moved into the doorway, glancing between the office and corridor, the front edges of her coat bunched in one hand.

"It's okay, Father," she said. "I can do it."

8

THE ADMINISTRATION BUILDING was suspended in quiet for a moment. The ringing phones, clack of Father Ian's computer keys, banging doors, and boots shuffling in the corridor as people came for counseling or meetings—the usual noises seemed to have stalled. Father John stood at the window and watched the blue sedan snake around Circle Drive, engine clanking, black clouds of exhaust spitting from the tailpipe. Then the girl was gone. The clanking blended into the hum of traffic out on Seventeen-Mile Road.

He stepped back to his desk, picked up the phone, and dialed the number to St. Aiden's.

"John!" Father Nathan Owens' voice burst down the line. "My God, are you all right?"

Father John assured the man that he was okay.

"The radio says you were wounded."

A small wound. Still assuring the man. Nothing that wouldn't heal in a couple of days.

"You could have been killed."

True, Father John was thinking. He might have died out there with the other three men.

"If anything had happened to you," the other priest was hurrying on, "I never could have forgiven myself. I shouldn't have gotten you involved, John. It was unconscionable. I should have figured out the message and gone there myself."

"You didn't know someone would try to shoot me, Nathan."

The line went quiet for a moment. Then the other priest said, "I don't like this, John. That frightening message, and three men shot to death. The moccasin telegraph says they're Shoshones. I hope it wasn't an Arapaho who did this. It'll tear the reservation apart."

"Listen, Nathan," Father John said, "Detective Burton from the sheriff's office will probably want to talk to you."

"He's already called. He'll be here in thirty minutes. I intend to give him the tape." The other priest paused. "Be careful, John," he said. "Whoever killed those poor men is very evil. There's no telling what else he may do."

Father John thanked the man and dropped the receiver back into the cradle. Then he went down the corridor in search of Father Ian. He found the man hunched over sheets of paper lined up in front of him, elbow braced on the edge of the desk, chin resting on one fist.

"How's it going?" Father John swung a wooden side chair around and straddled it, folding his arms over the back. He hadn't meant to leave the new priest alone so much. Here only a few weeks, still getting a feel for the place, and yesterday evening, it had been up to Ian to explain the bleak financial situation to the parish council and assure the members—this from the pastor, himself—that no programs would be cut in the summer. There had been no chance to talk to the man since the meeting. Ian had gone to bed by the time Father John had gotten back to the mission last night, and he wasn't around this morning. And Edie Bradbury had appeared first thing.

He could see that his assistant was poring over the budget, which the man had volunteered to handle. *Good at numbers, John. BA in finance, you know.* Father John had thrust the budget into the man's hands, wondering if it was just a stroke of good luck that his assistants usually had a background in finance or accounting that made them eager to take over the budget, or if the Provincial, knowing the pastor's lack of interest, made a point to send a man who might put St. Francis Mission in the black.

"You could say everything's hunky-dory." Ian looked up. Flecks of light seemed to have attached themselves to the man's eyes, like paint splashed on dark stones. His hair was mussed, as if he'd been combing it with his fingers. Beneath his eyes were the dark half-circles of a man who hadn't been sleeping well. "That, of course, is not the case with the budget."

"Sorry I missed the council meeting," Father John said.

"No problem." Ian backed his elbow off the desk and leaned into the armrest of his chair. "A couple of phone messages when I got in this morning. People wanting to know about the bodies you found at some-place called Bates." The man shrugged and cracked a thin smile. "Priest stumbles onto dead bodies in the middle of nowhere? I must have missed something in the job description. That the usual routine around here?"

Father John shook his head and looked away a moment. God, he hoped not. The images of the bodies were still there, floating in front of his eyes.

"So, how'd you get that?" Ian jabbed a finger toward the Band Aid on his face.

Father John lifted his hand and pressed at the edges of the small wound. A burning sensation ran through his cheek, which surprised him. Sometime during the night, the pain had receded into a dull throb, and this morning, the throb had dissolved into numbness. He locked eyes with the other priest and told him about the telephone message and the fact that he'd guessed the bodies might be at the site of an old massacre, all of which Ian seemed to take in with mute acceptance, as if figuring out the clue in obscure phone messages were just another part of the job that he would become accustomed to. He didn't want to talk about dead men. He didn't want to relive the horror. Father John asked how the meeting had gone.

"Ah, the meeting." Father Ian gripped the armrests, pushed himself to his feet, and walked over to the window. "I don't know how you've done it, John," he said.

"What are you talking about?"

"Run this mission on hope and prayer and convinced the parish council that hope and prayer are legitimate business tactics. The council is in complete agreement with you that there's no need to cut back on anything. What are we going to pay the religious education teachers with? Prayers?"

Father John drummed his fingers on the top of the chair, listening to the *click click click* noise that punctuated his thoughts. This was his fault. He'd never wanted to dive into the abysmal swamp of the mission's finances, never wanted to admit that St. Francis couldn't afford the programs it offered, never wanted to cut back. Just the opposite. He'd added programs every year, and he *had* convinced the parish council that the little miracles would arrive in the mail, unsolicited and unexpected—checks falling out of envelopes with return addresses in towns he'd never heard of and scribbled notes that read, "Use this to help the Indians." The funny thing was, the little miracles had occurred, and the mission had gone along, lurching from one potential financial disaster to the next, always bailed out at the last minute.

He got to his feet and, leaning over, gripped the top of the chair. Donations were always smaller as summer approached, but this year, they had been almost nonexistent. He should have been the one to break the bad news to the council that the miracles hadn't arrived. Ian was right. They would have to cut back.

He said, "We'll schedule another meeting."

"Already done." Father Ian jammed his hands into the pockets of his khakis. "I suggested that we revisit the situation next Wednesday evening. That work for you?"

Father John nodded. He waited a couple of beats before he said, "How are things with you?"

The other priest took a step backward, tilted his head, and stared up at the ceiling, as if the answer might fall out of the cracked plaster. "You mean," he locked eyes again with Father John, "am I avoiding the temptation of demon rum, whiskey, vodka and staying off the bottle?"

"This can be a lonely place."

"Loneliness." The other priest drew in his lower lip, considering. "Was that your excuse?"

Father John didn't take his eyes away. The man not only had a finely tuned way of avoiding uncomfortable subjects, he was also good at turning things around, so that, all of a sudden, the conversation between the superior and the priest under his supervision was about the superior.

He said, "There are a lot of excuses. Take your pick."

The other priest gave a dry, brittle laugh. "You want the truth, John? I never needed an excuse. I liked to drink, that was all. Do I want another drink? What do you think?"

Father John was thinking that they were a pair. The truth was, they could both get drunk right now. Drive over to Riverton, buy a couple of bottles of Jim Beam, and sink into the soft, quiet fog of alcohol. He said, "I guess we both have to make the decision every day to stay sober."

"What works for you, John? You've been making that decision every day for what? Nine years?"

"About that," Father John said. He could count the days. "The work here. The people. AA. Prayer." The list was short, he knew, and fragile. "Listen, Ian, we can help each other. Any time you want to talk . . ."

The other priest threw up both hands. "I had enough talking in rehab. Enough trying to invent my childhood anxieties. Truth was, I had good parents, good friends, good schools. The all-American suburban middle-class childhood, that was mine. Played soccer and tennis. Never hung out with the druggies, because, frankly, I had my own drug."

"I wasn't suggesting we explore your childhood," Father John said. "But if the thirst gets too strong . . ."

"We can have our own little rehab group."

Father John didn't say anything. He might have been facing a mirror. The cocky priest with a chip the size of Boston on his shoulder in his superior's office that afternoon—what? ten years ago?—and the superior had told him that he had a choice. Go into rehab at Grace House or take an office job in a back room someplace and drink himself to death. His choice. Odd, when he thought about it now. He'd replied that he wanted to think about it. *Think about it!* As if there really was any choice between life and death. He'd been at Grace House four months before he'd decided to choose life.

Watching the muscles work in Father Ian's cheek, he wondered if the man had left rehab too soon, before he'd made *his* choice.

"See you at AA tonight," Father John said, starting into the corridor.

"Hold on," the other priest called, and Father John turned back. Ian came across the office and thrust a wad of miniature sheets at him. "Telephone messages," he said.

Father John thumbed through the sheets as he walked back down the corridor: Jennie Antelope, Mary Blue Eagle, Les Walker. And all of the messages were the same: *Who could have killed those men? What happened, Father?* He could sense the undercurrent of fear in the questions, as if the fear itself had invaded the pieces of paper.

Father John dropped into the leather chair at his desk and stared at the name on the last sheet: Charles Lambert. *Please call back.* Next to the name was the phone number.

He swiveled toward the bookcases, running his gaze over the spines of the books wedged into the shelves. Novels, books of poetry among the books on opera, philosophy, theology, American history, the Plains Indians, the Arapahos. He could read the story of his own life in the titles.

There it was. *The Way of the Warriors.* The author's name was in small blue type: Charles Lambert, Ph.D. Father John pulled out the book, opened the back cover, and studied the black and white photo.

Probably in his seventies with white, curly hair, like the mane of an old lion, and piercing, intelligent eyes that stared into the camera. The man was a professor of history at a small college in New York, the author of dozens of scholarly papers and articles and five books on the American Indians. He had read two of them, Father John thought. And now the man was teaching at the local college.

He reached across the papers scattered over his desk, picked up the receiver, and tapped in the number. A couple of seconds passed before the buzzing noise stopped.

"This is Professor Lambert." A rich bass voice, with the resonant tones of an opera singer.

Father John gave his name.

"Ah, Father O'Malley. Kind of you to get back to me." The voice paused, then hurried on. "Perhaps you may have heard of me. I've been writing about the Plains Indians for many years."

Father John said that he was familiar with the man's work.

"Ah, splendid!" That seemed to please him. "Now that I've retired, my wife and I have come to the open spaces of the West from where I've drawn much of my inspiration. A wonderful place in which to write, wouldn't you say?" He hurried on, not waiting for a response. "Naturally I've missed teaching, so I'm giving a class at Central Wyoming College this semester on the Plains Indian wars. I see in the newspaper that you are the one who found the bodies at the Bates Battlefield. I was hoping we might be able to sit down for a chat about the unfortunate event."

Father John nudged his shirt sleeve back and glanced at his watch. Almost 10:30. He was thinking that Charles Lambert was one of the last persons to see Trent Hunter before he disappeared. "Where are you?" he asked.

"I'll be in my office at the college for another hour," the professor said, enthusiasm riding through the bass voice. Then he gave the directions to his office.

"I'll be there in twenty minutes," Father John said.

9

A LIGHT SNOW—more like rain than snow—started falling through the dim columns of sunshine as Father John drove to the campus that straddled a hill on the western edge of Riverton. He left the pickup in the parking lot and, pulling down the brim of his hat, plunged past the fountain with bronze figures leaping into the snow. Ahead was the beige brick building with the black, peaked roof streaked in white and the sign in front that said, "Main Hall." His boots cut fresh tracks, yet there were students about, floating like specters between the buildings.

He let himself through the heavy wood door that snapped shut behind him. Down a corridor of beige walls and plum-colored carpeting, past the half-wall of windows that overlooked the library, up the staircase into what resembled a waiting area with a couple of chairs pushed against one wall and a desk that looked as if it had never been used. The entire floor had a deserted feel, the faintest trace of something lingering behind—human smells—as if students and professors had hurried out minutes earlier. He walked down a row of closed doors. Next to each door was a small white placard that shimmered under the fluorescent ceiling light and announced each professor's name in black print: Egan, Mussey, Chandler, Lambert.

Father John rapped twice. The sound was muffled by his glove, and he gave a sharper rap.

"Yes, yes. Come in." The same bass voice on the telephone, tinged now with fatigue.

Father John opened the door and stepped into a closet-sized office that looked surprisingly neat. In a pair of bookcases against the opposite wall, books were lined up in neat rows, probably in alphabetical order, unlike his own books toppling against one another and jostling for space. A man could quickly put his hand on a book here. At a right angle to the bookcases was a small desk that protruded into the center of the room, the top as shiny as glass. It was bare apart from the telephone and a metal hook-necked lamp that threw out a circle of light. The man looking up at him from the desk looked much like the photograph on the book jacket: the white mane of hair framing a sculptured, still-handsome face, with the prominent nose, the strong chin that slanted forward, and the lines of concentration worn into the broad forehead, as if he had spent long hours pondering difficult questions. He had a slight build with thin shoulders and a stalklike neck that gave him the look of a man who had been much larger and still seemed to inhabit the space he had once taken up. The collar of a light blue shirt showed above the brown sweater that bunched over his shrunken chest.

"Professor Lambert?" Father John had stopped himself from calling the man "grandfather," the term of respect he'd gotten used to addressing Arapaho elders by. "I'm Father O'Malley," he said.

The older man had started to lift himself from his chair, a slow unfolding of elbows and knees, knobby hands curled around the armrests, the faintest shadow of pain crossing his face.

"Please don't get up."

Charles Lambert sank downward and righted his thin frame against the back of the chair before he reached out to shake Father John's hand.

"Good of you to come, Father." The man's grip was firm and definite, sinews of steel formed through the years. "Please sit down," he said, nodding toward a metal chair almost hidden behind the opened door. "I hope you won't mind that I made a few inquiries and discovered that you are another toiler in the field of history. A former history professor, I believe."

Father John had to smile at that. The mistaken notion clung to him like his own shadow. "I taught American history at a Jesuit prep school," he said.

The professor's eyebrows shot up, and Father John wasn't sure if the man was disappointed in the truth or disappointed in his source of information. He stuffed his gloves inside his jacket pocket and unsnapped the front. Then he nudged the chair over and sat down.

"Ah, well, no matter." Professor Lambert spread his hands on the polished desk and leaned forward. His eyes were light blue and very bright, laserlike, Father John thought. "You may be aware, Father," the man went on, "that I have been teaching and writing about the wars on the plains for a very long time."

"I'm familiar with two of your books."

"How nice." He seemed to take this in for a moment, glancing away and smiling to himself. "At any rate"—the blue eyes back again—"when I retired from my position back East, it seemed natural to remove myself to the place that has inspired my work. My wife and I have settled into a bungalow three miles east of town, a quiet, peaceful location on a lane off of Monroe, where I was able to finish writing *Tribal Wars*. I'm pleased that the book will be published in two weeks."

He paused—the professor allowing time for the student to absorb an important piece of information. "You may wonder why I am telling you this, Father. Be so good as to indulge me."

"Go ahead." Father John removed his cowboy hat and hooked it over one knee.

"*Tribal Wars* will upset the commonly held belief that the Plains Indian tribes were one happy family. As a history professor . . ." Another pause. "As a history teacher, you know that the Plains tribes were very different people. Different languages, cultures, histories. Ah, the sad truth is . . ." The professor shifted in his chair, blue eyes turning upward for a moment to the Charles M. Russell poster on the wall above the desk. "The tribes waged war with one another most of the time. Crow and Sioux. Cheyenne and Pawnee. Arapaho and Shoshone. Naturally I've included the Bates Battle in my book. I was able to uncover new information about the motivations for the battle."

The professor leaned forward as if he were about to take Father John into his confidence. Light from the desk lamp shone in the man's blue eyes. "Arapaho warriors had committed depredations on settlers in the area, which, naturally, alarmed Captain Bates, who was charged with protecting the white settlers. Shoshone scouts spotted the Arapaho village in a canyon in the badlands and informed the captain. Indeed, the Shoshones guided the captain and his troops to the village and joined in the attack, prompted on their part, I believe, by a pervasive fear. That fear, Father, became the motivation. There's no question but that the Shoshones feared the Arapahos were about to invade their land, which is ultimately what occurred. By the time of the battle, Shoshone lands had been greatly diminished. It was only natural that they should take steps to prevent any incursion onto the reservation."

"An attack at dawn on a sleeping village, Professor?" Father John didn't try to soften the irritation in his voice. "It was inexcusable."

"Yes, yes." The white head nodded, the knobby hands fluttered over the desktop. "One might make the argument that the long war for ownership of the Great Plains was inexcusable, but nevertheless, it was waged among the tribes themselves, and ultimately, with the United States Army. A war, of course, which the tribes were bound to lose. As scholars, we must do our best to lift the veil of confusion and reveal the motivations behind the actions. Sometime, Father, we must have a discussion on the purpose of historical research: to condemn or to illuminate?"

Professor Lambert took a moment to reposition himself in the chair. A trace of amusement moved through his expression at some new idea. "When a colleague at the college implored me to teach a class on the tribal battles, I acquiesced," he said. "Quite an exceptional gathering of students for a small college. Twelve of my thirteen students are Native American. Here on the plains, it is the descendants of the conquered who are most interested in the battles waged for the land. I suggested to the students that they visit the Bates Battlefield. When I read in this morning's paper that the dead men are most likely native, naturally I grew concerned . . ."

He let the rest drift between them a moment before he continued. "It has occupied my thoughts all morning, Father. It occurred to me that you may know the identities of the dead men."

Father John shook his head. He reached inside his shirt pocket, pulled out the folded sheet of paper with the telephone message written on it, and slid it across the desk. "The killer called the priest at St. Aiden's, Father Owens, and left this message. The voice was distorted, like the voice of a robot. It's impossible to know whether it was a man or a woman."

The professor picked up the paper and held it in the circle of light. A shadow flitted across his face. "How did you come upon this?" he asked.

Father John explained that when the other priest couldn't make sense out of the message, he'd taken a chance and called him.

Pushing the paper back, Lambert said, "I find the phrasing oddly familiar. Perhaps the creative endeavor of one of my students, although I hope that is not the case."

Father John waited while the man seemed to turn his attention to the Russell poster again. After a moment, Lambert said, "A young woman, the only nonnative student in the class, by the name of Edith Bradbury. I would say she fancies herself a poet, although I suspect her attempts at poetry may be crude. However, she does have a flare for brief, pithy images."

Father John refolded the paper and pushed it back into his shirt pocket. "Are you saying she could have written the message?" It was hard to believe. The girl had been so distraught—so lost—at Trent's disappearance.

"No. No. Absolutely not." Lambert was waving both hands over the desk. "I would not be qualified to judge her poetic endeavors, which, in any case, I have not seen. Naturally I do not require my students to write poetry. I can only say that the piece is . . ." He hesitated, as if he were choosing from the words tumbling in his mind. "Reminiscent of her writing. Nothing more. I'm sure the same could be said of many other students."

Father John let a couple of beats go by before he said, "I understand that Edie's boyfriend, Trent Hunter, is also in your class."

"A fine student, Father." A slow smile came into the old man's face, as if this were a more comfortable subject. "Very serious and dedicated young man," he went on, "but preoccupied, it seems to me. I surmise that he carries a heavy burden, between school and work. No doubt he also has family obligations. I don't have to tell you that tribal people place great emphasis on family relationships. Please tell me that Trent Hunter is not among the dead."

Father John explained that Edie hadn't seen Trent since Friday and that she had filed a missing person's report with the Riverton Police.

"Oh, my." Professor Lambert squared the chair to the desk and gazed up at the Russell poster again. "I'm afraid that I witnessed a very unsettling occurrence in the parking lot two weeks ago." He swiveled back toward Father John. "A carload of what I can only describe as toughs in black leather jackets drove into the lot, shouting and cursing, banging on the sides of the car as though it were a drum. They circled Trent and the girl in a menacing manner and began pelting them with empty beer bottles. I'm afraid the couple was quite helpless, clutching each other and attempting to duck the missiles. I got the impression that the girl may once have been involved with one of the toughs, who seemed to be in a jealous rage. I shouted at the assailants, but who am I?

An old man, unable to frighten them away. At long last, some fine sturdy lads came running into the lot, and the car immediately drove away. Naturally, I hurried back to Main Hall to call security, but when I returned, the culprits had vanished."

"Did Trent tell you who they were?" Father John asked. He had a good idea: Jason Rizzo and his white supremacist friends.

"When I returned to the parking lot, Trent and Edie were gone. At the next class, Trent assured me that the problem would solve itself and there was no need to report the incident to the police. I sensed that he had come to a resolution, but I chose not to pry. Oh, dear, Father. I'm afraid I made a terrible mistake. I should have reported the matter to the police myself. Now . . ." His head was shaking, and he clasped his hands together to stop the trembling. "Trent might be one of the men killed at the battlefield. And the others, they could all be my students."

"Detective Burton is handling the investigation," Father John said. "He'll want to talk to you."

"Of course." The professor patted at the folds of his brown sweater. A thin hand darted down the V-necked front and fumbled at the pocket of the blue shirt, finally drawing out a small container, which he flipped open. He touched his index finger to his tongue, then dabbed at one of the small white pills in the container and lifted it to his mouth.

"Can I get you a drink of water?" Father John got to his feet, wondering how he was going to carry water from the fountain in the hall.

"Water would be fine." The professor nodded at a cooler wedged between the desk and the bookcase.

Father John crouched down, opened the lid, and took out one of the cool, plastic bottles. He removed the lid and handed the bottle to the professor, who threw back his head and took a long drink. His Adam's apple bobbed up and down in his thin neck.

"Ah," he said, leaning back and wiping at his mouth, balancing the half-full bottle on the armrest. "I'm afraid that my doctor has warned me against getting upset. Naturally the possibility of my students having been shot is most upsetting."

There was a sharp knock, and the door swung open. An attractive young woman dressed in blue jeans and a long gray coat stepped into the office. "Ready, Charles?" she said, throwing a glance at Father John. "Sorry. I didn't know you had an appointment."

"Perfectly all right, my dear." The professor was leaning back in his chair, chin tilted up, a hungry look in the blue eyes fixed on the woman. "Allow me to introduce my lovely wife, Dana," he said, not taking his eyes away. "This is Father O'Malley, the mission priest we've heard about. A fellow historian."

The woman turned to Father John and thrust out a small, gloved hand. "Nice to meet you," she said. Her grip was nearly as strong as her husband's, the leather glove smooth and cool against his palm. She looked like one of the professor's students, still in her thirties and strikingly beautiful, with green eyes shot through with questions, a sprinkling of freckles across her finely shaped nose, and a mass of curly black hair that she'd fastened in the back somehow, except for a few loose strands that fell toward her cheeks. She was small, barely coming to his shoulder.

"Excuse me if I seemed surprised." She removed her hand and smiled up at him. "I always picture priests as rather stout and nondescript. Thick glasses, that sort of thing. Rather like some of your colleagues, Charles." Tossing a glance at her husband, she gave a little laugh that ran up the scale, like the notes of a brief melody. "I can wait outside, if you like," she said, a serious tone now.

"No need, my dear. We're finished here. You may as well know that the unfortunate men killed at the Bates site could be one or more of my students."

"Whatever makes you think so? The newspaper said the men haven't been identified." Father John realized that the woman was still observing him. "You're the one who found the bodies, aren't you? How dreadful. And you were wounded yourself." She paused, then hurried on. "Did you know the victims?"

"No," he said.

"How did you ever happen to wander onto the site? Is that what you do in your spare time, Father? Hike to old battlefields?"

Father John told her about the telephone message and the cryptic clues.

"How interesting." Dana Lambert lifted one hand and tucked a black curl back into place. "No doubt clues that only a historian could understand."

She pivoted toward the man seated behind the desk. "I hope this hasn't upset you, Charles. No sense in working yourself up until the authorities release the victims' names. They may not be your students at all. We must keep a positive outlook, as you always tell me."

"Nevertheless, I intend to contact the police and tell them about the altercation I witnessed in the parking lot."

"Are you sure you're up to the strain, Charles? You don't have to get involved in such a sordid business."

"What would you have me do, dear? If Trent Hunter has been shot to death, it's possible the culprits are the men who harassed him."

The woman shot a sideways look at Father John. "I hope you'll excuse us, Father. I must get Charles over to the newspaper. They're going to interview him about his new book, which is coming out soon."

Charles Lambert leaned toward the far side of the desk, slid a metal walking stick along the carpet, and jabbed one end into the carpet. Gripping the top in both hands, he pushed himself upward, a slow, jerky motion. "I may be retired," he said, leaning on the cane, "but my lovely wife is a slave driver."

"Nonsense," Dana said. "No one drives himself harder than you, Charles." The woman had removed a black topcoat from its hanger on the door. "My husband's an authority on Indian warfare," she said, holding out the coat. "No other scholar can match his accomplishments, yet he's still waiting for his best seller, while so-called popular historians publish shoddy history and make millions. It's hardly fair."

"My dear, please." Balancing on the cane, Professor Lambert managed to slip into the coat. He crooked his head around and gave his wife an affectionate smile while fumbling with the coat buttons. "I'm afraid Dana's my biggest fan," he said.

"You know it's true, Charles." The woman stepped around and began slipping the buttons through the slits, which the professor seemed to enjoy. Father John had the sense that all the fumbling had brought about the intended result. "*Tribal Wars* will be your best seller. It's truly brilliant."

"With your help, my dear."

"Nonsense, I'm only your assistant."

Professor Lambert shifted sideways and smiled at Father John. "And the most brilliant graduate student with whom I've ever had the privilege to work. Dana is now in the process of writing her dissertation." The man held out his hand. "Thank you for coming, Father," he said. His grip was still strong, despite the fact that he leaned on the walking stick as if he were holding himself upright against a wall. "It's unfortunate we couldn't have met under more fortunate circumstances. Be so good as to let me know when you learn of the identities."

Father John snapped up his jacket and set his cowboy hat on his head. "The names will be in the newspaper," he said.

"Yes, yes, the newspaper." The professor swatted at the suggestion, as if the interview he was about to have was a pesky annoyance. "We must have a chat again soon."

Dana Lambert had found a briefcase and opened it on the desk. She was arranging the stack of folders inside under her husband's fond gaze when Father John let himself out the door and headed down the deserted corridor, the muffled pounding of his boots bouncing off the beige wall.

10

"BOTTOM LINE IS, wolves are back." Bob Posey, director of the reservation's natural resources department, hunched forward and let his gaze roam around the perimeter of the small round table in the corner of his office. Vicky lifted her pen from the legal pad she'd been scribbling on and waited for the man to go on. Across from her, Adam had also stopped writing, his eyes on the director. Somewhere down the corridor, a phone was ringing. Gusts of wind rattled the window behind the table and deposited splotches of moisture on the glass.

"We've had sightings as far south as Rawlins," Posey said. The man was Shoshone, about her age, Vicky guessed. Black hair dipped over his forehead above a long, narrow face while graceful fingers flipped a ball-point like a cartwheel over the file folder in front of him. "Some of the gray wolves that the Fish and Wildlife Service reintroduced into Yellowstone have made their way south looking to establish new territory. Several packs could be settling into the Wind River and Owl Creek mountain ranges right now. Alpha wolf says, 'Hey, this looks like a good place. Lots of elk and deer and we can get an occasional lunch on calves and lambs. Let's hang around.' Now that they're on the reservation, we gotta make certain our plan to manage the population meets both state and federal regulations. Here's where you come in." He opened the folder and pushed a stack of papers across the table toward Adam.

For an instant, Vicky felt as if she were invisible, a specter at the table, like the specter of wolves that had been almost exterminated decades ago. "I'd like a copy," she said.

"Have one for you right here." Posey sent another stack of paper-clipped papers skimming over the table toward her. "We got ourselves some legal minefields to walk through. Soon's the federal government takes wolves off the endangered species list, the state's gonna manage the population in Wyoming. Except for the reservation. That's our jurisdiction."

Vicky began thumbing through the pages: synopsis of court decisions, Ninth Circuit, Tenth Circuit, federal regulations on managing the reintroduced wolves, and a copy of Wyoming's management plan.

"Whole reintroduction thing has been controversial from the get-go," Posey continued. "Tourists love the idea. Drive up to Yellowstone, stop on the highway, and watch the Druid pack gamboling about, like a wildlife zoo. Once the wolf population started growing and heading out of the park, it was a different situation. Ranchers don't appreciate their livestock gutted in the pastures, so folks started bringing lawsuits, asking the courts to halt the reintroduction of wolves to the northern Rockies. Tell you the truth, sometimes in the middle of the night out on my place, I hear wolves howling up in the foothills. So I get up—three a.m. or whatever—pull on my boots and go out into the corral. The horses are real skittish, like they hear the howling, too."

The man sat back and smiled off into the space. "Tell you the truth, I'm glad they're back. Maybe they never went away completely. That's what some of the old Indians say." He nodded toward the window and the reservation beyond. "Fact is, we need wolves to protect our forests.

Keep the trees and brush from being browsed to death by too many deer. They cull out the herds, too, keep 'em the right size for the range, only no rancher's gonna admit it."

"What about the reservation plan?" Adam was thumbing through the pages.

The director turned his attention back to the contents of the file folder. He pushed another pair of paper-clipped pages toward them. "We gotta comply with both federal and state regs, and we gotta manage the wolf population. Don't want them destroying all the elk and deer and other wild animals on the reservation. Of course, we gotta pay attention to the concerns of Shoshones and Arapahos trying to raise their cattle. We can designate wolves trophy animals and control the population by the number of hunting licenses we issue. Any wolves that become predators, however, can be shot. That doesn't mean anybody can pick up a gun and go looking for wolves, and we sure as hell don't want ranchers around the area coming onto the rez and doing any precautionary killing."

Posey snapped the empty folder shut and started tapping the pen on top. It made a muffled, skittering noise. "Naturally it's important that everybody on the rez rides the same horse about this issue. We've got to be united on our plan—Shoshones and Arapahos—'cause if we're not, the state's gonna want to take over the management. Any questions about our plan, I'm at your disposal. Any questions about the regulations or court decisions, you'll have to talk to wildlife people in Cheyenne. We want to get things into place so we can implement the plan the minute the wolves come off the endangered list. We'd like your opinion, let's say, yesterday." He stuck the pen into the pocket of his white shirt and got to his feet.

"We'll get back to you pronto." Adam was also on his feet, reaching across the table to shake the director's hand. "Appreciate the business," he said.

Vicky could hear the purr of satisfaction in Adam's voice. An important job with the Arapaho and Shoshone tribes, an important issue. She slipped the papers into her briefcase, stood up, and also shook Posey's hand. Then she brushed past Adam, who was holding the door open, and started down the corridor, conscious of his boots scraping the vinyl floor behind her, wondering if her name would have ever crossed Bob Posey's mind if Adam Lone Eagle hadn't been her partner.

VICKY STARED OUT the passenger window at the gray clouds crawling down the slopes of the foothills and the mixture of rain and snow drifting over Highway 287. She was vaguely aware of Adam's voice—something about how Wyoming's first management plan had failed to meet the federal standards, which delayed removing wolves from the federal endangered species list and turning management over to the states. A jazz piece was playing softly on the radio.

Her thoughts were on the wolves, out there somewhere in the clouds and trees, roaming wild. Sometimes in the night, when she was driving across the reservation, she thought she heard wolves howling, and she told herself it couldn't be true. Wolves had been exterminated decades ago. But some of the elders said no. A few wolves had managed to escape. They stayed close to the people.

There were so many stories, she was thinking, stories her grandfather told when she was a child about wolves circling the camps in the Old Time. They were hunters, quiet and fierce. They always found their prey. *We learned from wolf.* Grandfather's voice was in her head now. *He taught us many things. How to scent the buffalo. How to track the deer and elk. How to scout the enemy. How to work together so that no one was hungry. All of this, wolf taught us.* And when the warriors went out to track the enemy, grandfather said, they pulled wolf skins over their heads and shoulders. *They became wolves.*

Vicky realized that Adam's voice had gone quiet. "Where are you?" he asked.

"What?" She shifted around and stared at the feathers of moisture on the windshield.

"You're not here, Vicky."

"Sorry."

"You have a way of doing that, going off. I can't find you."

"I was thinking about the wolves out there. I'm glad there's still a place for them."

"The first cattle they kill on the rez will start an uproar. If a Shoshone owns the dead cattle, Shoshones'll have Posey fired. If it's an Arapaho rancher, they'll blame the Shoshones, since one of them is in charge of management. It's a no-win situation, as far as I can see. It's only a matter of time until wolves are killed off again."

"Is that why you want to see the Druid pack?"

He glanced over and smiled at her. "You still on for the weekend?"

Vicky nodded. "Looks like one of us will have to go to Cheyenne and meet with the fish and wildlife people."

"We'll both go," Adam said, rapping his knuckles against the edge of the steering wheel. "It'll give us another chance to get away together, get to know each other better."

Vicky leaned her head back onto the cushion. She felt lulled by the sense of well-being settling over her, like the snow tracing the sagebrush along the road and flouring the ground, the jazz riffling against the soft sounds of the tires. At the periphery of her vision was Adam's profile, the black hair streaked with gray, like rain, the prominent nose and firm set of his jaw, the large, capable hands gripping the steering wheel, and all about him, a calm, steady presence. Maybe we don't get everything we want, John O'Malley had once told her. God, she could still hear his voice in her head, summon it up, reintroduce it, the way wolves had been reintroduced. We don't get everything we want, but what we get is good.

"We interrupt this program to bring you late-breaking news." The woman's voice sounded small and hesitant. She might have been reading a note someone thrust into her hands.

Vicky lowered her head and glanced at the yellow numbers flickering in the little window of the radio. A half-second passed before the voice continued: "The Fremont County coroner has confirmed the identities of three Shoshone men found shot to death Monday at the Bates Battlefield. The victims are Trent Hunter and Rex and Joe Crispin, all from the Fort Washakie area. The coroner estimates that the men had been shot by a rifle at least forty-eight hours before their bodies were discovered by Father John O'Malley, the pastor of St. Francis Mission. Father O'Malley told investigating officers that he had gone to the battlefield after a suspicious telephone call."

"God!" Vicky lifted her bag off the floor and started digging inside until her fingers wrapped around her cell.

"You know them?"

"They filed the assault complaint against Frankie Montana," she said. Now she was fumbling for the little directory where she kept the telephone numbers relating to current cases. She found the book, flipped to *M*, and started punching in Frankie's number.

"You're telling me they're the three men who didn't show up at the hearing Monday?"

"They were already dead." She pressed the cell against her ear, listening to the electronic noise of a phone ringing in the stretch of whiteness behind her.

"This isn't your dogfight, Vicky."

The noise stopped, and Lucille Montana's voice came over the line. "Hello?"

"It's Vicky. Is Frankie around?"

"There isn't any trouble, is there?"

Adam's hand shot out next to her and punched the off button on the radio. "Why are you doing this?" His voice cut into the space between them.

"Please put Frankie on," Vicky said into the cell. She shifted toward the passenger window. Thank God Lucille hadn't heard the news on the radio.

"He's not your client anymore, Vicky. For Godsakes."

The cell had gone quiet, and for a moment, she wondered if she'd lost the connection. Was it her imagination, or were they driving faster, the wheels thumping at a louder rhythm?

"Yeah, Vicky, what's up?" Frankie was on the line, a mixture of boredom and annoyance in his tone. She could almost see the way he'd probably grabbed the phone out of his mother's hand, the hunched shoulders and insolent stance.

"Listen to me, Frankie," she began, and then she repeated what the radio announcer had said.

"No shit! You telling me they're all dead? Hallelujah!"

"Frankie!" She was pressing the cell so hard that the edge bit into her jaw. "Don't you get it? They were murdered. Who do you think the fed is going to think killed them?"

"What? Give me a break. They don't have nothing on me. I didn't kill them bastards. Wait just a fucking minute," he went on, the reality sinking in. "They can't come around here accusing me of something I didn't do. I ain't never killed nobody."

Vicky was aware of Adam beside her, the short, quick intakes and exhalations of breath. "They're going to come around," she said. "Are you hearing me, Frankie?"

"Yeah, yeah, I'm hearing you."

"They're going to come around and want to ask you a lot of questions."

"Like the police? I ain't afraid of talking to the police."

"Like the police, Frankie, and the Fremont County Sheriff. It doesn't matter. You don't talk to them. Understand? You don't say anything. You tell them . . ." Vicky glanced over at Adam. He was staring at the road, the muscle twitching along his jawline. "You tell them to call your lawyer."

"Well, you're my lawyer."

"I can't handle this, Frankie. Sorry." She paused. "There are other good lawyers."

"Samantha Lowe," Adam said.

"You're my lawyer, Vicky."

"Call Samantha Lowe in Lander. She'll do a good job for you."

"Then why the hell did you call me, if you ain't my lawyer?"

"Just call Samantha," Vicky said before pushing the end key.

"You didn't have to do that," Adam said.

Vicky took a moment, slipping the cell into the pocket inside her bag and closing the bag. "You know Frankie will be the number one suspect on the sheriff's list."

"He could be guilty."

"Frankie? Enticed three men who claimed that he'd assaulted them out to an old battlefield in the wilderness and shot them? How'd he do that, Adam?"

"I'm telling you, the man had a motive, and the investigator's going to zero in on that."

Vicky didn't say anything. She let her bag slide back onto the floor next to her boots and unbuttoned her coat, pushing the fronts back around her gray turtleneck sweater. It seemed hot all of a sudden, the warm air pouring out of the vents. She leaned forward and closed the vent blowing toward her.

"Don't worry." Adam reached over and patted her hand. "Samantha'll do a fine job. She'll make the investigator prove his case every step of the way. Last night at dinner . . ."

"Dinner?" Vicky turned toward him. "You had dinner with her last night?"

Adam took his eyes from the highway and stared at her a moment. "A business dinner, Vicky."

"Right." Vicky heard her own voice, small. A half-voice. She turned her head to the passenger window and the snow flitting by.

"I have a lot of colleagues, Vicky. Many of them are women. We go to lunch and dinner. We talk business. Last night Samantha and I talked about building a new practice. She needs clients, and I assured her that we'll refer all we can. Is that okay with you?"

"Why wouldn't it be?" Vicky kept her eyes on the snow, struggling to hold back the dam of memories flooding over her from that other time. Ben, coming home reeking of cheap perfume, the lipstick tubes in his jacket pockets, the hours out with the guys. *Just throwing back a few beers. For Chrissakes, Vicky, get off my back.* She tried to shut out the voice, but it rang inside her head. Of course Adam could have dinner with whomever he pleased. She didn't own him. She didn't own his time. And he wasn't Ben.

"I'm glad I have your permission," Adam said.

They were in the western reaches of Lander now, and the snow had let up. Adam turned off the wipers, leaving a wide swath of gray residue on the windshield. Traffic crawled down the slushy street, and people hurried along the sidewalks, huddled inside hooded jackets.

"Look, Vicky," Adam said, a conciliatory tone, "we're going to have our hands full with the wolf management plan. You can count on Samantha doing a good job for Frankie. She's very eager. Graduated at the top of her law-school class."

"When was that?"

"I don't know. Two or three years ago. She spent a couple of years at a firm in Cheyenne."

"So that makes her, what? Twenty-seven? How many murder suspects has she represented?"

"You're jumping to conclusions, Vicky. We don't know that Frankie's the only suspect."

Adam made a left into the parking lot alongside the office building. He pulled into the space with the sign at the front that read Lone Eagle, turned off the ignition, and shifted toward her. Then he was running his fingers along the edge of her jaw, pushing back a strand of hair. "We'll have dinner tonight and leave the office behind. Just the two of us."

Vicky pulled away from his hand, opened the door, and got out onto the snow-slicked pavement, lifting her bag after her. She grabbed her briefcase from behind the seat, aware of Adam outside the other door, leaning down for his own briefcase. His wife had left him, he'd told her once, because he liked women too much.

Oh, God, she thought, starting across the parking lot toward the back door of the building. Adam Lone Eagle and Ben Holden, shadows of each other. From behind her came the sharp crack of the pickup door slamming shut.

11

SOMEWHERE IN THE darkness a bell was ringing. Father John swam upward toward the clanging noise, flung out his hand, and groped for the alarm. It spun out of his grasp, and he patted at the surface of the nightstand until his fingers wrapped around the small plastic box. He pushed the top button, plunging the bedroom into silence, the faintest light from the streetlights tracing the blind. He swung out of bed, groggy from the half-sleep he'd been wandering through all night, images of the bodies at Bates still in his mind. Now there were names: Trent Hunter and two brothers, Rex and Joe Crispin.

The phone had started ringing in the late afternoon. It had rung all through the evening. *How come Shoshones got shot out at Bates?* Fear pulsated down the line. *Arapahos got massacred at Bates. Somebody's out looking for revenge.*

His own voice, saying the same thing over and over. Detective Burton would sort it out. They should try not to worry. And all the time, he was thinking about the girl, Edie Bradbury, and the stricken look in her face when she'd told him that her boyfriend was missing, as if some part of her had known that he was dead. He'd found a number for her in the phone book and tried to call throughout the afternoon and evening—three, four times. There was no answer.

Now he squinted at the little red numbers on the clock: 5:30. It was his turn to say the six o'clock Mass. The elders and grandmothers who would be scattered about the pews were probably already on their way to the mission, headlights on battered pickups flashing through the darkness. He pushed himself onto his feet and made his way down the hall to the bathroom.

Fifteen minutes later—coming alive after a shave and shower—Father John headed down the stairs. The steps creaked under his boots; the whole residence seemed to be groaning awake. He walked down the hall, flipping on light switches as he went. He could hear Walks-On's nails clicking on the vinyl floor in the kitchen. The dog stood at the back door, tail wagging, muzzle pushed against the wood panel. It had been almost four years since he'd found the golden retriever in the ditch beside Seventeen-Mile Road. He'd almost driven past—nothing more than a bunch of golden white straw. And yet . . . something was not right. He'd pulled over and run back to where the dog lay whimpering, his hind legs scraped and broken. The vet had managed to save his life, but not his mangled right hind leg.

"There you go, buddy." Father John opened the door, followed the dog out onto the back porch, and yanked open the outside door. A wall of cold air fell over him. He watched the dog skitter down the ice-crusted steps, then lift his nose into the cold, and dart through the snow. Father John stared across the yard. In his mind's eye were the three bodies, frozen and gray.

He turned back into the kitchen, shook out some dry food into the dog's dish, and refilled his water. He hadn't been looking for a dog. He'd thought he'd be leaving St. Francis, back on his own career track, finishing up his doctorate, teaching at a university. What would he do with a dog?

He'd collected the dog at the vet's and brought him back to the mission. It was as if the dog had been looking for him. Even the old kitchen rug where he slept seemed to have been waiting for him to arrive. Father John had named him Walks-on-Three-Legs, a name of honor, in the Arapaho Way, for his courage, as if having only three legs wasn't a nuisance at all.

The dog was scraping at the outside door, and Father John went back onto the porch and let him in. He bounded past, took a right in the kitchen, and slid toward the dish of food. Father John shut both doors and, leaving the light on for Elena, who would be arriving at any moment, went down the hall and took his jacket off the coat tree. He was still pulling on the jacket as he crossed the grounds. Stalks of wild grasses were pushing up through the snow. The sky was a dark curtain, but in another thirty minutes, it would be on fire, bands of crimson and gold streaming across the eastern horizon and the sun an enormous red ball lifting out of the earth. Lights glowed through the stained glass windows in the church, but darkness clung to the other structures—museum and administration building. A few pickups stood in Circle Drive, and other vehicles were turning in to the mission. The morning was silent, except for an animal howling somewhere. For a moment, he wondered if the animal might be a wolf, and he thought again of the three dead men, shot to death and left in the wilderness.

He hurried up the steps to the church. Leonard Bizzel, the caretaker at St. Francis since long before Father John had arrived, had already brushed off the steps, so that a thin trace of snow glistened red and blue in the light seeping past the stained glass windows. He stepped into the vestibule and headed down the center aisle, nodding at the handful of parishioners kneeling in the pews. Light from the candles at the sides of the altar flickered across the brown faces that turned up to him as he passed. He stopped to genuflect in front of the tabernacle—a miniature tipi the grandmothers had sewn out of finely tanned white deerskin—and hurried to the sacristy where he found Leonard lifting the Mass books and the chalice from the cabinets.

"You hear that those dead men are Shoshones?" the man asked.

Father John said that he had heard. He draped his jacket over the back of a chair.

"What I can't figure out is what made 'em go out there? Shoshones stay away from Bates like it was haunted. Don't want the ghosts of any Arapahos coming for them. I hear the bodies was arranged so they looked like people killed in the old battles. That true?"

Father John took his white alb off the hanger and slipped it on over his shirt and blue jeans. Somebody at the site—deputy, coroner's officer—had probably told somebody else about the bodies, and the moccasin telegraph had flashed the news across the reservation in minutes. No wonder last night's callers were worried that somebody had killed the Shoshones for revenge.

He could feel Leonard watching him, waiting for an answer as he put on his stole and chasable. "It's possible," he said.

"Come on, Father. Maybe people don't talk about the massacre, but we don't forget. Somebody might've decided it was time to make the Shoshones pay."

Father John faced the other man. "Let's pray that's not the case," he said. Because if it is the case, he was thinking, there would be a war between the two tribes.

He lifted the chalice and walked out to the altar, conscious of Leonard's footsteps padding after him. A few more people were in the pews, all working their way onto their feet amid the clunk of kneelers and the rustle of coats and bags. A cold draft floated like an invisible stream down the main aisle from the vestibule. He felt as if winter had set in again, pushing away the other seasons.

"Let us offer our Mass this morning for the souls of the men killed at Bates," he began. "Let us also pray for their families. And for everyone who loved them," he added, his thoughts moving to Edie Bradbury. "Let us pray that God in His mercy will give them the strength and the courage to go on."

A hushed chorus of amens wafted toward him.

* * *

THE PINK LIGHT of morning flooded the sky as Father John retraced his steps across the grounds. The residence was quiet, apart from the sound of subdued activity in the kitchen. He tossed his jacket onto the bench in the entry and walked down the hall, following the aromas of fresh coffee and sizzling oil. Elena stood at the stove, ladling pancake mix into a frying pan, back bent into the task.

"What's this?" Father John went over to the counter and poured himself a mug of coffee. "No oatmeal this morning?"

"You want the truth, Father?" Elena shot him a sideways glance. The woman was probably in her seventies—her age a closely guarded secret—part Cheyenne, part Arapaho, with wrinkles creasing her brown face and dark eyes shot through with light. "I'm pretty tired of cooking oatmeal."

He stopped himself from saying he was pretty tired of eating it. "Pancakes look good." He hoisted his mug toward the round globs of batter browning in the pan. The kitchen was filled with the hot, sweet smells. Then he pulled out a chair and sat down at the round table in the center of the room. The place across from him was vacant.

"Father Ian hasn't come down yet?"

"Haven't seen hide or hair of the man."

It wasn't unusual, Father John thought. In the weeks since Ian Mc-Cauley had arrived, they'd eaten breakfast together only two or three times. Even on the mornings when Ian took the early Mass, he preferred to pour himself some coffee and retire to his room for "a little quiet time."

"Knocked on his door a few minutes ago." Elena arranged a stack of pancakes on a plate and set it in front of him. "Tol' him breakfast was ready. He said he wasn't hungry. Man doesn't eat enough to keep a chicken alive, even when he bothers to come to the table. Tol' him I'd bring him some Alka-Seltzer or aspirin, if he needed something." She shrugged.

Father John dabbed margarine on the pancakes, then dribbled on some syrup, watching the margarine and syrup melt together into a stream that ran around the plate. "Thank you, Elena," he said, smiling up at the old woman who stood next to the table, like a penitent waiting in line for the confessional. "Why don't you join me?" He motioned to the other priest's vacant place.

Elena turned back to the counter and poured another mug of coffee. "People are real upset about them dead Shoshones," she said, dropping down across from him. "Looks like that fool Frankie Montana might've finally killed them, after all the harassing he's been doing. Now some fool Shoshone's liable to take after Arapahos. Soon's that happens, Arapahos are gonna be after revenge. Whole rez is gonna be taken over by fools, you ask me. Fools that ain't willing to let the past stay in its grave where it belongs."

The woman sipped at her coffee a moment. "That fool Frankie's been a trial to his mother since the day he came into this world," she said. "Nearly killed her doing that, and, you ask me, he's been trying to finish off the job ever since. Lucille can't see it, though. Thinks the sun twirls around that boy of hers."

Father John took another bite of pancakes, then a sip of coffee. It didn't make sense. Frankie Montana was a hothead, the kind who acted first and thought about it later, if he thought about it at all. He might have shot the Shoshones in the parking lot at some bar, that Father John could believe. But take them out to Bates? Pose the bodies? Record a message that sounded like a robot? Deliberately leave clues? The murders had been calculated to reopen old wounds. They had been *planned*. Frankie wasn't the kind who made plans.

"What makes you think he killed the Shoshones?" Father John asked.

" 'Cause he hated them." Elena dipped her head and took a draw of coffee. "They was going to college, gonna make something of themselves. Red apples, Indians trying to be white. Guys like Frankie, they hate Indians like that. You ask me, that's why he wanted to make their lives miserable. Make 'em pay for showing him up. That's why he shot 'em. They was supposed to go to tribal court Monday and show the judge how Frankie assaulted them. Only they didn't go, on account of they were dead."

Father John drained the last of his coffee. "You think Frankie got the Shoshones out to the Bates Battlefield to kill them?"

"That's the part that gets me, Father. I don't know how Frankie would ever come up with that, unless he was looking to make all the Shoshones real mad. If that's what he wanted, I hear he's got it. Shoshones got together for a big meeting last night over at Fort Washakie."

Dear Lord! Father John felt another stab of alarm. He got to his feet, picked up his plate and mug, and carried them to the sink. Behind him, Elena's chair scraped over the vinyl floor. He could hear the raspy inhalation of breath as she stood up.

He turned back to the old woman. "Try not to worry," he said, patting her shoulder, wishing he could shake his own worry. It was part of him now, a second skin. He walked back down the hall, pulled on his jacket, and started across the grounds. The sun burned yellow in a pale gray sky. The killer had set some inexorable force into motion, he was thinking, like a wolf flushing out its prey.

He was almost at the administration building when he saw the white pickup emerge from the cottonwoods. He waited until the vehicle pulled up beside him, Andy Burton peering over the lowering window.

"Got a minute?" the detective called.

"Coffee's still hot at the residence." Father John tossed his head back in the direction he'd just come from.

12

"WHAT DO YOU know about Trent Hunter and the Crispin brothers?" The detective was settled into the upholstered chair in the corner of the study, black leather jacket hanging open over a dark turtleneck sweater. He was a big man, with thick arms and legs that overflowed the chair, a round face with flushed cheeks, a nose that looked as if it had been broken a couple of times, and a brown crew cut peppered with gray. His eyes were quick and alert. They'd probably already catalogued the contents of his study, Father John thought.

He handed the man a mug of coffee, then carried his own coffee over to the desk and sat down. "Trent was a student at Central Wyoming. Maybe the others were students," he said.

"Yeah, they were all at the college. Tell me something I don't know, Father." Burton slurped at his coffee a moment.

"I got a call from a professor, Charles Lambert. Trent was one of his students."

The detective reached around and set his mug on the middle shelf of the bookcase. Then he pulled a small notepad and pen from inside his jacket and jotted something on the pad. "Anything else?" he asked, glancing up.

He told the detective about Edie Bradbury.

"The girl who filed the missing person's report with the Riverton police."

"She's also in Professor Lambert's class."

The man's eyebrows shot up. He went back to scribbling on the pad a moment. "I spoke with the families last night after we got the IDs. Not easy delivering that kind of news. Guess I don't have to tell you that."

Father John swirled the coffee in his mug, then took another drink. How many phone calls from the police in the middle of the night? *Father, we got an accident. Couple of kids got in a fight, Father. Possible suicide, Father.* Always the same request, *Can you go to the family?* He'd gone more times than he wanted to remember, numb with his own sorrow and the knowledge that he was about to transfer its terrible weight to the unsuspecting families.

"How are they?" he said.

"About like you'd expect. In shock, can't believe it's true. Said their boys were gonna meet somebody out at Bates. All I could do was tell them the truth. Their boys were shot to death out there. The coroner has ruled the deaths homicide."

The detective went quiet. He shifted around, took his coffee off the shelf and took another drink. "They're angry," he said. "It's to be expected, but this is different."

Father John sipped at his coffee and watched the man over the rim.

"They say an Arapaho must've killed them in revenge for what happened so long ago . . ." Burton shook his head. "Who cares what happened in the past?"

"The country of dead people," Father John said, almost to himself. The comment he'd heard from the time he'd decided to major in history at Boston College. "What kind of living you going to make if all you study is dead people?" his mother had wanted to know. But his father, sitting at the kitchen table, nursing a cup of coffee laced with whiskey, had grinned at him. "Always liked history, myself," he'd said.

"You're the historian, John," Burton went on. "Why in the name of all that's sane and logical would anybody want to kill three Shoshones at an old battlefield?"

Father John swiveled toward the window. The sun was glowing through the gray sky, and crocuses were poking through the snow at the edge of the sidewalk—spring trying to burst through. Still, it could snow again. And it occurred to him then . . .

It occurred to him that the killer had wanted the bodies found before they were buried under the spring snow.

He turned back to the man across the room. "I think the killer intended to link the three murders to the Arapaho massacre in 1874."

"Well, the killer did a good job of it. The families are saying things like, Arapahos did this and they're not gonna get away with it. They said it to me! With all the relatives coming around, they're just going to get more and more worked up. No telling what they might do. I talked to Chief Banner at the wind River Police and suggested he put more officers in the Arapaho areas." Burton paused a moment, concern working into the hard set of his jaw. "What do you know about Frankie Montana?"

"He comes from good people." Father John was aware of the footsteps in the hall. A half-second passed, and then the *whoosh* of the front door opening and faint ripples of cold air sweeping across the floor as the door thudded shut. Ian would be in his office if anybody stopped by.

"Doesn't mean Frankie's any good." Burton leaned sideways and set his mug back on the shelf. "Been in his share of trouble. Would've been in more trouble if Vicky Holden hadn't gotten the judge to let him go on a bond. She'll probably get the assault charges dismissed, my guess. If Frankie does go to trial and is found guilty, the judge'll banish him right then. Pretty serious, banishment. Doesn't happen very often, but I get the sense that his own people are fed up with Frankie Montana. Makes me think that maybe he decided to avoid a trial by making sure the complainants never showed up. Gives him a powerful motive, wouldn't you say? Coroner says homicides occurred sometime Saturday when Frankie says he was just hanging around. Not the best alibi I was ever handed. Then Saturday night, Father Owens gets that taped phone call."

Father John was quiet a moment. Maybe he hadn't given Frankie Montana enough credit. Maybe the man was capable of planning the murders, especially if he wanted to make certain the victims wouldn't testify against him. Still . . .

"Why Bates?" he said.

"Keep coming back to that, don't we?" The detective gripped the armrests and levered himself to his feet. Pulling on the fronts of his leather jacket, he jabbed the ends of the zipper together. "Think I'll have a talk with Hunter's girlfriend. Maybe she knows who Hunter and the Crispin boys were gonna meet at the battlefield." He zipped up the jacket, then patted at the pockets, finally extracting a pair of leather gloves.

Father John got to his feet. "Did anybody notify the girl that Hunter is dead?" She would take the blow hard, he was thinking.

"Riverton Police might've gone to her place," the detective was saying. "No matter. It's been all over the radio, and it's on the front page of this morning's paper."

Father John walked over and opened the door. He hadn't seen the paper yet, and last night, he hadn't needed to turn on the radio. The moccasin telegraph had delivered the news.

"Listen, Burton," he said, following the other man into the entry. "Before you go to her place, let me stop by and see how she's doing, will you?"

The detective pulled on his gloves and yanked open the front door. He glanced back. "I guess I can pay a call on Professor Lambert first, but I'll want to talk to the girl today."

"I'll go see her first thing," Father John said.

Burton nodded, then, head forward, like a bull shooting into the arena, he propelled himself outside. He'd reached the sidewalk when he turned around. "Something else," he called.

Father John stood in the doorway, his breath floating into the outdoors.

"Maybe you can visit the Hunter and Crispin families." The man thrust out a gloved hand, as if he wanted to forestall any objections. "I know they're Shoshones and you're the Arapaho pastor, but maybe you can help cool down some of that anger."

Father John told the man that he'd drive over to Fort Washakie after he saw Edie Bradbury. Then he shut the door, went back into the study, and riffled through the papers on his desk until he found the sheet on which he'd jotted down the girl's phone number. He lifted the receiver and punched in the numbers. The phone was ringing into a void, he thought.

He went back into the hall, set his cowboy hat on his head, and grabbed his jacket. He was still pulling it on as he hurried toward the pickup parked under the cottonwood in front and shrouded in a thin layer of snow.

FATHER JOHN FOUND the house in the middle of the block, a small cube with a sideways tilt, rails of melting snow on the peaked roof, stripes of gray paint peeling off the siding. The stoop looked as if it had detached itself from the front. The house had probably been an outbuilding at one time for the dilapidated Victorian on the corner, he thought. He'd driven down Pershing and halfway back before he'd spotted the blue sedan protruding from behind the house. Chances were that Edie Bradbury was home. There were no tire tracks in the drive, no footprints in the thin blanket of snow that lay over the front walk.

A woman had emerged from the Victorian and begun shoveling the driveway next to the house. He parked at the curb and headed up the sidewalk, conscious of the woman's eyes on him. When he glanced around, she turned away, lifted the shovel, and went back to scraping the driveway, the rasp of metal on concrete breaking through the neighborhood quiet.

He knocked on the door. A clothespin was clipped to the black metal mailbox on the wall that jutted at a right angle to the stoop. He could see the tops of envelopes in the box. He knocked again. "Edie?" he called.

No reply. Nothing but the clinking of the shovel. Maybe the girl wasn't home after all. She could be staying with friends. Friends would know that she would take the news of Trent's death hard. Why was it that he couldn't shake the feeling that she was alone and she was inside?

He cut a diagonal path through the snow in the front yard toward the woman still working the shovel.

"Excuse me," he said.

She propped the end of the shovel against the concrete. She was probably in her fifties, but she might have been older; it was hard to tell. A narrow, weathered face dipped into the collar of her oversized brown jacket. Her black galoshes were buckled halfway, and the flaps brushed at her baggy trousers like the wings of a crow. She stared at him with hooded eyes flooded with distrust.

He told her that he was the pastor of St. Francis Mission. Ignoring the look of surprise that flashed through her expression, he gestured with his head toward the little house with peeling paint. "Do you happen to know Edie Bradbury?"

It was like turning on a spigot. Oh, she knew Edie, all right. The woman cupped one gloved hand over the top of the shovel and listed toward the handle. Nothing but a lot of trouble since that girl rented the shack out back. People coming and going at all hours, cars ripping up and down the street. Hangs out with Indians, Edie does. One of them Indian's pickups was parked out in the front at night. Used to have a white boyfriend. Wore one of them black leather jackets with all them metal chains hanging about. Least he wasn't Indian.

Father John had to interrupt to ask if she'd seen Edie leave the house today.

For a moment, the hooded eyes followed a pickup passing in the street, leaving a trace of exhaust and the smell of gasoline rippling through the air. Finally, she looked back. "I guess I got better things to do than keep track of the comings and goings of trash like her."

He doubted that was true. Thanking the woman, he headed back along the trail of his boot prints. He pounded hard on the door, his gloved fist making a hollow noise against the flimsy wood. It struck him that anybody could put a shoulder to the door and knock it open. Out of the corner of his eyes, he could see the woman still leaning against the shovel, watching him.

He knocked again, then tried the knob. To his surprise, it rolled to the left. "Edie," he called, pushing the door open. He stepped into the small living room, with green and white webbed folding chairs scattered about the brown vinyl floor and, against the wall on the right, a desk made of upended cartons and a plank. Several books were stacked on top around a small lamp with a white plastic shade. Beyond the desk was a closed door, and beyond that, in the corner, a sink poised over a collection of metal pipes that bent into holes gaping in the wall. Next to the sink, a cookstove sat on top of a half-sized refrigerator.

He stood very quiet for a moment, listening, but there was nothing but the muffled noise of the scraping shovel and the sound of a vehicle moving through the slush on the street. He walked around the desk and opened the door.

13

THE BEDROOM WAS swallowed in a half-light, with what looked like a blanket tacked over the window. Edie Bradbury lay on the bed, dressed in blue jeans and a black tee shirt, head twisted into the pillows, her thin neck white against the edge of her shirt. Her arms were flung to the sides, like two thin, bloodied sticks, hands as small as a child's, curled into fists. Beneath her arms, strips of pink bedspread had turned brown with blood.

In two steps, Father John was at the bed. Leaning over the girl, placing his fingers along her neck, looking for a sign of life. He could see the slashes in the flesh of her arms, like markers made at one-inch intervals between the wrists and elbows, then disappearing under the sleeves of her shirt. The girl's mouth hung slightly open, her lips bluish white.

There it was, a pulse as faint as the breath of a whisper against his fingertips. He placed his palm in front of her mouth, his own breath stopped in his throat until he felt the exhalation of her breath on his skin.

"It's Father John, Edie," he said, running his hand lightly over her forehead and pushing back the damp, golden hair. Her forehead felt feverish. He glanced about the room. A column of daylight fell past the edge of the blanket over two cardboard boxes pushed against the wall, filled with books and papers. Another box with items of clothing spilling over the sides stood in the corner. Next to the box was a half-opened door. He could see the white corner of a bathtub.

"I'll be right back," he said.

The girl let out a breathy moan that sounded as if it had taken all of her strength. He smoothed her hair above her forehead, then went into the bathroom. There were two frayed pink towels tossed over the rim of the bathtub, and he gathered them up and carried them back to the bed. He folded the towels and laid them over the length of the girl's arms, pressing gently. Her eyes fluttered open, then closed again. She moved slightly. On the bedspread under her hip, he spotted the glint of a small razor blade.

He went back into the bathroom. In the little cabinet beneath the sink, he found a small towel, which he soaked in cold water and wrung out. Folding the towel, he carried it back to the bed and laid it on the girl's forehead. "I'm going to get help," he said, leaning over the girl.

She moaned again and rolled her head. Her lips began to move, as if she were struggling to give shape to the words stuck in her throat. "He's dead," she whispered.

"God, what's happened now?"

Father John looked around. The woman from the Victorian stood in the doorway, the flaps of her rubber boots hanging out. She gave the door a shove, clacking the knob against the wall.

"Stay with her," he said.

"Stay with her? What's going on?"

"I'm going to call an ambulance."

"Somebody try to kill her?"

Father John took the towel from the girl's head. The cloth was hot and sticky. "You can help by soaking this in cold water." He thrust the towel into the woman's hand. "I'll be back."

For a moment, he thought she wasn't going to move out of the doorway. She looked like a prison guard, bundled in the brown jacket snapped up to her chin, holding out the towel as if he'd handed her a dead animal. She stared up at him, her mouth forming a perfect O.

"The bathroom's in there." He nodded toward the other door.

Finally, pulling her mouth into a tight line, the woman moved past him, the jacket rustling as she walked. He could hear the water running as he headed across the front room. No sign of a phone. He searched the alcove that passed for a kitchen. There it was, almost hidden under a stack of plastic bags. He punched in 911 and counted the rings. Three. Four. "Come on," he said out loud. Finally, the operator's voice. He gave his name and said that a woman had cut her arms and needed an ambulance.

"Where is she, Father?" There was a calm steadiness in the voice.

He crossed the living room and stepped outside. God, there were no numbers on the house. He told the operator that he was on Pershing Boulevard, behind the Victorian on the corner.

"We're on the way," the operator said.

He pushed the off button, set the phone on the bookcase, and went back to the bedroom. The woman handed him the cold towel. "What happened to her?" she said, waving at the girl on the bed.

He ignored the question and set the towel on the girl's forehead. Then he ran his hand over the top of her head. Her hair felt moist, but she seemed cooler. "The ambulance is on the way," he told her.

The blue eyes fluttered open. "Let me die," she whispered.

"What'd she do? Try to kill herself?"

"Could you get a glass of water?"

"Not until you tell me what happened."

"She needs water, Mrs. . . ."

"Teters."

"You'll find a glass in the kitchen." He waited until the woman had backed through the door. Then, keeping his voice low and calm, he said, "I'm sorry about Trent."

The girl's eyes snapped shut. A thin line of tears ran back into her hair.

He took a corner of the towel and patted at the moisture. "Try to be strong," he said. "Try to live. You have Trent's baby." He hoped that was still true.

The woman came back into the room and handed him a plastic glass of water. "You don't have to tell me that she tried to kill herself," she said, her eyes fixed on the towels swaddling the girl's arms. "I can see what she done. Cut herself up again."

"What are you saying?" From somewhere in the distance came the wail of a siren.

"Oh, she tried this trick last fall. That young man, Jason, found her. Had the ambulance here. Whole neighborhood was out gawking."

Father John slipped one hand under the girl's head and lifted it off the pillows. Holding the plastic glass to her mouth, he said, "Try to sip a little water." He tipped the glass until she was able to draw in some water. Then, twisting out of his hand, she burrowed back into the pillows.

"You ask me," the woman said, "cutting yourself up is a mortal sin. That's what I learned in Catholic school. A mortal sin to defile your body, the temple of the Holy Spirit."

The clang of the siren came closer, bricks of noise battering the little house. "Would you mind going outside and directing the ambulance here?"

"It seems to me that anybody who . . ."

"Please, Mrs. Teters," he said.

The woman swung back through the doorway, the galoshes slapping as she walked across the living room.

The wailing noise cut off, and in another moment, two men and a woman, all in blue uniforms, pushed into the bedroom. One of the men was carrying a canvas stretcher rolled between two poles.

"You Father O'Malley?" asked the other man. He looked about twenty years old, slender with blond curly hair.

Father John nodded. Then he told them that the girl was Edie Brad-bury, that she'd slashed her arms with a razor, that she was conscious. And she was pregnant. He backed away as the medics closed in on the bed, lifting the towels on her arms and putting them back into place.

The blond man looked back at him. "We'll have to take her to River-ton Memorial," he said. "Want to ride along?"

Father John said that he would follow the ambulance. He walked back into the living room and waited. Through the open door, he could see the small groups of people forming out front, Mrs. Teters making her way from one group to the other, pointing toward the ambulance parked in the drive, waving toward the house. Other people were hurry-ing down the sidewalk, crossing the street around a couple of pickups that had slowed in front, drivers gawking at the house.

It was a few moments before the medics emerged from the bedroom, carrying the stretcher with the small body nearly lost under blankets. He followed them outside, closing the door behind him. The crowd was larger now, like tumbleweeds bunched together on the sidewalk. An el-derly woman with thin gray hair pulled the fronts of a red sweater around herself and came toward him. "Is she gonna be okay?" she asked.

He said he hoped so.

"I live across the street." The woman nodded at a tan duplex nearly hidden behind a row of bushes. "Sure don't like to see trouble come to young people."

A guffaw erupted from the crowd. "She brought it on herself, you ask me." It was Mrs. Teters' voice.

The ambulance had started backing out of the drive and into the street. There was the sound of gears crunching. Then the ambulance burst forward, siren screaming.

Father John started for the pickup, cutting around the crowd that still blocked the sidewalk. He slid behind the steering wheel, pulled a U-turn, and followed the ambulance toward Federal Boulevard.

* * *

"YOU MUST BE Father O'Malley." The woman standing in the doorway at the end of the corridor was probably still in her thirties, slim and beautiful with finely sculptured features and dark, intelligent eyes.

Father John got up from the hard plastic chair where he'd been sitting for almost an hour. The emergency waiting room was familiar: the worn chrome and plastic chairs lining the walls, magazines thumbed through and wrinkled, tossed onto small tables, green vinyl floor gleaming under the fluorescent ceiling light. Dear Lord, he'd been here so many times.

"I'm Eleanor Henderson, ER physician," the woman said. She held out a hand with clear nails at the tips of long, graceful-looking fingers. Her grip was surprisingly strong. "We have Edie Bradbury stabilized, but she lost a lot of blood. She's lucky she hasn't lost the baby." She paused. "It's possible that she might abort. I think it's best to keep her here for a day or two. In cases like this . . ." She paused again, and drew in her lower lip. "There's always the danger that the patient may keep trying until she succeeds. She's conscious, if you'd like to see her for a few minutes."

Father John followed the doctor down the corridor past a series of closed doors. Oblongs of white light washed over the beige walls and gleamed along the floor. A faint antiseptic odor hung in the air.

The doctor stopped and nudged open a door on the right. "You'll find her in there," she said.

Through the slim crack, Father John could see the foot of a gurney. He pushed the door back and stepped into a bright room barely large enough to accommodate the gurney and a bank of steel cabinets on the opposite wall. The contours of the slim figure made a slight disturbance in the white blanket draped over the gurney. The girl lay still, arms at her sides on top of the blanket, rows of gauze bandages running from her wrists to her shoulders. Dangling from a steel pole above the gurney was a clear plastic bag half full of liquid attached to a plastic tube that disappeared past the edge of the bandages near the girl's elbow. There was a skeletal look about her face. She kept her eyes closed, but he had the sense that she was awake, and that, past fluttering eyelids, she'd seen him enter the room.

"How are you feeling?" he said, touching her hand. Her fingers had dug into the folds of the blanket.

It was a moment before the lips started to move, almost an involuntary reflex, he thought, around whatever words were trying to emerge. "Why'd you come?" she managed.

"I wanted to make sure you were okay."

"To the house."

He understood then. Edie Bradbury hadn't expected anyone to stop by the house and find her in time.

"I'm glad I did." Her hand felt like a chunk of ice beneath his palm.

"You should've let me alone. I don't want to live anymore."

He was quiet a moment. Then he said, "What do you think Trent wants?"

"What?" Her eyes flew open, and she stared up at him with such a mixture of grief and surprise that he had to force himself not to turn away.

"Trent loved you," he said. "Don't you think he'd want you to go on? He'd want you to live. Try not to forget that."

The girl shifted her gaze away and stared upward into the light glaring through the plastic panels that covered the ceiling. "My baby?" she said, directing the question to the light.

"You didn't lose your baby, Edie." The girl's hand twitched beneath his own. It was a moment before he realized that she was crying. A faint sheen of moisture glistened at her temples.

"He killed Trent." She spoke so softly that Father John had to lean over to catch the words.

"Who, Edie? Who killed him?"

She stared up at him, eyes wide and bright with fear. "Jason said he was gonna make Trent pay, that he was nothing but an Indian. He went and shot him, so I wouldn't have him anymore. I wouldn't have nobody but Jason."

Father John started to say that she must tell Detective Burton what she'd just told him, then stopped himself. He knew by the fear burning in her eyes that she would never implicate Jason Rizzo in the homicides.

"Is there anyone I can call for you?" She was shaking her head, but he pushed on. "How about your parents? Brothers? Sisters?"

"My father, or whatever you want me to call him, took off so long ago, I don't remember what he looked like," she said, the words coming in a rushed whisper. "And Mom . . ." The girl tried for a laugh that sounded like a small hiccup. "Soon's I turned fifteen, her boyfriend told her to tell me to get lost, so that's what she did. So it was just me and Trent and the baby. Now it's just me."

"And your baby."

"It's not gonna be enough, Father." She was sobbing now, a skim of moisture running over her temples and glistening on her cheeks.

"If you like," he said, "you can come to the mission. There's a guest house . . ."

"Sorry, Father." The doctor slipped past the door. "We have a room ready for her now."

He pressed the girl's hand a moment, trying to impart as much reassurance as he could, and said that he'd be back tomorrow. Then he made his way past the doctor and the two attendants who had crowded into the room and headed back down the corridor.

As Father John walked into the waiting room, a large man spun around, blocking the path to the exit. He looked about thirty, with short reddish brown hair and a black mustache that curled upward toward flushed cheeks. He had on a black leather jacket that hung over the waist of his blue jeans and sported silver chains draped in a half-circle over the top of the sleeves and silver studs on the wide collar folded back over half of his chest.

"You the priest?" He hooked his hands onto his hips.

"Who are you?" Father John said. So this was Jason Rizzo, he was thinking.

"I'm here for Edie, okay? You got a problem with that?"

"What do you want?" Out of the corner of his eye, Father John saw the woman behind the counter on the left get out of her chair and step backward until she'd disappeared past the edge of a cabinet.

"How come they let you see her, and they won't let me? You must be special, that it? You being the Indian priest around here. Guess people like to lick your boots."

"Maybe she doesn't want to see you," Father John said.

"That what she told you?" The man started tossing his head, a horse fighting the reins.

Father John ignored the question. "How'd you know she was here?"

"I got friends. Neighbor lady gave me the news when I stopped by the house. I hear Edie's Indian sleazebag got himself shot. Few less red-skins around here, and that's okay by me. She should've listened to me. I warned her not to take up with Indians." He was shaking his head, emitting a strangled noise, like a half-laugh. "What's she thinking? That I'm gonna tolerate that kind of disrespect?"

Somewhere behind them, a door squealed on its hinges. Father John glanced around. A burly guard in dark blue trousers and a light blue shirt, holstered gun riding on his hip, walked over and stopped next to Jason Rizzo. "You're gonna have to leave," he said.

Rizzo's lip curled back into his mustache. "You ain't got no cause."

"Let's go." The guard took hold of the man's arm and, turning him around, walked him toward the exit. Leaning forward, he yanked open the glass door and waited until the other man had sauntered past.

"I'll be back," Rizzo was shouting. Then he was darting around a brown pickup parked at the curb, lowering himself behind the steering wheel. He turned his head and glared through the passenger window as the pickup shot forward, laying down a trail of black exhaust that floated toward the door.

14

QUIET HAD SETTLED over the office, except for the sound of warm air escaping from the vents and the dim hum of the fluorescent lights overhead. Traces of moisture clung to the window in the conference room. Vicky read through the last page of the Endangered Species Act, then set the page onto one of the stacks that she'd arranged in rows along the polished table. She had the office to herself. No clacking keyboard, no telephone ringing. Adam had left for lunch fifteen minutes ago, and a few minutes later, Annie had poked her head through the door and said she was going to lunch. And—just to let her know—Adam would be back later than usual.

Vicky pulled over a copy of the Wyoming Wolf Management Plan and thumbed through the pages. Then she fanned out the pages in one of the stacks. The sections matched. Ah, but here was the problem. In the first plan the state had submitted to the U.S. Fish and Wildlife Service, wolves would be trophy animals in the northwestern part of the state. Everywhere else, wolves would be predators. They could be shot on sight. And what kind of place would it be? she thought. Everything tamed and controlled, and no more wildness? No more wolves? The plan had been rejected.

She set the copy of the state plan to one side and picked up the folder marked "Proposed Wind River Wolf Management Plan." Leaning back in the rounded leather chair, she opened the folder against the edge of the table and skimmed the first page. They were walking a fine line, she was thinking. The tribal plan had to agree with federal regulations as well as with whatever new plan the state was drafting. Adam was right. They would have to go to Cheyenne and meet with both the federal and state wildlife people.

There was the smallest change in the atmosphere, an almost imperceptible stream of air rippling over the pages spread in front of her. Vicky sat very still. Nothing but the background noises of the office, the muffled noise of traffic on Main Street. Surely Annie had locked the front door when she'd left.

And yet . . . someone was here. Vicky could *feel* another presence.

She got up from the table, opened the conference room door, and walked down the hall that emptied into the front office. No one was there. The upholstered chairs, the small oak tables in the corners, Annie's desk facing the door, file folders stacked next to the computer, the oak chair pushed into the well—all normal. Yet there was something unfamiliar about the room. She had the sense that she was seeing it for the first time through the eyes of a stranger.

She was about to turn back into the hall when she heard the muffled scuff of footsteps on carpet. Across the office, next to one of the upholstered chairs, the door to her private office was closed. But Adam's door a few feet farther along the wall—Adam's door was ajar.

Vicky walked past the secretary's desk. "Adam?" she called, pushing the door open. The tentativeness in her voice hung in the air.

"Oh, hello." The woman across the room turned away from the window that framed a view of the redbrick building across the street, the gutters tipping forward under a ridge of snow. "I'm waiting for Adam. He must've stepped out for a moment." She paused and gestured with her head toward the front office. She could be an actress, Vicky thought. Tall and gorgeous and young—How old could she be? Mid-twenties? Light brown hair sharply cut in slices dipped to the shoulders of her dark leather jacket, and black boots wrapped around her legs all the way to the hem of her tweed skirt. "I've been dying to see Adam's office. You must be Vicky."

She was advancing across the carpet, past the desk, the side chair, blue eyes lit with enthusiasm, a slim hand extended. "I'm Samantha Lowe," she said.

She'd known who the woman was even before she'd heard the name. "Adam's at lunch," Vicky heard herself saying. She took the out-stretched hand, aware of the tiniest whiff of perfume.

"He's left already?" The light in Samantha Lowe's blue eyes dimmed with disappointment. "Oh, I was hoping to give him a ride to the restau-rant. She wrapped both hands around a green bag and began kneading the leather. "He's probably already there, wondering where I am."

"You're meeting Adam for lunch?" Vicky heard the note of surprise in her voice.

"Oh, I can't tell you how helpful Adam's been," the woman bubbled on with all the lightness and enthusiasm of a teenager. "I guess I was pretty naïve thinking I could just move to town, hang out my shingle, and clients would beat a path to my door. Lander seemed like a great town to live in. All those historic buildings restored on Main Street, and flower planters and old-fashioned streetlights. I loved it, but I really didn't know anything about the business side of setting up a practice. Thank goodness for Adam. He's taken me under his wing and kept me from making a lot of costly mistakes."

She paused and drew in a long breath. "Well, I guess I don't have to tell you," she said, waving the slim white hand toward the front office. "I'm sure he's done the same here. You and Adam must be very busy." A confidential tone now, as if they were two girlfriends discussing their latest dates. "It must be wonderful to be in a firm with a lawyer who has so much experience. Adam says you've agreed to send clients my way. I'm very grateful." She stepped forward.

Vicky moved to the side of the door. "I'm sure Adam's waiting," she said, weak with the sadness and disappointment washing over her.

The young woman slipped past. She was as slim as a shadow, Vicky thought, except for the high, rounded breasts that filled out the front of her leather jacket, the shapely hips, and the curve of her calf muscles beneath the leather boots. She opened the outer door and turned back. "We know," she said, as if she wanted to underline the unspoken comment hanging between them, "that Adam Lone Eagle isn't the type of man who likes to be kept waiting."

Then Samantha Lowe was gone, the blond hair and dark leather jacket moving past the rectangle of glass next to the door, starting down the stairs, as graceful as a ballerina.

Vicky walked across the outer office and threw the lock on the door. Then she went into her private office, took her coat off the hanger behind the door, and pulled it on. Leaning over the desk, she scribbled a note for Annie: "I'm working at home this afternoon." She lifted her briefcase and leather bag out of the desk drawer and went back to the conference room where she stuffed the management plans inside the briefcase before walking back through the quiet of the office and letting herself out, making sure the lock was set before she closed the door.

Fool. Fool. Fool. What was she thinking? She headed around the corner of the building and down the narrow walkway that divided the brick walls from the parking lot, lifting her face into the chilly, moist air, the briefcase rigid at her side, one hand gripping the handle of the bag slung over her shoulder. From behind her came the slushy noise of traffic and the faint smell of exhaust. Why had she thought that a man like Adam Lone Eagle—who stopped women in their tracks when he walked by—could ever be faithful? He was like the chiefs in the Old Time. It was their duty—responsibility—to take many wives. But that was the Old Time, when a woman needed a man to hunt and bring her food to eat and skins that she could make into clothing and tipis. So she looked the other way when he took other wives. But this was now.

Vicky stabbed her key into the lock of the Jeep until, finally, the lock button jumped up. She didn't need Adam Lone Eagle. She yanked open the door, threw her briefcase and bag across the front seat, and got in behind the steering wheel, shutting the door so hard that the vehicle seemed to rock. It was ironic, when you thought about it. After ten years with Ben Holden—ten years of lies—she'd sworn that she would never be so trusting again. So naïve, as naïve as Samantha Lowe peering out at the world through blue eyes that cast a lovely hue on everything.

She had to jiggle the key in the ignition before the engine sparked into life. She'd have to break things off. *That* was as clear as the red sedan parked ahead. There could be nothing more between them. No more late dinners and long nights where he made her feel warm and comforted and not alone. Where he made her forget all that had been with Ben and all that would never be with John O'Malley—all the memories and yearnings—as she and Adam had floated together in what was present and possible.

There would be nothing personal between them. Nothing but the law firm. Vicky shifted into reverse and shot backward into the lot. A horn blared. She hit the brake and glanced over her left shoulder at the orange sedan stopped behind her. Then she pulled back in and waited for the sedan to drive past, her thoughts on the law firm. Who was she kidding? Adam was not the kind of man to walk into the office every day, nod a pleasant good morning, sit down on the other side of the conference table, and hammer out some legal document, as if they'd never been lovers. There was a good chance he would want to dissolve the firm. He could open another office in Lander, go his own way. And take the tribal business with him.

God, the horn was still blaring, like a cow bleating into the cold. "I'm waiting for you to go," she said out loud. Then she dipped her head against the rim of the steering wheel. Adam would go, she thought.

Well, she had options. She lifted her head and straightened her shoulders. Now that was funny. She had to laugh at the options, and the choked sound of her own laughter caught her by surprise. She swallowed back the impulse to go on laughing, afraid that she might burst into tears. She could continue to be one of Adam's women, walking around with blinders on, like a mare at the edge of a cliff, or she could return to her one-woman law practice and spend her days working on DUIs, divorces, adoptions, and parking tickets, and forget about practicing Indian law.

She stared at the red sedan ahead, aware now of the silence that floated around her. The orange car must have driven past, and she'd been too preoccupied to notice. She'd started backing out again when a blurred figure appeared silently outside her window. A gloved hand tapped on the glass. Vicky stepped on the brake and looked into the brown eyes of Lucille Montana, head bent toward the window, breath making little gray clouds on the glass.

"I've got to talk to you." The woman looked as if she were mouthing the words, but the muffled sound of her voice cracked through the glass and metal.

Vicky pressed the window button. A shaft of cold air peppered with moisture drifted over the lowering glass. Lucille stuck her face into the opening. Her eyes were red rimmed, her cheeks flushed with cold and worry. If she invited the woman into her office, Vicky was thinking, Adam could return before they finished talking.

She said, "I'm on my way home. We can talk at my place."

"Can't we go to the office?" Lucille clasped her gloved hands together like a microphone in front of her mouth, which made her voice tremble, laced with hopelessness.

Vicky had to look away to keep from jamming down on the door handle and getting out. It was just as she'd expected. A sheriff's investigator was probably taking a hard look at Frankie Montana for the Shoshone murders. But she did not want to return to the office. She did not want to face Adam yet. She needed some time.

"I'm working at home this afternoon," she began, averting her eyes from the woman still pressing her face a few inches from her own. "We can talk there."

There was a moment before Lucille Montana began to drift back along the Jeep. Another moment before the orange sedan lurched across the parking lot and turned onto Main, bouncing in the rearview mirror, the woman's dark head bobbing over the steering wheel.

"FRANKIE DIDN'T KILL anybody." Lucille gripped her gloves in one hand and slapped them against her thigh. She was sunk into the middle of the sofa, the cushions angled upward on either side. "I don't care what the detective says. He wants to arrest some Arapaho for killing Shoshones, so he can make himself look like a big man. He don't care what Arapaho he arrests."

"Better tell me what happened." Vicky lifted a yellow notepad out of her briefcase and located the pen tucked in the side pocket. She sat down in the upholstered chair across from the other woman.

Lucille squared her shoulders, tilted her head back, and studied the ceiling a moment, as if the images were moving across the white plaster. "First thing this morning, he's knocking on the door."

"Who?"

"Detective Burton. Knocking on the door, and soon's I opened it, he says to me, 'Go get Frankie,' and I say, 'Frankie's still sleeping, so come back later.' He says, 'Go get him now,' and give me that look like he's gonna haul me off to jail if I don't do what he says."

Vicky held the pen close to the notepad balanced on her lap and waited.

After a moment, Lucille went on, "I told Frankie to get up 'cause Burton was there and wasn't gonna leave. Then I went back out to the door, and I said, 'Guess you better come in, so I can close the door and keep the cold outside.' The house was already getting cold from him standing there. Pretty soon Frankie comes down the hall. He's got his blue jeans on and the dirty tee shirt he was sleeping in. He's still half asleep, and he says, 'What're you doin' here?' and Burton says he has a few questions he'd like Frankie to answer."

"I warned Frankie." Vicky could hear the exasperation leaking into her voice. "He didn't have to talk to him."

"I told him. I said, 'Frankie, shut up. You don't have to answer questions,' but Frankie turns on me like I'm the one wanting to lock him up in prison for the rest of his life for killing people he never killed, and he says, 'I don't have nothing to hide.'"

"He should have told Burton to call his lawyer."

The other woman threw one hand into the air. "Well, that's just the problem, Vicky. He doesn't have a lawyer. He thought you were his lawyer, but you told him to call somebody else."

Samantha Lowe, Vicky thought. She tried to swallow back the bitter taste in her mouth. A lawyer out of law school for how long—two, three years? That was the lawyer she'd recommended to a man who could be looking at three charges for first-degree murder.

"Start at the beginning," Vicky said. "Tell me everything that Frankie said."

"You gonna help him?"

"I'll see what I can do." Well, this was perfect, she was thinking. A fitting way to sever all relationships with Adam Lone Eagle. She would have a client for her one-woman law firm, a troublemaker she could count on for a steady flow of business, which Lucille Montana would pay for out of tips from twelve-hour shifts over at a cafeteria in Riverton, while Adam Lone Eagle rewrote the Wind River Wolf Management Plan and went on to handle cases on the tribe's water, oil and gas, timber, and a lot of other important issues.

Vicky scribbled the date at the top of the notepad and tried to focus on what Lucille was saying. Something about Burton saying somebody killed the Shoshones with a rifle, and how Frankie had himself a deer rifle and how he had a grudge against the Shoshones, and Frankie saying, sure, he might've had a grudge on account of they'd told the police he assaulted them, when they were the ones that took after him. Who wouldn't hold a grudge?

Perfect. Frankie ignored her advice and dug himself deeper into a hole that she would have to wave a lot of magic legal wands to try to pull him out of. The man was a hothead. She could imagine Frankie Montana getting drunk and yanking his rifle off the rack in his pickup and shooting somebody. But getting three men out into the country— *planning* to murder them? That she could not imagine. Besides, she had believed him when he said that someone had stolen his rifle in the parking lot next to the bar in Riverton—in full view of the traffic on Federal. It was so preposterous she'd decided it must be true.

Vicky realized that Lucille had stopped talking. She was staring across the living room, as if she were trying to bring something else into focus. "Anything else?" Vicky asked.

The other woman closed her eyes a moment. "It's got me real worried," she said. "Burton kept asking Frankie where he was on Saturday, and Frankie kept saying he was home all day. The detective says, 'What about the afternoon?' and I'm thinking, that must've been when those Shoshones got shot. Frankie tells him that he was home all morning and afternoon and night. He says that he came home Friday after the Shoshones beat him up and went to bed. Next thing he knows, it's Sunday night and the cops are hauling him off to jail. Frankie tells Burton that he can ask me if he wants, 'cause I know he was home."

Vicky leaned back in the chair. "So Frankie has an alibi," she said, almost to herself. In the silence that pulled around them, Vicky knew that it wasn't true.

When the other woman started to say something, Vicky put up her hand. "What did you tell Burton?"

Lucille was quiet a moment. Finally, she said, "I gave Frankie his alibi, Vicky. He's my son. I can't let him go to prison for something he didn't do."

"Where is he now?" Vicky said. This was worse that she'd realized. Frankie expected his mother to lie for him, even perjure herself on the witness stand, if it came to that.

"Probably over at the house with the guys he's been hanging out with. It's that white shack on Trosper Road. They go there and get drunk." The woman's eyes were big with moisture. "Tell you the truth, I'm worried sick. I did all I could for that boy. I tried to raise him up to follow the Arapaho Way. I don't know what's gonna become of him."

Vicky slid forward and, reaching across the space between them, patted the other woman's hand. "I know, Lucille," she said. She was thinking that she had to find Frankie before he did himself any more damage.

15

FATHER JOHN SPOTTED the house from the top of the rise. Low and flat, hugging the earth, splotches of snow on the brown roof, like the mixture of snow and dirt on the prairie that stretched into the horizon. There were two or three other houses along the road, but *that* was the home of Trent Hunter. A house of mourning, with pickups and cars parked haphazardly in the front yard, as if the friends and relatives had stopped in the nearest empty space.

He slowed the pickup on the downhill. *Di quella pira* filled up the cab, blotting out the whir of the vents that emitted occasional gusts of warm air. This was Shoshone territory, the little settlements that crawled west and north out of Fort Washakie. He came here from time to time, usually when there was a death and someone had asked for him. He'd never been to the Hunters'. The familiar feeling of dread that had set in somewhere on Seventeen-Mile Road pressed down like a heavy weight. It was the hardest part of being a priest—searching for words to comfort the parents of a dead child.

The pickup had nearly crawled to a stop when he turned right and bumped across the logs laid over the borrow ditch. He parked between two sedans, turned off the tape player, and headed across the yard, zigzagging around the other vehicles. The front door swung open when he was ten feet away. Hanson Tindall, one of the Shoshone elders, stood in the opening, wrinkled and bent, leaning against the door frame. "Come in, Father," he called. His other hand flapped over the wooden stoop. "We knew you'd come."

"Good to see you, grandfather," Father John said. There had been several occasions when Hanson had met with Arapaho elders at St. Francis about the problems both tribes faced: alcoholism that ran through families, the need for more jobs, the importance of keeping the kids in school and teaching them their Indian heritage.

"Come with me." The elder made a stiff turn into the living room. The knobs of his shoulders poked through his white shirt. Father John followed the old man past small groups of people standing around, gripping Styrofoam cups with the dark stains of coffee running down the sides. The smell of coffee drifted toward him, and the hum of conversation ran like an electric current through the room. He removed his cowboy hat and nodded toward the elders and grandmothers seated on the sofa and chairs.

"This here is Trent's folks," Hanson said, nodding to the middle-aged couple with slumped shoulders and black hair streaked with gray, seated on straight-backed, wood chairs along the side wall.

The man jumped to his feet. "Tomas Hunter," he said, stretching out his hand. His palm felt wet, as if he'd been mopping moisture from his eyes. "This is my wife, Marie." A nod toward the woman. She looked exhausted, Father John thought, drawn and tight, an old woman still inhabiting a younger body, as if her spirit had grown old first and prematurely sapped her life.

"Here's Lou Crispin." The elder nodded to the stocky man with a black ponytail seated a few feet away, and Father John stepped over and shook the man's hand.

"Pull up a chair for yourself." Crispin tugged at his shirt pocket until he'd retrieved a full pack of cigarettes, then concentrated on unwrapping the cellophane. He tapped the pack on the edge of his hand until the tip of a cigarette sprang out. "Want one?" he said.

"No, thanks." Father John held a chair for Hanson, then sat down on a folding chair that someone had pushed toward him. The room had gone quiet, except for the hushed sounds of people shuffling about, assembling into new groups. "I'm very sorry about your sons," he said, his eyes taking in the Hunters and Lou Crispin.

Tomas nodded. "Detective says you went out to Bates." He stared at the Band-Aid Father John had smoothed on his cheek this morning, then took his chair and reached for his wife's hand. The woman kept her eyes on her lap. "How'd you happen to do that?"

"I told you this priest knows what them Arapahos are up to." This was from a young man slumped against the wall. He started pulling himself away, a slow unfolding of his slim, muscular frame. He was probably in his twenties, face hard set in anger and black hair sleeked back into a braid that hung down the back of his yellow shirt.

"Best for you to be quiet, Eric," Tomas said.

"I got a phone call," Father John began. Then he explained about the message and how he'd gone to the Arapaho elders.

Another snicker from Eric, louder this time, and Father John studied the man for a moment. He was more than six feet tall, close to his own height, with muscular shoulders and arms bulging through his shirt and big hands dangling from thick forearms. But he was going soft, with the flushed cheeks and the big-belly look of a boozer.

"You ask me, the priest knew what he was gonna find at Bates," he said.

Tomas turned in his chair and glared at Eric. "Nobody asked you."

"The priest got word of what went down," Eric went on, gesturing with one hand to the men who had begun crowding around him, as if he were the spokesman. "So he went out there to make sure that Frankie Montana didn't do anything stupid, like leave his rifle behind." He swung around toward Father John. "You pick up the rifle for him? What'd you do, toss it in a hole where it ain't never gonna see the sunshine?"

Tomas was on his feet. "You're my sister's son, Eric, but I'm not gonna stand for disrespect in my home. You know that Father John got shot out there, could've been killed. You and your friends better be on your way."

"I'm telling it like it is, Uncle," Eric said, a pleading tone now. "Maybe he just wants folks to think he got shot, maybe he's protecting Montana 'cause he's Arapaho. Don't matter that Montana's out to kill Shoshones. How many other Shoshones is that bastard gonna kill while this priest is protecting him?"

Father John stood up and faced the Shoshone. "Hold on, Eric," he said, aware of the crowd pressing closer, the quiet in and out of their breathing. "You've got it all wrong. I want to see the killer brought to justice as much as you do."

"Is that a fact! Well, I got a news flash for you," Eric said, his eyes narrowed into slits. "Montana wants war, and that's what he's gonna get."

"Enough." Tomas threw a hand in front of his nephew. "We don't need any talk of war around here. You better go someplace and cool off."

Eric stood motionless, shadows of disbelief and anger moving across his face. Finally he motioned to two other young men. Heads thrust forward, they started plowing through the crowd of relatives and friends, who peeled back as they filed past. The *whack* of the front door shattered the quiet. Then, as if the slammed door had jarred something loose, everyone started talking at once, voices hushed and insistent.

"We got ourselves one helluva tragedy," Crispin said. His voice was low, suffused with grief. "Only thing I'm grateful for is Rex and Joe's mother didn't live to see 'em dead." The man took another draw of his cigarette. "Now the young bucks are all stirred up."

Father John waited until Tomas had reclaimed his seat before he sat back down and took a sip of the coffee that someone else had thrust into his hand. It was strong and bitter, but oddly enough, he thought, the warmth of it seemed to calm something inside him.

"It's like the Old Time," Hanson Tindall said. "There was enough of Indians killing one another, and where'd all that killing get us? The white invaders just kept coming, and we was as busy fighting each other as we was fighting off the invaders. Lost our lands and buffalo. The brave warriors, they was lost. We don't need no more of that. We gotta pull together. Now we got three murdered boys, good boys, all dead." He nodded at the Hunters, then at the Shoshone drawing on the cigarette until there was a steady red glow at the end. "Eric and the others are chomping at the bit for revenge. Maybe we got ourselves a new kind of invader." Hansen went on. "Somebody wants to cause trouble and get up a new war."

Father John held the elder's gaze. It was a thought that he didn't want. He'd tried to push it away, but it hovered at the edge of his mind like a black shadow.

The room had gone quiet again. They might have been onstage, Father John thought, all eyes of the audience glued to them, waiting for the next line, the next aria that would express the fear pulsating through the theater. He took another sip of coffee. He could see that Tomas was considering the idea. Trent's mother looked up, as if she, too, were contemplating the possibility that whoever had taken her son's life wanted more killing. The killer had gone to a lot of trouble to link the murders to a battle that ran like a fault line through the reservation. Whoever it was, the killer was waiting for the plates to shift. Waiting for the earthquake to erupt that would destroy a century of carefully built peace.

Tomas looked over at the elder. "Don't worry about Eric, grandfather. He's hurting real bad right now, so he's talking crazy. He looked up to Trent, you know. Trent was his idol. Used to go into Riverton to see how Trent was doing. I think Trent was talking to him about going back to school. Eric would've done it, too, with Trent keeping at him.

Now . . ." He let the thought drift off and shook his head, a heavy weight rolling back and forth.

"Everybody looked up to Trent." Marie was staring at her lap again, threading and unthreading her fingers. "Working, taking care of himself, and going to college. Learning about the Old Time. You remember, grandfather?" she asked, lifting her eyes to the old man seated across from her. "Trent and Rex and Joe, they all loved stories about the Old Time."

Lou Crispin was shaking his head. "Rex told me some big shot from a college back East was gonna teach about the Indian wars at the college. The boys couldn't wait to sign up. Platte River campaign, Powder River campaign, Sand Creek, Washita, the Custer battle." The man worked at the cigarette a moment, the hint of a smile playing in his eyes. "They loved that class. That's how come they wanted to go to Bates. I never took Rex and Joe out there when they was kids. Bates was over and done, that was my feeling. No use bringing back hard feelings between Shoshones and Arapahos. Let the dead bury the dead, is what I tol' my boys. But they said, 'We gotta know the Shoshone side, 'cause Shoshones always get the blame, with people calling it a massacre.'"

He paused. Leaning over the armrest, he stubbed the cigarette into a glass dish. Then he pulled himself back into place. "Rex called last Friday. Said Joe and him was going to visit Bates Saturday and see what happened. Where the Arapahos was, where Shoshones rode in, where the troops went. My boys said they was gonna meet somebody out there. Trent was gonna go, too. I'm thinking that whoever else went was also in that class. I said to that detective, look at them other students."

The room was quiet again, and Father John realized that everyone seemed to be watching Hanson, waiting for the elder to speak. It was a moment before the old man said, "I used to tell the boys, it's good to hold onto the stories, but we gotta let go of the old grudges and the hate. They don't do nothing but keep us down." He shifted toward the couple sitting next to him. "Been awhile since Trent come around asking his questions about the Old Time."

"Since he got mixed up with that white girl," Tomas said, a hardness in his tone. "We tried to tell him," he paused, his gaze lingering for a moment on his wife, "that she wasn't any good for him. No reins on that girl, nothing to keep her going straight. We told him she was gonna pull him off track, but it was like he was drunk on her. Didn't want to give her up. We told him, don't bring her around the family. We was waiting for him to wake up and see she wasn't any good."

"I've met her," Father John said. "I think she really loved Trent."

Tomas shook his head and closed his eyes for a moment at this. "Girl like that don't love anybody but herself."

"Maybe nobody ever loved her," Marie said.

The man slid his gaze sideways toward his wife. "She was hanging around with them crazy white supremacists that want to kill off all the brown-skin people. That the kind of girl you wanted our boy getting mixed up with?"

"She took Trent's death pretty hard," Father John said. "She's at Riverton Memorial."

Tomas didn't say anything. He leaned forward and stared out across the room, as if he'd like to join one of the other conversations erupting now and then.

"What happened to her?" Hanson asked.

"She was pretty upset over Trent's death," Father John began, guessing now, struggling for some logical explanation. "I think she wanted to bring the pain into focus. She cut her arms."

Marie lifted one hand to her mouth. "She gonna be okay?"

"She'll recover, but she's hurting a lot."

"Ain't it enough our son's been killed?" Tomas said. "We don't need that girl's troubles. Why doesn't she go back to wherever she came from?"

"She doesn't have any family."

"Well, that figures." Tomas was shaking his head, as if he could shake away the topic.

"There's something you should know," Father John went on. "Edie is carrying Trent's child."

"Oh, my God." Marie dropped her face into her hands. A moment passed before she took her hands away. A sheen of moisture crept over her cheeks. "The baby?"

"The baby's okay."

Father John glanced at Tomas. His jaw was clenched. His hands lay like rocks dropped onto the thighs of his blue jeans. He might have been turned into stone.

"We don't need this," Tomas said finally. "Forget it, Marie, anything you're thinking. That girl's got a white supremacist baby in her belly, and we don't want anything to do with it. Trent never said one word about a baby."

"A child's always a blessing," Hanson said. "*Dam Apua dame mash. The Creator is with us.*"

"Not a white supremacist child. No way would Trent ever break up with that girl if she had his baby."

"Break up?" Father John heard the astonishment in his voice. Edie Bradbury hadn't said anything about a breakup. "When did that happen?"

"Two, three weeks ago, I guess," Tomas said. "Called here and said, 'Don't worry, Dad. I'm gonna break it off. Gonna tell Edie it's not working out and get my own place.' "

Father John sat back in his chair. The girl said that Trent hadn't been *home* since Friday, yet there hadn't been any sign of Trent's things at the house. "Do you know if he moved out?"

"Called me next day and said he'd found an apartment in a basement by the college. Said it was gonna be real convenient and quiet. No more trouble from the girl's white friends."

"She gonna be okay?" Marie moved to the edge of her chair.

"I tol' you, honey." Tomas patted her hand. "We can't be worrying ourselves about that white girl. Let her white friends take care of her."

"The detective will want to know everything you've told me," Father John said. He kept his voice low, although what difference did it make? Everybody in the living room had been listening in on the conversation.

The moccasin telegraph would be bursting with gossip the next few days.

Tomas nodded. "I already told that detective everything I know. I told him, take a good look at that girl and the gang of troublemakers she hangs with. Maybe they're the ones want to get a war started on the rez, so Indians can kill one another off."

Father John drained the rest of the coffee, then got to his feet. "Call me if there's anything I can do to help you," he said, setting one hand on the man's shoulder a moment. Then he turned to Lou Crispin who was staring up at him out of red-rimmed eyes. "Anything at all," he said.

Motioning for them to stay seated, he started back across the room.

"There's something else you can do." The elder's voice came from behind him.

Father John turned around. Hanson was holding onto the back of a chair, and one of the other men, Father John realized, had a hand on the old man's arm. For a moment, Father John thought the elder was going to ask him to stay in touch with the girl, make sure she was okay. Instead, he said, "Tell the Arapahos we don't wish 'em harm. And if you talk to that detective, tell him he's got to find the killer real soon. No tellin' how long we can keep the likes of Eric Surrell from goin' off and lookin' for their own revenge."

Father John shook the elder's hand, the palm as rough as rawhide. He could feel the old man's eyes trailing him past the groups of people—the nods and half-smiles—until he'd let himself out the front door.

FATHER JOHN TURNED onto Trout Creek Road and peered at the snow-streaked asphalt rolling toward him, unable to shake the image of Edie Bradbury curled on top of the bed, the blue-red slices in her arms, the blood crusted on the bedspread. A flare for capturing history in brief, pithy images, Professor Lambert had said of the girl. Edie, Trent, the Crispin brothers—they were all in the class. It was hard to imagine the girl with a rifle, pulling the trigger—one, two, three times.

Afterward, posing each body to look like a fallen warrior. Recording the message somewhere and placing the telephone call, wanting the bodies to be found before the snow covered them. A poet yearning for her work to be appreciated.

It was hard to imagine.

And yet, *no reins on that girl,* Tomas had said. And she was carrying the child of the man who had broken up with her.

He wasn't sure when the pickup had appeared in the rearview mirror, brown and weaving across the road. It was coming closer now, so close he could see the three dark heads bobbing above the dashboard, the white teeth flashing in brown faces. They were enjoying this, taking up the whole road and then speeding up until they were riding the tail of the Toyota.

The first hit was like a nudge. Father John felt the rear tires spin, knocked out of sync a moment. He let them settle back into a regular rhythm before he pressed down on the accelerator, trying to put space between himself and the brown pickup that was also speeding up. The next hit was a loud crash of metal against metal. He had the sense of being airborne, the pickup loping down the road and swerving to the side as the other pickup rammed the tailgate hard. His head snapped forward into the windshield and the front end plowed into the borrow ditch.

The engine whined for a moment, then shut off. In the rearview mirror, he watched the doors of the pickup swing open. He recognized the three men tumbling out of the cab: Eric Surrell and the men who had left the house with him. Eric planted both boots in the snow, leaned down, and lifted out something from behind the seat.

They were coming up his side of the pickup now, single file. Funny, he thought. Like baseball players marching out to the field, Eric in the lead carrying the bat.

16

FATHER JOHN PUSHED the door open and jumped out just as the bat rose in the air and smashed down onto the pickup. The thumping noise reverberated through the quiet. A dent the size of a baseball appeared on the top edge of the bed. The vehicle seemed to jump sideways, then settle back, shuddering under the force of the blow.

"Hey!" he shouted. "What're you doing?" He stepped around the door, placing the shield of metal and plastic and glass between himself and the three men who were crouching forward, like wolves moving in for the kill.

"Your turn, priest." Eric Surrell held the bat up and out, ready for another strike.

Father John waited, his breath an icy lump in his throat. He was barely aware of the moist air stinging his face and the dull throb of pain in his cheek. Everything was moving in slow motion. He didn't take his eyes off the man with the bat. Come on. Come on.

"We got a message for Arapahos," Eric shouted. He adjusted his weight from one leg to the other. The others pulled back, giving him room to swing. "You're gonna be the delivery boy."

One more step.

Eric pulled the bat up higher. The instant he stepped into the swing, Father John threw his weight against the door, crashing it against the man and knocking him into the side of the pickup. He stumbled sideways and jabbed one hand against the front seat, scrambling for balance. The bat dipped in his other hand, and Father John grabbed hold of the man's arm and yanked him forward, then sideways, pulling him against the edge of the door. The bat slid downward, planting itself like a pole in the snow as Father John rammed the man's arm up behind his back and slammed him into the side of the pickup. There was a snapping noise, like the sound of boots stomping on ice. Father John felt something in the man's arm slacken, and Eric gave a howl that ripped out of his lungs and cut into the air.

The other men were coming to life. Out of the corner of his eye, Father John could see the surprise slip from their faces, giving way to a red anger that glowed like burning coals through the gray cold. They started forward. Father John swung Eric around and shoved the man into them. Then he scooped up the bat and stepped away from the pickup, giving himself a good five feet from the men stumbling forward, trying to steady Eric, who was still howling with pain and screaming, "My shoulder! My shoulder!"

Father John fixed the bat into place over his right shoulder. He could feel his hands tighten into the familiar grip. It felt natural, except for the leather gloves he was wearing. He was the pitcher again, the rare pitcher who was damn good up at bat. He could bat at .382, but that was twenty-five years ago. Twenty-five years ago, but he could still swing a bat. He knew that for a fact.

One of Eric's buddies, a tall man with squinty eyes and black braids dangling over the fur collar of his jean jacket, had moved past the others. He looked like a wrestler, arms bent, elbows pointed outward, legs planted a couple of feet apart. His eyes were black slits in his brown face. "Okay, priest. Looks like it's you and me."

"You want to try me? Come on." Father John moved the bat up and down. With the right swing, he could break the man's arm.

The Indian hesitated. "Throw the bat down. Let's see what kind of man you are."

"The bat's mine," Father John said. "You're going to have to take your chances."

Eric let out another yelp. "Sonnuvabitch," he screamed.

"Get him, Lester!" The man holding onto Eric shouted.

A couple of seconds passed. The Indian kept shifting his gaze from the bat to Father John. Father John could almost read the argument playing out behind the squinting eyes. The man was weighing his odds. The priest was twenty years older, but he was taller and in better shape than he'd expected. Maybe he was fast with the bat. He could be real fast and strong. He could hit him. Maybe he'd get hit before he saw it coming.

Finally, something in the Indian's expression seemed to deflate, all the confidence and energy leaching away. He put up both hands in an awkward sign of peace. "We come to send a message to that Arapaho," he said. "Tell Frankie Montana we aren't gonna sit around and do nothing while he kills our people. He wants war, he's gonna get it. Tell him we're ready."

"That's all you want, then take off," Father John said, keeping his grip tight, his hands glued to the bat. "Get your friend to the hospital."

The Indian took a step backward and glanced around at Eric, who was doubled over, moaning, his good arm looped over his dislocated shoulder. The other Indian had an arm around Eric's waist, keeping him on his feet.

"Shit, Lester," the man shouted, steering Eric back toward the brown pickup. "Let's get out of here."

Lester kept moving backward, his eyes on the bat. When he reached the tailgate, he swung around and lunged for the brown pickup. He slid in behind the steering wheel as the Indian with Eric shoved the man into the middle and crawled in behind him. The doors slammed shut, the engine turned over, and the pickup started backing up. Then it pulled around and shot down the road in the direction of Fort Washakie.

Father John waited until the dark vehicle had blurred into the fading daylight before he stepped back to the stalled pickup. He set the bat inside, leaning it against the passenger seat, close at hand. Funny, he hadn't been aware of how chilly it was, but now the cold bit through his jacket and settled in his bones. The wind had picked up. He could hear it whining through the trees behind him like an animal. It made a whistling noise as it gusted through the cab.

He slid inside and turned the ignition. The engine sputtered and shut off. He tried again, and this time it caught. He shifted into reverse, then into forward and back into reverse, easing on and off the pedal, rocking the Toyota out of the mud and snow in the ditch, still watching the rearview mirror for the brown pickup.

It was no use. He was stuck. He was about to give up and get the shovel out of the box in back when he shifted again into reverse and stomped down on the accelerator. The pickup jumped backward, free.

He steered the vehicle into the lane, then shifted gears and drove east. Another couple of turns and he was speeding down Seventeen-Mile Road. There was no other traffic, no sign of life, except for the small houses set back from the road here and there. He gripped the steering wheel hard. He'd managed to stay calm and logical, but now that it was over—or was it over? Now Eric had another score to settle. He could feel the anger creeping like fire through his chest and into his throat. His mouth was as dry as dust. If Lester had made a move, he would have swung at the man with all his strength. God, he could have killed him, and he didn't care. *He didn't care.*

He made himself take several deep breaths to tamp down the anger. Gradually he felt his grip relax on the wheel. The muscles in his chest and arms also began to relax. He kept his eyes on the road unfurling ahead. He could breathe easily now. "Lord, help me," he said out loud, his own voice lost in the noise of the wind gusting over the half-opened window. Let me care.

THEY KNEW SHE was here.

Vicky had seen the blinds moving in the front window as she drove through the slush and mud into the yard. Frankie and his friends were inside the blocklike house with faded yellow paint and a wooden stoop with part of the railing hanging loose, she was sure. She'd parked the Jeep close to the stoop and waited for the door to open. Nothing had happened. The silence of the afternoon pressed down over the house, yet she had the sense that somebody was moving about inside and eyes were watching her through the slats. She left the engine running and waited. If Frankie Montana wanted to see her, he would come out. That was the Arapaho Way.

A couple of minutes passed. Still no sign of anyone. Vicky turned off the engine, picked her way up the soggy steps, and knocked on the door. Her knuckles made a heavy thudding sound through her glove. This was not the way she'd been brought up—pushy and loud and insistent—but Frankie was probably looking at three homicide charges and the man was too pigheaded to realize the danger he was in. It was his mother who was doing all the worrying.

Vicky knocked again and glanced around. Across the road, little gusts of wind kicked up powder puffs of snow that looked like white tumbleweeds blowing across the fields. This was foolish, she was thinking. Trying to find a client who didn't want to talk to her and had no idea he even needed a lawyer, when she should be working on the wolf management proposal. God, Adam was right.

Adam.

Adam wasn't always right, and, something else: she knew now that she couldn't trust him. Why couldn't she trust him? She pounded hard on the door. "Frankie!" she called. "Open up."

The door cracked open about two inches and a pair of dark eyes peered out slantwise. A whiff of something putrid and acrid floated past the opening.

"What do you want?" It was a woman's voice, sharp and suspicious.

"Tell Frankie I have to talk to him," Vicky said. A drinking house, she was thinking. Probably a drug house. The place where Frankie and his friends hung out and got stoned.

The woman opened the door wider, a mixture of distrust and curiosity moving through her thin face. She was still a teenager, Vicky guessed, dressed in jeans and a baby blue tee shirt that looked too small. She had the reddened eyes and the lifeless look of a meth addict.

"Who are you?"

"Frankie's lawyer. Will you please get him."

"Wait a minute."

Vicky placed one hand on the door trying to hold it open, but it slammed shut. She was conscious of the wind gusting around the yard now, pitting her face with little flecks of moisture. She gave the door another rap. "I'm not going away," she shouted.

A couple of minutes passed before the door inched open again. "He's not here." The girl was in the shadows, and her voice sounded far away.

"Right," Vicky said, starting down the stoop. "Tell him not to call me when he gets arrested for murder," she called over her shoulder.

"Wait!"

Vicky looked back. The girl had opened the door wider and jammed herself into the opening. "You think Frankie's gonna get stuck with them murders?"

"I'm positive of it."

"He's innocent."

"A lot of innocent people end up in prison."

"He's not here. I'll see if I can find out where he is. Okay?"

Vicky said that she'd wait in the Jeep. It was obvious the girl didn't want to invite her inside, which was just as well because she didn't want to go inside. She didn't want to see whatever was there. It was enough to get a whiff of the odor.

She crawled back into the Jeep and turned on the engine, trying to fight back the sense of futility that had dropped over her like a heavy blanket. At least the girl seemed to glimpse the trouble that Frankie could be in.

Warm air was exploding from the vents as the girl came out of the house. Coatless, hugging her arms in the cold wind, she loped for the Jeep, and Vicky realized that she was almost barefoot, nothing but thin-strapped sandals kicking and sliding through the mud and snow.

Vicky rolled down the window, and the girl stuck her head in the opening. Specks of moisture clung to her long black hair and speckled the shoulders of the blue tee shirt. Behind the masklike set of her face was evidence that the girl might have been pretty not long ago—the finely pointed nose and full lips, the sharp cheekbones. She kept rubbing at her thin arms, which were purplish red with cold.

"Frankie says he'll see you at the office." She seemed to find this amusing. For an instant the masklike face cracked into a barely perceptible smile.

"And where might that be?" Vicky asked. She was tired of this game.

"Cowboy over in Riverton."

"The bar?"

"He said you'll find him at his desk in back. Unless he feels lucky and decides to shoot some pool." Also amusing, judging by the little laugh that gurgled out of the girl's throat.

"Tell you what . . ." Vicky had to stop to swallow back the disgust, a hard knot rising in her throat. A beautiful, young Arapaho girl mixed up with Frankie Montana, hanging out at a drinking house, strung out on drugs. "Frankie can call my office and make an appointment."

"I know you're Vicky Holden." The girl was leaning into the Jeep. Her breath had the sour smell of someone much older, someone sick. A kind of terror had come into her eyes. "You gotta help Frankie. All kinds of deputies been asking questions around the rez."

"Did they come here?" Vicky gestured with her head toward the house. No one inside would have opened the door, she was thinking, and unless they had a warrant, Detective Burton could only guess what was inside. But the next step would be a warrant, and who knew what circumstantial evidence Burton would find that could tie Frankie to the murders.

"Not yet. But they're gonna come around. I just don't wanna . . ." She hesitated, a debate playing out behind her eyes. "I don't wanna be here when they show up."

"Is that why you want me to help Frankie? To keep the law from poking around?"

The girl flinched backward and blinked several times. "Frankie and me are in a relationship, you know what I mean? I'm his woman."

"You're his woman," Vicky said. The girl was probably all of seventeen.

"Yeah. Maybe Frankie's not the greatest, and maybe he gets a little crazy sometimes, and I don't always know what he's gonna do, but that's when he's . . ." Her features settled back into the lifeless mask, and it struck Vicky that the girl was good at donning the mask, like an actress.

"So if you're Frankie's lawyer," the girl hurried on, "you're not gonna tell anybody what I say, right? I mean, you're not gonna tell the deputies stuff that might hurt Frankie."

"You mean the fact that he drinks and probably uses drugs? I think they know."

"Well, that's the only time he gets crazy, you know, when he's drunk or . . ." She let the thought hang in the air between them.

"Using drugs," Vicky said. The girl blinked an affirmation.

"He can't go back to jail, Frankie can't," she said, the mask cracking again. "It about killed him when they locked him up over in Lander for hitting some guy. I mean, thrown into a cage like some animal in a zoo. I seen when he got out that he wasn't the same. That's when he started drinking big time and shooting up. That's what made him crazy, that stupid jail. Would've gotten locked up again last year for breaking and entering, if you hadn't got him off. Like them rich people's houses up in the mountains wasn't just begging to get broken into. I mean, they don't even need them houses, 'cause they got big houses someplace else. Most the time, they don't even go to them mountain houses, and all that stuff's sitting in there, nobody using it. So Frankie took a few things. So what's the big deal? No way was he gonna go back to jail. He'd do anything to stay out of jail. He'd even . . ."

"What? What would he do?"

"I don't know," the girl muttered. She started backing her head out of the Jeep, as if she'd like to reel back everything she'd said.

"What would he do?" Vicky persisted.

The girl was rubbing her arms hard and stomping her feet. Her teeth were chattering. "Forget it," she managed. At that, she turned and started running for the house, still hugging her arms. The backs of her legs looked purple. The tee shirt was plastered against the knobs of her spine.

"Tell Frankie to call me," Vicky called, then she rolled up the window, put the gear in reverse and backed across the yard and out onto the road. *That's what made him crazy. He gets a little crazy sometimes.* Vicky stared at the snow-splotched asphalt cutting through the patchwork of brown and white prairie. The girl's words ran through her mind like an endlessly looping melody. She wondered how crazy Frankie had gotten on Saturday—how much booze, how many drugs? Maybe Frankie had decided to end the feud with Trent Hunter and the other Shoshones once and for all out at Bates.

He'd do anything to stay out of jail. The rest of what the girl had said was rolling around in her head now. *He'd even . . .*

Vicky could guess the rest of it. There was nothing Frankie Montana wouldn't do to stay out of jail. He might even kill the three men who tried to put him there.

She could almost believe it, except that Lucille didn't think so. And that was the point, wasn't it? It was Lucille who had confided that Frankie lied to the sheriff about his whereabouts on Saturday. She wouldn't have mentioned that Frankie had lied if she thought her son might actually be guilty of murder. Lucille would have protected him.

She gripped the steering wheel, pumping the brake pedal and pulling to the side at the same time. As soon as an oncoming pickup had lumbered past, slush spitting out from the tires, the motor growling, Vicky yanked the wheel around, made a U-turn, and headed toward Riverton.

17

SHE HAD ONLY a vague idea where the Cowboy was located. Some-where on north Federal. She'd driven almost out of town and turned back before she spotted the square building with the peaked roof and brown shingled sides and the parking lot in front. An assortment of ve-hicles crowded around the pole that hoisted a rectangular sign: "Cow-boy Bar & Grill."

Vicky parked in an empty slot, grabbed her bag off the seat, and started around the old sedans and pickups. The muffled beat of a coun-try song floated past the wood door. She pushed the door open and stepped into a long room that resembled a log cabin, with chinked log walls and iron chandeliers with fake candles hanging from the ceiling beams and cowboy music coming from speakers over the bar. A pale light washed over the plank floor that vibrated beneath her feet. It took a moment to adjust to the dim, smoky air.

There was an odd mix of people about: three or four cowboys straddling the stools at the bar on the right and, sitting around the tables, groups of what might be college students—twenty-somethings with mussed hair and slept-in sweatshirts—hunched over books opened next to bottles of beer. The atmosphere was charged, as if each group resented the other.

Vicky scanned the tables at the far end. *At his desk in back.* No sign of Frankie. She had the same feeling of futility: Frankie and the girl playing a little joke, laughing their heads off back at the house.

Then she spotted him through the wide doorway across from the bar, standing next to a pool table, intent upon chalking a cue as if it were the most important thing he had to do.

Vicky made her way around the tables. A couple of the college students looked up with blank eyes, their thoughts on whatever was in the books, probably aware of a change in the atmosphere as she'd walked by. But the eyes of the cowboys at the bar, they were following her.

"Well, hellooo there," one called. "Haven't seen a classy lady like you around here." The others joined in a laugh that rumbled down the long polished wood.

"What can we get you?" The bartender leaned across the bar, joining in the fun.

Vicky shook her head and kept going: around a couple of more tables, through the doorway, past a group of men huddled together, counting out dollar bills.

Frankie looked up from the end of the pool cue. "Well, well," he said, a satisfied grin spreading across his brown face. "You must've wanted to see me real bad."

"We need to talk, Frankie."

"Wait for me in my office. I'm just about to lift twenty bucks off this here white dude." He poked the air with the cue toward the tall, blond man across the room.

"I'm not waiting." Vicky nodded at the pool table. "Your choice."

Frankie went back to chalking the cue. He crinkled his forehead and blew a little puff of chalk out over the green felt table. Then he tossed the cue to one of the cowboys who'd been peeling out bills. "Shoot this one for me, George," he said. "Show this here college boy how to pocket them balls. I got me some business to attend to in my office."

Frankie sauntered past her, brushing her shoulder—deliberately, Vicky thought. She started after him into the main room. The bartender uncapped a beer, and Frankie scooped it off the bar as he passed, not slowing a beat. When he reached the last table, he dropped down in the wooden, barrel-shaped chair and tipped back, wrapping his boots around the front legs.

"Be my guest," he said, motioning with the beer bottle toward the chair across from him.

Vicky glanced around. The nearest occupied table was a good twenty feet away. The music was still pouring out of the speakers over the bar—Willie Nelson, "Nothing I Can Do About It Now." She hooked her bag over the back of the chair, sat down, and folded her arms on the table. Leaning forward, she locked eyes with the grinning man rocking his chair back and forth. "Let's be clear about something," she said, keeping her voice low, the words distinct. "Your mother came to see me today. She's worried about you. That's the only reason I'm here."

"So now you're gonna be my lawyer again?" Frankie tossed his head back and gave a little snort. "Well, you don't have nothing to worry about. I didn't kill nobody."

"Detective Burton has you tagged as the prime suspect," Vicky said. "He thinks you had the motivation, and you owned a rifle, which happens to be the weapon."

"I already told you." Frankie dropped the front legs of his chair and leaned toward her, pressing his chest against the edge of the table. "What kind of lawyer are you, you don't remember things? My rifle got stolen out there in the parking lot." He lifted the beer bottle in the direction of the lot. "Some bastard broke my lock and took it out of the rack. You don't believe me, go look at the broken lock."

Vicky didn't say anything for a moment. Maybe Frankie was telling the truth. Maybe his rifle had been stolen, which meant that Trent

Hunter and the Crispin brothers had lied to the police when they'd said that Frankie had a rifle when he'd assaulted them. It made sense, she thought. The Shoshones were fed up with Frankie. They could have lied about the rifle to make certain that Frankie didn't slip out of the assault charge. Frankie would probably slip out anyway. She'd filed the motion to dismiss the assault charges, and the tribal judge had scheduled the hearing for next week.

"You had the time to shoot the men Saturday," she said.

"No way. I got an alibi. I was home, tucked in safe and sound from Friday to Sunday. Ask my mom. Just her and me, watching TV. She fixed me some chicken soup and we . . ."

Vicky held up one hand. "Stop it, Frankie. Tomorrow you won't remember what kind of soup she made you. You might start thinking she made you tacos."

"Tacos, yeah. That's good. She made me tacos."

Vicky waited a moment. Willie Nelson had finished and the clank of bottles filled in the quiet. Back in the pool room, somebody yelped, and somebody else let out a shout: "Okay!" When the music started again—some female singer that she didn't recognize—Vicky said, "You're willing to let your mother perjure herself for you?"

"She's gonna say what I tell her."

Behind her, Vicky heard the boots hitting the floor. She glanced up as the bartender walked up, leaned over, and rapped his knuckles on the table. Light gleamed on the man's bald head. "This Indian even offer you a beer?" he asked.

Frankie tilted back on his chair again and looked up at the man out of squinting eyes that barely masked contempt. Then the eyes turned to Vicky. "What d'ya want?"

Vicky shook her head. "I won't be here long." She waited until the clack of the man's boots was lost in the beat of the music before she said, "You know what I think, Frankie? I think you were at the drinking house." She pushed on, ignoring the bolt of surprise that shot through his expression. "You were high on something. Maybe you were stoned senseless, I don't know, but you don't want Burton or any of the police on the rez near that house. So when he came to talk to you about the three murders, you said you were home. And you knew that your mother would back you up. All of your problems would go away. The house would still be safe and, with an airtight alibi and a witness, you couldn't be charged with the homicides."

Frankie took a long swig of the beer and grinned at her, something like appreciation flickering in his eyes. "Maybe you're okay after all," he said. "You know, you're pretty good looking for an older babe. Hard to think you got kids as old as me. How old are you? Forty something?"

Vicky glanced at the fake-candle light dangling overhead. Then, looking back at the man, who was taking another swig from the bottle, enjoying himself, she said, "It won't work, Frankie, all your scheming and dodging. Sooner or later, Burton's going to find the house and talk to your girlfriend and whoever else hangs out there, and somebody's going to tell the truth. That you were at the house Saturday. But you know what? They might not remember you there the entire day."

"Jennie's gonna say what I tell her. She knows what's good for her." Frankie tipped the bottle back, drained the last of the beer, and, dropping the front legs of the chair onto the floor, set the bottle down hard on the table. "You're so smart, you got any better ideas?"

Vicky leaned back. Another female singer now, something about a foolish love. There was a long riff on the guitar. It was possible that Frankie had bought himself time with his fake alibi. Just possible that Burton might look somewhere else and maybe by the time he'd figured out that Frankie was lying, he'd have the murderer. Unless . . .

Vicky tried to push back the thought that she was sitting across from the man—the grinning, arrogant man—who had taken the lives of three human beings. She was aware of the smoke in the air, the acrid mix of beer and whiskey odors. She felt a slight nausea coming over her. A chair scraped over the floor, like a flat note on the guitar.

"The way I see it," Frankie said, still grinning, "I'm not going to prison for something I didn't do." The grin dropped from his face, replaced by a look of such hostility that Vicky blinked and pushed back hard against the rungs of her chair.

"You know what that's like? Locked up in a cage like a monkey? Nothing but concrete and steel everywhere you look. Concrete floor and walls, concrete bench, and concrete everywhere. A crummy cot with a crummy blanket and a stinking toilet. Noise twenty-four seven, shouting and cursing, and boots walking up and down outside, some smart-ass guard knocking his stick on the window and shouting, 'Wake up, Indian!' Like I was ever sleeping, and them bringing in some garbage on a tray and saying, 'Breakfast.' After the first two weeks, I couldn't remember what the sky looked like. You know what that feels like? Not being able to remember the sky? Get it pictured in your head. I'm not rotting in some cell 'cause somebody decided to take out those Shoshones."

"You could end up in prison on drug charges, Frankie. The tribal judge could schedule a trial on the assault charges, and you could be banished from the reservation."

"You gonna be my lawyer, or what?"

"It depends," Vicky said. She waited a moment, then went on. "Are you going to follow my advice? Don't say anything to anybody. Don't lie. Just don't say anything. If Detective Burton contacts you again, call me. And get yourself into a rehab program. Try to find a job." The man had held jobs before. A series of jobs over the last five years, most of them dead end and low paying, but at least he had worked. "Make yourself look like less of a murder suspect," she said.

"Well, here's my advice, *Mssss*. Holden." Hunching his shoulders, he leaned over the table. "You're my lawyer; you keep me out of prison. You understand that?"

Vicky got to her feet and yanked her bag off the chair. "Listen, Frankie. I don't give a damn if you rot in prison the rest of your life. The only reason I'm trying to keep you out is so that your mother won't have to cry herself to sleep every night worrying about you. She loves you. God knows why."

Vicky whirled around, walked back through the bar, and slammed out the door. It was almost dark and the air so cold that it stung her face like a thousand needles. Her eyes still felt raw from the mixture of smoke and alcohol fumes, her stomach still queasy. She crawled into the Jeep, started the motor, and waited, forcing herself to take several deep breaths. It was a few moments before she backed out of the lot and headed south toward Lander, her heart still thumping against her ribs. What had she gotten into? She could have taken on a client—a lying, conniving client—who was as guilty as sin.

18

PROFESSOR CHARLES LAMBERT was a more imposing figure than he'd realized, Father John thought. Looming in the doorway over the knobbed walking stick that he'd planted a foot inside the office, face red and puffy looking, he wore a long black coat speckled with moisture that gave it the look of tweed. A bulky blue scarf was tucked inside the V of his collar, and white hair sprung from beneath the dark cap pulled low over his ears.

"So sorry to bother you, Father O'Malley," he said, projecting the sonorous bass voice across the office. It occurred to Father John that students in the last row of an auditorium would have caught every syllable of the man's lectures. "Might we impose upon your good nature for a brief moment?"

"Of course." Father John snapped the checkbook shut—one last bill to pay, one last check, and just enough money in the account to cover it. Somehow the financial situation at St. Francis Mission always seemed to even itself out, although he'd given up trying to find the logic.

"It's nice to see you," he said, crossing the office. It wasn't until the professor shifted sideways that Father John saw Dana Lambert in the corridor behind her husband, nearly swallowed by the man's presence.

The woman swept past her husband, the skirt of her gray coat brushing against the walking stick. She was a small, slight woman who had mastered the trick of holding her head high so that she seemed taller. Her head was bare, and tiny flecks of moisture glinted like diamonds in her curly, dark hair. The bright red lipstick that she wore accentuated the paleness of her skin, the dark eyebrows above the green eyes, and the hollow spaces beneath her cheekbones. The red lips parted in a smile. "Hello again," she said.

"Let me help you with your coats." Father John stepped around the couple.

"No need, Father." The sonorous voice floated above the woman's head. "We won't take but a moment of your time. I apologize for barging in on you at the end of your workday."

Father John smiled at that. Another thing that he'd never fit into a logical sequence were the points at which his workdays began and ended.

"I called earlier. The other priest told me you were out for a while. Dana and I took a chance on catching you upon your return and drove over about four o'clock, I believe. We found the building open, but no one, I'm afraid, was here."

Father John wondered what had called Ian away. The other priest was gone when he'd gotten back this afternoon. Door unlocked, phone ringing into an empty building. No note, nothing to indicate an emergency. He hoped there hadn't been an accident, with the roads wet and slushy.

Charles Lambert had balanced the walking stick against the front of his coat and parted a space between his glove and coat sleeve. Peering down at a silver watch that hung loosely on his bony wrist, he heaved a sigh. "Oh, dear," he said. "The dinner hour, I'm afraid. Nevertheless, I do confess to a certain relief at finding you in."

"Please have a seat." Father John motioned to the two side chairs along the wall. "Can I get you anything? Coffee to take off the chill?"

"No. No. Don't trouble yourself." Charles Lambert waited until his wife had peeled off her leather gloves, settled into a chair, and unbuttoned her coat, allowing the fronts to drape to the sides. Then he dropped down in the chair beside her.

"Ever since Charles learned the identities of the dead men today," Dana said, "he's been insisting that he had to speak with you."

Her husband leaned forward on the stick planted between his boots. "The poor, dead boys," he said.

Father John nodded. "Your students."

"Yes, my students. Good boys, all of them. Eager to learn everything about their own history." The man was shaking his head. "They were sponges, couldn't absorb enough. I encouraged all the students to visit Bates, which is not only the closest battlefield, but a very important site since the massacre marked the culmination, if you will, of decades of hostility on the plains. The Arapahos were caught between two enemies—the Shoshones and the army troops."

"Charles explains all of this magnificently in his new book, *Tribal Wars*." Dana hadn't taken her eyes off the man. She'd shifted sideways and was giving him the rapt attention of a freshman student in the presence of a Nobel Laureate. "The book will be out in two weeks," she added, moving her gaze from her husband to Father John. Light pricked her green eyes. "It's a brilliant accomplishment, Father. My husband takes the Bates Massacre and places it within the broader context of the general war on the plains, with the many consequences for the Indian people and their leaders. Chief Sharp Nose and the Arapahos claimed victory because they'd managed to drive off the Shoshones. Yet it was the Arapahos who were left to bury their dead. As my husband demonstrates, Bates is symbolic of the fall of a proud people, who remained proud despite the disaster. Proud and determined to go on. Does anyone believe that Napoleon and his soldiers were not proud and determined as they were driven from Russia? That is the vision that my husband imparts. Arapahos represent people who may have been defeated but whose spirits were never conquered."

"Thank you for the kind accolade, my dear." Professor Lambert reached over and placed a gloved hand over his wife's bare hand. "Dana has been an enormous help with research and editing." He spoke into the space between Father John and his wife, keeping his gaze fixed on his wife. "Naturally her insights and comments were invaluable. Nevertheless . . ."

He let the word hang in the air a moment, like a final note of an aria. Turning back to Father John, he placed both hands over the top of the walking stick. "I am tortured with the realization that I sent the boys to their deaths," he said. His eyes clouded with sadness. "I can't help but believe that they well understood the importance of Bates, yet I suggested that they visit the site when there was no need for them to go. Terrible. Terrible," he said, shaking his head.

"It was not your fault, Charles." Dana Lambert scooted forward in her chair and turned toward her husband. "You couldn't have known what would happen. Tell him, Father."

"Your wife is right, Charles."

"I have dedicated my life," the professor said, still shaking his head, "to young people, trying to help them understand the past and the way in which the past has created the world that we know today. Isn't that an important thing? I always believed it so. How else can we hope for a better world if young people don't understand the terrible mistakes made in the past, the ill-considered decisions, and the way in which evil can spread if people do not have a frame of reference with which to recognize it. Now three fine young men are dead."

"You must stop this morbid line of thought, Charles." The woman's voice rose with insistence. "It isn't good for your heart. You have so much to look forward to now that the book is coming. Newspaper and radio interviews. The speaking engagements you've accepted at how many universities? Five? Six? You must save your strength for the book."

The man was quiet a long moment. "It is exhausting to contemplate," he said finally.

"But I will be with you, Charles. You must remain focused on the importance of your work. All the years of research and writing are going to be rewarded. You deserve the reward, Charles. You must try to forget what has happened. Please tell him, Father."

Father John rested his elbows on his thighs, clasped his hands, and leaned toward the man. "I'm very sorry," he said. "The death of your students is a terrible tragedy."

The man shot him a look filled with so much gratitude that Father John waited a moment before he went on. "Try to think about the deaths in the most rational way possible. You didn't send the men to Bates to be shot. You sent them to see the canyon and the slopes and the boulders so that they could better understand the way the massacre had unfolded. It was a logical suggestion that any professor worth his salt would have made."

"Yes. Yes. You Jesuits and your logic." The professor made a tight fist and thumped his chest. "There are places where logic doesn't matter. Here," he said, "in the heart."

"Father O'Malley is right, Charles," Dana said. "We must be rational."

"It'll take time." Father John kept his gaze on the man.

"Thank you, sir, for that." The professor gave him another look of gratitude. "My wife doesn't seem to realize that the heart has its own time and its own logic."

Dana Lambert seemed to shrink back against the chair. Her husband let a long moment pass before he said, "There is something else I find difficult to get out of my mind. I'm unable to stop thinking that one of the other students is responsible for this reprehensible act." He hesitated, staring into space, shaking his head. "The young woman. So talented and clever with words."

"You don't know that she's involved, Charles," the man's wife said, an edgy, impatient tone now.

"I don't *know*, but it is what I am coming to believe. I looked at each of the faces in class today. Is it you? I wondered. Or you? The seats of the murdered students were vacant, as was the seat of Edith Bradbury. One of the students said she'd heard that Miss Bradbury had been hospitalized. Naturally, my suspicions were aroused."

"She was very affected by Trent's death," Father John said.

The professor nodded. "I had seen the affection between them for some time. But recently . . ." He paused, then hurried on. "I believe that it had begun to cool, and I haven't been able to stop thinking about the message you showed me. Naturally, when I spoke to Detective Burton, I expressed my concerns. I'm sure he'll speak with her."

"You didn't tell me you had spoken with the detective," Dana said.

"My dear." Charles glanced over at his wife, still pressing herself against the back of her chair. "There is much that occurs each day. I couldn't possibly burden you with the details. Well," he said, leaning on the walking stick and levering himself to his feet, "we must take our leave. You've been most generous, Father O'Malley, indulging an old man's ramblings."

Dana Lambert jumped to her feet beside her husband, setting one hand on his arm to steady him. "Please stop saying that, Charles. You are not old. You have much to look forward to."

"My dear, it is your career that we will look forward to. My career is in the past."

"You will see how important your scholarship is when *Tribal Wars* reaches the bookstores. Everyone will flock to buy your book."

"Yes. Yes." The man waved one hand in front of him. "We've absorbed enough of your time, Father. Your words have been comforting, as I knew they would be. I would appreciate your keeping me informed of any information you may receive about the murder investigation. It would be a great relief if I were not the one who unknowingly sent the boys to their deaths."

Father John said that he'd let him know if he heard anything. Then he walked the couple out into the corridor and held the front door open.

"Watch your step," he said, gesturing with one arm toward the little clumps of slush.

He watched Professor Lambert and his wife pick their way across the stoop and down the steps, a solicitousness in the way the young woman gripped the arm of the old man, not for her balance but for his. It made him think that she knew her husband's health was precarious, even if she pretended that he had a bright and long future ahead, almost like the professor's theory, of proud people refusing to admit defeat. And yet, there was something about the man's walk that made Father John wonder if Professor Lambert really needed his wife's assistance as much as he enjoyed it.

He waited until the blue sedan had backed away from the front of the building and headed out toward Seventeen-Mile Road, a mixture of pebbles and slush spitting from behind the tires. Then he went back to the office. He wrote out the last check and set the envelope on the pile of envelopes to go out in tomorrow's mail. Then he reached for the phone and called Riverton Memorial.

Yes, Edith Bradbury was stable and improving, the nurse assured him. She was resting now, and if she had a restful night, she should be able to go home tomorrow.

Home. A shoebox filled with memories of Trent Hunter, memories that had led her to slash her arms with a razor. She has nowhere to go, Father John was thinking. He said, "Please tell her I'll be at the hospital tomorrow. Tell her she can come to the mission."

The nurse agreed to relay the message. He hung up, switched off the desk lamp, grabbed his jacket and hat, and let himself out the front door. Shrugging into his jacket, he crossed the grounds to the residence. A dim light twinkled in the living-room window. Ian's beige sedan was parked next to the pickup, both vehicles shimmering in the moisture that hung in the air.

The smell of alcohol hit him the instant he opened the front door.

19

THE SOUND OF the buzzer sent an electric jolt through the room. Vicky laid the pen across the top of the yellow legal pad, the first pages full of the notes that she'd been scribbling. Other pages from the tribe's proposed wolf management plan were scattered over the table. She glanced at her watch: 6:47. The window across from the table framed a dim rectangle penciled with the yellow glow of the streetlights below. It looked like it might snow again—little flecks of moisture had speckled the windshield on the drive back to Lander—and the outside of the pane looked smudged, as if someone had flung a wet towel against the window.

Vicky walked around the sofa and leaned into the metal grille of the intercom next to the door. "Hello," she said.

She knew who was there. For the last few minutes she'd sensed that he was on the way, picturing him hurrying up the sidewalk, letting himself into the entry. She'd felt his presence downstairs even before Adam said, "It's me."

Vicky hesitated. He would know that she knew. Samantha Lowe would have told him she'd stopped by the office. Vicky squeezed her eyes shut at the bagful of explanations he would be carrying. She could imagine them all. They had been drilled into her heart years ago. *Quit your worrying. She's nothing to me. So we had a couple of drinks, danced a little, had a few laughs. So what? Trust me. Trust me.*

And now, Adam. She'd thought they had a relationship. Wasn't that how Frankie's girlfriend had put it? *We're in a relationship. I'm his woman.* Why not face the truth? The truth was that she and Adam were sleeping together. And that was all there was. She'd thought it was going somewhere, that she was part of a couple again, no longer Woman Alone, as the grandmothers called her. No longer *Hi sei ci nihi.*

"Vicky?" Adam's voice came through the grille, laced with impatience. She pressed the door-release button. "Come up," she said.

He was there in minutes, bursting through the door, arms loaded with two brown bags. He must have sprinted up the stairs, Vicky thought. The elevator, cranking and crawling to the second floor, would have taken longer.

"Took a chance you haven't eaten yet," Adam said. He dropped the bags on the counter that divided the closet-sized kitchen from the small dining-room table with papers spilling across the top. "I know you like Chinese."

If only Adam Lone Eagle weren't so handsome, Vicky was thinking. So confident and strong, a warrior at home in the outdoors, the black leather jacket fitted across his shoulders, the cuffs giving way to the gloved, capable hands opening the brown bags.

"You okay?" he asked, looking at her for the first time.

"I'm okay." She didn't feel okay. She felt queasy with the sweet-sour smells of Chinese food filtering into the air and the presence of the man removing his gloves stuffing them into his pockets, unzipping his jacket.

"You didn't come back to the office after lunch," he said, tossing the jacket over a chair. "I got to worrying about you."

"I thought I'd work at home." Vicky stepped over to the table. Her legs felt shaky, and she gripped the back of the chair. "The problem, as I see it," she said, "is that the Arapahos and Shoshones don't have enough rangers in the field to enforce any management plan." She heard herself babbling on, like an eavesdropper listening in on the monologue of someone with a voice like her own. How would the tribes keep ranchers in the surrounding areas from tracking wolves into the Owl Creek or Wind River mountains and killing them? *Babbling. Babbling.* The fact they were protected wouldn't mean anything to a man with a rifle who'd just seen one of his cattle cut down, the insides spilling over the ground. There was so much hatred of wolves. It went back centuries, to the Europeans who first came to America, bringing their old hatreds with them. *Babbling.* So it made sense for the tribes to join forces with the state, but first, the management plans would have to be brought into agreement . . .

"Vicky!" Adam put up one hand. "Can we leave it alone for the evening? Let's just have a nice, relaxing dinner. You want to eat at the counter or the table?" He shot a doubtful glance at the litter of papers.

"I'm really not hungry, Adam. Maybe you should take the Chinese and go."

Adam didn't say anything. He focused on the two brown bags a moment, then brought his eyes back to hers. "Let's be honest, Vicky. What happened this afternoon?"

Vicky turned away and walked over to the window. Samantha had told him.

Before she could say anything, he said, "Lucille Montana called a couple of hours ago. She wanted to know if you'd had any luck finding Frankie this afternoon." A mixture of concern and irritation worked through his voice.

Vicky turned back. "Frankie could be charged with three homicides."

"Maybe he's guilty."

"Maybe he is, but I'm going to represent him."

"We talked about this. I thought we agreed."

"I'm sorry, Adam. I can't turn him away."

Adam drew in his lower lip and looked over into the shadows of the living room beyond the light that circled the dining area and kitchen. He was drumming his knuckles on the counter, and the sound was like a miniature herd of horses galloping between them. "Nobody can defend an Arapaho but you, is that it?" he said, fixing her with a look so intense and cold that she flinched. "Your mission is to keep every Arapaho charged with anything, from driving on the wrong side of the road to killing people, out of jail."

Vicky threaded the cord of the window shade through her fingers and looked past the blurred windowpane to the flare of yellow light over the street below. It was a moment before she felt the pressure of Adam's hand on her shoulder, and it struck her as odd. She hadn't heard him walk over.

"I'm sorry," he said. "That was out of line." His fingers kneaded into her skin now, warm and comforting through the soft wool of her sweater. "I want this to work between us, Vicky. You can't do it all. You can't defend guys like Frankie and still handle projects like wolf management. I need your expertise on the big cases. We're a good team, remember? We're unbeatable. Maybe we could hire another lawyer. Somebody to work for us and handle the Frankie kind of cases. That way, you could oversee them, make sure they're handled right. What do you think?"

Vicky shrugged away from his grasp and faced him. "Maybe we could hire Samantha," she said.

Adam stared at her a moment, then walked back to the counter and slammed his fist down. "So that's what this is about. Samantha Lowe. She told me she stopped by the office. So you jumped to your own conclusions and decided to go back to where you feel comfortable—representing losers like Frankie Montana."

"I want to trust you, Adam. I don't know how."

"You're right. You don't know how, and that's your problem." He was pulling on the leather jacket, zipping up the front, digging the gloves out of the pockets, jamming his hands inside the gloves. Then he walked over to the door and yanked it open. "Take your case, Vicky," he said, looking back. "See if you can keep your client from being indicted for homicide. I'm going to Cheyenne tomorrow and meet with the state fish and wildlife people." He started into the corridor, then stepped back. "Oh, and Yellowstone next weekend? Watching the wolves? I have to pass."

The door slammed shut. Vicky watched the small mirror hanging next to the intercom slide a half-inch sideways. All their plans, she was thinking, everything they'd talked about, the firm they were going to build, the important cases they would handle for tribes across the West, what a difference they were going to make—two Indian lawyers using the white man's laws to obtain Indian justice. And all the time, moving into the future together. Oh, she wanted to laugh, it was so preposterous, such a heavy weight hanging by such a fragile string as trust.

She would not cry, she told herself. She swiped at the wetness on her cheeks, turned back to the window, and pressed her face against the cold glass. Below, the door to the entry burst open. Adam emerged from the building, slightly blurred, as if he were a figure in a dream. He strode across the sidewalk to the pickup at the curb, got in behind the wheel, and pulled the door after him. The *thwack* sounded muffled and distant.

Nothing was as it should be, she thought, watching the pickup spin into the lane and start down the street, little smears of red taillights blinking. She'd wanted to make a difference for her people, but the tribal council had always found a firm in Casper or Cheyenne for the cases that mattered. Managing wolves and the other cases that were beginning to come would have all gone to one of those firms, too, if it hadn't been for Adam. They would be a strong firm, he'd told her. Arapaho woman, Lakota man. She was from the rez, and he was native. Both Shoshones and Arapahos could trust them. They would be unbeatable. And it was working. They'd hardly announced the opening of the new firm when the tribal officials had started to call.

She'd let her guard down, that was the problem. She'd begun to think about the future. Didn't he know she could tell when he got involved with another woman? Didn't he know she could sense the truth, as real as an odor of perfume or the thick, oily smell of the Chinese food bursting through the brown bags.

She needed to get out of here. She walked over to the closet, pulled on her coat and gloves, and fumbled in her bag until she found her keys. Then, moving out into the corridor, she let the door *swish* shut on its own. The building felt like a vault, her own footsteps on the carpet the only sound—a muffled, hurried rhythm. She took the stairs and plunged outside into the evening heavy with moisture. The air felt wet and warm on her face, until she realized she was crying. She ran her gloves over her cheeks and crawled inside the Jeep.

She'd lost track of how far she'd driven—ten miles, fifteen miles—before she realized that she was heading northeast on Rendezvous Road toward St. Francis Mission.

20

TELEVISION LIGHTS FLICKERED past the doorway and into the shadows of the entry, background voices unintelligible in the quiet. The odors of fried chicken and hot oil funneled from the kitchen. Elena would have left dinner in the oven, a plate wrapped in aluminum foil. Father John tossed his coat and hat on the bench and went into the living room on the right. Father Ian slumped on the sofa, head pillowed back into the cushions, long legs stretched out in front. He looked disheveled in the white glow of the television, denim shirt unbuttoned halfway down his chest and khaki slacks that could have been slept in. Hair standing out in clumps around his forehead and eyes at half-mast. He was thumping at his chest with his knuckles, the slow, hypnotic rhythm of a man trying to keep himself awake.

"Authorities in Wyoming have confirmed that the murders of three Shoshone at the site of a nineteenth-century battle between Shoshones and Arapahos could be revenge killings." The voice of an attractive, blond woman bundled in a bulky jacket, hair flying in the wind, floated from the television.

Father John stepped closer to the TV. The woman was at the Bates Battlefield, the canyon stretching behind her, the boulder-strewn slopes rising on either side. Then a map of Wyoming filled the screen, a red arrow pointing to the battlefield.

The voice went on, "A spokesman for the Fremont County Sheriff's Office, in charge of the investigation, says they are looking into the possibility that the homicides are the result of ongoing feuds between the two tribes on the Wind River Reservation. According to well-known Western historian Charles Lambert, Shoshones and Arapahos are traditional enemies. What is known as the Bates Battle was a massacre of Arapahos by Shoshones in eighteen-seventy-four."

The map dissolved, and the woman came back on screen. "The sheriff's office refuses to characterize the homicides as the first salvo fired in a new tribal war, but I've talked to numerous people here, and they fear that is exactly what has occurred. Back to you, Clint."

Father John walked over and pushed the power button. He watched the screen fade from gray into black, conscious of the hollow space opening inside him. It was if the blond woman's words had confirmed his own fears, made them real and imminent, like the past looming up in front of him.

He made himself turn back to the other priest on the sofa. "We'd better talk, Ian," he said.

The fist stopped thumping, but the man kept his gaze fixed on the TV. It was a moment before he pulled himself upright and leaned forward, slowly taking his eyes from the screen, as if he'd just realized that the news program had disappeared.

Father John turned on the table lamp and perched on the ottoman. This might be an interrogation, he was thinking; Ian, the suspect and he, the interrogator.

Well, get on with it.

"When did you start drinking again, Ian?" he asked.

For the first time, the other priest faced him, eyes tightened in contempt.

"Always the first to know, another alkie." He spit out the words.

"You could say we have the nose for it," Father John said. Oh, he'd developed the nose early. When was it that he'd first discovered it? Halfway up the flight of stairs to the apartment he'd grown up in—two bedrooms, sitting room, and Pullman kitchen hardly big enough to turn around in—over his uncle's saloon on Commonwealth Avenue? On up the steps, and the putrid stink from above hitting him with a force that rocked him backwards, and he knew his father was drunk again. It was so obvious, the smells, and yet he'd always told himself that no one could tell. No one else had the nose.

"When, Ian?"

"I had a couple drinks this afternoon. A drink now and then doesn't mean anything."

"We both know better. You want to talk about it?"

"You wouldn't get it," Ian said. An absent look had come into his expression, as if his thoughts had wandered somewhere else.

"Try me."

The other priest took a moment, then shrugged. "Okay, here it is. I'm going to hit a hardball straight at the guy on the mound." When Father John didn't say anything, he plunged into it. "I thought this would be a good assignment. I could get involved with the people, help them, maybe bring a little consolation and hope, and maybe they'd do the same for me. An isolated place out of the craziness where I could get my life back. It worked for you."

"So far."

"You know what I think?" Ian McCauley was warming up now, gripping the bat harder, ready to whack the fastball. "You got yourself a nice little fiefdom here, where you're the lord and master, and you can do anything you like."

"What?" Father John wasn't sure what he'd expected, but this wasn't it.

"Don't pull the denial act on me. I'm a priest, too, and I've put in my time in the confessional. I've heard it all. I know all the subterfuges and lies."

"What are you talking about?" Father John said.

"Everywhere I go, the social committee and religious ed meetings, AA, morning Mass, I get the same question: Where's Father John? Nothing can start around here, nothing's quite right unless the almighty presence graces the room. I'm your man, I tell them. Well, the look on their faces! The perfect picture of misery. What's it like to be loved like that?"

"It'll take time, Ian. Give the people a little time to get to know you."

"Over at the senior center yesterday, the elders said to be sure to tell Father John to come by again soon. Today at the hospital, I walked into Louis Birdsong's room and the man's face fell into the bedsheets. 'Hey, Father,' he says, doing his best to cover up, 'I thought you was Father John.' "

"I've been here almost nine years," Father John said. "They're used to me."

"Well, I drove out of the hospital lot and kept driving. Past the bars, and there are a helluva lot of bars in town when you're not looking for one, and pretty soon, I started looking and I ordered myself a double whiskey."

Father John leaned forward, clasping his hands between his knees, his eyes on his boots. "So what do you think, Ian? Is this going to be a problem?"

"What do I think? Alkie's lie, didn't you know?"

Oh, he knew. Father John kept his eyes lowered. He could lie with the best of them. One drink was all he'd had, he'd told the superior back at the prep school when he'd been teaching. One drink doesn't hurt anybody. Lies and lies.

"It's not going to be a problem," Ian said. "I've fallen off the wagon before and climbed back on."

Father John looked up. The man had been watching him, calculating the next move, the next lie. "I can call the Provincial and arrange for a short stay in rehab," he said. "A refresher."

"I said, it's not going to be a problem."

"It can't do any harm."

"You don't want me here, do you?"

Father John leaned back. "What makes you say that?"

"Let's be honest. You've run off every assistant the Society has sent out here. You don't want the competition. You call the Provincial, and I'll be out of here tomorrow."

"Not necessarily. I'll recommend . . ."

Ian cut in. "What I don't get is how you've managed to stay here so long."

"You're talking in riddles, man," Father John said, not trying to hide his growing irritation.

"I've heard the rumors."

Ah, here it was, Father John thought. The rumors about Father O'Malley and the Arapaho lawyer on the reservation, how there was something more than just friendship between them. Dear Lord, he'd thought those rumors had died a natural death.

"Whatever you heard is wrong," he said. "Vicky Holden and I have worked together. That's all."

Ian was smiling and shaking his head. "Soon as your assistants figure out what's going on, you get them out of here before they can blow the whistle."

Father John stood up. "Let's get something straight," he said. The other priest pushed himself to his feet and faced him. "There's no drinking at St. Francis Mission. No bars, no double shots of whiskey, no bottles. Nothing. You've got one last chance." He let this hang between them a moment, then, tossing his head in the direction of the kitchen, he said, "Get yourself some coffee and something to eat. I'll take the social committee meeting tonight."

"No way." The other priest shook his head. "It's my committee, and I'm the priest who should be there. You're going to have to get used to the competition, because I intend to stay."

Father John turned and walked back across the entry and into his study. He dropped down into the old leather chair that had adjusted itself to the contours of his back and snapped on the desk lamp, aware of the footsteps ascending the stairs and clumping down the upstairs hall, the sound of the shower coming on. His own little fiefdom, Ian had said. Well, that was a new idea. He'd only been aware that he was happy at St. Francis. He felt that he belonged here. And the trust in the brown faces looking up at him when he said Mass, the people hurrying over when he walked into a meeting at Eagle Hall, the expectant tone in the voices on the phone saying, *Can you come over, Father*? He felt *needed* here, that the Arapahos needed him more than he needed a drink. He felt safe.

He tossed a pencil over the stacks of papers on his desk. Which was the reason that the Society of Jesus didn't usually leave priests in one assignment more than six years. They might start to feel safe, secure in their own little fiefdom, start making plans—God, he had so many plans, so much he still wanted to do—new programs and classes, new coat of paint on the buildings, new pews for the church. They were the same, he and Ian McCauley, fighting the same thirst, wanting to belong.

He swiveled around and flipped through the stack of opera CDs on the bookshelf, then set *Il Trovatore* in the player, and tried to work his way through the stack of mail. Over the sounds of "Soli or siamo!" and "Il balen del suo sorriso" came the clank of dishes in the kitchen, the footsteps in the hall, and, finally, the front door thudding shut.

He was heading into the kitchen for his own dinner when he heard the knocking. He turned around and walked back down the hall. A cloud of wet air blew into the entry when he pulled open the door. Vicky stood on the other side, hands jammed into her coat pockets, flakes of moisture—or was it tears?—on her eyelashes.

"May I talk to you?" she said.

"Come in." Father John stepped back to give her room. Something must have happened. He could count on the fingers of one hand the number of times she'd come to the residence—only when she'd felt she had nowhere else to go.

"Let me take your coat." He closed the door behind her.

"I think I'll keep it," she said, hugging her arms now. Her face looked pinched with worry, and he wondered how long she'd been driving around.

"We can talk in the study." He nodded toward the doorway behind her, although she knew where the study was. When she came to the residence, they'd always talked in the study. It seemed safer there, less personal, an envelope of ordinariness and business. "I'll get you some coffee."

He hoped the coffee was still hot. He watched her turn into the study, struck again at how small she seemed, and vulnerable, beneath the steel armor that she'd taught herself to wear. Then he walked back to the kitchen, found a couple of mugs in the drain on the counter, and poured out the coffee. Plumes of steam rose over his hands. He could feel the heat working through the mugs as he walked back.

21

VICKY WAS IN the side chair across from the desk, strips of shadow and light playing over her face. "Mira d'acerbe" drifted through the study. She reached up and took the coffee that he handed her. Then Father John walked around the desk and turned down the volume. He came back and sat on the chair next to her. "You okay?" he asked.

"What about you?" Vicky gestured to the Band-Aid on his cheek.

"It's nothing," he said.

"A bullet is nothing? I heard you were wounded at Bates."

He shrugged, trying to put it aside, and finally she said, "I agreed to represent Frankie Montana today."

"I thought you'd represented him all along."

She gave a little laugh and took another sip. "I'd excused myself and suggested he find another lawyer. Adam and I . . ." Vicky paused and looked away. "We've been working with the Arapahos and Shoshones on a plan to manage wolves on the reservation. Looks like other big cases will come our way."

"You're a good team," Father John said. He used to think he and Vicky were a good team. "I'm glad it's working out."

She dipped her head toward the mug and took a long sip of coffee. Avoiding his eyes, he thought, not wanting to reveal something—whatever it was that had brought her here tonight. He'd had years of experience counseling people, watching the ways they avoided the truth.

"Things don't look good for Frankie," she said. He could hear the avoidance in her tone. "Burton's interviewed him."

"He's interviewing a lot of people. Probably everybody who knew Trent Hunter and the Crispin brothers."

"Frankie's the one the murdered men had filed an assault complaint against. Even Frankie admits they had an altercation Friday night at Fort Washakie. He claims they assaulted him, but if they were alive to show up at the tribal court, the judge might not agree." Vicky took another drink, then gripped the mug in both hands, as if she wanted to draw the warmth into herself. "It doesn't take a mind reader to figure out what Burton's thinking. Frankie had the motivation to shoot all three men. He owned a rifle, which conveniently disappeared before the murders. And he doesn't have an alibi."

Il Trovatore was still floating around them. Father John could feel Vicky's doubt working its way under his skin. It was contagious, like a virus.

"Frankie lied about where he was on Saturday, and he's counting on his mother to perjure herself, which she'll do, I'm sure."

Father John didn't say anything. He didn't want to press her for an explanation of why she was so certain Frankie had lied. There were ways in which she knew things, just as there were for him. Lawyer and priest. People confided in them, and they kept confidences. He sat back and took a long drink of his own coffee, his eyes on the woman next to him. She was staring straight ahead, her face almost unreadable, except for the tiny blue vein that pulsed in her temple and the slightest tremor in her lower lip.

"Why Bates?" She shifted toward him. "I keep asking myself, why would Frankie go to the trouble of killing the Shoshones at the Bates Battlefield? He could have shot them anywhere on the reservation. I'd be surprised if Frankie even cares about a massacre that happened a hundred and thirty years ago." She stopped, then hurried on. "The *Gazette* said you found the bodies after somebody had left a telephone message. What was it, John?"

Father John got to his feet. He set his mug on the desk, turned off the opera, and ejected the CD. Then he opened the side drawer, withdrew the tape of the telephone call, and inserted it into the player. He pressed another button and looked over at Vicky.

The crackling noise, like paper being crunched near the mike, burst out of the machine, then the mechanical voice. It could have been the voice of a robot moving stiff-legged across the floor. *This is for the Indian priest . . .*

The voice was as chilling as when he'd first heard it. He could feel the evil, like a presence, invading the space between them. When the message ended, he pressed the off button and turned back to Vicky. Her face had gone rigid, stonelike, drained of life.

"The killer," she said, nodding toward the silent tape player. "He must have had access to a recording studio. He knew how to change his voice. He knew how to get the exact sound that he wanted. That takes a pro, John."

"Burton's probably already checked the studios in the area." Father John sat on the edge of the desk, facing her.

"Two years ago," Vicky began, hesitancy in the way she was reeling out the words, "for all of three or four weeks, Frankie had a job at the radio station on the reservation. He was on the air for two hours every day playing Indian music. Carlos Nakai, Bill Miller, Joanne Shenandoah, people like that."

She stood up and walked past him to the window. Pulling the slats apart with her fingers, she stared out for a moment into the yellow glow of light shining over Circle Drive a moment. "Frankie's managed to land a half-dozen jobs in the last several years, which gives Lucille hope." She let the slats drop and turned back, something new settling behind her eyes, a mixture of weariness and resignation. "As soon as Burton finds out that Frankie worked in a radio station, he'll see that Frankie's charged with three counts of first-degree murder."

"Look, Vicky," Father John began, "just because Frankie once worked at the studio doesn't mean he had access recently."

"Knowing Frankie, he probably has an extra key." Vicky threw both hands into the air and walked over to the desk, then pivoted about and headed back to the window. Pacing. Pacing. "Somebody could have let him in, a buddy at the station who would never admit it. There's any number of ways Frankie could have recorded that message."

Father John was quiet a moment, watching her carve out a small circle on the carpet. She always paced when she was upset, when she was trying to work something out. He was struck by how much he remembered about her. Weeks went by when he didn't see her, then she appeared again, and so many little things popped into his mind, as if they'd only retreated into the background, waiting to be summoned.

He said, "You said yourself that Frankie probably doesn't care about what happened at Bates."

"He must have overheard the Shoshones talking," she said, making her way around the circle. "That's it, John." She stopped almost in midstep. "He overheard them at the bar talking about going to the battlefield. They were taking classes at the college. Maybe they had to visit the site for a class." She stepped forward and bent her head toward him. "That's it, isn't it? They had to visit the site."

Father John nodded. It was starting to make sense, everything she said. "They were in Professor Lambert's class. The man blames himself for the fact that they went to Bates."

"Oh, God." Vicky combed her fingers through her hair and resumed pacing. "What kind of lawyer am I, taking a client like Frankie

Montana. He's guilty, and he belongs in prison. They should throw away the key."

"You don't have to do this. There are other lawyers . . ."

She swung around and fixed him with a hard glare. "You sound like Adam. Let him hire a twenty-seven-year-old two years out of law school who needs the work. So throw Frankie to the wolves. You know what, John?" She walked over and stood in front of him. "Maybe I could go along with that, if I didn't mind seeing Lucille's face every night when I closed my eyes, and if I didn't know that, the day they locked up Frankie, it would destroy her. I'll defend him with everything I've got, and you know what? If we win, the bastard will probably go out and kill somebody else. So walking around right now is some poor fool who doesn't even suspect . . ."

"Whoa, Vicky! Stop!" Father John pushed himself off the desk and placed his hands on her shoulders. He could feel her shivering beneath the thickness of her wool coat. "What's going on? What's this all about?"

Slowly, her face began to crack, like a sheet of ice starting to break up, and little by little, the dark, distorted thing that was below the surface began to seep into the cracks. She was starting to sink beneath his hands, and for a second, he thought she might crumble to the floor. He pulled her close. His own breath felt warm in her hair. "What is it, Vicky? Tell me."

She was weeping silently against his shirt. It was a moment before she pulled back and began patting at her cheeks. Then she was running her fingers through her hair, tossing the strands sideways, as if she could toss away all of it, whatever had worked up from below the surface.

"I'm falling apart," she said.

"No, you're not." He kept his voice calm, reassuring.

"I'm looking for an excuse, any excuse to dump Frankie, as if that would make any difference between Adam and me."

This was about Adam, Father John was thinking, and he realized that somehow he'd known that. "What's going on?" he said.

"A man comes into your life." Vicky tilted her head back and was staring at the ceiling. "You think this is a good man. This is going to work. This time, I'll make it work. We have the firm and we have an important project, one that matters. If we do a good job helping the tribes come up with a plan to manage wolves, we'll continue to get jobs."

"There's no time for Frankie Montana."

"Right." Vicky was hugging her arms.

"Can't you and Adam work this out, Vicky? Frankie hasn't been arrested. And if he is, couldn't you take a little time from the firm to handle the case?"

"That's so like you, John. So rational."

Rational. It was the second time in the last couple of hours he'd been called that.

"It's not the kind of firm we are," Vicky was saying. "DUIs, divorces, rent disputes, defending the Frankie Montanas on murder charges. We've already talked to tribal officials about other projects. New oil leases, agreements to open natural gas deposits. Important issues, John, and the tribe will hire us, because Adam's one of the partners. He's Lakota and he's a man." She paused, then hurried on, her voice edging toward hysteria. "They like him and they trust him. People trust Adam, John. That's the thing about Adam. He seems so . . . so right on."

He had it now, Father John was thinking. Pieces of the puzzle locking themselves into place. "You don't trust Adam," he said.

"It's over between us."

"Because you're going to represent Frankie? Because you want to help Lucille?"

Vicky was shaking her head. "Adam's involved with someone else."

Father John had to look away from the pinpricks of pain in her eyes. A wave of disbelief and anger washed over him. What was the matter with Adam Lone Eagle? Didn't he know what he had?

"Are you sure?" he said, bringing his eyes back to hers. In the pain that was still there, he knew the answer.

"I know," she said. "I had years of experience with Ben. I learned my lesson well."

"Like a nose for alcohol," he said.

"What?"

Father John shook off the question. "Some things you just know," he said. "I'm sorry, Vicky."

She started crying, standing there so still, arms dangling at her side.

Father John put his arms around her and pulled her to him again. "I'm truly sorry, Vicky. I wanted it to work for you. I wanted you to be happy." What a waste of happiness, he was thinking. What a huge, sad waste.

"Oh, excuse me."

Father John lifted his eyes over Vicky's head. Father Ian was in the doorway, a mixture of incredulity and amusement in his expression.

"I didn't know you had a visitor," he said.

Vicky took a step back, patting at her cheeks again, then smoothing the front of her coat. "I was just leaving," she said.

"This is Father Ian McCauley," Father John said. "Ian, meet Vicky Holden." But his assistant already knew who she was. Father John could tell by the glance the man threw at him—like a fast pitch, daring him to take a swing.

"The social committee needs the list of parishioners released from the hospital in the last month," Ian said.

Father John turned away and began shuffling through the stacks of papers and folders on his desk, finally retrieving the file with "Hospital/ Home" on the tab. He handed the file to the other priest.

"Good." Ian dangled the folder from one hand and started backing up. "Nice to meet you," he said to Vicky before he disappeared around the door. His boots clacked in the entry, then a cold gust erupted into the study.

"That was embarrassing," Vicky said.

"You have nothing to be embarrassed about."

"I didn't mean to fall apart like that. I'd better get going."

"Take a few minutes. I'll get you more coffee."

Vicky put up the palm of one hand. "It's just going to take some getting used to, having my plans rearranged." She walked over and picked up the bag she'd dropped on the floor next to the chair. "Thanks for listening. I needed somebody to talk to," she said, fixing the strap of the bag into the curve of her shoulder.

Father John followed her to the front door. Reaching around, he pulled the door open. "Will you be okay?"

"I'll be fine." She reached for his hand and held it in hers a moment. Then she tugged her gloves out of her coat pockets and started down the sidewalk for the Jeep, pulling on her gloves as she went.

Father John waited until the Jeep had started around Circle Drive before he went back to the study. He dropped down at his desk and stared into the shadows washing over the bookcases. Well, this was awkward. The minute he called the Provincial to suggest that his new assistant go back into rehab, Father Ian McCauley would suggest that it was time for the pastor to be sent elsewhere.

22

THE RECEPTION AREA of Riverton Memorial felt muffled in the wet snow that had fallen during the night. Moisture glistened on the vinyl floor that ran across the lobby and down a wide corridor. A few people occupied the chairs against the walls, hushed conversations drifting toward the desk with the small sign that said "Information." Father John stopped at the desk and waited, drumming his knuckles along the edge, aware of the dull headache that seemed to have connected to the soreness in his cheek.

He'd slept badly, tossing in a wilderness of anger and sadness: anger at Adam Lone Eagle—what was the matter with the man?—and sadness at the raw hurt in Vicky's eyes. But another idea had hovered at the edge of his mind. Vicky was free again. She had no one to turn to—*Hi sei ci nihi,* Woman Alone—except for him. She'd needed him. Dear God, his assistant was right. He was a dry alcoholic who needed people to need him, just as he'd needed a drink.

Two minutes must have passed before a slim, dark-haired woman who looked about forty emerged from the door behind the counter, carrying a paper cup of coffee. "Hello, Father," she said, her face breaking into an easy smile. He recognized her. She was often on duty when he came in. "You here about the girl you brought into emergency" she said.

Edith Bradbury was the girl's name, he said, unsure of whether the woman had the information. Could she tell him what room she was in?

The woman looked over at a computer screen and tapped several keys on the keyboard. "Down the hall, first door beyond the nurse's station," she said without looking up. "Wait a minute." Her fingers ran over the screen. "Looks like Edith Bradbury's checked out."

"Checked out?"

The woman took her eyes from the screen and rested them on a spot beneath the counter where she'd set the paper cup, a faint look of longing in her expression. "Good news, I guess," she said. "She must've had a good night or the doctors wouldn't be letting her go."

"You're sure she's gone?"

Her gaze shifted back to the screen. "Well, the records say she checked out."

"Can you tell me where she went?"

The woman hesitated. "Well, Father, even if I could . . ."

"Edie's coming with me." It was a male voice, rumbling like a bassoon over the faint buzz of conversations.

Father John turned around. Jason Rizzo was striding down the corridor, dressed the same as yesterday. A uniform, Father John thought, black leather, silver chains and studs, blue jeans wrinkling around the thick legs, and high-top, snap-up black boots.

"Where are you planning on taking her, Rizzo?" Father John said. He could hear the alarm bell sounding in his voice. Professor Lambert could be right. If Edie Bradbury had gone back to Rizzo, then it was possible she'd helped Rizzo take out his revenge on Trent. Or was it that Rizzo had helped her?

He tried to push away the thought.

"Now let me just see here." The man ran one hand over his chin, as if he were searching for stubble. "I'm asking myself, is there any reason why this here priest needs to know my business? You know the answer I keep getting, coming through loud and clear?"

"Where, Rizzo?"

"Where? Where?" The man lifted one foot and took a step forward, then another, his boots stomping hard on the vinyl. He could have been a giant advancing toward the counter.

"We don't want any trouble, Mr. Rizzo." The woman's voice sounded faint and shriveled. "I can call security."

"You folks are good at calling security. I ain't forgot that little number over in emergency." Rizzo jabbed an index finger at the desk. "That's a little grudge I'm gonna worry about settling up later. Right now, all I'm worried about is getting my woman out of here and back where she belongs, with her own kind."

Father John shouldered past the man. He caught the look of surprise that flashed in Rizzo's eyes and kept going down the corridor. The blond head and white shoulders of a nurse floated above a nurse's station. A man in green scrubs was pushing a gurney through a side door, a limp plastic bag dangling from the top of a metal pole.

A heavy hand, like a weight, gripped his shoulder, and Rizzo's voice rang in his ear. "You hold up there."

Father John yanked himself free and turned around. Little black stubs poked from the pores in the man's face; his breath was fueled with a mixture of coffee and whiskey.

"You got a problem, Rizzo?" he said.

"Yeah, I got a problem with you sticking your nose in our business, Edie's and mine. Why don't you just get out of here."

"I will as soon as I see her."

"Maybe she don't wanna see you."

"Edie can tell me so." Father John headed past the station, and the blond head tilted up from the stack of paper on a clipboard, eyebrows lifting above the light-colored eyes.

"Everything all right?" she chirped.

The first door on the right stood ajar, a wide enough slot that Father John could see the thin arm with squares of white bandage resting on the armrest of a wheelchair. He rapped on the door, then pushed it open.

The girl seemed to flinch, or had he imagined it? She looked small and shrunken in the wheelchair. A talented student, Professor Lambert had called her. Creative, with a flare for words. Dear Lord, a killer? This small girl with a red coat draped over her shoulders, bunching up in back, holding a black plastic bag that bulged at odd angles, like a bag of captive animals trying to escape from her lap.

Edie kneaded her fingers into the plastic bag. "I thought you was Jason," she said, her voice a monotone.

"I'm here." Rizzo pushed past and stationed himself behind the wheelchair.

"You don't have to go with him," Father John said.

She rolled her head around and glanced up at Rizzo. "What difference does it make?"

"You ever think that maybe Edie knows what's good for her?"

"Jason's right." The girl seemed to be trying to make her voice bigger. "I gotta stick to my own kind. I shouldn't've gotten mixed up with that Indian."

"Listen to me, Edie," Father John said, leaning over the small figure in the wheelchair. "You need your family now."

"Yeah, like I have a fricking . . ." She stopped, pulled in her lower lip, and looked away. Finally she said, "Besides, I called my mom this morning, and you wanna know what she said? 'So what'd you do, Edie. Cut yourself again?' Then she says, 'I don't wanna hear about your trouble. You got nothing but trouble. Follows you around like a sick puppy. Bobby don't want any of your trouble around here, so just leave us alone.' That's what she said, and that's what I'm gonna do. Soon's I called Jason, he said he'd come over and get me after . . ."

"After what?"

The girl went quiet, as if she'd like to pull back the words.

"None of your business," Rizzo said. He set a glovelike hand on the girl's shoulder. There was the dark smudge of a tattoo above the knuckles. Then he was squeezing the girl's shoulder, and Father John caught her wince against the pain.

"Let her go," Father John said, and to his surprise, the man's hand seemed to relax until he was patting at her shoulder. Father John pushed on. "Let me guess, Rizzo, you wanted an apology, right? You wanted to hear how sorry she was for leaving you and going with an Indian."

"Mud people." Rizzo let out a snort. "We can't get ourselves contaminated by mud. Edie's gonna get herself back on track. She's my woman, and I'm taking her out of here."

Edie was gnawing on her lower lip, her teeth working it like a piece of leather, and Father John wondered if Jason Rizzo knew about Trent Hunter's baby.

"You ask too many damn questions," the girl said. "I don't know why you came to my place yesterday. I mean, if you hadn't showed up, it'd all be over. So you did your good deed. So forget about me, okay?"

"Let me help you, Edie."

"Why don't you just get out?"

"Yeah, good idea," Rizzo said.

"You know where you can find me." Father John set a hand on the girl's other shoulder. He could feel the bony knob poking through the red coat. She wasn't much more than a child, he thought.

As he turned toward the door, Rizzo lunged forward, blocking the way. Father John feinted right, and as the other man took a step in that direction, Father John went left. He reached for the doorknob, but Rizzo's arm shot past. His hand gripped the knob, and Father John could make out the tattoo of a wolf head.

The man leaned against the door. Folding his arms across his chest, he tilted his head back and ran his tongue over his lips, enjoying himself.

"What're you gonna do?" he said, flexing his shoulders, throwing a quick glance at the girl in the wheelchair, as if he expected applause.

"I'll tell you what you're going to do, Rizzo," Father John said. "You're going to step aside."

"If I get damn good and ready."

"Let him go." The girl's voice had a surprising surge of determination.

"Shut up." Rizzo sent her another glance, but there was no smile attached.

"You're going to step aside now," Father John said. "This is a hospital, man. You have a point to make, make it someplace else."

The other man stared at Father John a moment, then started laughing—a raw, hiccupy noise. "Well, I just might do that, Indian priest, next time you come around poking your nose into our business, me and Edie's." He took his time about peeling himself away from the door.

Father John threw the door back and started down the corridor. Another nurse—squat and gray haired—was heading his way, clipboard in one hand. She stopped in front of him. "You're Father O'Malley," she said, as if to confirm her own conclusion. "I gave her your message." She waved the clipboard in the direction of Edie's room, then shrugged. "Maybe she knows what she's doing."

He didn't think so. He gave the nurse a smile, thanked her, and walked the length of the corridor and across the reception area. Outside he brushed a trace of snow off the pickup's windshield with his arm and drove out of the parking lot, "Mira d'acerbe" mingling with the hiss of cold air spewing from the vents.

23

HE SPOTTED THE tan SUV parked in front of the administration building as he came through the canopy of cottonwoods that spilled onto Circle Drive. Not a vehicle that he recognized, but visitors were always dropping by St. Francis Mission, wanting to see the Catholic church with Arapaho symbols on the walls and in the stained glass windows. Whoever the visitors were, Father Ian had probably already offered to give them a tour. The man really did want to belong. Father John had to give him that.

He hurried up the concrete steps and let himself through the door. Ian's voice droned down the corridor. He was at the far end with a tall, broad-shouldered man in blue jeans and a blue jacket that hung open in the warmth of the old building. The priest was waving a hand toward the portraits of the past Jesuits at St. Francis Mission lining the walls—the pairs of solemn eyes behind wire-rimmed glasses that, Father John thought, seemed to be forever watching over the place. The other man gave his full attention to one of the portraits, as if it were the most interesting thing he'd seen today.

Father John shut the door behind him and stomped his boots, spattering moisture over the mat.

"Here's the pastor now." Ian started toward him, ushering the visitor ahead. "John, meet Liam Harrison, reporter for the Associated Press."

"Great to meet you, Father O'Malley." Liam Harrison thrust out a large hand. He couldn't have been more than twenty-five, with dark hair combed back from a handsome, intelligent-looking face and hazel eyes lit with curiosity. He had a grip like an iron vise.

"What's this about?" Father John asked. He knew the answer. He'd read it in the tone of the young man's voice, even before the other priest said, "Mr. Harrison's doing a story on the Shoshone murders."

"That's right," the reporter said. "Father McCauley here has been filling me in on the background of St. Francis Mission. I figure whoever shot those Shoshones out at the Bates Battlefield wanted everybody to know it was an Arapaho job. So the killer sent you a message, intending for you to find the bodies. What do you say, Father?"

"Sounds as if you've already made up your mind." Father John glanced at Ian. He wondered what his assistant had given the reporter along with the mission's history.

The reporter emitted a little laugh—the nervous laugh of a student unsure of the matter about to be discussed. His fingers curled around a pen, which he began tapping against a small notebook cupped in his other hand. "If you don't mind, Father, I'd like to ask you a few questions. Looks like the Shoshones were killed in revenge for an old massacre."

Father John gestured toward the door on the right. There was no getting around it—he was going to have to talk to this reporter. He followed the man into his office and asked him to have a seat. Then he took off his coat and hat and tossed them over the coat tree. "Where did you get your information?" he asked.

The reporter had shrugged out of his own jacket and settled his large frame into one of the side chairs, the notepad balanced on his thick thigh, pen laced between thumb and forefinger. Father John walked around the desk and dropped into his own chair. A red light was flashing on the phone.

"I'm sure you know the rules, Father O'Malley." Liam Harrison waved the pen into the space between them, a friendly, open smile on his face. "We're both in the confidential business." He paused and looked up at the ceiling a moment, considering. Finally, he said, "I can tell you this much: we received an anonymous phone call from somebody who thought we'd be interested in a story about two tribes squaring off against each other."

"Man? Woman?"

The reporter shrugged. "I probably shouldn't tell you this, but it was hard to tell. You know, a garbled voice. Doesn't make any difference. My editor thought the story worth pursuing so . . ." He shrugged again. "Here I am, pursuing it."

Father John glanced away a moment. The story on the national news last evening, and now the Associated Press running a story. He could see the headline: "Tribal War on Wind River Reservation." He looked back at the young man. "You should talk to Detective Burton," he said.

"Oh, I've talked to Burton and several deputies who went to the site. Had a long interview with the coroner. Pretty gruesome, from what I hear, the victims being posed like the bodies on an old battlefield. Whew! There's got to be somebody sick out there. Who do you think could have made that taped message that Father Owens got?"

"I don't know," Father John said.

"You don't know, or you won't tell me?" The reporter bent his head and jotted something on the notepad.

"The investigation is still going on."

"Can you confirm the caller left a message that led you to the battlefield?"

"You seem to have everything you need for your story."

"I need your confirmation."

Father John didn't say anything for a moment. In the back of his mind, he could hear Eric Surrell's voice: *Montana wants war, and that's what he's gonna get.* And now this—a reporter chasing down rumors and anonymous calls for a story that would sell newspapers and feed the kind of mindless hysteria that could run like a wildfire through the reservation.

"Look, Harrison," Father John said, leaning forward and clasping his hands on the desk. "You don't have a story yet. I suggest you wait until the investigation is completed."

"You're entitled to your opinion." The reporter was grinning again. "My editor and I disagree. If those Shoshones were killed out of revenge, there's no telling what might happen next. The way I see it, this is one helluva story that could start a cycle of revenge, you get my drift. Revenge killings leading to other revenge killings, just like in other tribal areas around the world. Africa. Balkans. Middle East. Turns out, we got our own tribes holding onto old grudges. This story resonates with current events, and we intend to be out in front with it."

The man drew in a long breath and leaned forward, one hand pasting the notepad to his thigh. "I would think you'd welcome the story, Father. Nothing like a little publicity to get the detective motivated to solve the case. We can help get out the truth."

The truth, Father John thought. Frankie Montana out for revenge? A pregnant girl left behind and a white supremacist thug, either one of whom could be out for revenge? The truth could be anything.

"How about the phone message?" The reporter pushed on.

"No more comments."

"Ah. Well, in that case, it looks as if I've been wasting my time. I had hopes that since you're a former history professor . . ."

"High school teacher," Father John said. Lord, let the man get one fact right.

"Historian, all the same. I had hopes you'd be concerned about old tribal animosities showing up in the twenty-first century."

Father John got to his feet. "I think we're done here," he said.

Harrison stood up, slid the notepad and pen into his shirt pocket, and bunched his jacket under one arm. Then he jammed his fingers back into the shirt pocket and pulled out a white business card, which he snapped down on the desk. "Should you have second thoughts, I'd be interested in anything you have to say."

"I'll see you out." Father John walked around the desk and motioned the man ahead. He followed him across the corridor, past the watchful eyes in the portraits, and opened the door. The man hurried down the steps, stuffing his arms into his jacket as he went, shoulders squared, as if he already had the story.

"You're going to want to listen to the call that came in while you were out." Father Ian's voice came from behind him, the man's boots clacking on the wood floor.

Father John headed back to the office, the other priest a few steps behind. "I didn't want to say anything while the reporter was here," Ian said.

Father John walked over to his desk and stared at the phone. There were usually messages when he got back to the office, the red light flashing. What was it about this message that seemed so different? So like an ominous intruder. *You're going to want to listen . . .*

Not again, he thought. He glanced over at the other priest waiting in the doorway, hands jammed into the pockets of his khakis. "I was just coming in when I heard the phone ringing," Ian said. "The answering machine took over before I could get it."

Father John pressed the mailbox key and bent over the desk. The scattered papers, the folders and envelopes, the paperweight and stray pens all blurred around the black plastic telephone. "You have one new message," the telephone voice announced.

A half-second passed, and then the high-pitched, scrunched voice of the robot, "Listen, Indian priest." A pause, then,

Now the killing time.
Revenge is mine
At last.
Blood runs in the gorge,

Memory of the past.
A debt to pay.
Wolf sees the way.

"Another body at Bates," Father John heard the hollow note in his voice.

"I decided to . . ."

The other priest hesitated, and Father John glanced up. "To do what?"

"I called the sheriff's office right away and played the tape for Detective Burton. He's probably out at the battlefield by now. I would have gone myself, but that wouldn't have left anyone at the mission." An accusatory note had seeped into the other priest's tone.

Father John nodded. There was nothing at the mission Ian McCauley couldn't do, no need he couldn't meet. He could even stop by a bar for a drink. Who would know? Not the Provincial, Father John thought as he crossed the room.

"I'm going to the battlefield," he said, grabbing his jacket and hat and heading for the door.

IT WAS THE same caller, he was sure, the same distorted, alien voice. He'd sensed the malevolence wafting down the line like a bad odor. *There's got to be somebody sick out there,* Liam Harrison had said. Whoever had made the call had access to a recording studio, and, according to Vicky, Frankie Montana had worked at the reservation radio station. Father John wondered about Jason Rizzo and his gang of supremacists. Which one of them worked at a studio? It was a question he intended to bring up with Burton.

He could see the vehicles ahead, huddled among rocks and brush at the mouth of the canyon. Exhaust from one of the vehicles curled into the air. Dark uniforms were darting about. Other figures moved through the shadows in the canyon. An ambulance was parked between two SUVs, and what looked like the coroner's van stood over to the side. He could feel the muscles tightening in his stomach. How many bodies this time?

Father John left the pickup behind an SUV and started past the vehicles. Burton had stepped away from a couple of uniforms and was heading toward him. He looked like a bull plowing over the snow, his bulky frame encased in a black coat, a black cowboy hat tilted back on his head.

"Figured you'd show up." He waved a bulky arm toward the canyon. "Another homicide. Looks like a replay of the last massacre."

Father John winced at the man's choice of words. And yet . . . it was true. Trent Hunter and the Crispin brothers *had* been massacred.

"Who is it?" he asked.

"Maybe you can tell us." Burton cocked one shoulder in a "come on" sign, swung around, and headed back into the canyon.

Father John started after him. Their boots crunched the snow and the wind hissed through the boulders. The air was colder in the shadows of the canyon, washed with ice. His fingers felt numb inside his gloves, and he lapped his gloves together to work the circulation back.

There were other deputies ahead, close to the place where he'd found the three bodies. They glanced around and started pulling back. One officer peered into a camera pointed toward the ground. Light flashed over the snow.

It was then that Father John saw the body, snow drifting over the blue jeans and dark jacket, around the dark head. A single black braid dug like a thick finger into the snow. He stepped past Burton, moving in closer, swallowing hard against the nausea in the pit of his stomach. He forced himself to look down at the body and the purple mass of blood, tissue, and fabric in the center of the man's chest. There were dark splotches of blood in the snow.

And the body had been posed. Right arm bent upward over the head, left arm folded below the hole gaping in his chest, and both legs crooked backward with the knees ahead of the rest of the body, as if he'd been running.

Father John knelt in the snow and made the sign of the cross over the body. "God have mercy on you," he said out loud. "God forgive you whatever wrong you might have done and show you His infinite mercy. May you rest in peace."

He stayed in place for a long moment, still fighting down the surge of nausea. The smell of death filled his nostrils.

"Any idea of who he might be?" Burton asked.

"I know him," Father John said.

24

FATHER JOHN GOT to his feet. He looked from Detective Burton to the deputies, all of whom had moved forward, tightening the circle around the body.

"Trent Hunter's cousin," Father John said. "His name is Eric Surrell. I met him yesterday at the Hunter place. I ran into him later on Trout Creek Road."

"Ran into him?" The detective thrust his head forward and began pounding his gloved fists together. The rhythmic sound was like that of an animal digging into the earth.

"Eric and two other Shoshones . . ." Father John hesitated, his gaze on the posed body. The right arm angled upward. "They ran me off the road," he went on. "Took a bat to the pickup. Trying to send a warning that Shoshones weren't going to let Arapahos commit murder and get away with it."

Burton was staring down at the body. "Ironic. Surrell's the one who was murdered. You report the incident?"

Father John didn't say anything.

"Let me rephrase that," the detective said. He moved into the edge of a shadow, giving his face the look of a skull, eyes sunken beneath the ledge of his forehead. "Why didn't you report it?"

"It was a one-time occurrence. They made their point. Besides, they were frustrated and angry and . . ." He understood. "Three Shoshones had been murdered. It could happen to any of them."

Something moved on the right of his vision, and Father John looked up. His muscles tensed. The last time he'd been at Bates, someone up the slope had shot at him. Now he could see the uniforms making their way over the boulders, leaning over, examining something, moving on.

"So another Shoshone's been shot. Probably hit with a rifle, like the last bunch." Burton blew into the tunnel of his fists a moment. "We found a brown pickup over in the trees, cleaned out, no plates. Probably belongs to the victim. You know what this means, John?"

Father John didn't say anything.

"The rez could come apart. Shoshones and Arapahos will be tearing at one another's throats like a pack of wolves. It's a bad scene, no matter what spin you try to put on it. Shoshones are already convinced that Arapahos are bent on revenge for a massacre that took place so long ago that nobody oughtta give a damn."

The man let his gaze roam over the slope. Two of the deputies seemed to be working their way down. "We've got a psycho on our hands," he went on. "Somebody who gets his jollies killing people, leaving crummy messages, watching us run around trying to figure out what's going on, and digging up a helluva lot of bad feelings that oughtta stay buried."

The detective started back through the canyon, and Father John fell into step, their boots crunching the snow. Finally, the man said, "You better not go back to Shoshone territory. No sense asking for trouble.

Soon's we get the ID confirmed, I'll see about getting a Shoshone pastor to pay the family a visit. You'd better stick with the Arapahos, see what you can do to keep them from getting riled up and start thinking Shoshones might look for their own revenge."

Father John nodded. He was thinking that he'd have a talk with the elder, Ethan Red Bull.

"Think we've got something here." A deputy intersected their path and stopped in front of Burton. He gestured over his shoulder toward the two uniforms behind them, both breathing heavily, the sound of air gusting from their lips. The older-looking man, with a bull neck and red face, stepped ahead. His gloves were wrapped around a rifle, the muzzle pointed into the sky. "Killer left us a souvenir this time," he said, glancing around at the slope of boulders. "Winchester deer rifle, 30-30. Found it about a quarter of the way up."

Burton's gaze ran upward over the slope. "Any sign of boot prints?"

"Maybe." Another uniform stepped forward. He wasn't more than twenty-two, with the tall, gangly look of a kid who'd gotten his growth in six months.

The red-faced man nodded. "Couple places in between the rocks where it looks like a boot could've gone into the snow. We marked 'em. We'll show the evidence team. Maybe they can get some prints."

Burton nodded, then started trudging again. Father John stayed with him, trying to concentrate on the investigation. That was logical, rational—weapon, boot prints—not the robotic voice of a psychotic killer.

He said, "The killer wanted the weapon found."

They'd reached the vehicles before Burton stopped and turned to him. "You got it. The killer's been leaving clues. Two phone messages he thinks are exceedingly clever. So clever, as a matter of fact, that we're chasing our tails trying to figure out who sent them. We're not moving fast enough for this guy, so he wants to help us along."

Father John looked off into the shadows falling among the vehicles. His jeans felt frozen and stiff. He knocked his knuckles together, a prizefighter loosening up his fists. "It doesn't make sense," he said. "Psychos don't want to get caught. They're laughing up their sleeves at how clever they are. Way too smart for the law." He hurried on, working it out, the logical pieces tumbling into sequence. "He wants you to get close, but not too close. He wants to signal who he *might* be, but he won't give you anything to prove it. He thinks you'll never be able to prove it, and that only proves how smart he is."

The detective was nodding. "You ever get tired of your job, we can always use a good man."

"There won't be any fingerprints on that rifle," Father John said, watching the man's eyes drop to half-mast in confirmation.

"Keep my offer in mind." Burton lifted a hand in a quick wave, then started trudging back toward the body. Father John could see that the coroner had already joined the deputies. They were spreading a gray bag over the snow.

He threaded his way around the vehicles to the pickup. He was about to swipe his sleeve over the laccy film of snow on the windshield when he saw the light-colored SUV plowing along the road. It spun to a stop and the driver's door swung open. The crackle of a police radio burst into the quiet, then shut off. Liam Harrison ducked out of the SUV and started toward him, jamming his hands into the pockets of his jacket.

"We meet again, Father," he called out, a cheery note, as if he were on his way to a hockey game. "I hear another man's been shot to death out here. You the one that found him?"

"Talk to Detective Burton." Father John tossed his head toward the canyon.

"I don't get it." The reporter stepped closer, his mouth drawn into a tight, determined line. "Indians getting murdered on this old battlefield, and you don't want the public to know what's behind it? Don't you think citizens have a right to know if we got our own tribal war in the States?"

"There's no war, Harrison."

"Well, it looks to me like we got the battlefield, and now we got four dead bodies. So what would you call it?"

Father John got in behind the wheel of the pickup and pulled the door shut hard. He fished his keys out of his pockets with stiff fingers, turned the ignition, and shifted into reverse. Then he was making a U-turn and hurtling up the narrow road, the reporter framed in the side-view mirror, arms hanging at his sides, shaking his head.

ETHAN RED BULL stood in the doorway of the small, blocklike house with gray siding that melded into the morning haze hanging over the reservation. Steadying himself against the door frame, he thrust his arm outside. He might have been shooing a horse into the corral. "Come on inside," he hollered as Father John got out of the pickup.

Two minutes ago, he'd turned off the road and driven across the borrow ditch, tires grinding, engine racing. For an instant, he'd thought the pickup would stall nose down in the ditch, but the front end had crawled up the far side and the rear wheels had spit the old pickup out into the yard. He'd stopped close to the front stoop and waited.

He'd tried to call Ethan from his cell three or four times on the drive over from the battlefield yesterday evening. Finally, the call had connected. Eva, the old man's daughter, was on the line. "Dad's not feeling so good, Father. But he's been saying that he wants to talk to you. How about stopping by tomorrow morning first thing?"

"Want some coffee to warm your bones?" Ethan said, ushering Father John into a small, tidy living room, with crocheted doilies draped over the top of the brown sofa under the window and the recliner chair over in a corner.

A small, middle-aged woman with black hair streaked in gray and a face that was still pretty, despite the worry lines digging into her forehead, got up from the desk across the room. She came toward him, holding out her hand. "Nice of you to come by, Father. You eaten lately?"

The way the woman looked up at him reminded him of Elena, checking to make sure he'd eaten the dinner she'd left in the refrigerator. He had to smile. Arapahos were always trying to feed him. *Come in. Eat. Eat. Eat.* They were known for their hospitality in the Old Time. Nobody left an Arapaho village hungry.

"I'm fine," he said, trying to ignore the hollow feeling in his stomach. He'd gulped down a bowl of oatmeal and a cup of coffee for breakfast, hurrying to take care of whatever awaited him at the office this morning before driving out to Ethan's.

"Let me get you a sandwich to go along with the coffee," the woman said, as if she'd read his thoughts. Then she disappeared around the doorway to the kitchen in back.

"Make yourself at home." Ethan had stepped around a small coffee table to the recliner and was hesitating, stopped in the motion of sitting down. The moment Father John took a seat on the sofa, the old man dropped onto the cushion.

"You go to the battlefield yesterday?" he asked. The man's eyes looked like black coals sunken between the cliff of his forehead and the sharp bones of his cheeks.

The question surprised Father John. Ethan had gotten right to the point. None of the polite preliminaries that were usually exchanged. What about all the snow? Spring sure taking long to get here. None of that. The murders at Bates had eclipsed the pleasantries. The moccasin telegraph had probably spread the news before he'd gotten back to the mission last night. "I was there," he said.

From the kitchen came the dull clank of metal against something hard and the sound of a faucet running. The smell of coffee wafted across the living room, and Father John tried again to ignore the hungry feeling nipping at him.

"Same as before?"

Father John nodded.

The old man was quiet a moment, the black eyes fixed on the window above Father John's shoulder. "Another Shoshone massacred, like we was massacred at Bates," he said finally.

Father John tried to muster as much confidence as possible. "Every law enforcement agency in the area is working with the sheriff's office," he said. "People just have to stay calm."

"Well, they're not calm." Eva emerged from the kitchen, holding a plate with a sandwich and a bunch of potato chips in one hand and a coffee mug in the other. She set them down on the coffee table. "My boy's scared to death," she said. "So are his buddies. Scared to go to Fort Washakie. Scared to pull into the filling station for gas or stop at the convenience store. Looking over their shoulders all the time, waiting for some Shoshone to jump 'em, maybe kill 'em, 'cause of some crazy Arapaho that's living in the past. There's going to be more killings, Father. Everybody's on edge, keeping their guns loaded."

The woman had spun around and returned to the kitchen. In a moment she was back with another sandwich and another mug of coffee, which she set on the lamp table next to the recliner.

Ethan glanced up at his daughter. "You just fed me breakfast."

"You might still be hungry." She waved away the protest, went back into the kitchen, and returned with another mug. She pulled a hardback chair over and sat down. "Eat, eat," she said, motioning toward the sandwiches with her mug.

"Thank you, Eva," Father John said. He picked up the bologna sandwich and took a bite, then another. The cold, gray morning, the images of the bodies reeling in his mind—he was more tired and hungrier than he'd realized.

"Oh, I know there's crazies out there," Eva said, crossing her legs and working her shoulders into some kind of comfortable position against the rungs of her chair. She took a sip of coffee and went on. "But crazy as Frankie Montana is, carrying on his grudge with Shoshones, nobody thought he was *that* crazy."

"Killer's not Arapaho." Ethan's voice boomed through the room, the voice of a chief speaking to the village.

Father John looked over at the old man, aware that Eva had lowered her mug and was also staring at her father. A moment passed. The house was quiet: nothing except the raspy sound of Ethan's breathing. The muscles in his jaw flexed before he said, "We didn't have no place to go when we came here to *he'teini:ci'e*. Our lands gone, all the places that we called home, gone. Government kept telling the chiefs, 'Don't worry. We're gonna find you a reservation,' and the chiefs kept saying, 'Let us go to the Powder River country. Let us go to the Platte.' There was water in them places, not like the no-water land down in Colorado where the government wanted to send us. The chiefs said, 'How we gonna live without water?' So they kept pestering the government. Things was desperate. The people was hunted all across the plains, like we was wolves the soldiers wanted to exterminate. Some of the young men, they'd get fed up. They was scared. They started going on raids, stealing food and livestock. Some ranchers got killed down by where Lander is now. So Shoshones went to Captain Bates and said, 'We seen the Arapaho village out in the canyon in the badlands. We can get revenge on those killers.' That's how come Captain Bates and the Shoshones went out there."

The old man closed his eyes, as if he were watching the images playing across his eyelids. "It wasn't Arapahos that killed them ranchers," he said after a moment. "My grandfather was hunting in the area. He seen a raiding party of Sioux goin' to the ranches. It was Sioux that killed them people. The Arapahos that died at Bates, they was innocent."

The elder took another drink of coffee, allowing what he'd said to drift through the room, like a shadow from the past. He stared over the rim of the mug a moment, then set it on the table. "Maybe that's the reason Chief Washakie said yes and let our people come to the reservation. 'Cause he'd found out that they'd killed innocent people. No Arapaho's gonna kill Shoshones, make them start thinking about how the reservation used to be theirs, and how, maybe, that's the way it oughtta be."

Father John took the last bite of his sandwich and washed it down with coffee. He'd been worrying about Shoshones and Arapahos killing one another; he hadn't thought about *this*. . . . He took another swallow of coffee before he said, "You think the Shoshones might ask the government to remove the Arapahos? Send them somewhere else?"

The elder threw his head back in a single nod. "They could file one of them lawsuits against the Bureau of Indian Affairs. Claim their lives was in danger, that the reservation wasn't safe no more. There's government land all over the place they could move us to, if that's what suited them."

Father John was aware that Eva had dropped her head, her gaze fixed on the mug cradled in both hands. They'd already discussed this possibility, he was thinking. He wondered how many other Arapahos were looking at their houses, their barns and pastures, and wondering if the government could do that. Transfer them over to some other lands. Ten acres someplace else for the ten acres they had on the rez.

He set the mug down and stared at the shadow it cast on the table. If the Shoshones could prove that Arapahos were behind the murders of their people, the government might settle a lawsuit by moving the Arapahos.

"What's got me worried," Eva began, a reluctance in her tone, as if she didn't want to contradict her own father, "is that some fool like Frankie Montana doesn't realize what he's doing."

Ethan looked over at his daughter. "*Tihko':no:ku'no: nihno':howo' ho'xei'hino*," he said. Then—a glance at Father John— "When I opened my eyes, I saw wolves." He paused a moment before going on. "There was wolf scouts that brought Washakie and the soldiers to the village. The *ho':xei* always sees what he's doing."

It was a few minutes before Father John got to his feet, thanking Eva again for the sandwich and coffee, thanking the old man for his time. A few minutes, in which he'd talked about how the investigation hadn't proved anything, how they shouldn't worry about what might happen until the killer had been found. Platitudes. The logic of platitudes. And all the time, he was aware of the polite masks that had come over the faces of Ethan and his daughter. They hadn't wanted to contradict him.

He motioned the old man to stay in his chair, saying that he'd find his way out, but Eva reached the door ahead of him and held it open. "I hope you're right, Father," she said, as he stepped out under the gray sky.

25

"Tribal War on Reservation."

Vicky spotted the headline splashed across the front page of the *Gazette* the minute she walked into the coffee shop. She stood suspended in the doorway, forgetting to shut the door, until the cool air sweeping past caused heads to turn in her direction, eyes glazed in impatience. She closed the door, walked over to the newspaper rack, and lifted out the top paper. Folding the newspaper in half to hide the headline, she walked over to the counter. Who was she kidding? Newspapers were spread open on every table. Everybody in the shop was fixated on the story. She could feel the eyes following her with new interest, boring into her with the obvious questions: Arapaho? Shoshone? Which side did she fall on?

Vicky asked the bored-looking girl behind the counter for a cup of coffee, black. She slid the newspaper under her arm and fumbled in her bag for her wallet, withdrew a dollar bill, and pushed it across the glass countertop.

No, thank you, she didn't care for anything but coffee, she heard herself saying, although she'd planned on a Danish, something to get her through the morning. She no longer had any appetite. The sugary smells made her stomach jump. A hiss of conversation ran through the sounds of coffee sloshing into a mug. Yesterday, the news had been filled with the murder of another Shoshone, Eric Surrell. And now this! Headlines screaming what everybody on the reservation feared, giving the fear substance, making it real.

God, she hoped Frankie Montana had a solid alibi this time.

The eyes were still following her as she carried the coffee over to a table near the door and sat down, letting her bag drop at her feet. *Normal. Normal.* She would read the newspaper article. Drink the coffee. Go to the office just as she'd planned. Saturday morning—she'd have the office to herself. No phone calls, no interruptions. She would pack her files and take a final look at the notes she'd written for Adam on the wolf management plan. Everything neatly pulled into place before she left. And this afternoon, she'd look over vacant office space in Lander with a realtor.

She shrugged out of her coat and unfolded the newspaper. Halfway down the front page was the photograph of a middle-aged man and woman leaning on each other, faces contorted in grief. The caption said, "Martin and Lois Surrell, members of the Shoshone tribe, fear their son was murdered in old tribal feud with Arapahos."

Vicky started skimming the article itself. It was worse than she'd expected, pounding out the same points over and over. Shoshones and Arapahos, traditional enemies. Ancient animosities resurfacing. Four Shoshones murdered where Shoshones had massacred Arapahos in nineteenth century.

And the quotes from people across the reservation: Shoshones saying that they never did trust Arapahos, that Arapahos had always been out for revenge, that they'd waited a hundred years for the chance. And

Arapahos talking about how Shoshones never wanted them on the reservation, how it must've been Shoshones themselves that shot those three other Shoshones, so they could blame Arapahos and have an excuse to get Arapahos off the reservation.

The article ran into the inside. More quotes and interviews with the families of the murdered men, all of them saying what fine young men they had been. Three of the victims had been students at Central Wyoming, the article said. Trent Hunter. Rex and Joe Crispin. They'd gone to the site as part of a class assignment. Investigators were not certain as to what took Eric Surrell there, except that he was Hunter's cousin and may have wanted to see where his cousin had been killed.

Another photo appeared on the inside page, an elderly man, with a full head of white hair, looking out over rimless glasses that sat partway down his prominent nose. The perfect picture of a professor, Vicky thought. Hovering near the man was a young-looking woman with black, curly hair. Professor Charles Lambert and his wife, Dana, according to the caption. Three of the Shoshone victims had been enrolled in the professor's class on the war on the plains.

Vicky read quickly through the rest of the article. Professor Lambert, described as an authority on the Bates Battle. The professor himself describing Trent Hunter and Rex and Joe Crispin as excellent students who immersed themselves in the details of various battles. They had been especially interested in the Bates Battle, and the professor had suggested that his students visit the site. Bookstores in the area had ordered large numbers of Lambert's latest book, *Tribal Wars*. According to Lila Benson at Books on Main, the publisher had moved up the shipping date by almost two weeks in order to accommodate the interest in a nineteenth-century massacre that threatened to reignite a tribal feud.

Vicky closed the paper and studied the byline, somebody named Liam Harrison. An AP article, it would be published in newspapers around the country, around the world. She was beginning to think she would be sick. She folded the paper down until it was a narrow, thick stack, as if she could fold the story away, then pulled on her coat, lifted her handbag off the floor, and walked out of the shop, leaving the folded newspaper on the table.

She moved through a wall of cool, moist air that parted as she headed down Main Street. An imitation of the sun glowed through the layer of gray clouds. There was little warmth in it. She caught sight of the reflection moving beside her in the store windows: Indian woman clutching the top of the black bag slung over her shoulders, crystals of moisture glistening in her black hair. There was no one about, except for the occasional vehicle grinding down Main. There were so many issues, she was thinking, important issues such as managing the wolf population, handling the oil and gas leases, and preserving the water rights and the timber rights, that Arapahos and Shoshones had to work together on. They had to trust one another, or they couldn't live together at Wind River.

Who are you? Why are you doing this to the reservation?

Vicky let herself in the main door of the brick office building and climbed the stairs, the sound of her footsteps clacking into the quiet. In the office, cool air streamed through the vents, and she kept her coat thrown over her shoulders as she worked at her desk, organizing and shuffling papers, trying to concentrate, unable to push out of her mind the fear that the newspaper was right, that a tribal war was about to erupt on the reservation. Detective Burton was good at his job, she told herself. He'd arrest the murderer and everything could return to normal. Normal.

The sound of her voice in the silence startled her. She was talking to herself.

She slid some papers into file folders and set them in the cardboard boxes that she'd brought to the office last night, then taped the tops closed. The movers would bring the boxes when they came for her furniture. The other file folders would stay: They were part of the firm, hers and Adam's. Theirs. She laughed out loud at the idea that there had been a "theirs."

The phone started ringing. She reached for the receiver, then pulled her hand back. An old habit, that was all. Emergency calls came on the weekend. There was no need to take an emergency call to a firm of which she was no longer a part. The ringing stopped; the call went to the mailbox. Whatever it was, Adam would get the message Monday.

She taped up the last box and was about to crawl back into her coat when she heard a faint metallic sound, like keys clinking together, coming from somewhere in the building. There had been noises yesterday evening, too. When she was leaving, she'd run into the dentist from the office downstairs, on his way out after treating a patient with a toothache.

The ringing started again. She stared at the phone, counting the rings. Three. Four. She leaned across the desk and picked up the receiver.

"Vicky Holden," she said.

"Oh, thank God you're there." Lucille Montana's voice was edged with barely controlled hysteria. "I been calling your apartment, and I been calling the office. I didn't know what . . ."

Vicky cut in, "Tell me what happened, Lucille."

"They came for him."

"Lucille, start at the beginning."

"Busting into the house, like that, Detective Burton with two deputies and some rez cops. What right do they got to bust in that way?"

"Wait a minute. You're saying they broke through your door?"

"Soon's I opened the door after I hear somebody pounding, they bust right in, not waiting for me to say it was okay, and that detective shouting, 'Where's Frankie?' It scared the shit outta me. I think I said, 'What d'ya want him for?' I can't even remember for sure. One deputy looks in the kitchen, then heads down the hall to the bedrooms, and Burton's saying they got a warrant for Frankie's arrest and they're executing the warrant."

"On what charges?" Vicky sank onto the edge of the chair. She could feel the answer in the pit of her stomach. Burton had found the evidence to link Frankie to the murders.

"Homicide!" The woman was shouting down the line. "Four counts of homicide. I told that detective he was crazy, and all the time, I'm looking down the hallway expecting to see that deputy dragging Frankie into the living room, and I'm praying, Vicky, like I never prayed in my life, that Frankie heard all the commotion and got himself hidden in the closet or something."

"Try to be calm," Vicky said. "They'll take him to the county jail. I'm on my way over. Frankie will have a court hearing first thing Monday, and I'll do my best to get him released. Can you put the house up to secure the bond?" She'd done that before, Vicky was thinking.

There was hesitation, then a sputtering noise, like a small engine trying to turn over. "There was gunshots, Vicky."

"Gunshots!"

"Frankie must've heard the racket, 'cause the deputy comes running down the hallway and says, 'He jumped out the window,' and they all went running outdoors. I went after 'em, and I see Frankie's footprints dug into the ground, like he was pounding hard, all the way to where he parked the pickup. I seen what the gunshots was all about. There was a cop out back, like they expected Frankie to run, and that cop went running after him. He was shooting off his gun, like he's a real big man gonna shoot Frankie in the back. It made me sick, Vicky. I thought I was gonna throw up, thinking Frankie could've been dead, but he made it to the pickup and he was out on the road. Those cops jumped into their cars and went after him, but he was gone, Vicky. It was like that road was bare."

Except for the tire tracks, Vicky thought. The police had probably already caught up with Frankie Montana. The man was probably in custody, with more charges piled onto the homicide charges: resisting arrest, eluding officers. Burton would come up with a whole list of charges, enough to ensure that, even if Frankie beat the homicide charges, he was looking at prison.

"Listen, Lucille," Vicky said. "I'll find out where Frankie is."

"They didn't get him."

"How do you know?"

"I called the sheriff. They said he didn't get arrested. They called him a suspect at large. They're looking all over the rez for him right now. They're gonna shoot him, Vicky."

"Don't let yourself think like that."

"I'm telling you. They blame him for all the trouble them murders have stirred up, and they want to put an end to it, so they'll just shoot him."

"I'll get back to you," Vicky said, then punched the off button. The receiver felt like a piece of lead in her hand. A crackling noise came from somewhere in the building, barely registering on her consciousness. Suppose Lucille was right? She could imagine the scenario. A couple of cops spot Frankie's pickup out in the middle of the reservation somewhere and force him off the road. Frankie takes off running again, and the cops shoot. Shoot to kill the crazy Arapaho who wants to start a war on the reservation. It would be over with, wouldn't it? The best solution for everyone, except Lucille. And Frankie . . .

Vicky closed her eyes a moment and pressed her thumb and forefinger against her eyelids, unable to stop the idea working its way into her mind: Frankie Montana could be guilty.

She tapped out the number for the sheriff's department and listened to the intermittent buzzing noise. "Fremont County Sheriff." A woman's voice.

"This is Vicky Holden," she said. "Put me through to Detective Burtton. It's an emergency."

"He's not in the office," The woman said. "I'll connect you to his voice mail."

"Hang up!"

Vicky swung around in the chair. The receiver slipped from her hand and crashed against the edge of the desk before thudding onto the floor. Frankie Montana was bracing himself in the doorway, a hand on one side, as if he were holding up the frame. He was coatless, his blue shirt plastered against his chest with perspiration. The Velcro tabs on his boots hung at the sides. In his hand was a small, black gun.

"Now you're gonna help me," he said, holding out the gun.

Vicky took a couple of seconds, trying to slow down the thoughts tumbling through her head. She was alone in the office, probably in the whole building, with a man running from the police, a desperate man with a gun.

"Come in and sit down, Frankie," she heard herself saying. It surprised her, how calm her voice sounded. "We've got some options. Let's talk about them."

"Yeah, we got an option, all right. You're my option."

"Sit down, Frankie," she said again.

"You and me, we're gettin' outta here."

"Frankie." She drew out the man's name, reaching for the next words. "Don't make things any worse than they are. I can talk to Burton, tell him you're ready to turn yourself in, and maybe he'll agree to overlook what happened at the house . . ."

"You gone psycho or somethin'? Well, ain't that just great. All I need's a psycho lawyer. You and me, Vicky, you're drivin' me out of here."

"How far do you think we'll get, Frankie? Every cop in the area is looking for you right now. It won't take them long to trace you here and figure out that you took my Jeep."

"Wrong on all the above. Them dumb cops are gonna find my pickup in back of a motel up on the highway, and it's gonna take 'em awhile to figure out which piece of crap I hot-wired to get outta there. Even if they get real smart and figure I got you with me, they're not gonna be shooting at no vehicle that you're inside. Besides, by the time they know what happened, you and me are gonna be in a real safe hiding place. You're my stay-out-of-prison pass. Get my drift?"

"You don't want to do that, Frankie. You'd be making a huge mistake."

"They're not sending me to prison, I tol' you before." The gun was waving back and forth, like a pendulum. Vicky tried to pull her eyes away.

"You didn't listen to me," Frankie went on. "You tol' me to go find another lawyer, when you should've been talking to the detective and telling him how I'm innocent so he'd get off my back. I figure you're to blame for everything that's come down, so you're gonna keep me out of prison."

"Let me call your mother." A new tack. God, let it work. "She's worried sick."

The man dropped his hands and took a step inside the office. "You ain't so high and mighty now, are you? Not like you was in the bar a couple days ago." He let out a low guffaw. "She loves you, and God knows why," he said, switching into a falsetto voice. Then he threw his head toward the outer office. "We're gettin' outta here now," he said, pointing the gun at her face. "Let's go."

26

VICKY STOOD UP slowly, not taking her eyes from the black pistol that Frankie Montana was waving in her direction. The man was crazy. His eyes burned like coals in his skull; sweat glistened on his face. He was high on something. Alcohol? Drugs? Probably both. The slightest twitch of nerves and the gun would go off.

Vicky kept her gaze on the black metal gun moving back and forth. "Put the gun away, Frankie," she said again, struggling to keep her voice steady. The calm courtroom voice, the one she reserved for the hostile witness who wouldn't give up anything until, worn down by calmness and persistence, he might reluctantly let go of whatever he had been clinging to.

"I said we're gettin' outta here, you and me."

Vicky didn't move for a moment, and then she started to pull on her coat still draped across her shoulders.

"Hold it!" The gun protruded into the room, the muzzle gaping like an endless black tunnel.

"I was just getting on my coat," she said, her gaze still fixed on the weapon.

"Real slow." Now Frankie waved the gun up and down. "Don't try any funny stuff or I swear, I swear I'll pull the fucking trigger."

Vicky stuffed one arm into the sleeve. Slow motion, pulling up the collar—how familiar it felt, the soft, comforting wool. "Can I get my handbag? It's on the floor."

Frankie seemed to consider this, the brown brow wrinkling with arguments playing out inside his head. He nodded finally, then motioned her forward with the gun. "Get a move on."

Vicky reached down and picked up the black leather bag. "I'm going with you, Frankie," she said, locking eyes with the man. A crazy, drugged murderer. God, God, God. "So put the gun down. Those things can go off. I don't think you want that to happen."

Frankie didn't move for so long that she feared it was exactly what he wanted to happen. Finally, he lowered the gun. His arm hung at his side, the gun brushing his pant leg, pointing to the floor. "You try anything . . ."

"I know, I know." Vicky walked around the desk, across the office, and through the doorway, moving past the man who took a half-step back. She felt him lurch after her as she crossed the corridor and turned toward the elevator, the raspy sound of his breathing close behind.

"Take the stairs." A sharp object poked through her coat into the small of her back, nudging her in the direction of the stairway. She went weak-kneed with the realization that he was poking the gun into her.

She dragged one hand along the corridor wall to steady herself and tried to hurry ahead. Frankie Montana stayed with her, the gun burning into her back. Their boots pounded on the stairs, an out-of-sync rhythm, and rising from below was a metallic clinking noise. Through the rails, Vicky caught the glimpse of dark hair above a tan overcoat leaning into one of the doors on the first floor. The dentist who'd been in yesterday evening was letting himself into his office. She grabbed hold of the top rail and hurled herself down the remaining stairs. Now she could see that standing about two feet farther down the corridor was a heavyset man bundled in a dark coat with a scarf hanging down the front.

A moment. She needed only a moment.

"Working this morning?" she called.

The dentist turned the key in the lock, pushed the door open a couple of inches, and glanced along the corridor toward where the stairs spilled into the entry at the same time that the man standing next to him also threw a pained, impatient look her way. In that moment, in the look she tried to hurl back at them both, she hoped they would see . . .

God, let them see!

"Toothaches never respect weekends, I'm afraid," the dentist said.

Vicky felt as if her legs had turned to air. She had to hold onto the bannister knob to stop herself from crumbling to the floor. *They didn't see!*

"Shut up and keep going," Frankie hissed into her ear and gripped her arm hard. The gun pushed so hard into her ribs that she gasped with the force of it.

"What brought you in today?" The dentist was walking toward them now, the other man moving like a shadow behind him, something new flooding through their expressions—a mixture of interest, curiosity, and wariness.

"Move," Frankie hissed again, pushing her forward.

Vicky felt herself propelled toward the wood-paneled door that rose before her like a barrier. The gun was still pushing into her ribs. Frankie's free hand reached around and slammed against the door, sending it swinging on its hinges out into the gray morning. In an instant they were through the door and scrambling along the sidewalk, Vicky's boots skipping and sliding on the wet pavement. Frankie's fingers dug into her arm, pushing and pulling her forward. A pickup drove past on

Main, tires whining, the distinct sound of hip-hop bursting through the unopened windows.

They swung around the corner of the building. Frankie pulled her off the curb and down the dirty, uneven tracks of snow and mud carved out by the vehicles parked around the lot. He steered her to the driver's side of a battered tan pickup, looking back over his shoulder toward the front of the building as he did so. Vicky glanced back. Before he yanked her around, she'd caught the slightest movement, like a disturbance in the air, of someone pulling back from the corner. A wave of weakness and disorientation came over her, as if she were in a nightmare where everything should be familiar. Wasn't that Main Street? The brick buildings across the street looming into the gray morning? The windows of the shops facing the sidewalk? And yet, nothing was familiar. Nothing was as it should be.

"Get in," Frankie said, yanking open the door. "You're gonna drive."

It was then Vicky realized that the humming noise she'd only half registered was the motor running. Warm air funneled from the cab.

She felt Frankie's fist clamp hard around her arm. Pain shot through her jaw as her face smashed against the steering wheel. She sprawled onto the front seat, the lump of her handbag digging into her stomach, and fought to right herself, finally managing to pull in her legs an instant before the door slammed shut.

She had a sense of being underwater. She was drowning at the bottom of a murky lake, unable to see anything, except for the dark smudge moving in the rearview mirror that had to be Frankie running around the pickup. She put the gear shift in forward and jammed down on the accelerator. The vehicle jumped ahead and slammed into something hard, pitching her forward. She threw up her hand to stop herself from hitting the windshield. The steering wheel dug into her chest. From far away, like noise traveling underwater, came the sound of crunching metal and breaking glass.

The passenger door flew open. Frankie jumped onto the seat. "I oughtta break your neck," he said, slamming the door behind him. Then he stuffed the gun under his belt. "Get out of here," he shouted. "Take the alley."

Vicky shifted into reverse and pushed on the gas pedal. Whatever she'd hit gripped the front bumper a moment before the pickup rocked free. She swung left, steered around her Jeep and headed down the alley toward the side street, where there would be even less traffic than the handful of vehicles on Main.

"I'm not gonna forget your little trick back there," Frankie said when she reached the end of the alley. She was aware of him settling back into the seat, removing the gun from his belt, holding it in his lap, pointed at her.

"Where are we going?" Vicky asked. A sharp pain pulsed through her jaw. She strained forward, staring through the windshield.

"Just drive," the man beside her said.

FATHER JOHN STOOD at the door to Eagle Hall, shaking hands, patting shoulders, trying for an encouraging word, as Joanne Thornton, Don Menlo, Judy Pretty Horse, and the five other members of the education committee filed outside into the cool, moist air that seemed to have settled in. He waited until the last pickup had sputtered to life, backed across the gravel, and pulled out into the driveway that led to Circle Drive before he walked back to the front of the meeting hall and began gathering up the copies of the agenda.

Agenda. He shook his head at the idea that the committee might have actually gotten around to discussing the education programs for the summer. Religious education, high school tutoring, Head Start—everything would have to wait. The committee had huddled together in a circle of folding chairs under puddles of white fluorescent light that flooded down from the ceiling and talked about the murder of another Shoshone at Bates, and Liam Harrison's front-page article in this morning's paper about the tribal war on the reservation. Worry, shock, fear—

all of it was there in the brown faces turning toward him, black eyes pleading for some explanation, some words of assurance. Four Shoshones had already been murdered and more violence would end . . . where?

After sliding the papers inside a file folder and pulling on his jacket, Father John was locking the door outside when a green pickup squealed into the driveway and skidded to a stop a few feet away. Even before Leonard Bizzel, the mission caretaker, jumped out, Father John had started toward him, all of his instincts switched to alert.

"What's up?" he asked.

"You heard what happened?" Leonard gestured with his head toward the opened door of the pickup and the sound of a radio voice trailing from inside.

"What is it?" he asked.

"I was just heading home and turned on the radio. Hadn't even gotten out of the mission when this announcer comes on with a news bulletin." Leonard leaned closer. "Frankie Montana's on the run from the police. They tried to arrest him this morning for shooting them Shoshones, and he took off."

"Took off?" He could hear Ethan Red Bull's voice in his head. *It wasn't an Arapaho.* But if the police went to Montana's with an arrest warrant, there must be some new evidence to tie him to the murders. The rifle. Dear Lord, the rifle must be Montana's.

"Jumped out of the window," Leonard said. "Made it to his pickup and drove off. Cops followed him to Lander before they lost him. Got an alert out, roadblocks everywhere." The Indian hunched his shoulders and swept his eyes over the ground a moment before he said, "There's something else."

Father John waited. He could feel the knot tightening in his stomach. Whatever it was, Leonard didn't want to tell him.

Finally, the man locked eyes with him again. "The cops say a couple of witnesses spotted Montana at Vicky's office. They say he's got her with him."

"No!" Father John heard someone shout. But it was his voice, he realized. He was the one shouting. Then he was running, boots pounding down the alley, past the church, and across the grounds to the pickup parked in front of the residence. He got inside and jammed the key into the ignition. Stomping on the gas pedal, he shot around Circle Drive, barely aware of the rear tires spinning in the slush and the mission buildings flashing past the pickup's windows.

27

"ROADBLOCKS!" FRANKIE MONTANA shifted around on the ripped passenger seat of the Ford pickup he'd stolen and tossed his head back. A loud guffaw erupted from his throat that sent a cloud of foul-smelling air across the dashboard.

Vicky kept her fingers wrapped around the rim of the steering wheel and tried not to breathe in the foulness. The stink of evil, she thought, what you read about in science fiction books, some imaginary stink that didn't actually exist.

"Them cops are putting up roadblocks on every highway in the county, and we ain't on the highways. What d'ya say? Ain't that a laugh?" He was gloating now, congratulating himself that he'd directed her through alleys and down the streets of sleepy bungalows with blinds still drawn over the windows. The engine clanked and squealed, as if the metal parts were rubbing together.

"What d'ya say?" he demanded.

"You're brilliant, Frankie."

"Ha!" He let out another smelly guffaw. The sarcasm had rolled right by him. "Damn right I'm brilliant. And they're so fucking stupid, all of 'em. Wasting time trying to put them murders on me, just so they can brag how smart they are, and the killer's out there laughing at 'em, and all of 'em, the killer, too, thinking how I'm the one gonna be sitting in prison. Well, they're not dumping me in no prison."

Vicky threw a sideways glance at the man. "If you didn't kill the Shoshones . . ."

"Bitch!" Frankie slammed a fist into the dashboard. The suddenness and unexpectedness of it, the hard thud of bone and flesh on the inert object made her give an involuntary jump. "I been telling you I didn't do it. You're not listening. My own lawyer, and you think I'm guilty like the rest of 'em. If you'd just listened to me, the cops wouldn't've busted my door this morning. Good thing I got my gun right by the bed. You wanna know why you're here? 'Cause you screwed up, and now you're gonna help me escape, whether you like it or not."

"Help you escape? That's no way to help you, Frankie." Vicky was trying again for the calm courtroom voice, but she couldn't pull it off. Instead, the voice she heard was shaky and scared. "You're acting like you're guilty. Instead of looking for whoever killed the Shoshones, Burton's going to spend every moment trying to find you. We should turn around, go back, and . . ."

"Shut up!" He was leaning forward in the seat now, turned toward her, the gun bobbing up and down between them. "You had any good ideas, I never heard 'em. All I heard from you was, 'Get another lawyer,' and 'I don't care if you rot in prison.' "

All true, Vicky was thinking. A part of her had decided that Frankie Montana was guilty. She should have found him another lawyer. Not Samantha Lowe with the eager sheen in her eyes. An experienced lawyer who would have *believed* in Frankie and argued with Burton over every piece of circumstantial evidence that he came up with, thrown up enough stumbling blocks and enough alternate scenarios about what might have happened out at Bates to make it impossible to charge Frankie, instead of sitting back and waiting for it to happen, as she had done, content to defend the man after he was arrested. For his mother's sake, for Godsakes.

Neither one of them spoke. Frankie seemed spent. He leaned his head back on the seat, and for an instant, she feared that he would see the gas needle jumping around empty. She'd noticed that the gas was low when they were still in town. She'd been silently praying that the pickup would grind to a halt. Nothing to do but get out and walk through a neighborhood where someone might see them, wonder who they were—Indians. A man in shirt and jeans—in this cold weather— pulling a woman along, someone might have called the cops. Even if no one had, she could have watched for a chance to get away.

But the pickup had kept clanking and lurching forward, and now they were climbing a narrow, winding road that switched back on itself, the pickup balking at the trackless snow that spilled into the ditches. She couldn't tell where the road ended and the ditch on her side began. The pines dipped under the wet snow, branches bending into the road and scratching at the sides of the pickup. Every once in a while, she caught sight of Lander below, the gray smudges of smoke rising above the roofs. It was like catching a glimpse of another world. She felt as if she'd been sucked into an alternate universe running parallel to the reality of an ordinary Saturday morning.

In the combination of cold and silence and utter solitude that pressed around the pickup as it took another turn upward, Vicky felt a wave of hysteria coming over her, the scream rising inside her throat. For a moment, she feared she couldn't hold it back. She forced herself to swallow hard. Breathe, breathe, she told herself. Stay in control. If she became hysterical, the crazy man beside her would also become hysterical. Hysteria was contagious. And if Frankie Montana became hysterical, the gun could go off.

She was barely aware that the pickup had started bucking, little jumps at first, the pines rising and falling outside her window. She gripped the wheel hard, her fingers glued to the plastic, and watched the fuel needle bobbing below empty. The pickup shuddered and seemed to buck into the snowy road.

Frankie sat up straight and turned to her. "What the hell did you do?"

"We're out of gas," she managed, automatically bracing herself for the blow, the thud of flesh and bone into her face as she turned the key in the ignition. The engine coughed and sputtered, gasping at the last drops of gasoline, then stopped. They were left in a silence so profound that it was like the silence at the end of the world.

"What the hell!" Frankie shouted. "Fucking out of gas! I don't believe the fucking luck."

The blow didn't come. Vicky felt a mild sense of surprise. Her muscles were still tense as she watched the man thrashing around beside her, knocking his fist against the dashboard, flailing at unseen enemies.

After a couple of minutes, Frankie tucked the gun inside his belt. "Get out," he said. "We're gonna hike."

Vicky waited until he'd opened his door and stumbled onto the road before she grabbed her handbag from behind the seat and got out. There was no one around, no sound except for the soft hiss of snow falling off the branches. She could see the blue puffs of breath in front of her, and the breath of the man stomping around the pickup, swinging his arms to keep up the circulation.

Vicky slung the bag over her shoulder. Inside was her cell, which probably wouldn't work in the mountains, but you never knew. She prayed that Frankie wouldn't notice the bag and become curious about what was inside. Pushing it back behind her arm, she weighed her options. She could start running down the tracks that the pickup had plowed through the snow and take the chance that he wouldn't shoot her in the back.

He would shoot her. It wasn't an option.

She had to stay with him and wait for a chance to try the cell.

"Come on," he shouted, waving her forward. "It's around here somewhere."

It? "What are you talking about? What's around here?

"A real nice house." He was smirking at her, arms doing a windmill. "Let's go."

Vicky started after him. She understood now. He knew exactly where they were going. He'd had it all planned from the minute he'd forced her into the pickup. They were going to one of the mountain houses that he'd broken into last fall, a charge that she'd gotten dropped on a technicality. She was the one who'd kept him out of jail! And now he was taking her to one of the houses.

It was funny when you thought about it. She felt the hysteria bubbling up again and clamped her teeth together against the laughter that threatened to burst forth, laughter that she knew would leave her weeping helplessly. She focused on planting her boots, one after the other, in the footprints that he was making through the snow.

They must have gone a mile, she thought. Frankie was still ahead, but he'd slowed his pace, walking stiff-legged now, arms hanging like logs at his side. His shoulders were hunched up so far that his head and body looked welded together. He hadn't said anything for twenty minutes, for which she was grateful. Just breathing, keeping one foot in front of the other—that was enough. It took all her energy. She didn't need the conversation of a crazy man. The sense of weariness tugged at her legs, making them seem like stone pillars moving beneath her. She was breathing hard, her heart doing double time in her ears. Beneath the layers of her sweater and coat, her skin felt hot and clammy, and yet—this was the surprise!—she felt as if she might be freezing to death.

As they came around another switchback, the road took a steeper pitch upward. Vicky stopped and tried to catch her breath, but each inhalation felt like an icicle stabbing her chest. Frankie was barely moving, nearly bent double into the rising road and swaying side to side, one foot shuffling in front of the other.

He must have spotted the house at the same instant that she saw it, because he veered off the road and started wading through the snow piled around the trees, arms paddling like oars at his sides. And howling out some gibberish that she couldn't make out, like the howling of a wolf.

Still trying to stay in his footprints, Vicky started after the man. The drifts were deeper among the trees, bunched up in mounds of white powder that looked as light as air but felt like wet cement pulling at her boots as she struggled through. There was more snow here than in town, the air felt colder, and the sun was lost in the leaden sky. Ahead, nestled in a stand of pines, was a two-story house washed in shadows, roof heavy with snow. There was a deadness about the place, an absolute absence of life or activity, as if it had been standing empty for eons, and yet, from what she could see, the house looked well maintained, flower boxes piled with snow at the windows, a fresh coat of gray paint on the siding.

She realized that Frankie had made his way around to the side of the house and was leaning against a door, rubbing and hugging his arms and blowing out huge clouds of breath. She forced herself to keep walking, across the front of the house and around the side. She set her shoulder against the siding a few feet behind Frankie.

"Take off your coat," he shouted.

Vicky stared at the man.

"You heard me. Get it off."

She wasn't sure she had the energy to comply. Her fingers were clumsy sticks trying to push the buttons through the buttonholes.

"Hurry up!" he shouted again.

Finally the top button fell through the hole, then the next and the next. She was still slipping the coat off her shoulders when he reached around and grabbed it, tangling it with the strap of her bag. She staggered back along the side of the house, gasping at the blast of cold air that swept over her as he ripped the coat away. She stooped over and reached for the bag that had fallen into the snow. Her fingers kept sliding off the leather until, finally, she had hold of the strap and managed to drag the bag upward. She was shivering. She struggled to focus on what Frankie was doing. He'd wrapped his right arm and hand inside the front of her coat, letting the sleeves and collar trail down into the snow. Lifting his arm—a thick black club—he smashed it into the corner of the window set in the door. There was a muffled tinkling, like wind chimes, as the pane shattered and collapsed inward, falling out of the frame.

"All right!" Frankie let the coat fall into a pile at his feet, and Vicky swooped forward, picked it up, and threw it over her shoulders, hugging it close against the shaking that had taken over her body like some invisible force.

"They never learn their lessons, rich people." Frankie slipped his hand through the hole and, moving into the door until his face was pressed against one of the upper panes, stretched his arm downward. With a faint clicking noise, the doorknob started turning, and Frankie was dancing inward with the door. He retrieved his hand, slammed the door back, and plunged inside.

Vicky followed him into a large kitchen wrapped in dark wood cabinets and long expanses of tiled counters. She closed the door behind her. The house was almost as cold as the outside. She slipped her arms into the sleeves of her coat and wrapped it around her, as if the soft wool might absorb the cold that had settled inside her. She couldn't stop shivering.

Frankie was already across the room, punching the keys on a small plate attached to the wall. "Get us some heat in a minute," he announced, and almost as if he had ordered the snow to fall or the wind to pick up, a motor kicked over somewhere in the house and the faintest tremor rippled through the tile floor.

Frankie disappeared for a moment around a doorway that led into an interior of shadows and silence. Then he was back, shrugging into a heavy-looking plaid jacket, a wool cap pulled down over his ears. He started rubbing his hands together, and she realized that he was also shivering, even though, with his arm stretched past the needles of glass still clinging to the frame, he'd seemed quiet and in control.

He threw open a door on one of cabinets and pulled out a full bottle of Wild Turkey. "Nice of them to get me the expensive stuff," he said, fumbling with the red top for a longer time than seemed necessary. He was having trouble gripping the top, unscrewing it. His fist looked like a claw, frozen halfway open.

Finally, the top was off. Frankie threw his head back and tilted the bottle into his mouth, making a loud, slurping noise. His Adam's apple moved up and down as brown threads of whiskey rolled down the sides of his cheeks and dripped into the collar of the plaid coat.

"Want some?" He held out the bottle.

Vicky shook her head.

"Nothing like a little turkey to warm up your insides." He waved the bottle in her direction again. "No? Good. More for me," he said, kicking back a chair from the table in the center of the room and flopping down. "We fucking made it," he said, before tilting the bottle into his mouth again. Then he got up and walked over to the counter as if he'd just remembered something. He picked up the phone and tossed it across the kitchen. It slammed against a cabinet and thudded on the floor, pieces of black plastic skittering under the table.

He went back to the table and sat down. "Now, all I gotta figure out is what to do with you for the next couple of days until Burton decides I'm already outta the county and calls off the hunt." He took another long drink and swung the bottle by the neck in her direction. "I think I'm gonna have to tie you up."

Oh, God, no. Vicky pulled up a chair and sat down across from him. "Where am I going, Frankie? There's no gas in the pickup. I didn't see any other houses on our hike, and you can bet I was looking. I didn't see anything but snow. So we're up here miles from anywhere with a lot of snow on the ground and freezing temperatures. You think I'm going back out there? Looks to me like I've got only one option, and that's to stay here."

Frankie held the bottle close to his chest and stared at her. "You expect me to buy that? You think I'm stupid?" He pointed the bottle toward the door. "The minute I take my eyes off you, you're gonna be outta here. You know what I'm thinking?" He took another swig of whiskey, his eyes watching her over the raised bottle. "I'm thinking you're a lousy lawyer, that's the kind of stuff you come up with." Another swig of whiskey, and his voice switched into a falsetto: "Where'd I go, Frankie? I'd freeze my butt out there." He started shaking his head, hiccupping and laughing at the same time.

"How long can we stay here?" Vicky said, trying another tack. "How do we know there's any food?"

"Trust me, there's food." He held out the bottle toward a full-length door next to the cabinets on the adjacent wall. "Pantry's full of stuff. Spent three days here last summer and had me some real feasts. Chicken soup and chili. Lots of chips and popcorn and soda pop. Man, rich people know how to eat. We can sit out two, three weeks here, 'cause I don't think they're gonna be coming up through the snow to get to their fancy mountain house 'til warm weather sets in. But I got me a problem."

Vicky sat very still, not taking her gaze off the man. There was a clicking noise somewhere beneath the floor, like mice scurrying through the vents, and the first hint of warm air drifted up along the table.

"You," Frankie said. "You're the only problem I got right now."

"I told you, I'm not foolish enough to try to get away from here on foot."

"You got a cell, don't you?" He nodded toward the bag that she'd let drop on the floor on the other side of her chair. "Let's have it." A hand stretched across the table.

Vicky kept her eyes on his as she leaned over, lifted the bag, and set it in front of him.

He studied the bag a moment, pleased with himself, a half-smile playing at the corners of his mouth. "Just what I thought." He set the bottle on the table and started digging through the bag, pulling out the contents—wallet, lipstick, comb, dayplanner, keys—like an animal rooting in the ground. Then he had the cell. He held it up like a trophy and waved it over the table a moment before he pulled it toward his face and pressed a button. A couple of seconds passed before he began laughing silently, his chest rising and falling in spasms of amusement.

"So sorry, ma'am," he said, tossing the cell onto the deflated bag and leaning over the table. The sourness of his breath made her flinch. "Seems there's no service in your mountain hideaway. And I suggest you don't try again. That's it." He slammed down an open hand on the tabletop and the cell phone jumped off the bag and clattered against the hard surface. "You're getting tied up."

"Listen to me, Frankie. You resisted arrest, fled from the police, took me at gunpoint." Vicky tried to ignore the shakiness in her voice. "You broke into a house, and now you're holding me hostage. For a man who doesn't want to go back to prison, that's where you'll be spending the rest of your life."

She was talking to his back. He'd jumped up and was throwing open drawers, working his way down along the counter, the drawers hanging into the room. "I'll tell Burton that I came with you willingly, that we had to talk privately, lawyer to client." Vicky pushed on, trying to make herself believe what she was saying. "You won't be looking at a kidnapping charge. Resisting arrest, yes. Breaking and entering." She shot a glance toward the door with the draft of icy air tunneling past the broken pane. "I'll see what kind of deal I can make. You plead guilty to a couple of charges, and a prosecutor might consider dropping the others. Trials cost a lot of money and time. Any good prosecutor . . ."

Frankie pulled a stack of kitchen towels out of the last drawer. He swung around and started toward her, shaking out the towels. "These are gonna work just fine," he said.

Vicky sprang to her feet, grabbed the top of the chair, and set it down between them. "I'm not going to let you do this, Frankie."

Quiet. Nothing but the scuff of his boots on the floor as he moved toward her and the sound of his breathing—the sound of a bellows. He shook out the last towel, tossed the others onto the table, and started toward her.

Vicky picked up the chair and slammed it hard into his chest. He tottered sideways over the table, shock and surprise fixed in his expression, and for a half-second, Vicky thought he might fall to the floor. She lifted the chair again, but before she could crash it onto his head, he sprang up and lunged at her, like a wolf on the attack, teeth bared, brown eyes lit with hatred. She felt the force of his body hit her, the sharp edge of the counter in her spine as she stumbled backward, and the explosion of pain as his fist slammed into her face. The cabinets and countertops were spinning around. She wasn't sure which direction was up and which was down, only that she was sliding somewhere. Sliding off the edge of the world.

28

FATHER JOHN SPOTTED the blue and red lights shooting like fireworks through the haze ahead. He had to jam on the brake pedal to slow the pickup behind the line of vehicles snaking into the eastern reaches of Lander. He pounded his fist against the rim of the steering wheel and inched forward behind a truck, waiting for an oncoming car to pass. He swung out. It was then that he saw the sedan stopped in the oncoming lane, two police officers leaning into the front windows. They stepped back, waving on the sedan, and Father John pulled in again behind the truck.

Roadblock. Which meant that the police were still looking for Frankie Montana.

His mouth had gone dry; he could hear his heart thumping. Frankie Montana still had Vicky. He waited until the sedan flashed past, then pulled out again and leaned on the accelerator while passing the snaking line of vehicles. His heart hammered in his ears. She could be tied up under a tarp, thrown into the trunk of a car. Montana was a madman. She could be anywhere.

He was past the roadblock now, in the traffic moving down Main Street, making up lost time. Ahead was another flash of blue and red lights, and he realized they were flashing in front of Vicky's office building. He pressed hard on the accelerator, followed a sedan through the red light at the intersection, and pulled into the curb in front of a line of white police vehicles.

Father John got out and walked back to the first vehicle. Through the fogged windows, he could see an officer hunched over, peering at something in his lap. Father John tapped on the window. Slowly, the dark head swiveled around and the glass cranked down.

"What can I do for you?" The officer had a thin face with a nose that dipped over the top of his lip. He gripped a small notepad in one hand.

"Where's Burton?" Father John asked.

"Who are you?"

"Father O'Malley."

A light of recognition flickered in the officer's eyes. He tossed his head toward the building. "Inside," he said.

Father John crossed the sidewalk and opened the wood door. He took the stairs two at a time and hurried down the corridor toward the opened door and the low hum of voices.

"Hold on." A blue uniform sleeve blocked the doorway as Father John started into the office. He knocked the arm aside—his eyes on Burton standing in the doorway on the right—and strode across the carpeted waiting area.

"Hey! You heard me!" The officer was behind him, so close that Father John had to sprint a couple of steps to escape the hand brushing at his arm.

Burton had turned around. He held up a fleshy palm, like a traffic cop at a busy intersection. "It's okay, Thompson," he said.

"What do you know?"

"Take it easy, John. We'll find her."

"What do you know?" Father John said again, the sharpness in his voice slicing through the stillness. Crowded in the office behind the sheriff was a platoon of police officers and deputies. A tall man in blue jeans and blue jacket was spreading green powder over the top of the desk. Cardboard cartons were scattered about the floor, stacks of file folders stuffed inside.

"We think Frankie was here." Burton nodded sideways, and for the first time, Father John noticed the faint trail of green powder down the side of the door frame. "Looks like he took Vicky."

"What's that supposed to mean? She's either with him or she isn't."

Flexing his shoulders inside his coat now, Burton lifted his chin, eyelids at half-mast. "She's with him, John. Dentist from downstairs saw them leaving. He thought it looked suspicious, like maybe Montana was forcing her."

Father John ran his hand over his chin. He'd pulled on his gloves somewhere back on Rendezvous Road. Still his fingers felt like ice. "He must've had a weapon. Did he have a weapon?"

"We think so." The detective gave a little nod and glanced back into the office. "She was calling my office when he showed up. She must've dropped the phone. We found it on the floor. My voice mail picked up what was going on."

"What was going on?" Father John thrust his fists into his coat pockets to keep from grabbing the man's shoulders. "Tell me, Andy."

The man shrugged. "By taking Vicky hostage, Montana thinks he bought himself a 'go' card out of the county, maybe the state. He thinks he's gonna skip out on four homicide charges. That rifle we found out at Bates? Montana purchased it eighteen months ago. He won't get very far. We got roadblocks set up on every road out of town. He hasn't left Lander. No way he would've gotten past the checkpoints."

"He could've gotten out of town before you set up the roadblocks." Father John had to swallow back the anger rising inside him—a hot, bitter taste. What did the man think? That Montana was sitting around waiting until the roadblocks went up before he tried to get away?

"Lander PD had cop cars at every exit road two minutes after they got the call from the dentist. Trust me, John. Montana's still in town."

"This is police business." The voice of the officer boomed behind them, and Father John glanced around. The officer had planted himself in the doorway, blocking the way of a tall, black-haired Indian man. It hit Father John that Adam Lone Eagle had the look of a war chief in the Old Time.

"This is my office," Adam said. He didn't flinch. "Get out of my way."

"Okay," Burton shouted.

In three steps, Adam was across the waiting room, his eyes boring into the detective. "What the hell's going on?" he said.

Burton started to explain, but the Indian waved a gloved hand between them. "I heard the news on the radio. Just tell me where Vicky is."

"We'll find her," Burton said. "Every law enforcement agency in the county is looking for her. Like I told Father John, we don't think Montana's left town."

Adam turned his head and stared across his shoulder at Father John, as if he realized for the first time that someone else was in the office. His body was still squared toward the detective. "This is your fault, Father O'Malley," he said. "Vicky's too good a lawyer to waste her talents on scum like Montana. She wouldn't have taken on a client like that if it weren't for you. You've filled her head with a lot of noble bunk about helping the poor and downtrodden. All those DUIs and assaults and drug cases that you've dragged her in on. For some reason I haven't been able to figure out, she never can say no to you. Well, I'm saying no for her. Vicky Holden has more important things to do."

"You finished, Lone Eagle?" Father John moved around until he was wedged halfway between the Indian and Burton. "Vicky makes her own decisions. I don't know any man who tried to tell her what to do and stayed around very long."

"Wait a minute here." Father John felt the detective's fingers digging past his coat sleeve into his upper arm. "This isn't helping Vicky. Just go home, both of you. I'll call you the minute we find her."

"If you find her." Adam spit out the words. He looked from Father John to the detective and back. His face was frozen in anger. Then he turned around and headed back across the outer office.

"Hothead," Burton said, almost under his breath, the minute that Adam had disappeared into the corridor. The thud of his boots started down the stairs, like a pounding drum. "That's all we need now is another hothead, like Montana isn't bad enough."

"He loves her." Father John stared past the uniformed officer into the vacant corridor. For the first time, he felt the force of the truth. No matter what Vicky felt about placing her trust in Adam Lone Eagle, the man loved her. Just like Ben had loved her, he thought, and she hadn't been able to trust him, either.

He reached past the front of his coat and fished the small notepad and pen out of his shirt pocket, then ripped out a page and scribbled his cell number. Thrusting the page at Burton, he said, "Call me if you hear anything." He waited a second for the glint of agreement in the man's eyes, then retraced his steps across the office, past the officer, and down the corridor.

A dark green pickup with wedges of snow on the roof and hood shot out of the parking lot as Father John got to the sidewalk. He watched the pickup slide into the turn onto Main and accelerate through the snow, engine roaring, clouds of snow and ice trailing it down the street.

He loves her. The truth of it pounded in Father John's head like a sledgehammer. A man she cannot trust loves her.

He crossed the sidewalk, digging his keys out of his coat pocket as he went, and waded through the slush at the curb. He got into the pickup, made a U-turn, and drove east toward the kaleidoscope of blue and red lights flickering ahead. The green pickup was nowhere in sight.

He had to wait behind six or seven vehicles to get through the roadblock—the officer peering into the cab and checking the bed. Still checking. They hadn't found her yet.

He should go back to the mission and wait for the call, he was thinking as he drove north on Highway 287. He should sit at his desk and

stare at the phone until the image burned into his eyes. Oh, yes, the rational, logical thing to do. Scruffy mounds of sagebrush flashed past
outside the windows. Back at the roadblock—he wasn't sure when he'd
known what to do—he'd simply turned the pickup in the direction of
Ethete where Lucille Montana lived. She knows, he said out loud. His
voice sounded unfamiliar, strained with worry. She knows. She knows.
Dear Lord, let her tell a priest.

THE HOUSE LOOKED deserted, curtains closed, no cars in front. The
pickup bounced across the yard, through the churned snow, and
stopped at the stoop. Father John tried to fight back the sinking feeling
that the woman wasn't home. Maybe she hadn't talked to the police, although the police had probably been here, judging by the tracks criss-
crossing the yard. Maybe she hadn't talked to anyone, just gone away
with whatever she might know that could lead him to Vicky. And there
was no one else. Dear Lord, he couldn't think of anyone else.

Father John got out of the pickup and slammed the door hard into
the stillness. He stepped onto the stoop and pounded on the door. Nothing. No sounds of footsteps inside. He pounded again. "Lucille," he
shouted. "It's Father John. I have to talk to you."

He bent his head close to the door, listening for the slightest sound of
life. When it came, it surprised him, so small and quiet, like the scuff of
slippers over carpet. Then the door began inching open and Lucille
peered up at him. Stripes of shadow fell over her face. Still he could see
that she'd been crying—the puffy face, the red-rimmed eyes.

"May I come in?" he said.

She pulled the door back, and he followed her into the dark living
room. He shut the door behind him and took a moment for his eyes to
adjust from the white glare outside. She had already walked across
the room and was leaning over the shadowy hulk of a table. A lamp
came on, throwing a circle of light over the small table and one end of
the sofa. Lucille hovered at the edge of the light. She was dressed in a

dark bathrobe that bunched up around the belt cinched at her waist. On her feet were white fluffy slippers that made her look as if she were standing in snow.

"I'm not feeling up to company right now, Father. Sorry." The woman dropped onto the far side of the sofa, away from the light.

Father John perched on a chair. "You know why I'm here, Lucille," he said. "Frankie has taken Vicky hostage. We have to find her. I think you can help."

The woman didn't say anything for a long moment, just bobbed her head up and down, as if she were trying to absorb what he'd told her. Finally, she said, "I don't know where he went, if that's what you're after. You and them cops that come around thirty minutes ago, asking the same question. Where he'd take her? It's their fault, them and the detective. If they hadn't come busting in here trying to arrest Frankie, this wouldn't have happened."

"Listen to me, Lucille," Father John said. "What Frankie's done is very serious. It will go better for him if he lets Vicky go and gives himself up. The longer he holds her hostage, the more likely it is that something might happen . . ."

"He's not gonna hurt her," Lucille cut in.

"He's scared, Lucille. He's running. Anything could happen."

"You got that right. Only reason he ran outta here this morning is 'cause he's scared. Frankie's so scared of going to prison, he don't know what he's doing. You don't know what it's like for an Indian locked up in a cell. The cops are gonna hunt him down, like he was a wolf that dragged off one of their lambs. He's not responsible, Father."

Father John felt a stab of panic. That was the point. Frankie Montana wasn't responsible. There was no telling what he might do, and the longer he had Vicky. . . . He squeezed the tip of his nose hard to block out the sense of fear—like a physical pain—surging through him. He said, "Help me, Lucille. Tell me where he might be. I'll do everything I can to help him."

"The cops'll just go shooting their way in. That's what happened out at the Bates Battlefield where the sheriff says Frankie killed those Shoshones. Bunch of soldiers and Shoshones shooting into the village, didn't care who they killed. That's what they'll do, Father. They'll kill him."

"I'm not the police, Lucille." He tried to tamp down the fear that surged inside him. He could imagine a SWAT team surrounding wherever Frankie was, going in with guns drawn. Frankie and Vicky could both be killed.

"You'll talk to him?"

It was difficult to nod at her, difficult to remain patient. "Yes," he said.

"You won't tell the cops?"

"I'll talk to him."

She was considering this, he could tell. Her eyes got darker, two black stones shining in the shadows. "I been thinking and thinking where he might've gone," she said finally. "He's scared out of his mind, so he's not gonna be thinking straight and coming up with some new place. He's gonna go where he knows." She hesitated so long that he started to think she'd changed her mind. He had to fight back the urge to shout at her, "Tell me, tell me!"

It was then that she told him.

29

YES, THE DRINKING house was most likely. Lucille had dabbed the tissue at her face, closed her fist around it, and jammed her fist against her mouth. Father John had to lean forward to hear what she was saying. She'd been thinking about it all morning. Frankie would go someplace that was familiar. What was more familiar than the rez? He wouldn't bring her *here*. Not with his mother being home. There wasn't anybody else he'd go to. He doesn't trust a lot of people. But the drinking house on the dirt road off Trosper, he'd go there.

The house was just ahead, a quiet, yellowish cube with a wooden stoop and an abandoned look. Father John turned in to the yard, the pickup bouncing across the ditch. There were no vehicles around, yet the skin of snow in front of the house had been churned up and the tracks looked fresh. He could see the squiggly lines of tires.

He slid to a stop, slammed out, and pounded on the hollow wood that bowed slightly under the blows. He waited, listening for the slightest sound. Nothing. He knocked again, waited another couple of seconds, then started walking along the front of the house to the rectangular window. Cupping his hands around his eyes, he leaned into the glass and peered through the crack at the edge of the curtains. He saw the shadowy outline of a sofa and a small table with a lamp turned on its side.

He retraced his steps and pounded again on the door, then tried the knob. It surprised him how loosely it turned in his grip. The door slid back against his weight, and he was inside the small, dimly lit room with a sofa and a couple of chairs scattered over the bare vinyl floor. No sign that anyone lived here: no papers or magazines, nothing on the table apart from the overturned lamp. An acrid smell permeated the air. He reached around the door and flipped on a light switch. Nothing happened. The only light came from the narrow columns of daylight shooting past the curtains into the shadows.

He crossed the room into the kitchen and flipped on another switch. The ceiling light stuttered for a moment before casting a yellowish glow into the middle of the room. Nothing on the counters. Nothing in the cabinets when he yanked open the doors except for the traces of what might have been salt or sugar scattered over the shelves.

He started down the hallway, checking the bedrooms on the left, on the right. He checked the bathroom. Nothing. Nothing. Just pieces of furniture left behind, cheap and flimsy looking, with dark stains on the thin, bare mattresses. Whoever had been here had left. Left in a hurry. One proposition followed the other to the only logical conclusion. Whoever used the drinking house had heard the news about Frankie and had figured that, sooner or later, the police would be at the door. They'd gotten out and taken everything that might identify them.

He went back outdoors and got into the pickup, aware of the heaviness inside him, like a weight dropped into his stomach. He worked the ignition until the engine finally turned over. The logic went further. If Frankie's friends reached that conclusion, so would Frankie. This wasn't where Frankie would bring Vicky. This wasn't the place.

If not the drinking house, where?

Father John stared over the hood at the front of the house, slabs of brown paint peeling off the siding, and tried to put the rest of it into a logical order. No one knew Frankie Montana better than his mother. He wasn't thinking straight, Lucille had said. He was too scared to think at all. Therefore, he would fall back on something familiar.

Logical. Logical.

Something familiar, somewhere else. Friends, maybe. *He doesn't trust a lot of people.* The bar in Riverton where he hung out. *He wouldn't bring her here, with me at home.* He wouldn't take her to a bar where someone would see them.

Dear Lord! Where, then?

He was half aware of the ringing noise at the edge of his thoughts—far off and out of place. A couple of seconds passed before he realized that it was his cell. He lunged for the glove compartment, his fingers tearing past the papers and maps, until they gripped the phone.

"Burton?" he said, pressing the cool plastic to his ear.

"We got a break, John." A surge of confidence in the man's voice.

Father John felt his heart turn over. "You found Vicky," he said.

"They're on their way out to Bates. We had a call from a witness who spotted an Indian couple out by Lysite in the tan pickup Frankie hot-wired. He's taking her where he took his other victims." There was a pause at the other end, almost as if the man had regretted what he'd said. "Don't worry," he hurried on. "We got deputies on the way. They'll stop the pickup before it gets to the battlefield. I'm heading there now."

"It's not the right pickup," Father John heard himself say. Logic. Logic. It was beginning to make sense now, all the propositions falling into place.

"What are you talking about?"

"Whoever killed the Shoshones," he began, feeling his way toward the conclusion, "planned to kill them at the battlefield so it would look like revenge."

"What's the point, John?"

"You said yourself that Montana's a hothead. He's not the type to plan anything. He's taken Vicky someplace that's familiar. He's fallen back on what's familiar, Burton. Bates isn't familiar to him."

"You're making a lot of assumptions, John." A horn bleeped over the man's voice.

It was true. All he had was an assumption. A logical assumption, he was thinking, and in that moment, he knew where Vicky was. "What about the houses that Montana broke into last fall?" he said. "He knows the houses, and he knows how to get inside. They're in the mountains, isolated. There won't be anybody around for another month."

"They're isolated all right. County doesn't clear the roads. Probably a foot of snow up there. He wouldn't get far."

Father John was already backing across the yard, the wheels whining in the snow. He shifted into forward, pressed down hard on the gas, and rammed the pickup across the ditch and out onto the road. "Where are the houses?" He was shouting.

"You're wrong, John. Montana and Vicky were spotted."

"Which road are the houses on?"

"Look, I don't have that information with me."

"It has to be in the files."

"Take it easy, John," Burton said. "We got a lot of men working this, and right now, they're heading toward Bates. Montana's got a gun, remember? We can't take any chances, not with witnesses saying they saw them. We don't want any more deaths. If this is a bum steer, we'll check out the houses later."

"Later! You just said he's got a gun. Vicky could be dead later."

Silence on the other end. The silence of exasperation. "Try to hold on, John. I'll get back to you the minute we know anything."

There was a click in his ear. Father John tossed the cell to the side. It clanked against the tape player and slid onto the passenger seat. He was barreling down Trosper, sliding in the mud and slush. He could feel the rear end swaying, the tires lifting off the road and plunging down. He reached over, grabbed the phone again, and punched in the numbers for information, glancing between the keys and the road. The pickup was weaving all over the place. He might have been drunk.

It was a long moment before he had the sheriff's office, with a woman's voice at the other end, breaking up. "Don't break up," he shouted. To the operator. The phone. Heaven itself. "Don't break up."

"How can I help you?" The voice was clear now.

He gave her his name and said he had to know the location of the houses that Frankie Montana had broken into last summer.

"Well, Father . . ."

He cut in over the woman's hesitation. "Montana was charged. It's a public record."

"I know, Father. The problem is, there aren't any deputies in the office right now. We've got an emergency situation. Maybe you heard. Some Indian is holding a lawyer hostage."

"He's holding her at one of those houses!"

"I don't think so, Father. He's driving north of Lysite. Soon as one of the officers gets in, I can have him look up the info . . ."

He hit the off button, then punched in the number to Vicky's office, jamming the phone to his ear, trying to hold the pickup steady through the curve onto Highway 287. He counted the number of rings: one, two, three. Then came the smooth, mechanical voice of a machine: "This is the office of Lone Eagle and Holden, attorneys-at-law. Please leave your name and number . . ."

He could feel the tightness in his jaw, the twitch of protesting muscles. Finally the message gave way to the beep. "Pick up, Adam," he shouted. "If you're there, pick up. I know where Vicky is, and I need your help. I'm on my way to the office." He pushed his coat sleeve back with the edge of the phone and glanced at his watch. Almost three o'clock, and he was thirty minutes away. "Meet me there at three-twenty," he said.

* * *

THE LIGHT WAS somewhere above, a small, round glow in the blackness. Vicky floated upward toward the light until, she realized, she had reached it, and she was staring at the gray squares of tile on the floor. And interrupting the flow of tile were wooden legs—table legs, she realized, chair legs. And something else, two brown boots were planted under the table. Above the boots, blue jeans were stretched around thick legs. Rushing over her was a rhythmic, rasping noise. Breathing, maybe. Breathing and snorting. She struggled to remember. Why couldn't she remember? She was conscious of the pain sawing into her head, breaking through the warm, cocoon feeling. She realized she had on her coat. She tried to move her arms—logs submerged in water. Finally, holding her head in one hand to keep it from breaking apart, she began pulling herself up along the hard face of a cabinet.

She remembered now: trudging up the snowy road, the cold, and Frankie Montana wrapping his arm in her coat and crashing it through the window of the house. He'd come at her with the towels that she could see dangling off the edge of the table. And the gun, she remembered it all, the gun in Frankie's belt. He'd intended to tie her up when she'd hit him with the chair before she had sunk into the blackness.

He was sitting at the table, snoring into the stillness, an arm flung out next to the whiskey bottle with about two inches of brown liquid winking at the bottom. His arm kept twitching, as if he wanted to grab something or keep something away.

Vicky kept her eyes on him for a long moment, then slowly lifted herself to her feet. Her head was pounding. She gripped the edge of the counter to steady herself, still watching the man slumped on the chair, neck twisted around, head bent into his shoulder. The stench of whiskey on his breath floated toward her and made her stomach turn. She could get out of here, she realized, head down the mountain. But he would come after her the instant he woke up, and he had a gun. How far could she get—half-mile, mile?—before he forced her back to the house.

Still watching him, half expecting his eyelids to slide open, she pushed off from the counter, moved to the table, and picked up one of the towels. She carried the towel around the table, twisting it into a rope as she went. She was floating, feet barely touching the floor, boots skating silently over the tiles.

Gently, she took hold of a corner of his shirt sleeve and pulled the arm that was hanging at his side toward the back of the chair. She looped the rope around the chair rung, then around his lower arm, and—slowly, carefully—pulled his arm next to the rung. After making another couple of loops, she tied the ends of the towel into three hard knots.

She reached around, grabbed another towel, and twisted it into a rope before tugging at his other sleeve and dragging that arm across the table. The black tattoo crawled out from beneath the cuff of his sleeve. Frankie's head swung around. She held her breath. Finally he made a grunting noise and dropped his head forward until the folds of his chin pleated against his chest. She waited a moment before easing the arm down and tying it to the chair. His head lolled over his chest. He was shifting about, leaning outward, pulling at the constraints.

Then he was quiet, even relaxed looking, leaning into the constraints, head thrown back, Adam's apple bulging. Vicky swept the other towels off the table, dropped down onto her knees, and went through the motions: tugging on his jeans, dragging his legs back to the chair legs, looping and tying the towels.

She got back to her feet and stared at the black handle of the gun showing above his belt. All she had to do was take it, but her hands were shaking. It was hard to focus past the pain in her head. She had to get out of here. He'd started snoring again, a loud, menacing noise that propelled her around the table. She picked up her bag and started for the door. Then she went back, slipped the gun past the man's belly, the dampness of his shirt clinging to her hand. She stuffed the gun inside her bag, crossed the room again, and threw open the door. Daylight was starting to fade; it would be dark soon. A shower of sharp, moist crystals blew over her.

"Don't leave me." The voice might have emerged out of a fog.

Vicky glanced around at the man slumped back against the chair, arms tied at his sides. He looked pitiful. Not the man who had held a gun on her, forced her to drive up here into this isolation of snow and cold, the man who had knocked her unconscious.

"Please don't leave me." He couldn't conceal the panic. "Tied up like this. Don't, Vicky. Please. I'll go nuts tied up like this. I'm not an animal, Vicky. Don't leave me in a trap like this just waiting . . . waiting for them to come and kill me."

"I'll send Burton," she said. "Nobody's going to kill you."

"It don't matter. They're gonna put me away, Vicky, and it's the same thing, 'cause I'm gonna die in prison. I didn't kill them Shoshones. I swear to you by all the ancestors. I swear it."

"You assaulted Hunter and the Crispin brothers; then you shot them out at Bates. You called Father Nathan Owens with the first weird tape."

"What are you talkin' about?" Alarm and questions mingled in the man's expression.

"You figured out that you'd called the wrong mission, because you made the second call to Father John. He was the priest you wanted to send the message to. You knew he'd understand the clues and go to Bates. You wanted the bodies found, didn't you? You wanted to gloat. What a big, smart man you are."

"Tapes?" Frankie said. "I don't know nothing about tapes."

"Come on, Frankie. The taped messages you made at the radio station. What? A buddy of yours let you in? Or did you keep a key?"

Frankie tilted his head back and blinked up at the ceiling. "You're crazier than I am," he said. "Couple computers went missing when I was working at the station, so they fired me. Tol' me if I so much as drive into the parking lot, they're gonna sic the police on me. You think I got buddies there? They hate me there."

Vicky gripped the knob and leaned into the door. The cold air had already penetrated her coat. She closed her eyes a moment against the dull throbbing in her head. She had it all wrong.

"Who, then, Frankie?" she said. "Who wanted the Shoshones dead?"

"I don't know. I don't know." He was shaking his head so hard that she thought he might turn the chair over. "Somebody took my rifle at the bar, like I tol' you. You never listened."

She was still gripping the knob hard. She could see the puffs of snow blowing off the trees, and beyond the line of trees, nothing but the shadows of boulders climbing the slopes. Somewhere in the distance, an animal was howling into the silence. A freezing gust swept past her that even made Frankie flinch. He was tied up, she told herself. Helpless.

Except that Frankie Montana wasn't helpless. He was playing for time. She could see his fingers curled up toward his wrist—working on the knots. He could burst free at any moment.

She buttoned her coat, pulled the collar up around her ears, and, gripping her bag close, trying to ignore the pain coursing inside her head, went outside.

"Vicky!" Frankie shouted behind her as she slammed the door.

30

ADAM LONE EAGLE stood behind the fogged window in the entrance, a hulking presence in a sheepskin jacket, everything about him tense and impatient. Father John spotted the man as he pulled into the curb. Before he got across the sidewalk, Adam had flung open the door and stationed himself in front, half in and half out of the building. He squinted out into the wind gusting along Main Street.

"This better be good," he said, stepping back into the building ahead of Father John, then reaching around to shut the door. His eyes were locked in a hard stare. "I was on the way to Bates when I checked my messages. If you dragged me back here when Vicky's out there with a madman . . ."

"They're not out there," Father John said, wishing that he had the confidence he heard in his own voice. All he had was a logical assumption, but logic wasn't always the same as fact.

"Then where the hell did Montana take her?"

"I think he headed into the mountains to one of the houses he broke into."

"You gotta be joking. There's a lot of snow up there, and another storm's coming in. The back roads'll be impassable."

"That's why we have to get up there, Adam," Father John said. "It could take hours before Burton digs out the information and sends a car. If the pickup they're in gets stalled, Frankie might force her to get out and walk. If the temperature drops . . ." He didn't have to finish the thought. The Indian was peering through the fog growing over the window, the mixture of warmth in the building and their own breaths and worry.

"Frankie was Vicky's client. The location of the houses is in her files," Father John hurried on, but Adam had already turned and was starting up the stairs. Father John followed him. Doors to the offices on the first floor were shut tight against any weekend intrusion. So were the doors coming into view beyond the railing on the second floor. The thud of their boots rumbled through the emptiness.

They reached the top and started down the corridor. Father John was aware of the other man digging underneath his jacket and pulling a ring of keys from his jeans pocket. The keys clinked together like a ringing bell. He stopped at the third door, gave the key a quick turn in the lock, and, pushing the door open, went inside. Father John stayed with him, across the waiting room, through the opened door to the private office on the right.

Adam stopped in the middle of the room. He was surveying the cartons scattered about the floor, file folders bulging over the tops, a look of regret in the way that his eyes moved from one to the other. "We have to find the closed cases," he said, dropping to one knee, both hands rifling through the files in the nearest carton.

Father John crouched beside another box and began looking through those files, checking the names on the tabs: Blackwater, Buttress. He reached the Ms. Many Horses. Menton. Miner.

He went to the next carton, aware that Adam had already moved on. He flipped through the files again, more slowly now.

"Montana," Father John said, hauling out a thick file. He stood up and plopped it on top of the desk, smeared with a greenish powder.

Adam was at his side, opening the file, rummaging through the sheets inside. "A record of petty offenses as long as his arm," he muttered, still rummaging. "Spent a month in the BIA jail for battery. Another four months in county jail on an assault charge. Would have been there longer if Vicky hadn't gotten the charge reduced. Here it is," he said, pulling out several pages stapled together. "Breaking and entering charges dismissed on a technicality." He glanced down the top page, then flipped to the next, talking and reading at the same time. "The bastard had the sense to ask for an attorney after he was arrested. The deputy ignored the request and continued firing questions." He paused, still staring at one of the pages. "Three houses about a mile apart on a dirt road up in Sinks Canyon."

"It'll take most of an hour to get there." Father John could hear the anxiety in his voice. He headed back across the office, down the corridor, and down the stairs. Adam's boots thudded behind him. An hour! The thought banged in Father John's head like a drum. Frankie had taken her at least five hours ago. They'd been up there hours. People died in the cold. If they'd stalled, if they'd tried to hike . . .

Dear Lord. Let them be in a house.

"We'll take my pickup," Adam said when they reached the sidewalk. "I've still got winter gear in the lockbox." The Indian headed around the building toward the parking lot. Father John stayed in his footsteps.

VICKY WASN'T SURE how long she'd been hiking. Time blurred, like the trees and snow and sky around her. It was starting to snow again, and darkness was coming on, metallic blue shadows dropping over the mountain slopes and sweeping through the trees. She'd kept to their tracks, trying to step where they'd stepped, but sometimes the steps were too far apart. She couldn't reach the next one—how had she managed before?—and she had to tread through the unbroken snow, pain bursting through her head with each step.

She pulled the cell phone out of her coat pocket where she'd put it after the first time she'd tried to call out. "No service" had blinked red in the window and she'd tried again and again. Each time she came around a switchback, she punched in 911, and each time she got the same message. Her fingers kept sliding off the keys. She tried to grip the phone harder, feeling a wave of panic at the idea of dropping the phone and watching it disappear into a drift, but her hand had gone numb. She couldn't tell if she was gripping it hard enough. *She had to grip it hard enough.* She managed to press the three keys. Same message. She wrapped her other hand around the bottom of the phone and held on tight as she slipped it back into her pocket. God, it was her only lifeline. It might work as she got farther down the mountain. It had to work!

She reached the pickup and veered through the drifts. There was a chance that the owner had stowed a blanket or extra gloves, even fleece-lined boots, in the back. The lockbox was beneath the rear window— she could see it as she waded toward the rear. She reached over the metal edge, conscious of the deep, sharp stab of cold that cut into the flesh of her arm that touched the metal. She tried to lift the lid. Frozen in place, locked. It might as well have been welded shut. There was nothing else in the pickup bed: no loose tools, no hammer or crossbar that she might use to pry open the box, nothing but the ribbed floor of the bed under the snow. She felt the tears curling down her cheeks, warm at first—it surprised her—then a sharp sting of ice.

She started off again. An easier trek now, she told herself. Just stay in one of the tire tracks. One foot in front of the other, down, down. She could sense the elevation dropping beneath her and she tilted forward with her own momentum. Flecks of snow were sticking to her eyelashes, and she had to keep brushing them away. The snow-covered ground seemed to reflect whatever remained of the daylight, so that she was moving through a double world: darkness pressing down on light, as if night and day had butted up against each other.

"Crazy!" she said out loud, and the sound of her own voice, oddly enough, was almost comforting. She had to think straight, stay rational, keep moving. Her head was now a concentrated mass of pain. She could no longer feel her feet. Her legs were like fence posts that she dropped into the snowy track, one after the other. So heavy, the weight of them—these fence posts, dragging her down with them.

She made her way around another switchback, scarcely aware that she'd made the turn, only that the shadows had gotten deeper and that the snow had turned blue. She fumbled again for the cell phone and dragged it out of her pocket. Then, cradling it in both gloves, she pushed in the keys. No service. No service. No service. She could feel the warmth trickling down her cheeks again, then the swift change to ice. Ice against ice, she thought. She managed to stuff the phone back into her pocket and kept going. Waves of exhaustion had started moving through her, the weight of the fence posts bigger and heavier with each step. Each breath cut like a blade into her chest. She cupped her hands around her nose and mouth and made a pocket of air, warmed by the exhalation of her own breath, which she tried to suck back in.

Another switchback—a wide, wide curve that took so long to work around. She would rest here, she thought. Sink into the snow just for a moment. It struck her that the snow would be warm, a thick blanket in which she could wrap herself against the cold. Just for a moment, until the exhaustion passed and the heavy weights became lighter.

She would die then. The truth hit her like a blow that she hadn't seen coming—a blow from another world, a world of warmth and sunshine. If she let herself stop, she would die within minutes, that was the truth.

She would not die here. Not on this mountain in the darkness and blue snow. She would keep going and keep going until the cell started to work, until she reached the highway and caught a ride. For a moment, the exhaustion seemed to fade and the weight became lighter before they returned with a force that crashed into her. She had the sense that she was folding downward, floating with the snow, and there was nothing she could do.

THEY'D DRIVEN MOST of the way in silence. There was no need for words. Father John felt as if their thoughts were tethered together, the same thoughts running in both of their heads, the same dread coursing through them, watching the gray dusk sink into darkness and snow starting to fly in the headlights.

He smoothed out the map folded on his thigh and traced Highway 131 with his index finger in the dashboard light. Another mile and they would start into the sharp curves. "The road should be up ahead," he said. What was he trying to prove? Adam knew where the dirt road intersected the highway. Still, Father John had dragged the map out of the glove compartment, folded it down into the slice of Sinks Canyon and the little dotted lines that represented the maze of dirt roads. What was that all about? A pathetic attempt to reassure himself, a thick, gloved finger tracing their progress, as if the tracing itself would hurry them on.

"There it is," Adam said, and in the sense of relief sounding in the man's voice, Father John realized that Adam had also been trying to reassure himself, gripping the wheel as if he could push the pickup forward, staring into the headlights for some sign that they were right, that the tan pickup was ahead.

There they were—parallel tracks veering to the right onto a narrow road that snaked upward through a dark corridor of pines. Father John could feel the pickup begin to slow as Adam steered into the tracks. They started climbing immediately. The snow was coming down harder; the trees were thicker, with snow mounded around the trunks. Branches tipped with snow knocked against his side of the pickup. The engine growled through a switchback, then another. They bumped over a boulder hidden under the snow, and Father John gripped the dashboard to keep from being pitched into the windshield. He stared ahead at the mountain looming over them, the gray sky pressing down. If Vicky were out in this—Dear Lord!—how would they ever find her? He struggled to push the thought away, forcing himself to concentrate on the parallel line of tracks running ahead, as if he were the one driving, gripping the steering wheel, pushing on the accelerator.

They'd come around another switchback when Father John saw the hump in the middle of the road, black strips, like the fur of an animal, poking through the snow. Adam had seen it too because he was pumping the brake pedal. The rear tires were whining and spinning, the bed of the pickup shimmying sideways.

Father John was out of the cab before the pickup came to a stop. It was no animal—he could see that now. It was a human shape in the snow. There was an absolute stillness about it, like the stillness about the bodies at Bates.

31

FATHER JOHN DROPPED down on his knees beside the body and started brushing at the snow, barely aware of Adam on the other side. Both brushing until the black hair began to emerge, then her face, as still as the snow wedged inside the collar of her black coat.

"Vicky!" It was Adam's voice edged with panic, or maybe his own. Father John wasn't sure. He'd taken off his glove and was running his fingers along the side of her neck, searching for a pulse. Her face looked still and gray. Strands of black hair looped into the snow.

He had the pulse now, slow and regular and faint.

"Vicky!" he shouted. "Wake up!"

A couple of seconds passed, the blur of a nightmare. Adam shouting her name over and over, still brushing away the snow, and the dark expanse of sky and trees looming over them. Father John wrapped his hands around hers and began massaging them. Her black gloves felt as brittle as glass next to his palms. "Wake up, Vicky," he said, keeping his voice soft, as if the softness might slip into her dreams and bring her back. It was another moment before he saw her eyelids flicker, the tiny crystals clinging to her eyelashes. Slowly, slowly, her eyes came open. Dark, uncomprehending eyes stared up at him.

"We've got you," he said, his voice still soft. "Adam and I are going to take you to the hospital."

She stirred a little, gathering her forces, and as she did so, she turned her head toward Adam.

"You'll be okay, honey," Adam said.

Father John got his feet under him. He slipped his arms around her and began lifting her up, aware that Adam was also lifting her. It didn't take both of them, he thought. She was as light as the snow. "Get the blankets," Father John said.

He carried her around the passenger door, still hanging open toward the trees, slid her onto the seat, and got in beside her. He pulled the door shut and began adjusting the heat, adjusting the vents. Hot air started to pour around them. Over the hum of the motor came the brittle sound of metal creaking and thumping in the cold. He glanced back. Adam's shadow moved past the rear window.

Father John slid his arms around her and began rubbing her back, the small knobs of her spine beneath the thick layer of her coat. Even the coat felt stiff with frost. He picked up her hand, removed her glove, and started massaging the fingers that felt like dead twigs, the small, stiff palm, the bare wrist. He did the same with her other hand. She seemed to be coming back to life a little, rolling her head about, looking around the cab. "How did you know?" she said.

The driver's door flung open and a block of cold air crashed into the warmth. Adam ducked inside with the cold and began draping a blanket around Vicky, tucking it in at the sides, wrapping it around her feet. Like a father tucking in his child, Father John thought, as he tugged at the edge of the blanket and wrapped it about her head, leaving a small space for her nose and mouth, then reined her to him again. "You're going to be okay," he said.

Adam was settled behind the wheel now, the driver's door shut, a cocoon of warm air enveloping the cab. He started shifting the gear: forward, reverse. They were rocking back and forth, the engine growling. The heater sputtered a moment, then went back to emitting a stream of hot air.

Father John tilted his head sideways until he could see around the dark edges of the blanket. Vicky was staring at him from out of the shadows. "Do you know where Frankie is?" he asked.

"We're taking her to the hospital," Adam said. The words were strained, spoken through clenched teeth. He twisted around and stared out the rear window as the pickup started bumping backward, the tires scrambling for traction.

"He didn't kill the Shoshones." Vicky's voice was so soft that Father John had to lean closer to hear.

"Listen to me, Vicky," he said again. "Do you know where he is? We can't leave him out in the cold."

"We're leaving him," Adam said. The tires had settled into the tracks, and the pickup was rocketing dangerously backward down the road.

"Hold up, for Godsakes!" Father John heard himself shouting. His own sense of disbelief filled the cab like an unseen presence.

"All I care about is getting Vicky to the hospital and making sure she's okay." Adam didn't take his eyes off the rear window.

"Stop the pickup and let me out."

"What? Are you nuts?" For the briefest moment, Adam glanced across Vicky and locked eyes with Father John. "You want to die out there with a murderer?"

Father John felt the pressure of Vicky's hand against his and he realized that she was trying to say something. He bent his head close to her.

"The house," she said, her voice little more than a whisper. "We ran out of gas. We had to hike to the house."

"Frankie's in a house?" He repeated, making certain he'd heard it right.

"Up there." Vicky tossed her head sideways toward the mountain sloping into the darkness. "I got away."

For the first time, Father John felt himself begin to relax. Vicky was beginning to sound like herself. She was herself. Somehow she'd gotten away from Frankie Montana. She'd fled whatever house he'd taken her to. The man might not even know she was gone, but when he figured it out—when he figured it out, he would come after her.

Father John held her close for a moment. Thank God. Thank God. They'd gotten to her before Frankie had found her. He could almost sense the same wave of relief washing over Adam, still twisted around, peering out the rear window, one hand gripping the wheel.

"Frankie's innocent," Vicky said.

"You don't know what you're saying," Adam said, but in a gentle way. He might have been correcting a child. "You want to believe he's innocent, that's all. He took you hostage at gunpoint. Drove you up here where there's nobody around. God knows what he might have done if you hadn't gotten away. The man's capable of anything."

"What makes you think he didn't kill the Shoshones?" Father John kept his eyes lowered on Vicky. She'd reached up, pushed away the blanket, and leaned her head back against the seat. Light from the dashboard glowed on her face. There was a hint of color coming into her cheeks.

"He didn't do it, John," she said.

They might have been the only ones in the pickup, Father John thought, or maybe it was just that she sensed that he was the one who believed her.

"He's scared," she went on. "He's out of his mind with the fear of prison."

"So he kidnaps you?" Adam didn't try to hide the disdain. "He just bought himself a one-way ticket to prison, Vicky. He's guilty as hell."

"Not of homicide." She hesitated. "I feel sorry for him."

"My God, Vicky," Adam said.

"He didn't make the tape recording, John," Vicky said. They were alone again.

"What are you talking about?" Adam slowed the pickup until it skidded to a stop. Squaring himself to the front, he shifted into forward and, giving the wheel a sharp turn, began maneuvering the pickup around a depression in the road. Then they were hurtling forward down the tracks.

"The taped messages about the bodies at Bates," Father John told the man. The tracks emptied into the highway ahead, and Adam eased on the brake and pulled the steering wheel into the turn. The tires made a thumping noise against the asphalt under the snow. Far below, flashing through the trees, were the signs of life: headlights flashing, dots of lights flickering through the black expanse of trees.

"The radio station threatened to call the cops if Frankie showed up in the parking lot," Vicky went on, as if the interruption hadn't occurred. "He says he hasn't been near the place."

"He's lying," Adam said.

Maybe not, Father John was thinking. Vicky had spent most of the day with Frankie. He'd held her at gunpoint. She had every reason to hate him, and yet . . . she felt sorry for him. She had the sense that the man was desperate. Father John had learned to trust her feelings, even when he hadn't understood, even when they had seemed so— What was it? Illogical? Someone could have gone to a lot of trouble to make Frankie Montana look like the killer. A perfect setup with the perfect fall guy.

They were plunging down the highway, the glow of lights in Lander rising toward them. Adam had pulled out a cell and was holding it in one hand, the tips of his gloved fingers working the keys while his other hand gripped the rim of the steering wheel. He pressed the cell against one ear. "Patch me through to Detective Burton," he barked. A moment passed, then, "Adam Lone Eagle here. We found Vicky in Sinks Canyon. Montana took her to one of the houses he broke into last fall. He's still holed up there."

"I left him tied up," Vicky said.

Father John dropped his head and peered at her, aware that Adam had taken his eyes off the road and was also staring at her. "You tied him up?" Adam said.

The incredulity in the man's voice matched his own surprise, Father John thought. Beneath the layers of the blanket and her coat, he could feel Vicky give a little shrug of her shoulders. "Frankie was passed out," she said.

"Montana could be tied up," Adam said into the cell. "That's right. Tied up." Another pause. "Yeah, maybe he's gotten himself free by now. The pickup's out of gas. He can either try to hike out or stay put. I'd say he'll stay put."

Adam hit another key and slipped the cell across his chest into the inside pocket of his sheepskin coat. "It'll be awhile before Burton can get a couple of cars up there," he said, his eyes glued to the windshield and the snow-slicked street running into the western edges of town. "They'll get that bastard."

A couple of blocks back, Father John had spotted the blue sign with the white *H* and the arrow pointing in the direction of the hospital. The inside of the pickup was beginning to feel like a sauna, but Vicky was still shivering. He could feel the sudden, jerky spasms beneath the layers of blanket and coat. He stopped himself from telling Adam to step on it. There was no need. Parked vehicles, trees, bungalows flashed by in a blur of falling snow and shadows. The man had the accelerator floored.

FATHER JOHN AND Adam left the hospital and walked together in silence across the parking lot to the spot where Adam had left the pickup after they'd taken Vicky to the emergency entrance. She would be fine, the doctor had assured them. A big man, blond hair, reddish face, green scrubs, and white athletic shoes, exuding confidence. Just fine. Oh, she'd been close to hypothermia, but they'd gotten her body temperature back up, almost normal. She had some frostbite on her toes and fingers, a little frostbite on her nose and ears. And a mild concussion. They'd keep her for observation tonight. If all went well, and he certainly expected that would be the case, she could go home tomorrow. She should rest a few days, take it easy.

"I'll get Vicky at the hospital in the morning," Adam said.

They were at the pickup, and Father John opened the passenger door and got inside.

"Look, John." The Lakota settled himself behind the steering wheel and went on. "I owe you an apology."

"You don't owe me . . ."

The man cut in, "I owe you an apology." He started the engine, guided the pickup across the lot, and turned onto Bishop Randall Drive. "I knew you'd figured out where Montana had taken her the minute you called me. I didn't want to admit that you knew where to find her. I wanted to find her, you see. I wanted to be her hero. I'm in love with her. I'm sure you can understand that." He'd hurried on, not waiting for a response, and Father John had been grateful for that. There was no response. "I'm hoping she can learn to love me," Adam said.

Father John left his eyes on the man a moment, then turned back to the windshield. They were on Main Street now, pickups and sedans lumbering past, snow fanning from the wheels. The reflection of headlights shone in the storefront windows. "I'm not holding onto her," he said.

"Oh, but you are," Adam said.

IT WAS WHEN the road bent into Circle Drive and the headlights switched through the trees that Father John saw the vehicles in front of the administration building: a white van with a satellite dish fixed to the roof, two SUVs, and a couple of sedans. He pulled in next to the van with black letters sprawled across the side—KLTV—and slammed out of the pickup.

A half-dozen people began rising off the bench and peeling themselves away from the walls as Father John came through the front door.

Father Ian was paddling through the crowd. "You have visitors, John," he said.

Liam Harrison stepped around the other priest. "A few questions, Father O'Malley. Hope you don't mind." He ran his tongue over the tip of his index finger, flipped back the pages of the small pad cupped in his fleshy hand, and hurried on. "Looks like Arapahos and Shoshones are at war again, just like in Professor Lambert's book. Shoshones are looking for revenge for the four men killed at Bates. What can you tell us, Father? They send you any clues, like the Arapahos did?"

"Clues about what?" Father John let his gaze run over the reporters craning around Harrison, two women, four men, clutching notepads and pens, with the stretched faces of wolves catching the first sniff of prey in the air.

"I tried to explain, John." Ian elbowed past Harrison. "I told them you probably haven't heard the news, but they insisted upon hanging around."

"You'd better tell me, Ian." Father John said. He could feel the tenseness in the atmosphere.

"Bunch of Shoshones went on a rampage in Ethete." This from Harrison, waving the notepad. "Smashed up seven or eight vehicles with bats, hurled rocks through the windows at the gas station. Police arrested two men, but the rest got away. Hightailed it back to their own territory. Folks over in Fort Washakie are claiming they don't know anything about the attack, putting on real innocent faces."

"Looks like the first counterassault in a modern tribal war," one of the women put in, dark haired with a bony, hawklike face, and the note of authority in her voice. "Did they send you any messages, Father?"

Father John was still trying to get his mind around the news. Skulking like a shadow at the back of his thoughts, he realized, was the possibility that Shoshones might retaliate for the murders at Bates, but he hadn't wanted to admit it. He hadn't wanted the shadow to emerge into the light.

"Was anyone hurt?" he asked.

"Not this time," Harrison announced. Then he began hammering the questions: What do you know about Montana's escape? Is it true his lawyer helped him get out of the county? You and Vicky Holden are friends, right? What's their plan? Keep Montana out of jail while they plot a defense? Where d'ya think they went?

The questions rang like a gong in Father John's head. And his answers would determine what came next: the black headlines waving like banners in tomorrow's newspapers, proclaiming war between the tribes, *summoning* people to war. He could imagine the television news, the urgent voices filled with regret about the war that they had proclaimed.

He stole a glance at his watch. Ten minutes before the religious education meeting. Pickups would start rattling around Circle Drive at any moment. The reporters would have a field day swarming over his parishioners.

"You're asking the wrong man." Father John stepped back and pulled the door open. The cold whipped through the corridor, and a couple of the reporters set about turning up their collars and snapping the fronts of their jackets. New questions were crowding into his mind, now. If Frankie Montana didn't lure the Shoshones out to Bates and murder them, who did? Who wanted to cause trouble on the reservation? Set Arapahos against Shoshones? Rip open old wounds and give the reporters the story they'd been hoping for?

He was only partly aware of ushering the reporters through the door, one arm swinging back and forth like a traffic cop—get out, get out—as if the motion of air could propel them outside. "Take your questions to Detective Burton," he heard himself say, his thoughts stuck on Edie Bradbury and Jason Rizzo. He could see the girl, small and pale and blond, scared and hurt because Trent was going to break up with her. Turning to Rizzo . . .

She had turned to Rizzo at the hospital, it was true. Now the image of the man was in his head: big and round shouldered in his black leather jacket with all the metal studs and chains, the squinting eyes that had watched an Indian take his girl, the tattooed wolf running across his knuckles. Maybe Rizzo had worked out an elaborate scheme to get revenge, prove to Edie how tough he was. Maybe he'd overheard Trent Hunter and the other Shoshones at the Cowboy Bar and Grill, talking over plans to visit the Bates Battlefield last Saturday. Or maybe Edie had told him . . .

Maybe. But where was the evidence? It was Frankie Montana that Burton had charged with the homicides.

He's not guilty. The sound of Vicky's voice kept punctuating his thoughts, like the underlying rumble of a drum.

The reporters were out the door now, filing down the snow-swept steps glistening in the streetlamps, shoulders hunched against the falling snow. Liam Harrison was the last to leave, and Father John could see the reluctance in the forward pitch of the man's head. He was halfway down the steps when he swung around. "You surprise me, Father O'Malley," he said, turning his face up into the glow of light. "You think that not telling us what you know is gonna stop the war? You got your head stuck in the sand, Father. This war's just getting started."

Father John shut the door hard. He could still feel the tremor in his hand as he turned to the other priest stationed a few feet down the corridor. "The religious ed meeting is yours tonight," he said.

Ian stared at him a moment. "Oh, that's great," he said. "What am I supposed to tell them when they ask where the pastor is?"

"You'll think of something." Father John reached around for the knob, pulled the door open, and headed out. He was backing the pickup into Circle Drive when he caught a glimpse of his assistant standing in the doorway, tracks of surprise and anger shadowing his face.

Father John shifted into forward and followed the other vehicles out to Seventeen-Mile Road. A few minutes later he was heading north on Highway 789 toward Riverton.

32

"COWBOY BAR AND Grill." The red and yellow neon letters blinked into the snow from the sign over the parking lot. Pale streams of colored lights ran over the two or three pickups nosed against the brick building and across the snow churned up in the parking lot. Father John parked close to the front. The minute he opened the door, the smells of whiskey and beer slammed into him. He held his breath a moment and peered through the dim, smoky light of what might have been a log cabin, with log walls and plank floor. A couple of cowboys and their girlfriends sat at tables in the middle of the room, lingering over the remains of hamburgers and fries in plastic baskets with paper napkins poking over the tops, sipping at tall glasses of golden colored beer. Through a wide doorway, he could see other cowboys shooting pool.

Father John unsnapped his coat, headed over to the bar that hugged the wall on the right, and straddled a stool. The bartender moved down the other side of the bar. He had the look of a drill sergeant with a pale, clean-shaven face and a bald head that shimmered in the lights flashing from the Coors sign over the bottles lining the back wall.

"What'll it be?" He slapped a white napkin onto the bar and fixed Father John with an annoyed stare. "You planning on eating, better get your order in right away. Kitchen's getting ready to close."

"Coffee," Father John said.

The man drummed his knuckles on the bar. The knocking sound cut through the buzz of conversations behind them. "You come into a bar for a cup of coffee and that's it? How about something to warm up the coffee?"

Father John lifted the palm of one hand off the bar and pushed away the suggestion. "I'm looking for somebody," he said.

"If you're a cop, you gotta be new around here. I know all the cops. What're you? New FBI agent?"

"The pastor at St. Francis Mission."

The man rocked backwards. New flecks of interest came into his eyes. "No kidding! You wouldn't be looking for your partner, now would you? Haven't seen him tonight, but sometimes he comes in later. Not looking for food, just like you. Only he likes a couple shots of Jim Beam."

Father John didn't say anything. He glanced around at the smoke wafting over the tables, the cowboys leaning on elbows, balancing cigarettes between thumb and first two fingers, never moving the cigarettes more than an inch from their lips. It explained so much, he was thinking. It explained everything: the evenings away from the mission—just visiting folks, Ian said—the visits to the hospital that turned into long afternoons and missed dinners. Ian was here. But then, hadn't he known? Ian was a controlled alcoholic, wasn't that what he called himself? He could *control* his drinking, and it wasn't his fault—now was it?—that Father John couldn't do the same.

He turned back to the bar. A mug of coffee sat in front of him, a little ribbon of steam curling upward. He picked up the mug and took a sip. He could feel the hot liquid burning a line down his chest. "I'm looking for a man named Jason Rizzo," he said. "Does he come around here?"

"Ah!" The bartender thumped his fist on the edge of the bar. "I know who you are now. The Indian priest that found those dead Shoshones at Bates. You ask me, them Indians was nice guys. Never give me any guff. Used to come in here two, three times a week, order up hamburgers and coffee, maybe some beer, sit over there." He nodded toward the table near the door where a cowboy had slipped his arm around the woman beside him and was blowing into her blond hair. "They was students at the college. Liked to sit around here and kibbitz, you know what I mean? Talk about whatever they was studying. Sometimes they'd sit over there with their books propped up in front of 'em, eating their hamburgers and not talking, just reading. Cops get that Arapaho that killed them yet? Hear him and his Arapaho lawyer hightailed it out of the county."

"You know him?" Father John took another sip of coffee.

"Frankie Montana? Yeah, I know that Arapaho and that piece of shit, Rizzo." He leaned down over the bar, and the sour smell of his breath floated upward. "They're the same, you ask me. Troublemakers. Couple months ago, I made Rizzo persona non grata, you get my drift. Shows his butt around here and my buddies"—he tossed his head toward the cowboys shooting pool in the back—"are gonna make him wish he'd gone someplace else."

The man pulled a white towel out from beneath the counter and began snapping it against the edge. "Should've tossed Montana out the same time. Sitting over there." He nodded toward the table in back. "Hell, I didn't mind pouring his beer, long as he was paying. He was always watchin' the Shoshones. Sometimes he'd start shouting how he was gonna beat their asses, show 'em Arapahos was boss, stuff like that. One night he came roaring in here shouting how the Shoshones stole his rifle out of his pickup and how it was my fault 'cause I don't run a secure parking lot where folks can leave things without them damn Indians making off with 'em, and how I was gonna pay him for his rifle. That's when I said, 'Montana, shut up, or you're outta here.' Hell, should've run him out then, except I'd get charged with discriminating against Indians. Should've done it anyway. Turns out he's a fucking killer. They ain't never gonna catch that Indian. Guy like that knows how to run and hide."

"Why did you ban Rizzo?" Father John said.

The bald head was shaking, lights dancing across the scalp. The towel snapped two or three times. "Started a fight out in the parking lot with the Shoshones, 'cause one of 'em, Trent Hunter it was, took up with his girlfriend." He gave a snort that sounded like he was blowing his nose. "White supremacist sure as hell didn't like that! One time he barged in here, took hold of the girl, and dragged her out of the chair. Dragged her across the floor like she was a rag doll. Would've dragged her on out the door, you ask me, if them Shoshones hadn't jumped up and went after him. I jumped over this here bar, and me and my buddies let him have a taste of this." He made a fist and shook it over the bar like a club. "That's when I tol' him, 'Don't show your butt around here.'"

Father John kept working at his coffee. He didn't say anything. He knew from years of counseling not to interrupt a train of thought after it had started.

The bartender rolled his thick shoulders and went on, "She was a pretty thing, real thin and pale. Looked like a good wind would knock her over. Looked scared all the time, but for a couple months there, Hunter seemed to be looking out for her, you know what I mean? After a while, that Shoshone cooled off, you ask me. Maybe got tired of taking care of her, how do I know? Maybe got tired of waiting for Rizzo to jump out of the shadows, but I seen that she wasn't coming in with him lately. Couple of times she came in looking for him, that's all I know."

"When was the last time you saw Montana?" he said.

"Bastard didn't show up for last couple of weeks. Happiest weeks in my life. Then, three, four days ago, he's back there in his so-called office, drinking beer." He jammed a finger at the coffee mug. "Want a refill?"

Father John gave the mug a nudge. It was making sense, he thought, watching the steaming liquid arch out of the pot. Then the bartender turned around and began swishing the empty pot through the water in a sink. Frankie's story about somebody stealing his rifle out in the parking lot, and Lou Hunter's story about Trent breaking up with Edie. All making sense, adding up to . . . what? He was juggling a lot of propositions, none of which fit into a logical pattern. There was no logical conclusion.

But there was something. He took another draw of coffee. It washed down easily, lukewarm now. Neither Rizzo nor Montana had come to the Cowboy Bar and Grill before the murders, which meant they couldn't have overheard the Shoshones talking about going to Bates. And there was something else; Father John could still hear the voice of Lou Crispin: *My boys said they was gonna meet somebody.* Trent and the Crispin brothers had gone to Bates to meet somebody they had trusted. They would never have trusted Montana or Rizzo.

But there was still the girl. Hunter would have trusted the girl.

Father John drained the last of the coffee, pulled a dollar bill out of his jeans pocket, and pushed it across the bar. "Thanks," he said to the bartender's back.

The man was still swishing the glasses. He stopped and turned around, wiping his hands on the towel tied at his waist. "You ask me, neither of them white girls oughtta be hanging around them Indians. Sooner or later, there's gonna be trouble. See what happened to them Shoshones? Shot dead out on some old battlefield. Could've happened to them girls, too, you ask me."

"There was another girl?" Father John straddled the stool again.

"A real looker." The bartender spread his hands under his chest, as if he were palming two basketballs. "You get my drift? Every cowboy in the place had his eyes bugging out when she came in the place."

"Any idea of who she is?"

"Student, like them others, you ask me. Always carrying books. Propped 'em up on the table like the rest of 'em."

"When was the last time she came in?"

"Right before them Shoshones got themselves shot. I remember it real clear, 'cause after I read about the murders, I got to wondering if she was ever gonna come back. Sure enough, I haven't seen hide or hair of her since. What a shame. Always tried to treat her real good. Fill up her Coke glass for nothing. I was hoping maybe she liked more about the place than just them Shoshones. It was good for business, with her popping in. Like I say, the cowboys got themselves a real eyeful."

"What did she look like?"

"Like I say, a real eyeful. Some kinda body, I mean, like in your dreams. Real pretty, lots of dark hair and big, gorgeous eyes."

Father John thanked the man again. This time he got to his feet and crossed to the door, one eye on the table where the cowboy and his girlfriend had their heads bent together, drawing on cigarettes, blowing smoke out of the corner's of their mouths. The same table where Trent Hunter, the Crispin brothers, Edie Bradbury, and another girl—*a real looker*—liked to sit.

He hurried past the building to the pickup, the wind whipping the snow about, pushing him along. There was another student, a girl. Somebody else who might know about Bates. Somebody else who might have had reason to lure the Shoshones to their deaths.

THE MISSION LOOKED deserted. The windows in the administration building were dark and no vehicles were outside Eagle Hall; the meeting was over. Father John parked next to Ian's sedan in front of the residence. A faint light from the television flickered in the living-room windows.

Walks-On was waiting in the entry. He scratched the dog's ears, then set his coat and hat on the bench and went down the hall, the dog's nails clicking beside him. Through the arch to the living room, he glimpsed the figure of his assistant slumped on the sofa, legs extended across the coffee table. The man might have been asleep; Father John wasn't sure. Quiet, peaceful even, the dim light washing over his face.

In the kitchen, they went through the same routine, he and Walks-On. He shook out the dog's food, waited until he'd finished slurping the bowl clean, and let him out the back door. His own dinner was waiting in the oven, the odors of grease and fried chicken hanging in the air. After a few minutes, the dog was scratching at the door. Father John let him in and went back down the hall. He walked into the living room and stared at the television. The hawk-nosed, dark-haired woman on the screen, brushing at the snow blowing into her face, stood outside the convenience store in Ethete. Brown boards covered the store's windows. "This afternoon, a mob of Shoshones attacked the Arapaho community of Ethete. Authorities believe the attack was in reprisal for . . ."

Father John had lifted the remote from the coffee table and pushed the power button. He turned to the priest slumped on the sofa. "I want you to go back into rehab, Ian," he said.

The man jerked upright and planted his feet on the floor. "We've been over this."

"You're stopping at bars several times a week."

"So what's the big deal? I can control it."

"You say you like it here," Father John said. "I think you hate it. So you're setting yourself up. You know you can't stay here and drink."

The other priest began studying the dark television screen, as if he were trying to figure out what had become of the program. "You plan to take this up with the Provincial?" he said.

"I don't want to."

"Yeah, I'll bet you don't."

"I don't care what you tell the Provincial about me, Ian." Father John went over to the phone on the table under the window. He picked up the receiver and held it out to the other priest. "Call him now, if you like."

"He'll reassign you."

"He's going to do that sooner or later."

Ian waved the receiver away. He set his elbow on the armrest and blew into his fist a moment. "What're we talking about? How many weeks?"

"There's an outpatient program in town," Father John said. "You could start there, see how it goes."

It was a couple of seconds before the other priest said anything, and when he did, his voice was so low that Father John had to lean over the back of the sofa to catch the words. "I'll think about it," he said, leaning forward, patting the surface of the coffee table. Finally, his fingers wrapped around the remote, which he pointed at the television. The news returned, a gray-haired man behind a desk, another story.

33

IT WAS ALMOST noon by the time Father John drove out of the mission grounds and turned toward Riverton. The sky was gray, shot through with white streaks from the sun that lingered somewhere behind the clouds. It had stopped snowing sometime in the middle of the night, but it might start again; there was the feel of snow in the silence pressing over the trailers and warehouses that passed outside the pickup's windows.

He'd said the ten o'clock Mass and spent an hour over coffee and doughnuts in Eagle Hall, trying to calm the fear and worry in the eyes of his parishioners. There wasn't going to be any tribal war. Yes, a gang of Shoshones had gone on a rampage yesterday, but the police would arrest them. And the Sunday newspaper—the black, inch-high headline—had stated that the killer had been arrested. Last night, at a house in Sinks Canyon, Frankie Montana was taken into custody.

And all the time that he was assuring his parishioners, he'd tried to shake off the sense that the truth was something else, that the killer was still walking around free.

He slowed into the rhythm of the traffic moving north on Federal. He wasn't sure where he'd find Edie Bradbury. A couple of miles back, he'd punched in her number on the cell. Three rings, then a mechanical voice at the other end: "The number you have reached has been disconnected." He'd tossed the cell onto the passenger seat and headed west for the little house behind the Victorian.

"WHAT'RE YOU DOING here?" The voice was low and wispy. The door had slid inward as Father John was knocking, and now the girl was moving backward, pulling the door open. She reminded him of a child again, swallowed up in dark sweatshirt and baggy pants. There was a disheveled look about her: mussed hair, lips set in a thin white line, and dark shadows under eyes that looked hard and hopeless.

"I'd like to talk to you, Edie," he said.

She took a half-step forward, craned her head around the door, and peered up and down the street. "Okay." Still the wispy voice. Then she pivoted toward one of the webbed folding chairs with clothes and towels stuffed onto the seats and spilling over the armrests. Her sneakers made a scraping noise on the floor. Above the chairs, the oblong window with the crooked shade framed a view of the elm branches. There was a musty odor about the place—dirty clothes, spoiled food, and stale air.

"Sit down, if you want," Edie said, giving a little wave toward the futon across the room.

Father John waited until she'd swept the pile of clothes from one of the chairs and dropped onto the seat, and then he perched on the futon. He took off his hat and, bracing his elbows on his thighs, leaned forward, holding the hat between his knees. "How are you getting along?" he asked.

"You come over here for that?"

"Partly."

"Partly!" Her head started shaking, almost like an involuntary spasm. A faint red flush moved up her throat and into her cheeks. "I know what you want. You wanna help that Arapaho that killed Trent. Well, he's going to prison for what he done, and I hope he rots there."

"I want to know how you're getting along, Edie," Father John said.

She leaned into the webbed back of the chair, something new moving behind her eyes, as if she wasn't so sure now that the two realities fit together: the Indian priest sitting in her living room and the Arapaho arrested for homicide. "Jason's looking out for me," she said finally.

"You and the baby?"

The girl looked away, her gaze traveling across the wall, the dark spots in the vinyl floor, finally moving to her hands clasped in the lap of her baggy pants. "He doesn't want the baby. You can't blame him none. I mean, an Indian baby. Everything's gonna be okay. I got an appointment at the clinic."

Father John waited until she'd brought her eyes back up to his. "You don't have to stay with him, Edie," he said. "You can come to the mission. You can come with me right now."

She gave an abrupt laugh that sounded almost like a sob. "Then what? Where do I go?"

"You'll go on, Edie. You and the baby will go on." He waited a moment, and then he said, "You know what Moses said?"

"You gonna quote the Bible to me now?"

"No." Father John smiled at the girl. "Just Moses. When you have a choice between life and death, Moses said, choose life." He let another couple of beats pass. The girl's face was rigid, her lips pulled again into the hard line, but her hand—he noticed her hand—lay flat against her belly. "Nobody knows where they're going in the future," he said. "That's the thing about life. Life is full of possibilities."

"I made up my mind." She was staring again at the wall. "So maybe you oughtta go. Jason could show up, and he wouldn't like your being here."

Father John got to his feet. "There's something else, Edie," he said.

The girl tilted her head back and turned her face up to him, one hand still on her belly. "Did you know that Trent planned to go to Bates on the day he was killed?"

"What, so I could go out there and shoot him?" She started shaking her head again—another spasm. "You don't get it, do you? I loved Trent. I really loved him, and he loved me. So maybe he was pulling away; so what? Maybe he was scared about the baby. Maybe he needed some time to think. Everything would've worked out." Her voice was cracking now, and she started to sob. She lifted her hand and pressed it over her mouth.

"Then he went and got killed," she managed. The words were blurred and broken. "I wanted to go with him to Bates. The professor said we all ought to go, and I wanted to see the place. I would've gone if Trent had told me he was going. I would've been with him. I would've died at Bates, too. I wish I'd died there."

Father John walked over and set his hand on the girl's shoulder. He could feel the tremors erupting from someplace deep inside her. "You're alive, Edie. You have your life, and your life is important and necessary. You must remember that."

It was a moment before she nodded, wiping the palm of her hand over her cheeks, pushing away the moisture. When she looked up at him again, he said, "I know you loved Trent."

She squeezed her eyes shut a moment and bit at her lower lip. "Frankie Montana killed him," she said. "He killed all of them. He's the one tried to cause trouble over at the Cowboy Bar. Why don't you just forget it?"

Father John took his hand from her shoulder. "There were other students who came to the bar with you and Trent, weren't there?"

"Rex and Joe," she said. "We all hung out together, until Trent started getting weird on me, saying go back to the house, he'd catch up with me later. I knew he was gonna go get a burger with the others and didn't want me around." She shrugged. "So I just came back here, and I waited."

"Anybody else?"

She lifted her eyes, as if the names were scrawled on the ceiling. "Different guys. I mean, it wasn't like we were some kind of exclusive club. Class got over just before five, and whoever felt like it would head for the Cowboy and something to eat."

"What about the other girl."

"Other girl?" Edie's head snapped back. "What other girl?"

"Another student. The bartender told me he saw both of you there a couple of times."

"Oh, God." She looked away and shook her head. "You had me worried for a minute. She isn't any student, not at the college anyway. I guess she's writing her dissertation. You mean Mrs. Lambert, the professor's wife."

"The professor's wife hung out with students at the Cowboy Bar?" Father John could hear the incredulity in his voice.

"It wasn't like she was one of the gang." The girl laughed at this. "I mean, she helped out the professor a lot in class. Passing out papers, giving exams. You ask me, Professor Lambert's not in great shape, so sometimes she was looking after him, like if he was having a bad day. She'd be there, hovering over him. I mean, she'd look like she was ready to pick him up off the floor. So we got to know her, that's all, and she was real interested in the class. I heard she helped the professor write his book on the tribal wars. Couple times she showed up at the bar and had a hamburger with us. You ask me, she liked being with people closer to her own age once in a while. I mean, the professor's a great man and all, but he's so . . ."

She hesitated. "He's so old," she managed, but in the way she said it, he knew that her thoughts had already jumped to something else. Her body seemed to stiffen as she gripped the edge of the chair and stood up. She barely came to his shoulder. She lifted herself on the balls of her feet, then stretched her neck until the top of her head reached his chin. She was staring up at him. "Mrs. Lambert's the reason Trent started getting all weird, isn't she?"

"What makes you think so?"

"Tell me the truth!" She spit out the words. "She got tired of the old man and got the hots for Trent. That's why he told me to go back to the house, so he could meet her at the bar."

"Listen to me, Edie." Father John placed his hands on the girl's shoulders. "The bartender said you were the one who was Trent's girl-friend. Obviously, he never saw anything to make him think differently."

The girl seemed to take this in. He could feel her shoulders begin to re-lax. "Don't torture yourself," he hurried on. "You said yourself that Trent would've come back to you. You knew him. Trust your own instincts."

She started nodding, and for a moment, he thought she might break into tears again. He was barely aware of the sound of an engine cutting off. "You'd better go," she said, throwing an anxious glance at the window.

Father John reached past his coat and withdrew the small notepad and pen from his shirt pocket. He flipped the pages until he came to a blank page; then he wrote down the mission's number, tore off the page, and held it toward to the girl. "If you change your mind," he said, "call me. I'll come and get you."

She hesitated, eyes darting between the small piece of paper and the window. Then her fingers closed around the paper. Keeping her gaze on the window, she lifted the bottom of her sweatshirt and stuffed the pa-per inside the band of her sweatpants.

Father John turned and let himself out the door. The white suprema-cist was coming up the sidewalk, making an arc around the elm. "What the hell you doin' here?" Rizzo stopped, blocking the way.

"I don't see that it's your business," Father John said. The man was all leather, metal, and reddish brown head. His arms hung out from his sides, fists curled like clubs.

"I'm making it my business," Rizzo said. "You stay away from her. She don't need no more Indians around here. You might be white but you're one of 'em."

Father John started walking toward the man. He was close enough to touch him—close enough to smell the odor of leather—before Rizzo stepped sideways, forming a narrow corridor between himself and the elm branch.

Father John slapped back the branch and kept walking. "I'd suggest you take good care of her, Rizzo," he said as he passed.

He could feel the man's eyes boring into his back as he got into the pickup and plugged the key into the ignition. Then he made a U-turn and started back toward Federal, the man's eyes still following him. He could see him in the side mirror—one boot on the sidewalk, one in the snow, the elm branch slicing across his face.

A man who hated Indians, Father John was thinking. A man who might be willing to kill the people he hated. A sociopath. There was no guessing what a sociopath might do. Turn a rifle on human beings, pull the trigger. But . . . first he had to know where to find the victims, and Edie Bradbury didn't know when Trent and the others had planned to visit the battlefield. *I would've gone with him. I wish I would've died there.* If the girl didn't know, neither did Rizzo.

But somebody knew. He could picture Lou Crispin, propped on the straight-backed chair, drawing from his cigarette, grieving for his two sons, saying that Rex and Joe and Trent had gone to meet somebody at the battlefield on the day they had died. Somebody had planned to kill the Shoshones and pose the bodies to look like images in the old photographs of Indian battles. Somebody had wanted it to look like revenge killings—revenge for a massacre that happened more than a century ago.

The traffic was blurring past the side windows. The parking lots and storefronts and convenience stores, all were a blur. In his mind now was the image of Dana Lambert—the mass of curly black hair, the green eyes, and something in those eyes—an elusive quality, like a shadow passing through, that had struck him the first time he'd met the woman, as if she were watching the far distances that no one else could see. A young, beautiful woman married to an old man with a last chance at a best-selling book that could make them rich, watching, watching for a way to make it happen. What better way than to instigate a tribal war, like the century-old wars in the book. Dana Lambert understood the Bates Massacre, the tribal feuds, the old animosities that her husband had written about. *She has been a great help to me.*

And she'd gone to the Cowboy Bar and Grill, gotten to know the Shoshone students, earned their trust. At what point had she said, I can show you the battlefield. Show you how the wolf scouts had found the village in the canyon. Show you how the Shoshones and the troops had attacked, how Arapaho warriors had climbed over the boulders and fired down on the enemy to drive them away, but not soon enough. Not before the massacre had taken place.

Logical, he thought. The pieces fell into a logical pattern, but it was a theory; that was all he had. Where was the evidence? He had no evidence that Dana Lambert had taped the messages—how would she have done that? No evidence that she'd stolen Montana's rifle.

Father John eased up on the accelerator, waiting for a break in the oncoming traffic. Then he jerked the pickup around in a sharp U-turn and drove north a quarter mile. He wanted to talk to the woman, test his theory, listen to what she might have to say about going to the Cowboy Bar and Grill. And there was so much you could tell by *watching*.

He took a right onto East Monroe Avenue and headed east out of town.

34

FATHER JOHN HAD circled the neighborhood twice—the tidy ranch-style homes, the clusters of elms and limber pines—before he spotted the blue sedan in the driveway of the redbrick house that squatted back from the road, across an expanse of open, snowy fields, as if the house had once commanded a larger plot of land and was holding on to what was left. He followed the drive across the yard and stopped behind the sedan. The front door to the house had a glass and metal storm door that gave the place the look of a bastion. The storm door rattled as he knocked.

It was a moment before the inside door opened. The professor's head snapped backward. Little lights of recognition seemed to snap on in his gray eyes. "Father O'Malley," he said, his voice muffled against the metal and glass. Bracing himself on his walking stick, he pushed the storm door open. "I had no plans for visitors this Sunday afternoon, but do come in."

Father John ignored the veiled reprimand. "I'd like to talk to you and your wife for a few moments, professor," he said. "It's important."

A second passed before the man stepped backward and swung his thin frame into the living room, reaching for the top of a chair, the edge of a desk, before dropping into an upholstered chair against the far wall. "I'm afraid you'll have only me for company," he said. "Dana has gone to take care of a few errands. Have a seat." He waved a knotted hand at a chair.

Father John sat down, took off his hat, and hung it over one knee. He recognized the reproduction of Charles M. Russell's *Crossing the Missouri* above the sofa. Bookcases lined with neat rows of books crawled to the ceiling on the left. Other books were stacked next to the lamp on the side table, and pieces of painted pottery had been arranged around the books on the coffee table. A clock was ticking somewhere, and odors of roasting meat drifted out of a doorway on the right.

But Dana Lambert wasn't here. He felt his jaw clench with the sense of futility. What had he expected? To look into the woman's green eyes and read the truth? Had he thought she might break down when she realized that he *knew*—a woman with nerves of steel, within reach of her goal? Did he expect her to confess? A penitent in the confessional? Had he really thought that she would hand him the evidence to prove his theory?

"I must warn you," the professor was saying. "A few minutes is all I have. I have telephone interviews scheduled with radio stations around the country this afternoon." He slid his gaze to the steel watch that hung like a bracelet on his thin wrist. "In ten minutes, I expect a call from a station in Washington, D. C. It has been most gratifying to see the tremendous interest in my new book. The publisher was forced to increase the print run to meet the great demand."

He gave a sudden smile; then, just as suddenly, the smile disappeared. "Most unfortunate coincidence, I suppose, that *Tribal Wars* should appear when an actual tribal war is underway, due to the dastardly actions of an Arapaho." He was shaking his head. "I'm very sorry about the strife, of course, but on the other hand, it comes at a propitious time. It has already drawn attention to my book, which will help people around the country understand the many differences among the Plains Indian tribes. It will finally dispel the stereotype of Indians—that they are all the same."

The man drew in a breath and hurried on. "The reason you're here, is it not? The local tribal war? I understand the Arapaho murderer was finally apprehended yesterday evening. Inconceivable to me that he and his lawyer were able to elude the police for so many hours."

"Montana took Vicky Holden hostage."

"Yes, yes, so they say." Lambert flapped his hand toward the coffee table, as if he were slapping at a pesky fly. "How can I help you, Father O'Malley?"

"It's possible the wrong person was arrested." Father John was studying the man, watching for a reaction—the smallest twitch of a muscle, the pulsing of a vein, the sudden shift of his gaze. There was nothing.

"News reports suggest there is much evidence against this Montana." The professor leaned back in his chair and clasped his hands over his chest, on firm ground now, confident of his opinions. The front of his tan shirt bunched against his flabby sleeves.

"Circumstantial evidence, Professor." Father John pushed on. "If Detective Burton is wrong, the murderer could kill again. The conflicts between Shoshones and Arapahos could just be starting."

"I must ask you again, Father. What is it you want from me?"

"I think that the killer was very familiar with the Bates Massacre."

"Yes, yes." The knobby hand flapped in the air. "One of my students. So you indicated earlier. I'm sure Burton has investigated each of the class members. When you showed me the message you received, I admit that I thought of Edith Bradbury. She has a way with words, which might suggest her as the author, and she had that horrid tough in black leather hanging around her. Naturally it made me suspicious."

"What made you change your mind?"

"She came to see me after Trent Hunter and the Crispin brothers were killed. She told me she had to drop out of the class. I couldn't help but notice the gauze bandages showing below the cuffs of her sweater. She sat in my office and wept, Father. Wept for quite some time, I would say, until I thought I would have to call for assistance. It was not an experience I wish to repeat. I have always made it a policy not to involve myself in the personal lives of students. She said she couldn't imagine living without Hunter. It was then, I believe, that I came to the conclusion she was incapable of having had anything to do with the young man's death, or with the deaths of the others, I might add."

"It comes back to your class, Professor," Father John said.

Lambert sniffed in a couple of quick breaths. "Why are you belaboring this point, Father O'Malley? The guilty Arapaho has been arrested. Frankie Montana shot four Shoshone men at the battlefield and left you the taped messages. The television news reported that Montana had previously worked in a radio station on the reservation where he must have made the tapes."

"He hasn't been to the station in two years."

"He says?" The professor began to chuckle. His arms rose and fell on his chest. "And why, may I ask, would you believe anything the man says?"

"I understand your wife often assisted you in class."

The professor tilted his head to one side. His brow furrowed in confusion, and the light eyes became a thin line, as if he were trying to bring an explanation into focus. "Why do you ask about my wife, Father? She is a professional in the classroom. She maintains the appropriate distance between herself and the students at all times. She wouldn't know anything about their personal lives. She certainly wouldn't know why the unfortunate men were murdered."

"She joined your students for hamburgers at the Cowboy Bar and Grill."

The professor's head snapped back as if he'd been slapped. He gave a shout of laughter. "Preposterous! My wife at a place called the Cowboy Bar and Grill? That is the most ridiculous statement I have heard in some time. Please, Father, be so good as to not insult either of us with such an outrageous accusation. My wife does not associate with students."

"There are people who can identify her, Professor." Father John kept his voice low, the counselor's voice, encouraging, nudging the man toward a reality he didn't want to accept.

"Those who say that Dana was at a bar are liars. Let me guess." Lambert seemed to settle back into the cushion, relaxed, on solid ground again. "The liars are students, are they not? They are lying for their own reasons. Perhaps they wish to besmirch the reputation of a beautiful and brilliant scholar who has already achieved much more than they can ever hope to achieve. Perhaps they think that by lying about my wife they can diminish her. Gossip!" He spit out the word. "The oldest trick in the world, as you must know, Father. Diminish someone with gossip and you make yourself feel bigger. No thinking person takes lying, hateful gossip for anything other than what it is."

The professor readjusted his arms over his thin chest, his gaze leveled on Father John for a moment, as if the matter were settled. Then he seemed to have a second thought. He said, "This is a matter of jealousy. Oh, don't think I haven't seen the way the young men's eyes follow my wife in the classroom. I can read their thoughts: How did that old man get her?" He began chuckling, but there was a forced, unsure note in the sound gurgling in his throat. "They know so little and understand less. My wife has no interest in the immature antics of boys. It is a calumny that she ever joined them at the Cowboy Bar and Grill."

The professor planted his walking stick in front of him and began pulling himself to his feet. He started listing to the side, and Father John jumped up. Reaching across the table, he took hold of the man's arm to steady him, but Lambert yanked himself free. He straightened his shoulders and lifted himself to his full height. "I'm afraid this discussion is over," he said.

"There's something I'm wondering about, Professor," Father John said, ignoring the man's comment. "There's a recording studio at the college, isn't there?"

There was a long moment—the clock ticking into the quiet, the walking stick trembling beneath the professor's grip, the blue vein pulsing in the center of the man's forehead. "How dare you." He spit out the words. "How dare you imply that my wife had anything to do with the homicides. If you ever utter such a slander again, I will see that my lawyers take the appropriate action. Do we understand each other, Father O'Malley?"

The phone had started ringing on the small table in the corner, but the man seemed not to hear. The gray eyes remained locked on his own. Finally, he said, "Get out."

Father John turned to the door, aware of the man's boots clumping across the room behind him. The ringing stopped as Father John pulled the door open.

"Yes, this is Professor Charles Lambert." The strong, confident voice almost concealed the effort the man was making. Father John let himself outside and closed the door behind him.

He drove back into town, past the motels and warehouses and mobile parks. He knows. He knows. The words drummed in his head. Lambert knows his wife is responsible for taking the lives of four men, but he will never admit it. He will convince himself that Frankie Montana is the killer. He will watch Frankie Montana stand trial, be convicted, and sentenced to a lifetime in prison, and Charles Lambert will go on denying that his beautiful young wife was involved in any way.

And the woman would get away with it. That was the thing. Father John pounded against the rim of the steering wheel and struggled to contain the disgust and anger boiling inside him. There were people who could place Dana Lambert at the Cowboy Bar and Grill, maybe even place her there the night that Montana's rifle was stolen. The Shoshone students, the bartender, Edie Bradbury. But the Shoshone students were dead. The bartender? Different faces passed through the bar every day.

How reliable could the man be? Edie Bradbury? A student jealous of the way her boyfriend had looked at the beautiful Mrs. Lambert.

Charles Lambert was clever, Father John thought, clever and protective.

But there was someone else who could place Dana Lambert at the bar, someone Lambert didn't know about.

Father John turned into the mission and drove down the tunnel of cottonwoods. Through the trees on the left, he spotted a green pickup parked in front of the administration building—someone wanting to talk to a priest this afternoon. He turned right, followed Circle Drive around to the residence, and slammed out of the pickup. Across the yard and through the front door, taking a diagonal path through the entry to his study. Once there he dropped to one knee and began shuffling through the newspapers piled in a basket next to the side chair. There it was, Saturday's paper with the photos of Trent Hunter, Joe and Rex Crispin, and Eric Surrell lined up beneath the headline: "Shoshones Murdered at Bates." He yanked the newspaper out of the stack and headed back outside and across the grounds to the administration building. He could see the pickup flashing past the cottonwoods on the way out to Seventeen-Mile Road.

He found his assistant at his desk, chair tilted back, receiver tucked between his ear and shoulder, fingers tapping at the keyboard. "Uh-huh, uh-huh," Father Ian said, eyes fixed on the computer screen.

Father John perched on the wood chair at the front corner of the desk. He opened the newspaper and folded it at page two. The faces of Charles and Dana Lambert stared up at him. He slid the paper across the desk.

"I'm sure the right man has been arrested," Father Ian said, glancing up. Then he lifted his eyebrows and shrugged. "No, I don't think you have anything to worry about. I'm sure there won't be any more attacks on Arapaho communities." A long pause. "You're welcome." He dropped the receiver into the cradle. "That would make call number six this afternoon," he said. "Will and Lucy Storm just left. They're worried about their kids getting attacked by some crazy Shoshone. People don't know if it's safe to leave home. A couple of callers weren't so sure that Montana's the killer. They think the Shoshones might still be looking for revenge." He nodded at the newspaper. "What's this?"

"Take a look at the photo," Father John said. "Have you seen the woman before?"

Ian pulled the newspaper over a pile of papers and glanced at the photo. "She's the wife of the man who wrote the book on tribal wars, just like the war we've got going on now."

"Take a good look. Have you ever seen her?"

The other priest stared at him for a moment before lowering his eyes again to the photo. He picked up the newspaper and, holding it up in both hands, leaned back. Then he tossed the paper onto the desk. "What is this, the Inquisition? We had this discussion yesterday evening. Do we have to keep going over it? Yes, I stop in a bar now and then and have a drink. I confess. What more do you want?"

"I want to know if you've seen the woman before."

"I think you already know the answer."

Father John didn't say anything.

A couple of seconds passed before the other priest said, "I saw her at the Cowboy Bar and Grill a couple of times. She came in with the students who were murdered. I saw their photos in the *Gazette*. She looked different, not like this photograph of her and her husband. Younger, like a student herself. If I remember right, she had on jeans and a sweater, not the fancy suit she's wearing in the photo. Her hair looked longer. It hung loose around her face, not pulled back like that." He reached over and tapped the photo. "She was laughing a lot, like she was really enjoying herself, or maybe she was just enjoying the beer. She sure had the attention of the guys, I noticed that."

Father Ian paused, then picked up the paper and studied the photo again. "I read this article last week. I must have glanced at this photo, but I never connected the professor's wife with the girl in the bar. They're the same."

"Thanks, Ian." Father John stood up, reached for the paper, and started for the door. It was a start, he was thinking. Enough to take to De-tective Burton and maybe convince the man to continue the investigation.

"Thanks?" Ian said behind him. "That's it? What's going on?"

Father John turned back. "I'm not sure yet," he said.

There was the *whoosh* of the front door opening, and Father John stepped out into the corridor. For a half-second, Vicky stood in the doorway, backlit by the gray daylight. "I've got to talk to you, John," she said.

He was halfway down the corridor when she stepped inside and slammed the door. The noise rippled through the old walls. She was staring at him, as if she were seeing him for the first time. "You know the truth, don't you?" she said.

35

FATHER JOHN FOLLOWED Vicky into his office where she swung around to face him. "They're going to charge Frankie with four counts of homicide."

"How about taking a hostage at gunpoint, breaking and entering? Shouldn't you be home?" Father John felt a spasm of alarm at the drawn look in her face, the hollow spaces beneath her cheekbones. Her eyes were on fire. She knows the truth, he was thinking. He said, "The doctor said you should rest . . ."

She cut in, "They're going to charge Frankie for murders he didn't commit, John. Burton's probably falling all over himself, congratulating himself for stopping a tribal war before it tears the reservation apart. The investigation is closed, and the killer is still walking around free." She waved the notepad. "The evidence is here."

"Will you please sit down?" Father John took hold of her arm and steered her toward a side chair. "Frankie's not your worry anymore," he said. But the Arapaho *was* her worry, he was thinking. She couldn't put it out of her mind that the man was innocent any more than he could. They were alike, he realized. Maybe he had influenced her, encouraged her to care about her people, but he doubted it. She was the one who had influenced him.

She sat forward in the chair and started thumbing through the notepad, pages filled with scribbling in black ink. "Frankie was telling the truth about the radio station," she said.

Father John nudged another chair over with his boot and sat down beside her, close enough to see the date on the top of the page she was looking at. Today's date.

"I talked to the station manager this morning," Vicky said. "He fired Frankie almost two years ago. Not for incompetence. He said that Frankie was one of the most talented mikes they'd had. Lively, spontaneous. He had a large audience." She slapped the pad against her thigh. "Unfortunately, things started disappearing. Coffee mugs, sweaters, the latest Coldplay and Hoobastank CDs. Then bigger things, like computers. An employee saw Frankie carrying a large carton out to his pickup. The manager made Frankie an offer. Frankie would leave quietly and the manager wouldn't file a complaint. Frankie's been good at riding away from trouble, until now." Vicky was shaking her head. "The point is, John, the manager assured me that Frankie hasn't been near the place. He said that's what he told Burton."

Vicky thumbed to the next page, today's date also scrawled on the top. She'd already put in a busy morning, Father John was thinking.

"I spoke to the managers at the radio stations in Lander and Riverton. They'd heard of Frankie Montana." She shot a glance at him. "Who hasn't heard of Frankie by now? They said he'd never been in their studios."

Vicky flashed a sideways smile up at him. "Took a while to get ahold of Mavis Clooney, who manages the station at the college, but I finally got her cell and tracked her down at the grocery store. She'd also heard of Frankie, but he never came near the studio. I was about to hang up when I remembered how Professor Lambert had encouraged his students to visit the Bates Battlefield. So I asked about the students. Did any of Lambert's students happen to work at the studio? She started stalling. You know, private information, that kind of thing. She'd already given a copy of the schedules to Burton. I reminded her that I was Montana's lawyer, and that I was investigating the charges he faced."

She gave Father John another sideways smile, and this time, she shifted around until she was facing him. "I confess," she said. "I told a lie. I can't very well represent the man who took me hostage. But it worked. She agreed to check the schedule and call me back from her office. An hour later, she called. None of the students who work at the studio is in Lambert's class. I asked about students who might have make a recording in recent weeks. That's when she told me the studio isn't available for student use. But get this, John," Vicky hurried on. "It's available for faculty."

"Lambert?" It wasn't possible, Father John was thinking. He could see the man moving across the living room, reaching one hand for the top of a chair, the edge of a table, gripping the walking stick with the other. It struck him again that maybe the professor was stronger than he wanted to appear. The killer had hiked a steep slope, clambered among boulders and rock outcroppings.

"Close," Vicky said. "Two weeks ago, the professor's wife booked the studio. She wanted to record material for her husband's class. That's what she told the manager."

Father John looked away: the papers and folders crawling over his desk, the oblong of daylight framed in the window, the tiny specks of moisture flecking the glass. Dana Lambert recorded the robotic voice? It didn't make sense. Something was off, like the sound of an out-of-tune violin accompanying the soprano.

He brought his eyes back to Vicky's. "There were reports in the newspapers about the telephone messages and the robotic voice. Engineers at the studio would have known that Dana had made the recordings. They would have told Burton."

"That's just it, John." Vicky was shaking her head again, fingers rif- fling the edges of the pages. "Dana Lambert arranged to use the studio late in the evening. She said that it was the only time she had. Mavis Clooney gave her a key. After all, she's the wife of the most prominent man on campus. It wasn't necessary for the staff to be on hand. Mrs. Lambert had been a radio personality in Philadelphia for several years."

Vicky was quiet a moment, not taking her eyes from his. "There's more, John. Mavis told me that Dana Lambert had met her husband when she interviewed him about one of his books. They'd hit it off im- mediately, since they both had a great love of history. She had a master's in history and was thinking of starting a doctorate. At least, that's what she said, and Mavis seemed quite pleased that the wife of the great man had chosen to confide in her. There was no need for an engineer because Mrs. Lambert could operate the board herself."

Vicky stopped. She seemed to be holding her breath, allowing her words to fill up the space between them without interference. Finally, she said, "No one else was in the studio."

Father John stood up and walked over to the window. Across the mission, Walks-On was scratching at the front door of the residence. He could hear the dog whining, or was he imagining it? He was so used to the sounds that Walks-On made. So used to the mission and to the reser- vation and to the way things always were, except that now they were changed. Now four young men were dead, and Shoshones and Arapahos were locked into opposing camps. Tribes that had lived together in peace for more than a hundred years suddenly were thrust into the past.

He turned back to Vicky, and in her expression, he could read his own thoughts. It was *her* people, *her* place that could be destroyed. And for what purpose? He knew the answer, and the weight of it was like an avalanche of boulders crashing over him. He could see Professor Lam- bert settling into his chair, talking about the radio interviews around the country, the growing demand for *Tribal Wars*—the demand caused by the outbreak of a real tribal war. Oh, yes, the perfect logical syllogism.

Father John stepped over to the desk and perched on the edge, his gaze still on Vicky. He told her about his visit to Professor Lambert's earlier. "Dana Lambert saw the chance to promote her husband's new book, turn it into a best seller, make a lot of money," he said. Then he told her the rest: how the woman had met the Shoshones at the Cowboy Bar and Grill and arranged to take them to Bates, the perfect guide.

"My God, John." Vicky stared across the office. "Frankie fit right into her plans. He might have even given her the idea—Arapaho harassing Shoshones at the bar. She saw the way to kill the Shoshones, put the blame on an Arapaho, and cause a lot of trouble on the reservation. She made the tape, intending the message for you, knowing that you'd figure it out and go to the Bates Battlefield immediately. She was waiting for you, John. She intended to kill the Indian priest, too. Think of the publicity! Priest shot at historic battlefield along with three Shoshones. Oh, she's clever, John. She worked every angle to get as much publicity as possible for her husband's book. She had planned everything. She even stole Frankie's rifle out of his pickup in the parking lot at the Cowboy Bar and Grill."

Vicky got up, walked over, and leaned back against the edge of the desk next to him. "But with all of Dana Lambert's planning, the war didn't start soon enough for her. So she convinced another Shoshone, Eric Surrell, to go with her to the battlefield. Probably told him that she knew who had killed his cousin Trent and the Crispin brothers."

Father John reached behind her and picked up the receiver. "We have to talk to Burton," he said, pressing a series of keys.

"There's no physical evidence," Vicky said.

"There's enough for him to get a search warrant for the Lamberts' house." He leaned his head against the receiver. A phone was ringing at the sheriff's office in Lander. "They might get lucky and find the taped messages."

"Fremont County Sheriff's Department." A woman's voice answered, bright and almost relieved. Relieved that a killer was behind bars, he thought.

He said, "This is Father O'Malley. Let me talk to Burton . . ."

"Hold on, Father. I'll see if he's around."

The line went dead, and for a moment Father John thought they'd been disconnected. Then the detective's voice was at the other end, familiar and matter-of-fact. "What's up, Father?"

"Vicky Holden and I . . ." Father John began.

"Yeah?" the man interrupted. "How's she doing today? We got Montana, you know. He's not going to be hurting anybody else."

"Listen, Burton," Father John said. "We've found evidence that links Dana Lambert to the Shoshone murders."

"Dana Lambert?" the detective said. "We talking about Professor Lambert's wife?"

"We'll be in your office in thirty minutes."

"Hold on a minute, Father. Something just came in on the Lamberts. Let me get it." The line went dead again, and he had the sense that he and Vicky were alone with nothing, really, except a theory about a killer who might never be brought to justice.

"What is it?" Vicky said. Father John could feel her eyes on him.

"I don't know. Something about the Lamberts."

"Here it is." The detective's voice again, breaking over the crinkle of papers. "Thirty minutes ago, we got a domestic disturbance call from the Lambert residence. The professor himself, asking for assistance. A car responded immediately, but nobody was at the house. Neighbor down the road says she saw the couple drive away in a blue Pontiac sedan. We're looking for the car."

Father John pushed himself upright, the realization crashing through his mind. Dear Lord, he'd laid a trap for the man. He'd told the professor about his wife meeting the Shoshones at the bar. He'd said there were people who could identify her. He'd made it impossible for the professor to continue to deny the truth. The man knew that his wife was capable of making the tape; he knew it wasn't a coincidence for the Shoshones to be murdered at Bates at the same time his book was due out. But he denied the truth, until . . .

Until he'd realized someone could link Dana to the murder victims. He must have confronted her when she came home.

"Dana Lambert's taking her husband out to Bates," Father John said. "She probably has a gun on him. She'll kill him on the battlefield." It was so logical, the perfect logic. Book sales would go off the charts if the author was killed at the battlefield where the Shoshones had died.

"Whoa. Hold up there, Father," the detective said. "What are you talking about? Why would she take him all the way out there if she wants to kill him?"

"How long ago did they leave?" Father John said. Vicky had jumped up and was leaning in close, straining to hear the other end of the conversation.

"Wait a minute. This still isn't making sense."

"How long?"

"Maybe twenty minutes."

"They've got a twenty-minute head start. There's still time to stop them before they get to Bates. For Godsakes, Burton, get a car out there."

"Listen, Father. We've got one deputy in the vicinity. He could be thirty miles away. I can't guarantee . . ."

Father John slammed down the receiver and strode over to the coat tree in the corner. He was shrugging into his coat when Vicky said, "I'm coming with you."

"Go back to your apartment, Vicky. You've been through enough." Father John grabbed his hat and went into the corridor.

"I said I'm coming." She brushed ahead, flung open the door, and headed down the steps.

36

TWENTY MINUTES! TWENTY minutes could mean the difference between life and death for Charles Lambert. Father John swerved through the traffic on Federal, passing a truck, taking a sedan on the inside lane. It was starting to snow again, squishy flakes—part water, part snow—plopping on the windshield. He jammed down hard on the accelerator and raced through the intersection as the light flashed red. Finally, the outskirts of town, the strip malls and flat-topped buildings fell behind, and then nothing but the empty asphalt that stretched into a billowing curtain of snow ahead.

"I don't get it, John," Vicky said. Neither of them had spoken since they'd driven out of the mission, and now, the sound of her voice, punctuating the thrum of the engine, the swish of the wipers, and the rhythm of the tires, took Father John almost by surprise. He'd gotten used to the silence, to his own thoughts, even though he'd been aware of her in the seat beside him, staring straight ahead, one arm braced on the curve of the windowsill.

"Why did he wait until now to confront his wife?" she said. Her voice was low, percolating up out of a deep space. "Surely Lambert guessed that his wife might have been responsible for the murders of his students."

"He didn't want to know, Vicky." Father John glanced over at her. She had lifted her hand from the sill and was combing her fingers through her hair. "He didn't want to believe it. He probably told himself it couldn't be true, so that he and Dana could go on with their lives. Nobody had suspected her, and there was a warrant out for Frankie Montana. Everybody assumed Frankie was guilty. It made it easy for the professor to go along with the same assumption."

"Easy to live in denial," Vicky said.

Out of the corner of his eye, Father John could see that Vicky had turned away and was looking out the passenger window at the snow billowing over the open fields. He wondered who she was talking about now, Professor Lambert or herself.

She brought her gaze back to the front. "The professor saw his new book getting a lot of attention that it wouldn't have had if the Shoshones hadn't been murdered. A man who'd been writing books for years now had a best seller. Then you showed up today and told him that his wife had been seen with the Shoshones at the Cowboy Bar and Grill. He must have realized it was only a matter of time before Burton figured out that Dana had a world of experience with recording studios and that she'd recorded a tape at the college two weeks ago. There would be a search warrant and police shuffling through their home. They might even find the tapes. You forced the man to face the truth."

And if the man is killed, Father John was thinking, Dear God, how would he live with that?

"It's not your fault, John," Vicky said, as if she'd seen into his mind. "Whatever happens, you're not the one responsible. Dana Lambert is the one with the gun. Her husband must have threatened to expose her. He has his reputation to think about. He's a well-known scholar. Better to denounce his wife than for people to suspect that he might also have been involved in the murders. She has no choice but to shoot him. And she'll find a way to make it look like a Shoshone committed the murder. Some poor dupe she's probably already lined up. She's smart, John. She's clever and she's desperate."

Father John glanced over again. What Vicky said was logical, and Dana Lambert was following her own logic to its horrible conclusions.

And they were twenty minutes behind, he was thinking. Twenty minutes, an eternity.

Vicky's arm flashed in front of him. He felt her hand tighten over his against the rim of the steering wheel. "Just drive," she said.

They were passing through Lysite now, but Father John didn't slow down. After half a block, general store on one side of the road, abandoned gas station on the other, and they were out of town, careening onto dirt roads with nothing but the expanse of empty bluffs and canyons and white, sagebrush-studded flats melting into the leaden sky ahead. A layer of new snow clung to the rock-faced ridges in the canyons below. He could feel the rear wheels skidding and lifting off the ground as they bounced over the ridges.

Another vehicle had been here ahead of them. Not long ago, a single vehicle had left two clean lines of tire tracks in the snow. Father John struggled to hold the wheel steady while he pulled the cell out of his coat pocket. "See if you can get Burton," he said, handing the cell to Vicky. "Tell him we're on the way to Bates and there are tracks ahead of us. Unless a deputy's on the way, the tracks were made by the Lamberts."

He was aware of Vicky tapping the buttons, pressing the cell to her ear, then removing it and studying the readout. "Roaming," she said. She set the phone against her ear again. A couple of moments passed before she said, "Get me Detective Burton." Then, an anxious note in her voice, she said, "It's cutting in and out, John."

Father John kept his eyes glued on the road ahead, trying to steer the pickup around the ruts. They were swerving from side to side, he realized, and he could see that Lambert had done the same—an old man driving with a gun in his ribs.

"Hello?" Vicky said. "Hello? Hello?" Then she was giving their location to whoever was on the line, talking about the tracks. "Is there a deputy on the way? Hello? Hello? Damn it!"

Vicky slammed the cell against the palm of her hand, then pressed it again to her ear. "Are you there?" She was quiet a moment. Turning sideways, she said, "Burton's been trying to radio the deputy out here. The man's on another call, away from his truck."

"Get somebody else out here, Burton." Father John heard himself shouting. "A man is about to die."

He was pounding his fist against the wheel. They were in the middle of nowhere. The badlands, locals called the area. A few ranches ten miles apart, dry bluffs, and scrubland with barely enough grass for the straggling flocks of sheep and the antelope whose tracks intersected the tire tracks now and then, and nothing else, no other sign of life. A place of death, he thought, good only for a massacre.

"It's dead." Vicky was staring again at the readout. She tossed the phone on the seat between them.

The snow was heavier, as if the sky had opened up and was showering white flakes through the gray daylight. They were coming off the top of a bluff now, winding downward toward the thin lines of trees that ran along the canyon floor. The tracks were getting harder to spot, layered between the snow and the shadows of the canyon closing in. Bluffs rose on either side, topped with the sheer rock faces that loomed overhead.

Father John kept the pickup heading down the middle of the canyon, climbing over rocks and brush, bouncing through the ruts. Sometime back the engine had begun sending up a faint knock of protest, which was getting louder, more persistent. He ignored the knock and gripped the steering wheel hard, willing the old pickup to keep going. The battle-field was just ahead now. He knew by the rocks and boulders starting to climb out of the canyon floor and up the steep slopes of the bluffs.

"There's the car." Vicky jabbed an index finger against the windshield.

He'd seen it, too, the dark shadow rising out of the white earth, parked at the mouth of the canyon. He steered the pickup for the shadow.

"Maybe we're not too late," Vicky said. He could hear his own des-perate hope in her voice. Footprints churned through the snow on either side of the blue sedan, footprints leading farther into the canyon. He eased on the brake and skidded to a stop. "Listen to me, Vicky," he said, turning toward her. "I want you to stay here."

"So Dana Lambert can shoot her husband and then shoot you?" Vicky pulled her black bag off the floor and began rummaging inside. "What are you planning to do, John? Stop her with words?"

He stared at her. He would have to sneak up on Dana Lambert the way a wolf approached its prey—silently, swiftly. He would have to knock the gun out of her hand before she realized he was there. The chance was slim, nonexistent. What other choice did he have? Talk to her? Try to reason with her? Dear Lord, Vicky was right. The woman would shoot him and her husband.

"This works better than words." Vicky extracted a small, black pis-tol from the bag. She held it in the palm of her hand. "We'll take this," she said, glancing over at him. "I took it from Frankie. I didn't give it to Burton yet. To be honest, I forgot it was still in my bag. I wasn't think-ing too clearly when he came to the hospital last night."

"You didn't tell me you had a gun," he said, but Vicky was already out of the pickup.

"You would have insisted I leave it at your office," she said.

Father John followed her into the falling snow, heading past the sedan along the zigzagging footprints, as if they had gone in single file: the professor first, his wife behind him. Every few feet on the right was a round indentation where Lambert had planted his walking stick.

The quiet of the canyon swallowed the faint sound of their boots. There was the occasional *whoosh* of snow dropping off the brush or falling from the branch of an isolated tree.

He could see the couple now, standing close together, like trees bent into the snow. He looked back at Vicky and motioned toward the figures, but she had already spotted them. She was nodding, pulling the gun out of her coat pocket.

He started off again, walking faster, aware of the sound of Vicky's breathing behind him and the thumping of his own heart. The Lamberts hadn't spotted them yet. They seemed to be talking, a couple out on a hike, caught in a spring snowstorm, discussing whether to turn back.

It was then that the gunfire erupted, like a cannon exploding through the quiet.

"No!" Father John shouted, and then he was running, running toward the dark figure still standing and the other figure crumpled into the snow. They were too late! They were too late! The words pounded in his head, like the thud of his boots in the snow.

The figure began turning toward them, lifting one arm. And at the end of the arm, Father John could see the black pistol. They were in the line of fire, he and Vicky, like ducks in a shooting gallery, easy marks for Dana Lambert. Except . . .

Except that it wasn't Dana Lambert. Father John could see the woman's dark hair splayed in the snow. The person aiming the gun was the professor.

Father John stopped. He reached around for Vicky and brought her up close behind him, as if he could protect her. The thought made him want to choke. "Don't shoot, Professor," he called out. "We want to help you."

The man started walking forward, holding out the gun, stabbing the walking stick into the snow, closing the space between them until he was no more than a dozen feet away. Snow fluttered between them. Snow sat like new hair on top of the white mane.

"Not even God can help me, Father O'Malley." His voice was

calm, the professor making an obvious point. "I suppose I shouldn't be surprised that you were the one to follow us here, although I expected Burton would come to find us. You have made this unfortunate affair your business, although I admit to being stymied as to your reason. Who is that hiding behind you?"

Father John kept one arm behind him, his hand wrapped around Vicky's. He felt her pull free and move to his side. Then he saw the pistol come up, both hands gripping the handle.

"Drop your gun, Professor," she said. She was trembling, Father John realized. He could see the slightest tremor in her hands.

"Well, what is this?" Professor Lambert said. "Shall we have a shoot-out at the OK Corral? Would this be our *High Noon*?" He snorted with laughter. "I suggest you drop your gun, or I shall be forced to shoot the good father here. Shall we have a contest? Would you care to wager a bet on whether you can shoot me before I shoot Father O'Malley?"

Vicky didn't move for a moment. Then she dropped her arms at her sides, and Father John heard the soft thud of the gun in the snow. "You don't have to kill anyone else," she said.

Lambert's face contorted into a smile, like ice cracking on a pond. "Let me guess," he said. "You're the lawyer who ran off with Frankie Montana. Am I correct? And you are determined to prove the man innocent when he is nothing but a blight on the human community. It's unfortunate that you and Father O'Malley couldn't have let justice take its course. It's of no consequence that Montana doesn't happen to be guilty of murdering the young men out here. He was guilty of other crimes, was he not? Crimes, I might add, for which, I believe, you had a hand in helping him evade responsibility. It would have been right if he had finally been brought to justice."

"You're insane," Vicky said.

"Hardly." The man gave another snort of laughter. "I have never been more rational or, may I add, more determined."

"Your wife needs help, Charles," Father John said. "We have to get her to a hospital before we're snowed in."

The man tilted his head toward the prone body a few feet behind him. Snow lay in the folds of the woman's coat. The toes of her boots were covered in snow. "I assure you that no powers on this earth can help my wife. She is quite dead, which, again, is only just." Lambert took a half-step closer, moving the gun until, Father John realized, it was pointed at his heart. "She has deserved her fate."

"You're wrong, Professor," Father John said. "No one deserves to be murdered. The Arapahos who were murdered here long ago didn't deserve their fates. Neither did the Shoshones. Your wife would have been brought to justice."

The man emitted a growl of laughter that bubbled up like phlegm from somewhere deep inside the narrow chest. "Brought to justice? Spare me your platitudes, Father O'Malley. With attorneys like your friend here to assist her in avoiding her fate, I very much doubt she would have even faced charges, never mind a trial and conviction. I was left with no choice except to avenge my students and my own honor. You understand, I've spent my entire career, the most important part of my life, in the service of students who have relied on me as a guide into history. Surely you, as a former teacher, can appreciate my devotion. It consumed me to the extent I am afraid, that I did not give the proper consideration to the character of the woman whom I had decided to make my second wife."

The man paused and glanced back at the prone body. "I admit that after the death of my first wife, I was felled by loneliness," he said after a moment. "And, yes, I also succumbed to the siren call of lust. Dana was a beautiful woman. I was under the delusion that she would share in my devotion. I could not have been more mistaken. She assumed a man of my reputation must have a large bank account. I realize now how disappointed she must have been to find that my assets consisted of a modest retirement and meager royalty checks from my books. Naturally, she saw that the only asset which might be increased was the income from *Tribal Wars.*"

Lambert stared at the gun in front of him and listed sideways toward the walking stick. His jaw jutted forward, the muscles in his face seemed to tighten, and his eyes began to look bleary—an old man's eyes blinking into the snow. "She dishonored me," he said finally, his voice cracking with emotion. "Can either of you understand what it is like to be dishonored?"

"Put down the gun, Professor," Vicky said. "We'll take you back to town. You won't face anything more than a temporary insanity charge."

"Quiet!" Lambert shouted. His voice echoed from the bluffs. Then, in a calmer tone he continued, "I am Professor Charles Lambert. I am the foremost expert on the tribal wars of the Plains Indians. I will not be locked up in a grimy jail, dressed in orange clothing, and paraded around with my hands cuffed behind me. I will not cooperate with lawyers who seek to paint a false picture of what I have done and absolve me of my own responsibility. I will not prostrate myself in a public courtroom before an inferior man in a black robe. I will not dishonor myself."

The professor started moving backward, leaning on the walking stick—a slow, jerky motion. He looked down for a long moment, as if he were studying the still body, attempting to make out how it came to be as it was. There was the faintest look of surprise in his expression. Then, he bent his arm upward and placed the gun against his right temple.

"Don't!" Father John started to lunge for the man. The sound of the gunshot came like a blast of fireworks that filled the space between them and rocketed through the canyon. The man's head had exploded into the falling snow.

Father John froze in place, scarcely able to believe what he was seeing. The old man folded downward, knees buckling, arms swinging at his sides, blood pooling into the dark scarf pulled around the collar of his topcoat. There was a loud thumping noise, and someone was screaming—a sustained howl, like the howl of grief. It was a half-second before he realized that it was Vicky who was screaming, and that the thumping in his ears was the sound of his own heart.

He felt himself moving forward, his boots dragging like chains through the snow. He went down on one knee beside the bodies of Charles and Dana Lambert, so close together, they were almost touching.

He dropped his face into his hands. Snow tipped off the brim of his hat and pricked the skin between the top of his gloves and the edge of his coat sleeves. He was aware of the snow falling everywhere, ridges of snow tracing the bodies, clumps of snow on the branches of the sagebrush all around. "God have mercy on us," he whispered. The other words would come on their own. The usual prayers would form on his lips. He waited. There was nothing except the white void closing around them.

God. God. God. Where are You?

He lifted his head and stared through the snow at the steep slopes rising over them. The stillness was as deep as the canyon—the stillness of eternity. Then, the faintest sound, a staccato sobbing. He glanced around. Vicky was sitting in the snow, head buried in her arms, snow outlining the contour of her back.

Father John got to his feet and went over to her. He knelt beside her and gathered her to him. She shivered against him, small and light as if there was nothing to her at all except the shock and grief. Her sobs sounded muffled against his chest.

After a moment, he lifted her to her feet and kept his arms around her to steady her. "We have to get out of here," he said, guiding her back along their footprints to the pickup.

37

SO MUCH DEATH, Father John was thinking. Too much death. They'd driven back from Bates in numbed silence, he and Vicky. At some point, the cell had clicked in and he'd told Burton what had happened—jarred at the sound of his own voice in the silence. Ten miles later, a phalanx of white pickups and an ambulance, sirens blaring, red and blue lights flashing, had sped past. He had kept going, back toward the reservation, back toward life, not saying anything. He and Vicky, eyes fixed on the headlights flaring ahead, both of them seeing the same images of death, he knew. He and Vicky, each locked in their own worlds, and yet he had never felt so close to her.

Now he watched the dark shadow of her Jeep turning around Circle Drive and threading through the cottonwoods, taillights blinking in the snow. Then it was gone. He lifted his face to the snow; he could taste the snow, and for a moment, the sensation dulled the thirst that had started over him at the battlefield. He tightened his fingers around the keys in his coat pocket, walked over to the church, and let himself into the dark vestibule. He flipped on the light switch. Faint white lights stuttered into life over the altar and cast columns of light across the pews and stucco walls. The church seemed set apart and self-contained, a world unto itself.

Father John walked down the center aisle, slumped into the front pew, and buried his face in his hands. He closed his eyes, staring at the image in his head. Dear Lord, would it never go away? The prayers were coming now, all the prayers engraved in his heart, and yet they seemed new and insistent, as if he'd just discovered them. Have mercy on all their souls, he prayed. All of those who died at Bates. Have mercy. Have mercy.

He wasn't sure how long he had stayed in the pew. Time had collapsed into the flickering light, the quiet and the sense of the eternal that closed about him. The thirst seemed to withdraw into that place where he managed to keep it most of the time. He finally lifted himself off his knees.

It was when he turned around that he saw his assistant in the back, half sitting, half kneeling, hands clasped over the next pew. Father John made his way down the aisle. "I didn't hear you come in," he said, when he was a few feet away.

Father Ian pushed himself upright and headed into the vestibule. "I didn't want to disturb you." He threw the explanation over one shoulder as he pushed the door open and stepped outside.

"Heard you drive in," the other priest went on, still holding the door, half in shadow, half in light, until Father John flipped the switch and the other priest was enveloped in the shadow. "The news has been all over the radio and television about two more bodies found at Bates, and the phone has been ringing all evening. I figured that's where you and Vicky went this afternoon. Right?"

"Right." Father John moved past and went down the steps, conscious of the other priest's boots scuffing the steps behind him.

"Thought you might like to talk," Father Ian said, falling in beside him as they started across Circle Drive.

Father John jammed his hands into his coat pockets. The front of his coat was open, and he left it that way. The cold air swept over his face and neck and bit through his shirt, calling him back to life. After a moment, he explained how Dana Lambert had murdered the four men, hoping to start a tribal war that would promote her husband's book, how the professor had seen his world crumbling and had shot his wife, then himself.

Ian stopped walking. "You thought you could prevent what happened, and now you blame yourself, don't you? How did you plan to stop it?"

Father John could still see the gun pointed at his heart. They might have all been dead, and that was the thing, wasn't it? That was the thing that had propelled him into the church. It had made him open his coat to the cold, all to assure himself that he was alive. He was alive.

"When you drove in here," Father Ian said, "there wasn't anything you wanted more than a drink, right?"

Father John turned around and faced the light-colored eyes shining out of a face striped with shadows. "Yes," he said.

His assistant was shaking his head, everything about him looking satisfied and vindicated. "Alcoholics love guilt, John," he said. "We seek it out, look everywhere for it, and if we can't find it, we invent it, because when we have the guilt, we have the excuse. I've found all the guilt I needed here at the mission. It was you that people wanted at meetings, you patients wanted in the hospital, so I told myself, I must be doing something wrong. It must be my fault. If I'm at fault, I must be guilty. And . . ." He shrugged. "There are a lot of bars. But I can't change the fact that people here love you, and you couldn't prevent a man from committing murder and suicide. Face it, John. We're a couple of alkies trying to stay sober and looking for the excuse to drink."

"We?" Father John said. It was the first time that his assistant had actually admitted to being an alcoholic.

"Had a long talk with the Provincial today," Ian said. "Don't worry," he hurried on. "I didn't mention you and Vicky Holden."

"It wouldn't have mattered."

"I understand that, John. I've been watching you. I'm starting to understand some things. You'd like to stop in at the bars, that's what I started thinking, but you don't. Maybe you'd like to have an affair with her . . ." He tossed his head back toward Seventeen-Mile Road. "I have to believe what you say, that there's never been anything between you. You've made a life for yourself here and, well . . ." He hesitated, his gaze roaming over the grounds and the buildings settled into the shadows and the quiet. "I'd really like to do the same. It's like you said, whiskey won't let it happen. So I'm going to a clinic in Casper."

Father John clasped the man's shoulder. "That's good, Ian," he said. "I need you here. The people need you. You'll see."

"I hope nobody's going to need me in the next three weeks." Father Ian started toward the residence again, then turned back. "There was another call after you left," he said. "A young woman named Edie Bradbury. Sounded scared. Said you'd told her she could come to the mission. I offered to go and get her, but she said that she'd drive over. She's at the guesthouse."

"She's here," Father John said. Thank God, he thought.

He followed the other priest up the steps to the residence, waves of gratitude flowing over him for this assistant, after the years of hoping for another priest who would want to be here, and for Edie Bradbury and life and all the possibilities that lay ahead. The minute he and Father Ian stepped into the entry, Walks-On came scampering down the hallway.

Familiar, Father John thought. Everything familiar. He stooped over and scratched the dog's ears as the other priest tossed his coat over the coat tree and started up the stairs. Then Father John hung up his own coat, set his hat on the bench, and started after the dog, who was already in the doorway to the kitchen, looking back at him with dog patience. Familiar and normal and expected, all of it—Walks-On and the old house creaking around them, the thud of the other priest's boots on the steps, the faint odor of stale coffee lingering in the air.

* * *

VICKY JANGLED THE key in the lock, aware of the dim, orange glow of light in the empty corridor. She opened the door into her apartment and reached for the light switch. It was then that she saw the flicker of light in the living room. She gripped the doorknob, every muscle poised to bolt back down the corridor, but the figure rising off the sofa was familiar: the shape of the dark head and curve of the shoulders, the dark, thick forearms dangling from the rolled up sleeves of the light-colored shirt.

"I've been worried about you," Adam said.

Vicky closed the door and leaned against it a moment. In all the hurry to end the law partnership, move out her things, find a new office, and—yes, this was the main part of it—end everything between them, she hadn't gotten around to asking Adam for her key.

"Are you all right?" His voice seemed to come from far away, breaking through the torrent of her own thoughts. Vicky felt the gentle pressure of his hands on her shoulders, but still she clung to the door. Would she ever be all right? Would anything ever be all right?

"Have you eaten?" Adam tried a different tack.

"I'm not hungry." Finally, she found the strength to push off the door and walk past the man into the living room. She sank onto the far end of the sofa, away from the imprint of his body in the cushion. The television was lit, but Adam must have pressed the mute key because there was a man standing in a floodlit circle, hair blowing onto his forehead, lips moving, arms flapping about in a grotesque mime.

Adam dropped onto the cushion that he'd just left and, reaching forward, picked up the remote on the coffee table. He pointed it toward the TV and, as if he'd willed sound to erupt, the man's voice filled the room. A siren wailed in the background, mixing with the busy, purposeful noise of footsteps crunching snow and the sound of voices.

"We're still waiting for positive identification of the two bodies here at Bates tonight." The man's voice cut through all the noise. "So far the spokesman for the Fremont County Sheriff's Office has confirmed that the bodies are those of an elderly man and a woman most likely in her thirties . . ."

Adam pointed the remote again, and the sound went off. The screen went dark. For a half-second, they sat in the darkness, until Adam shifted around and flipped on the table lamp, sending a circle of light over the sofa. "Tell me about it," he said.

Vicky turned toward him and let her gaze take a slow turn of his face, trying to glean from his eyes, the set of his mouth, the flare of his nostrils, some explanation of how he knew that she had gone to Bates. She was aware that he was also studying her, and after a moment, Adam said, "I called two or three times to see how you were feeling. There was no answer, so I came over to check on you. It surprised me that you weren't here. The doctor said you should rest. I decided to wait for you and turned on the TV." He shrugged and looked away before hurrying on. "Two more bodies found at Bates. I called St. Francis Mission and learned that the good pastor wasn't in. I can do the math, Vicky. What I can't figure out is what made you and Father John go out to the battlefield today."

Vicky leaned against the back of the sofa and stared through the circle of light at the small table and bookcase and desk swimming out of the shadows toward her and told him how she'd found out that it wasn't Frankie Montana who had made the tapes at a recording studio, but Dana Lambert. She'd gone to John O'Malley, she said, rushing through this part. She could never explain to Adam Lone Eagle. She should have gone to Burton; surely that's what Adam was thinking. But she and John O'Malley were stronger together, more convincing than either of them could be alone.

She rattled off the rest of it, all the way to Bates and the dead woman and Charles Lambert threatening to shoot John O'Malley until she'd let Frankie's gun drop into the snow where the deputies would find it. They had probably already found it. It was at this point that she was aware of Adam reaching over and taking both of her hands in his. She told him how the professor had put the gun to his temple, but she didn't try to describe the sound of the explosion or the shell burst of tissue and blood in the falling snow. As she talked, she felt a kind of relief coming over her, a lightening, as if she were setting down a burden. Finally, she said, "Frankie won't be going to prison for homicide."

"No," Adam said, a thoughtful note in his tone. The warmth of his hands flowed into her own, and she realized that she no longer felt the chill of death. "But he'll go to prison for resisting arrest, taking a hostage at gunpoint, breaking and entering. Frankie's mother has retained another attorney, since you'll be the prosecution's star witness."

Vicky turned to him. "Samantha Lowe?" she said.

He nodded. "She left a message on my answering machine a couple of hours ago that she'll be representing Frankie. She's already arranged to consult with a firm of criminal lawyers in Casper. She'll give Frankie a good defense, Vicky."

Vicky tried to pull her hands free, but Adam tightened his grip and held on. "There never was anything between Samantha and me," he said. "I was her adviser, that's all. A father figure."

"Right, Adam." Vicky yanked herself free at this and jumped to her feet. She walked over to the window and began threading the cord of the shade through her fingers. The sky was silver, lit with stars, and a faint glow lay over the snow covering the street and sidewalk below. Everything seemed fresh and new, almost as if spring were pushing through the snow.

"I'm not going to lie to you," Adam said. "I was attracted to her, damn attracted. I got the feeling that Samantha might have been interested, and you had become so . . ." He hesitated. "A big space has opened between us lately, Vicky, and I haven't been able to figure out why."

"You know why." Vicky looked around. Adam had moved sideways into the corner of the sofa, arm draped along the back, leg crooked over the middle cushion. A polished black shoe dangled in the space between the edge of the sofa and the coffee table. A spark of anger flared inside her. They might have been chatting about the spring snow. "We want different things," she said. "You want to be Crazy Horse riding in to save the village. You want to be the one people count on. You want to take care of the big problems, make them go away in the courts."

Adam didn't move, still relaxed, sitting back, comfortable. "So do you," he said.

It was the truth, Vicky thought. She snapped her head back to the window. She wanted to lash out, tell him he was wrong, but it was the truth. He knew her. She wanted to be involved in the important cases that affected her people's future—cases that involved the land and the natural resources. She wanted the cases that dealt with civil rights and tribal sovereignty. She wanted to advise the business council on issues such as wolf management. She wanted all of that.

She said, "I can't turn my back on the Frankie Montanas. They still have rights."

"I understand that." Adam's voice drifted behind her. "You were right about Montana. He's not a murderer, but he probably would have been convicted."

"Even if he were guilty . . ."

"He would still deserve all the protection of the law. I know that, Vicky." She felt the slight change in the air. Adam got to his feet, and walked over. His arm slipped around her waist. "I want you to stay in the firm, Vicky. We'll find a way to take both kinds of cases. We might have to hire another lawyer . . ."

"Not Samantha," she cut in.

His laughter was low, a slight brush of air against her ear. "We can find someone else. This thing about the wolves is heating up. A rancher shot a wolf a couple of days ago out in the bluffs on the eastern edge of the rez. You know what that means. Wolves are here. I need you to stay with this, Vicky. The tribes need you to stay with this."

She turned inside the circle of his arm and, at the same time, pulled away, the edge of the windowsill creasing her back. "The moving truck is coming tomorrow."

"Cancel it."

"I have to think about it, Adam."

"Cancel the truck and think about it, and while you're thinking about it, we have a meeting in two days with the fish and game people from Cheyenne."

"Adam . . ." She started to protest, but she could hear the crack of indecision in her voice. "I'll stay on the wolf issue until it's settled," she said.

"What about us, Vicky?" Adam said. "I want to be part of your life; I want you to be part of mine." There was such intensity in his eyes that it took all of her strength not to look away. "I want to be the one you turn to when something comes up. I want to be the first one you think of."

Vicky looked back at the window and the white world spreading below. She felt the cold air coming off the glass pane and wondered how it could be possible that the first man she thought to turn to was not John O'Malley but Adam Lone Eagle. It seemed as impossible as putting the snow back into the sky. And yet Adam kept his hand on her waist, his fingers pressing into her skin. He was here, and John O'Malley was at St. Francis Mission. Where they wanted to be, both of them.

Now moving around again within his arm, tilting her face up to his, laying her hands on his chest, the soft fabric of his shirt, waiting. "We can try, Adam," she said. "We can try."

38

THE SOUND OF drums and singing swelled through the canyon, bouncing off the slopes as if there were other drums, other singers among the boulders. Traces of snow lingered here and there, like the memory of winter, but the sun was warm in a sky scrubbed of clouds and as still and blue as a mountain lake. Father John led Edie Bradbury over to the crowd bunched together at the mouth of the canyon. The smell of burning sage drifted through the air. Father Nathan Owens, wearing a black raincoat, an umbrella poking out of the side pocket, as if the man couldn't believe that warm weather had finally set in, stood a few feet away. The moment that Father John ushered the girl into a vacant spot, the Episcopalian priest stepped over.

"Can't tell you how happy I am to see you alive and well." He clasped Father John's shoulder and reached for his hand. Then he gestured toward the front of the crowd, past the group of Arapaho and Shoshone elders around the small campfire, his gaze focusing on the canyon beyond. "A terrible tragedy," he said. "I've lain awake nights worrying that I had sent you in harm's way and praying for your safety."

Father John thanked the man. He needed all the prayers he could get, he was thinking. You can't pray too much, an elder had once told him.

People began shuffling about, pulling to the sides, and Father John saw Ethan Red Bull coming down an aisle of marshy grasses and sagebrush. The elder stopped in front of him. "Join us at the campfire, Father," he said.

Father John motioned for Edie to follow him, but the girl shook her head and pulled back, shrinking into herself. He gave her a smile of encouragement, took her hand, and led her through the crowd to the front. The family of Trent Hunter and Eric Surrell stood together on one side, the relatives of the Crispin brothers on the other.

It was where the girl belonged, he was thinking. The mother of Trent's unborn child, one of the family, and she was grieving, her face blanched and tight, eyes lowered, studying her hands clasped over her belly. She'd ridden out to the battlefield with him this morning, although at first she'd said that she couldn't bear to see the place where Trent had died. Then, just as he was about to drive off, she'd flung open the passenger door and climbed into the cab.

The music stopped, the faint sounds of the drums and the voices lingering for an instant before receding into the stillness of the crowd. From far away came the noise of an engine throttling down.

The elders turned toward the crowd, and Ethan Red Bull lifted his hands toward the sky. "We ask the Creator to bless this place where the blood of our ancestors and the blood of the young Shoshones mixes with the earth," he said, his voice strong and firm, the voice of a chief in the Old Time, Father John thought. "We ask the Creator to take the evil from this place so that there may be peace between our peoples and that we may go into the future as friends. We ask *Hixce'e' be niho'3o'o*, the white man above, our Lord Jesus, to bless this place. *Ani'qa he'tabi'nuhu'nina, Hatana' wunani'na na hesuna'nin*."

Father John closed his eyes a moment, the old man's voice rolling over him, a comforting sound. He recognized some of the words: "Our Father, we are poor. Our Father, take pity on us."

The voice drifted into the sound of the wind sighing through the canyon. Then the only sound was that of the wind. Ethan stepped back, and now it was the Shoshone elder, Hanson Tindall, moving forward, lifting his hands. "God is with us," he said. "*Dam Apua dame mash.* God's spirit fills everywhere on earth and above us. *Dam Apua Swap bash meripegan oiont dam sogovant des damevant.*" He went on for another few moments, asking the Creator for forgiveness and peace, and when his voice had faded into the quiet of the wind, the music started again, the drumming and the singing somehow louder and freer than before.

The two elders were stooping over the fire. Finally they stood upright, each holding out a large pan, smoke pouring over the rims. Inside the pans, Father John knew—there had been so many ceremonies—sage burned in the hot coals of cottonwood chips. They held up the pans so that the smoke floated toward the sky and the Creator before it began drifting into the crowd. Then the elders turned and held the pans toward the canyon, moving toward the right, and then the left, until the cleansing smoke seemed to be everywhere, reclaiming the canyon floor and slopes above. Facing the crowd again, the elders kept the pans aloft, letting the smoke bind all of the people together.

The blessing ceremony was over now. Knots of people began drifting back toward the vehicles parked outside the canyon. The noise of engines bursting into life erupted over the scuff of boots in the grass and brush and the subdued buzz of voices. Father John made his way among the small groups hanging back, reluctance in the slope of their shoulders, as if in leaving the place where the young men had died, they would sever contact with them. He told the families again how sorry he was, grasping hands, patting shoulders. He lingered with Trent's parents for a few moments, and when other people who had come up to pay their condolences had finally peeled away, he said, "Trent's girlfriend is here."

"Figured that's the white girl you brought along." Trent's father said, and his tone had a forced note in it, punctuating the point that the information had nothing to do with the family.

"She's staying at the mission awhile," Father John pushed on.

Trent's mother looked up from the ground that she'd been studying, eyes lit with interest, as if a new thought had started growing. "Where is she?" the woman said.

Father John scanned the groups of people still picking their way out of the canyon. He saw her then, the blond head weaving through a cluster of black heads. "She's going to the pickup," he said, aware that the woman's gaze was following his own. Then he told the woman about Edie. A job as a receptionist in Riverton. Plans to return to school in the fall. Plans for the future.

The man looked away and launched into a commentary on the ceremony and how the evil spirits would no longer dwell at Bates, how the spirits of his son and the other dead men could now rest in peace.

Father John said he hoped that was the case. He searched the man's eyes, looking for the faintest shadow of interest in Edie Bradbury. There was none. Finally, he shook the Shoshone's hand, patted the woman's arm, and fell in with the other relatives who had started toward the vehicles. Walking alongside them, step by step. Thinking this was right, the Indian priest at this time and in this place, the brown faces turning to him filled with the expectation of comfort and understanding and he trying to summon the words.

He spotted Edie Bradbury's blond head again, bobbing among the black heads clustered around her. And he realized that Trent's mother and father had moved ahead somehow and were talking to the girl. And they were smiling. My God, they were smiling and nodding, and Trent's mother was patting the girl's belly. Father John watched them for several moments. A lightness had settled over the battlefield, it seemed, as if the last of the darkness had been banished. It was *right*.

He found himself looking around.

Vicky would be here. Surely, she was here. It wasn't until he glanced back at the canyon that he spotted her, standing alone near the spot where he had found Trent Hunter's body, the spot where the Lamberts had died. He broke away from the others and retraced his steps, past the place where he'd stood, past the place where the elders had made the circle and blessed the battlefield.

"How are you?" he said when he came up to her.

"I'll be fine." Not looking up, her gaze trained along the canyon, and he had the sense that she'd been waiting for him. "I'm giving Lone Eagle and Holden another chance," she said, turning to him, an almost imperceptible flash of hope in her eyes.

"I'm very glad, Vicky," he heard himself saying, and he meant it. Yes, he meant it, he told himself. It was right that she and Adam should build a life together. Partners in a law firm, partners in life. It was right that it should work out.

Footsteps were coming up on them. Those would be Adam's footsteps, he knew, even before the man stepped next to Vicky. Then Father John heard his own voice again, the stream of platitudes: congratulations, good luck, wish you both well. Grasping their hands for a moment, his and hers, he backed away. Finally, he turned and headed toward the groups of people converging on the few pickups that were still left. He did wish them well, God knew that was the truth. He wished Vicky a happy and fulfilling life. He wished her—everything good.

He hurried to catch up with his people.